Love in the City

THE *Love in the City* SERIES
BOOK ONE

JEN MORRIS

First edition October 2020

Kindle ISBN: 978-0-473-54166-8

Paperback ISBN: 978-0-473-54164-4

Cover illustration by Elle Maxwell

www.ellemaxwelldesign.com

For Carl and Baxter, my happily ever after.

One belongs to New York instantly. One belongs to it as much in five minutes as in five years.

— Tom Wolfe

AUTHOR'S NOTE

Please note that this book contains sensitive topics such as difficult parental relationships and divorce. I hope I have treated these issues with the care they deserve.

1

I'm dead. That's what this feeling is. My whole body aches and my head is about to explode.

With great effort I manage to crack one eye open, wincing as the light shoots straight through to my brain.

How much did I drink last night?

I spy the almost-empty tequila bottle on the counter and my stomach lurches. Fuzzy memories start to surface: Face-timing my best friend Emily, drinking tequila shots, something with my laptop... What happened? And why am I here alone? Usually Travis is—

Oh. Travis.

The scene in the parking lot behind the Italian restaurant comes rushing back to me, his words hitting me all over again: *You're happy with a small life, but I need more.*

Right. He's leaving me to travel the world. Five months together—our whole *future* together—gone, just like that.

My chest tightens as misery crashes over me. I pull a pillow over my head, desperate to fall back asleep and forget everything, but there's a thump on the door.

Heaving a sigh, I peel myself from the bed. I notice I'm

still wearing last night's dress, the fabric rumpled and creased from where I passed out. I catch sight of my reflection as I stumble towards the door and pause to try and tidy myself up, but it's no use. My shoulder-length brown bob is matted up on one side, mascara is smeared down my face and my hazel eyes are bloodshot and puffy.

Shit, I hope it's not Travis at the door. The last thing I need is for him to see me like this. My stomach lurches again and I realize that at least if it *is* him, I can puke on his shoes. You know, to thank him for dumping me on my birthday.

But it's my parents. Or rather, it's my mother, marching my father in by the arm. He closes the door behind him with an apologetic look while Mum stands there, hands on her hips.

I groan. This is the problem with still living in this tiny, rural New Zealand town: my parents live five minutes up the road and pop in any time they bloody well feel like it.

"Alexis." Mum gives me a stern look. "What on earth is this New York nonsense?"

I press a hand to my forehead. The room is spinning and my head is thundering and last night's tequila is hovering near the back of my throat. "Hold on." I stumble into the bathroom to grab a packet of painkillers, then stagger into the kitchen for a glass of water.

"Honestly." Mum's voice drifts into the kitchen. "This is crazy."

No, fuck the glass. I lower my mouth and drink straight from the tap, gulping back huge mouthfuls of water.

"So Travis ended things. That doesn't mean you—"

"Wait," I say, straightening up and turning to them. I don't remember telling them that. It only happened last night. "How do you know Travis ended things?"

Mum's brow wrinkles. "You announced it on Facebook, darling."

Oh *God*. I can't have done that, surely?

I push away from the kitchen sink, glancing around for my phone. Maybe if I can just delete the post, there's a chance no one else will have to see it.

Jesus, Alex. Way to go down in flames.

"But that's no reason to throw your whole life away," Mum huffs.

"What?" I mutter, yanking up the couch cushions, groping around for my phone. Where did I last have it?

"I just think quitting your job and moving your whole life overseas is a *very* dramatic response to a little break-up."

I stop, turning back to Mum. "What?" I ask again, feeling an icy chill run down my spine. Mum can be theatrical, sure, but she's not one to make stuff up. I glance between her and Dad. They both look anxious and there's a twist in my gut.

Shit. Please tell me I didn't do something stupid last night.

I return to my phone search, desperate to find it. Then I spy my laptop on the coffee table and lunge at it, turning it on. Mum and Dad are watching with concern and I almost want to cry. By the looks of it I *did* do something stupid.

I open my browser and go to Facebook, loading the notifications. Apparently I made a post last night and everyone has something to say about it. With a wave of trepidation, I open the post and read it.

Happy 30th to me! Got dumped by loser Trav the Man so it's time to move on. Goodbye New Zealand, hello New York! Leaving in a week,, going to become a best sealing author if you don't like it you can go duck yourself—

Oh God.

Mortification floods me. I don't even remember posting that. I must have been drunk out of my mind—the multiple errors are proof of that. I wouldn't be caught *dead* using such poor grammar in real life. And I *tagged* Travis in the post? I shudder in horror.

Glancing up at my parents, I give them a weak smile. "I was a bit drunk last night. Yes, Travis and I broke up, but the rest of this is just a joke." I gesture to the screen with an unsteady laugh. People post shit on Facebook all the time— maybe I can just say I was hacked? That happens, right?

Mum straightens up. "Really?"

I scroll down through the comments. A few people are asking if I got hacked—there you go, it's totally plausible— then there's one from Emily saying, *Yes! You go girl! This is going to be awesome!*

Well. I'll need to have a word with her about that, encouraging me when I'm that drunk. What kind of best friend is that?

I scroll further, my eyes landing on a comment by my boss, Julie. My stomach turns over when I read her words: *We're going to miss you girl, but this sounds like a wicked adventure.*

Oh fuck. No. I didn't *actually* quit my job, did I?

I open my email sent folder, and my heart sinks. There's an email to my boss, announcing my immediate resignation from the role of "Asitant Manger." My pulse accelerates and the tequila swirls treacherously in my belly. Because now, this is starting to feel a bit too real.

With shaking hands, I log into my bank account, and my fear is confirmed. Last night I spent $6000—basically all of my savings—on a one-way ticket to New York and something called the Wilson Rental Group.

The Wilson Rental Group.

The words register in the depths of my brain and every-thing starts to come back to me in fragments. I found a last-minute fare to JFK Airport two weeks from now. I put down a massive deposit on an apartment in the West Village. And yes, I quit my job as assistant manager at the local bookstore before announcing to the world what I was doing via Facebook. I distinctly remember deciding to announce it, so I couldn't back out.

Holy hell. I bury my head in my hands as the room starts to spin around me. I can't believe what I've done. What was I thinking? I *wasn't* thinking, obviously. I was wasted.

I look up at my parents, feeling my gut heave. Tossing my laptop aside, I push to my feet and flee the room, making it to the bathroom just as the tequila exits my stomach.

2

I spend a good few minutes with my elbows on the toilet seat, the cause of last night's mental breakdown pouring out into the toilet.

Because that's what this is, right? A mental breakdown. It has to be. No one does this sort of shit when they're sane.

I sink back onto my heels, reaching for a towel and dragging it across my mouth. Then I spy my phone sitting up on the bathroom vanity and grab it. There are a million notifications on the screen, but one jumps out at me, from Emily. I unlock the phone and read through the message thread.

Emily: I just read your Facebook post. Sorry about Trav.

Alex: Yeah he's a deck. But I'm exited about New York!!!

Emily: Are you seriously going?

Alex: Yes!!!! I just bought ticket!!! I'm going!!!

Emily: How drunk are you?

Alex: Really drank.. But I know what I'm doing. I've wanted this forever and now the time!!!

Emily: Are you sure?

Alex: I've never been more curtain of something.. In my life.

Emily: I think this will be really good for you.

Alex: I know, I can't wait!!!

Emily: I'll message my friend Cat, she can show you around.

Alex: Great!!!!

Emily: I'm so excited for you! I think this is exactly what you need. It's going to change your life.

Oh God. So many exclamation points. But I remember, now—I remember sending those texts. I recall the buzz I felt last night when I made the announcement, when I bought the ticket. I *did* want to do it. And in my wildly drunken state it seems that I, too, thought it was a good idea.

"Alex?" a voice calls through the door. It takes me a second to recognize who it is.

What the hell?

"Harriet?" I stand, flinging the door open, and come face to face with my sister.

Her eyes are wide behind her black-rimmed glasses. "Are you alright? Mum said there was some sort of emergency. What's going on?"

"Oh for fuck's sake," I mutter, pushing past her into the living room. "Everything's fine. I just did something silly while I was drunk." My empty bank balance flashes into my mind again and dread creeps over me. I sink down onto a chair, pushing the thought from my mind. This has to be a bad dream, surely.

Harriet drops onto the sofa beside my parents, still looking bewildered. Dad pulls a tiny box out of his pocket and hands it over.

"This is for your birthday, sweetheart. Open it."

I hesitate, then take the box. Inside is a silver necklace

with a book charm on it, and I smile. I do love my books; I've always wanted to be a writer. This is a nice surprise, because the last time I mentioned to my parents I wanted to write novels they brushed it aside and told me I wasn't being realistic. But now that I've made this Facebook announcement about wanting to write, maybe they're finally taking me seriously. Are they giving me their blessing?

"It's because of the bookstore," Mum explains. "Well, it *was*."

There's a ripple of disappointment in my chest. Of course.

"I know you're not feeling great about things right now," Dad says. "But we're proud of you, Alex. Assistant manager is a good job. You're hardworking and you don't expect too much."

I frown, glancing down at the necklace. I know he's trying to pay me a compliment, but somehow it feels like he's pointing out a flaw. So I was assistant manager at our crummy little bookstore. Big deal. It's hardly the writing career I imagined myself having at thirty.

I look at Harriet for support. Her hair is wound up tight in a bun on top of her head like always, her brow furrowed in thought. Of course she doesn't get it; she's worked at the same cafe since leaving high school and never complained. Is it just me who's so ungrateful?

Dad smiles at me warmly and I feel a pang of guilt. "Thanks, Dad," I mumble. They're so proud of me and I quit, just like that. Did I make a big mistake?

"Thirty is a big milestone." Mum pats me on the arm. "It can be a bit scary, but you've achieved a lot, darling. You have a lot to be proud of."

"I do?"

"Yes!" Dad chimes in. "You have your flat." He gestures

around the room and I wince. The peeling salmon-pink wallpaper and stained carpet do nothing to support his enthusiasm. Why on earth is he mentioning my flat? It's a tiny, run-down crapheap and I don't even *own* it.

"And you live alone, an independent woman!" he adds with a proud smile. Mum is nodding in agreement, her eyes gleaming.

I exhale. Yes, I'm a single woman who lives alone. What a bloody achievement. And now I don't even have a choice in the matter, what with Travis taking off.

"Yes, well. Thanks." I eye them warily. They must be quite panicked about this New York thing if they're feeling the need to scrape together this pathetic highlight reel of my life. But in all honesty, it's just making me feel worse. Because none of the things they've pointed out are what I imagined for myself at this age. They're all piling up to create a very dire picture indeed.

"And of course you have your degree," Mum says.

God, they're still going.

I mean, okay, the degree is good: a Bachelor of Communication. I worked hard for that, even if it wasn't quite what I'd wanted to do. What I *had* wanted to do was get a degree in literature then a Masters in Creative Writing, but my parents assured me that was pointless and wouldn't get me a job. I compromised with the communications degree, figuring I could still write. And while I did work at the local paper for a while, five years ago they had huge budget cuts and I was made redundant, forced to take a job at the bookstore. I've been there ever since. So again, not something I'm extremely proud of.

Mum leans forward to squeeze my hand. "I'm sorry about what happened with Travis, darling. That was awful. And on your birthday, of all nights."

Harriet screws up her face. "Yeah, that sucks. What a dick."

I give her a thin smile, swallowing against the bitterness in my throat. Because that's the icing on the cake, isn't it? My writing career is non-existent and my flat is awful, but at least I had Travis. And now I don't even have that.

"Do you like the necklace?" Dad asks.

I glance down at it with a little nod. "Yeah. Thanks." It's cute and it suits my love of reading and writing, but now it feels like a symbol of everything that's wrong with my life. I pull it out of the box and clasp the chain around my neck. It sits low on my chest and I stare down at it, my head spinning.

"See, darling? You don't want to move to New York," Mum says. "Your whole life is here."

I look around at my shitty flat and my body sags with disappointment. My whole life? *This* is my life? A job I don't care about, a boyfriend who's left me, parents who don't understand me, this hideous flat. Hell, even my best friend doesn't live here, she's in Auckland. Travis was right: I *am* living a small life. I'm living a tiny, insignificant life—one that doesn't even remotely measure up to what I imagined for myself at this age.

"Why don't you get dressed," Dad suggests, "then we can take you out for a birthday breakfast?"

Right now I want nothing more than to crawl under the covers and die, but they're all looking at me hopefully and I feel another spasm of guilt. It's hardly their fault I've fucked up my entire life, is it?

"Okay," I mumble, pushing to my feet and shuffling off to the bathroom. The minute I'm out of the room I hear them start whispering, but I'm too hungover to care.

I slip the bathroom door closed behind me and stare at

my reflection above the sink. I look dead. Actually, I *feel* dead. It's not just the booze, or the fact that I did something incredibly stupid last night. It's everything. I never expected I'd be here. I figured I'd be married by now, maybe with a kid or two. And that's on top of my successful writing career.

But I don't have any of those things. As Mum and Dad so clearly pointed out, I'm alone. Alone in this awful flat with no man, no career—and now, I don't even have a job.

I'm just about to peel my clothes off when I notice I don't have a clean towel. There's another surge of misery through me at the injustice of it all. It's like *nothing* is going right in my life.

With a gusty sigh, I open the door and step into the hallway. I go to grab a towel from the linen closet when Mum's voice floats down the hall.

"That was close. Moving to New York, what a ridiculous idea!"

I can hear the kettle boiling as she makes a cup of tea, and from here I can see the back of Harriet's head where she's still sitting on the sofa. It must just be Mum and Dad in the kitchen. I know I probably shouldn't stand here listening, but I'm rooted to the spot.

"And now she's quit her job, the silly girl," Mum continues. "Maybe I can call Julie and help her get her job back."

Dad sighs. "I don't think that's what she wants."

"That's the problem with this girl! She wants things she can't have. She gets one little job at the newspaper and next she thinks she can be an author. She goes on one date with a boy and she thinks they'll be getting married. And now this moving to New York business? I swear, she lives her whole life in a fantasy."

I stand frozen in the hallway, a cold, prickly sensation washing over me, suffocating the air from my lungs.

"I assumed she would have grown out of this by now. It's those stupid bloody romance novels she reads," Mum adds. I hear the fridge open and close. "They fill her head with nonsense. She just needs to learn that life isn't like that, that it's not realistic to expect—"

"Audrey," Dad says soothingly, "why don't we try and sit down with her—"

"That will never work. You know how *sensitive* she is. She'll just fly off the handle."

Tears sting my throat and I realize I'm almost shaking with shock. My parents have been saying this sort of thing to me for years—and I've *always* been derided for reading sappy romance novels—but there's something about the way people speak about others when they think they're not listening. Mum's voice is laced with such disgust, such revulsion, that for the briefest second I wonder if she's talking about someone else.

But she's not. She's talking about me.

I suck in a shaky breath and Harriet twists around on the sofa, her eyes locking with mine. And I can tell she knows I've heard everything.

I duck back into the bathroom, dropping down onto the edge of the bathtub. I'm reeling from the sting of Mum's words, from the way she laid out everything I've secretly believed to be wrong with me and said, in no uncertain terms, that it is wrong—that *I'm* wrong.

"Hey." Harriet pops the door open, slipping inside. "You okay?"

I press my lips into a thin line and nod, unable to meet her gaze. I know if I do, I'll start crying.

Oh look at that, my parents are right: too damn sensitive.

Harriet takes a tentative step towards me. "Don't listen to them. You know Mum's always a bit dramatic."

I stare down at the tiles, replaying Mum's words in my head. Because while Harriet's right, I also know Mum wasn't that far off. I *had* imagined I would be an author, that I was working towards that, eventually. And, as much as it hurts to admit this now, I had also imagined myself marrying Travis at some point in the future. Not just Travis; several previous boyfriends had dressed up in a tux and said heartfelt vows somewhere in the grand wedding venues of my daydreams.

And what happened? Nothing. It was all in my head.

A tear escapes down my cheek and I quickly brush it away. I have nothing to show for my life, but that's not even the worst of it. The worst part is that I'd convinced myself, somehow, I did.

Harriet lowers herself onto the tub beside me. "Did you really buy a plane ticket to New York?"

I nod numbly.

"Do you want to go?"

I shrug. Because Mum's right, isn't she? That was just another fantasy.

"Maybe you should."

Wait. What? Of all the people who might encourage this, I'd never expect it from her. She's always been the more pragmatic one, the more sensible of the two of us. She's never been the type to get swept up in flights of fancy like me.

"You heard Mum," I mumble. "It's crazy."

Harriet nods slowly. "Yeah, it is. And I'd never do it. But..." She adjusts her glasses, thinking. "If you're not happy here, then maybe it's time to do something different. You know they say the definition of insanity is doing the same thing and expecting different results." She gives me a nudge. "So maybe the crazy thing would be to *stay* here."

I snort a laugh and wipe my nose, studying her. She's

three years younger than me and we've never been especially close, but now I'm glad to have her here, sitting in my
bathroom while I battle a hangover and the intense urge to
do something life-altering.

She gives my arm a squeeze. "That sucks about Travis.
I'm sorry. But that's beyond your control. If you want to go to
New York, or write, or make some other big life change…"
She shrugs. "That's up to *you*."

I look down at the bathmat, absorbing her words. She's
right; the only thing stopping me is myself.

My pulse quickens at this realization. Because I could
actually *do* this. I could. Hell, I already have the ticket and
the apartment. It's halfway done already.

"Harri…" I glance at her again. "Do you really think I
should do this?"

"Well, do you want your life to change or stay the same?"

Emily's words flash into my mind—*this is exactly what
you need… it's going to change your life*—and a thrill runs
through me. Because I think it's about damn time to change
my life.

"You're right." I stand, conviction gripping me as I stride
into the living room with Harriet trailing after me.

Mum looks up from her cup of tea in surprise.

"You know what?" I raise my hands to my hips and look
squarely at my parents. "I'm going. I'm going to New York to
become a writer." I take in their aghast expressions and feel
another surge of conviction. They think my dreams are
absurd, that I should stay here and live a small life, but
they're wrong. It's one thing for Travis to hurt me, but for my
own *parents* to not even believe in me…

But they've never believed in me, have they? They don't
understand me at all. They've never even tried. And
suddenly, I realize that leaving here isn't so much about not

wanting to be here—it's about feeling like I don't even *belong* here.

I lift my chin. "I'm moving to New York," I say again, glaring defiantly at my parents. "And if you don't like it, you can go duck yourselves."

3

This can't be right.

I'm standing on the corner of West 10th and Hudson Street in New York's West Village. It's been two weeks of madness, packing and sorting out a visa and saying goodbye, before hauling myself all the way over here. And now, I find myself staring in confusion at a Starbucks.

Don't get me wrong; I love coffee. I never start my morning without it. And fuck, standing in front of a Starbucks Coffee shop in the middle of Manhattan is like standing on a film set or something. It's awesome. Surely any moment Meg Ryan and Tom Hanks will walk out.

But I can't *quite* enjoy it, because this isn't supposed to be a Starbucks. It's supposed to be the Wilson apartment block, where I put a deposit on my new studio apartment.

I dump my suitcases against the side of the Starbucks and pull out my phone, trying to ignore the sensory overload around me and focus on the matter at hand. Scrolling back through my email inbox, I pull up the confirmation from the Wilson Rental Group.

"Yes," I say to myself under my breath, glancing back up at the street signs. "Corner of West 10th and Hudson." Both signs match, and I stuff my phone into my pocket, turning to survey the street around me. Everything looks familiar, but somehow wrong: the cars are on the opposite side of the road, the sounds are different, the air is cooler but thicker. There's an NYPD car parked at the curb, a handful of yellow taxis cruising by, and the street has an acidic sort of smell I can't pinpoint.

But most alarmingly, there's no Wilson apartment building.

An uneasy feeling stirs in the pit of my stomach and I push it away, reaching for my suitcases and hauling them into Starbucks. The familiar smell of coffee wafts over me and for a moment, I feel comforted.

Right. I just need to get this mix-up sorted and everything will be back on track.

Trying not to look too flustered, I approach the counter and smile at the barista, whose name badge says "Steve." He flashes me a grin and picks up his pen, ready to write my name on whatever drink I order.

"Uh, hi." I take a deep breath, attempting not to sound like the lost, hopeless girl from the middle of nowhere that I feel like. "I was wondering if you could help me?"

He lowers the pen. "Sure. What's up?"

Well. This is a good start. I'd always heard that New Yorkers are rude and unfriendly, but his warm smile eases my nerves a little. I'm sure everything is going to be okay.

"This might sound a bit weird, but I thought there was an apartment block at this address." As I speak I can't help but be acutely aware of the twang in my New Zealand accent and I cringe, feeling self-conscious. "Have you, um, heard of the Wilson apartments?"

Steve cocks his head to one side in thought and I turn and give a sheepish smile to the man behind me, tapping his foot as he waits to place his coffee order. He's one of those classically good-looking men: early forties, I'm guessing, and easily over six feet tall. His shoulders are broad, his hair is a dark chocolate-brown and cut stylishly, and he has a short, tidy beard. He's the sort of man I might have pictured myself ending up with when I'm a proper grown-up. He looks like your typical New York businessman with his expensive suit and serious expression. Probably worrying about the merger, or something.

"Sorry," I mouth. He rolls his eyes and I shrink in embarrassment, quickly spinning back to Steve.

"Hey Dave?" Steve calls to a guy further behind the counter who saunters over. "Do you know the Wilson apartments?"

Dave stops, his brow pulling into a frown. "You're the second person this week to come here looking for them. But I've never heard of them."

"What? They must be around here somewhere." A nervous laugh sneaks out of me. "Here, I have this email." I fish out my phone and pull up the email again, showing it to Dave. "It says it should be right here."

Dave takes my phone and examines the screen, scrolling down. "Well, it's definitely not at this address. I've lived in this neighborhood for ten years and I've never heard of them. And"—he gestures to an image on the screen—"I've *never* seen this building around here. This looks like a stock photo." He glances up at me. "Did you pay for this?"

I nod. The man behind me in line clears his throat audibly and I throw him a look of annoyance, no longer impressed by his good looks. Clearly, I'm in distress here.

Dave shrugs, handing my phone back. "It might be a scam."

I stare at him, dumbfounded. A scam? That's absurd. I wouldn't get scammed. Although come to think of it, I was pretty hammered when I found the apartment.

"It can't be a scam," I whisper.

Dave and Steve exchange a pitying glance and my palms begin to sweat.

"You've really never heard of it?"

"No, sorry." Dave shakes his head again, pressing his lips together. "This sort of thing happens, you know. Where are you from, anyway?"

"New Zealand."

Dave shrugs again and gently motions for me to step aside so he can serve the businessman behind me who's about to give himself an aneurysm with his impatience. He glares at me as I shuffle my suitcases out the way.

So that's it? I glance from Dave to Steve, waiting for them to say something more. But they just make coffee, don't they? It's not their fault some random stranger is in here asking for an apartment block they've never heard of. They can hardly be held responsible.

Dave gives me a sympathetic look as he takes the businessman's drink order. "Sorry we can't help. Good luck." He turns back to the line of people that has accumulated behind me.

I stand frozen to the spot for a second, unable to process this. A scam? My lovely apartment is a scam? This can't be happening.

Dragging my suitcases over to a table, I slump into a chair. My gut is churning and I force myself to take a couple of deep, soothing breaths. It's going to be okay. It has to be. I'm sure this is all just a huge misunderstanding—one I'll laugh about when I'm snuggled up in bed in my new apartment tonight.

I pull my phone out and scroll back through the email. Maybe if I call the company they'll set me straight. But as I search the email, then the website, I notice there is no phone number. The only information I can find is an email address. This strikes me as odd and dread prickles across my skin as I send off an email. Because—shit. I hope Dave wasn't right.

I open my browser and search for the company name along with the word "scam." And my heart plummets as I read the screen. There it is, in black and white. There is no Wilson apartment block; it's a scam that has seen dozens of people lose thousands of dollars. I have to read it three times for it to sink in. *I've been conned.*

Fuck.

I drop my phone onto the table with a thud. How could I have been so *stupid*? Why on earth did I think this was a good thing to do blind drunk? Not only am I out thousands of dollars, I also have nowhere to live. I've been in New York for less than two hours and I'm homeless.

Tears prick my eyes before I can stop them, and I raise a trembling hand to hide my face.

Of course I don't fucking belong here. What the hell was I thinking? My parents were right—it was a fantasy, and it's only taken a couple of hours for the whole thing to come crashing down.

My phone buzzes on the table next to me and I reach for it with a sniffle. It's a text from Emily, asking if my plane has landed. Seeing her name flash up on my phone sends homesickness rushing through me. I'd give anything to be back in my flat, on the sofa in front of the TV with Travis's arm around me. I push the image from my head and press Emily's name in my contacts list.

"Hey hon!" she sing-songs on the other end of the line. "How's it going?"

God, I love Em. We met when we were seven years old and a teacher put us in the same reading group. We've been besties ever since.

"Not great. I, er, don't have anywhere to live."

"What? What about your apartment?"

"It doesn't exist." I lower my voice as a couple at a nearby table give me an odd look. "It was a scam."

"Oh my God. Are you serious?"

"Yes."

"Shit." She sounds distant over the line and it feels like I'm on another planet. "Alright, don't panic. We'll figure something out. Have you—"

"I should never have come here," I blurt, my voice catching in my throat. "It's a mess. I think I should just try and come home." As I say it, a weight settles on my heart. There's nothing I want back there, and my parents are only going to make me feel a million times worse. But what other option do I have?

"Oh, hon," Emily says. "It's okay. Don't come home."

"You don't think coming here was totally crazy?"

"No! Well, okay, it was a bit crazy, but in a good way. Your life needed some crazy. I know it isn't quite going according to plan right now, but you can figure this out. It's all part of the adventure! I think this is absolutely the right thing for you."

I sniffle.

"Hey!" she says brightly. "Let me call my friend, Cat. I'm sure she can help you."

"Cat?"

"Yeah, remember the friend I told you about in New York? I met her a few years ago when I went to that yoga course."

"Right," I murmur

"She's great. I'll call her right now." Emily's voice softens. "You'll be fine, honey. Don't worry. You've made it all the way over there. I'm not letting you come back yet."

I hang up and inhale slowly, taking a moment to compose myself. My fingers go up to touch the book charm necklace from my parents as Emily's words replay in my mind: *this is absolutely the right thing for you.* I repeat them over and over like a mantra, until my phone buzzes again.

Emily: Cat says you can stay at her place tonight. Where are you right now? She'll come meet you.

Oh, thank God.

I'm limp with relief as I text her the address. At least I won't be forced to sleep under a bridge tonight.

Setting the phone down again, I glance up, letting my gaze drift out the window to take in my surroundings for the first time. I can't believe I'm finally here, in New York. If only I wasn't homeless.

My gut clenches again—at the money I've lost, at the thought of somehow trying to find a place to live, at the realization that now I'm going to have to find a job ASAP when I'm not even sure if I can, given I don't have a working visa. When I had the apartment sorted—or thought I did—it gave me some time to settle in and formulate a plan. And now? Shit.

But I've got a bed for tonight, I remind myself, trying to stay positive. I push my chair back and stand to order a coffee, determined to distract myself until Cat arrives.

Dave looks up hopefully when I approach the counter. "Any luck?"

I shake my head, giving him a grim smile. How humiliating. He must think I'm some idiot tourist who falls for this kind of thing all the time. This is *not* the sophisticated world traveler image I was going for. Though let's face it, nothing about me is sophisticated—and now that I'm here in the city, that is painfully clear.

I mumble my coffee order and rifle through my bag, knocking my EpiPen to the ground. I hastily scoop it up and shove it away for safekeeping. Not that I'm likely to be stung by a bee in New York, but I can't be too careful.

"Right," I say, pulling out a wad of bills. God, they all look so similar. I sense someone approach the counter behind me and turn to see the same handsome businessman from earlier, a sandwich in one hand, his head bowed as he's engrossed in something on his phone. He glances up to see me ahead of him again and heaves out a sigh, shoving his phone in his pocket.

"Can I just pay for this?" he asks Dave, right over my head.

Heat sweeps across my cheeks. I might not fit in with this New York crowd, but how bloody rude to act like I'm not even *here*.

Dave's eyes dart between the two of us. "Uh..."

I thrust some bills onto the counter, taking my coffee. Flustered, I spin around to get out of the guy's way just as he steps up to the counter. But I've turned the wrong way and our bodies collide: my head hitting his chest, his foot crushing my toe.

And crumpled between us, in my hand, is the paper cup that held my coffee.

I gasp as the hot liquid soaks into the front of my dress, scalding my stomach. That's when I notice it's soaking into the businessman's crisp, white shirt too.

Oh God.

I glance up into his deep brown eyes. His face is seething with fury, as if I somehow did this on purpose.

"Shit. I'm so sorry," I stammer, my heart thudding hard. I pull my dress away from my skin, trying to ignore the burning sensation through the thin fabric.

He takes a handful of napkins from the counter and attempts to mop up his shirt, cursing under his breath. His jaw is clenched like he's trying to stop himself from yelling at me.

Mortified, I grab a napkin and dab at his shirt, attempting to stop the stain from spreading, because—good *God*, that's a firm stomach. I pat at the stain, following it down his torso where the liquid has spread, mentally cursing myself. I should have been more careful, I should have—

He leaps back, shooting me a look of surprise.

Whoops. Perhaps I went a little low with the napkin there. Accidentally, of course. It's not like I was *trying* to go feeling around his crotch.

"Fuck. Sorry," I mumble again, my face flaming. This could *not* get any worse.

He huffs, pulling out his wallet to pay for his sandwich.

I really do feel bad. He could have been more patient, sure, but I didn't do this on purpose. And now he'll have to wear a stained shirt to his board meeting or whatever.

"Here." I take the pen off the counter and write down my number on a napkin. "Please, send me the dry cleaning bill." I hold the napkin out to him and mop at my own soggy dress with another, wincing as I pat against my stinging skin.

He snorts. "Dry cleaning? You're kidding. I'm going to need a new shirt."

I gulp. A new shirt for him will probably cost the same as my apartment deposit. I open my mouth to protest, but he's glaring at me and I shrivel. "Okay," I squeak. "Send me the bill."

He snatches the napkin, glowering. "Fine." And with that he strides out of the coffee shop.

Dave hands me a fistful of napkins and a new coffee. I give him a weary smile and retreat to my table, thoroughly humiliated.

Sipping my coffee and mopping at my dress, I sigh. This is so far from how I wanted my first day to go, I'm on the verge of tears.

The door swings open and a short woman with chin-length gray-blond hair, ripped black jeans and chunky combat boots steps in. A tiny pug dog follows in after her and she scoops it up into her arms before surveying the coffee shop. Her eyes land on me and my suitcases, and she heads over.

"Alex?"

I nod.

"I'm Cat. I came as quickly as I could."

4

F inally, a friendly face.

I'm so relieved to see Cat, I have to hold myself back from throwing my arms around her. "Thank you. Oh my God, it's been a nightmare, I'm so sorry Emily had to bother you..." I start rambling, but she holds up a hand.

"It's okay, I understand," she says brusquely. "But I have to get back to the shop, so can we go?"

"Oh. Of course." I rush to gather my things, knocking over one of my suitcases which nearly crashes into the table next to me. I try to apologize but Cat is already marching out the door and I scramble after her.

"I just live a few blocks from here," she calls over her shoulder, her short legs moving fast. The little pug trots along beside her and my luggage bumps over the pavement as I struggle to keep up.

Even though we're powering along, I can't help but take in everything around me. The streets are short, all one way, criss-crossing over one another. Some are even cobble-stoned, lined with trees and brick townhouse-style apartment buildings, steps leading up off the footpaths—no, *sidewalks*. That's what they call them here. And being mid-October, the ground is covered in a layer of orange and yellow leaves. It's kind of jarring after just being in spring back home, like I've somehow skipped summer. But I don't mind. I love the way the West Village looks like something out of a movie, and—oh!—on some steps there are even pumpkins and Halloween decorations!

Despite the awful morning, I'm buzzing as we thread through the streets, hearing the distant sound of sirens. I can't believe I'm actually here, in America—in *New York*. It's like I'm walking through a dream, it's so surreal.

We round a corner and stop outside a redbrick building with steps up to an arched doorway and a black fire escape zig-zagging down the front. It's everything I've pictured a New York apartment to be and a thrill runs through me.

We head up the front steps, push through the heavy door and turn right into an apartment on the first floor, opposite the lobby.

"This is my place. You can put your stuff over here." Cat waves an arm at the living room. "And you can crash on the sofa tonight." She looks at me, a smile flitting over her lips before her eyes flick back to the front door.

"Oh, thank you. Are you sure—"

"Of course. Emily told me what happened. Look, I've got to run back to the shop." She steps into the kitchen and rummages in a drawer. "Here's a spare key." She thrusts a silver key into my hand and strides back to the front door. "I'll be home later."

"Thank you so much. It's been awful," I start again, but she just flaps her hand.

"Sorry, I can't chat. Gotta run." And with that, she pulls

the door shut behind her. I jump as it almost slams, the pug narrowly escaping through the gap.

I stare at the back of the door, feeling unease creep up my spine. I'm certainly glad not to be spending my first night on the street, but given that Cat doesn't seem to want a house guest, I'm not sure it's going to be much more comfortable here.

With a sigh, I tuck my suitcases into a corner of the living room and collapse onto the sofa, wanting nothing more than to sleep. The jetlag and stress from the morning have combined into a powerful cocktail of exhaustion. Despite the midday light coming in through the windows, my eyelids grow heavy and I drift off.

I'M NOT sure how long I sleep for, but when I wake it's still light outside. I prop myself up on my elbows, letting my eyes wander around Cat's apartment, taking it in properly for the first time. It's nice: bright white walls through the open living room and kitchen, with a breakfast bar separating the kitchen from the living space. Two windows in the living room let in light, both covered with sheer white curtains. I'm lying on a big, red sofa and there's a matching recliner chair, both facing a small television and a low wooden coffee table, strewn with bits of fabric and fashion magazines. Off to the left side of the living room is a partition-wall, creating a small alcove area with a sewing machine, a few bolts of fabric and a mannequin.

I pull myself up to sitting and glance down at the coffee stain on my dress. The whole horrible ordeal comes screaming back to me and I cringe, picturing the coffee soaking into the shirt of that businessman. I feel bad, but I hope he doesn't *actually* expect me to buy him a new shirt. It could bankrupt me.

"Hey."

I spin around to see Cat entering the apartment and my body goes rigid. "Hey," I say warily.

"I got takeout." She smiles and holds up a couple of containers of food; the kind of Chinese takeout boxes I've seen on TV.

I eye the food, wondering if I'm better off heading out instead. She must be able to sense my hesitation, because she sets the food down on the counter with a grimace.

"Listen, I'm sorry about earlier. I know I was a bitch."

I give an uneven laugh. "No, you—"

"I was, and I'm sorry."

She grabs some forks and flops down on the sofa, holding one out to me. I take it gratefully, reaching for some food. I didn't realize until now, but my stomach is growling.

"I had to deal with my ex at the store and he's such a jerk. It was the worst day." Cat shovels a fork-load of fried rice into her mouth, chewing absently, then swallows and turns to me wide-eyed. "Fuck, sorry. Obviously your day was *much* worse because of your apartment and everything. Listen to me rambling on after what you've been through." She rubs her forehead with the back of her hand, then looks at me earnestly. "I'm sorry I didn't give you the warmest welcome, I was just preoccupied with my own shit. I didn't mean to take it out on you."

"It's okay." I smile, feeling the last of the tension drain from my body. "I'm so grateful that you came to my rescue. I know it was out of the blue but you totally saved me."

"Happy to help." She pushes to her feet and heads to the kitchen, pulling some wine out of the fridge. "You want a glass?"

I nod vigorously. After the day I've had, I could use a bottle.

"So, you have a store?" I ask, taking a glass from her as she sits again.

"Yeah, in the East Village. I sell vintage clothes and some of my own bits and pieces I design."

"Oh, that's so cool." I take a long sip of my wine. "Your ex... did you guys break up recently?"

"No, we got divorced three and a half years ago. But he's in real estate and he manages the lease on the shop. So he uses that as an excuse to hang around." She rolls her eyes, reaching for a wonton. "He managed the lease on this apartment and got us a great deal, otherwise I'd never be able to afford to live around here. When I found him cheating I managed to get it in the divorce, and he's been pissed off ever since." She shakes her head, then focuses her attention on me. Her brown eyes sparkle and there's a dusting of freckles across her button nose. "Anyway, enough about me. Why are you in New York? Emily said you moved here."

"Oh, well... I went through a breakup a couple of weeks ago."

Cat nods, her expression intense. "Aren't men just the *worst*?"

"Yeah." I give a humorless laugh. "I guess I should have seen it coming, but I didn't." I feel a little pang as I think of Travis, and quickly shake it off.

"Maybe you'll meet someone new over here."

"Maybe," I murmur, trying to ignore the strange feeling that thought stirs in me. I probably shouldn't be thinking about meeting anyone new right now, given that I'm reeling with heartbreak. Well, maybe not *heartbreak*, exactly, since Travis and I were only together for five months and never actually said the L word. But I feel worse than I usually do after a break-up.

I've been sitting with this feeling over the past couple weeks, not turning to my usual distraction devices, like tequila—in case I accidentally put down a deposit on a penthouse in Paris, or something—and I think it's not so much about Travis as it is about all men. About dating, and wanting to meet someone, and failing. I'm still single after ten committed years of trying to meet my other half. Sure, I've had boyfriends, but each time I've hoped it would lead to happily ever after, it only led to disappointment.

Case in point: Travis.

Although now that I've had the distance of two weeks— and thousands of miles—I can see things with Travis more clearly. And the fact that I even *imagined* there could be a fairy-tale ending there shows me how deluded I've been. Which makes me think my mother is right.

And now that I'm thirty it's all starting to feel a bit pathetic. I might not have much control over whether or not I fall in love, but I can take back control of my career, and *that's* why I'm here in the city.

"I don't know if I want to meet anyone right now," I say, staring down into my wineglass. "I came here to focus on my career. I'd always wanted to live here and write. I'm sort of... a writer. Well, I want to be."

"Wow." Cat raises her eyebrows. "That's awesome. And I can't believe you just packed up and moved here to do that. That takes real guts."

She's right, actually. It did take guts. Or rather, it took me being so drunk I didn't know what I was doing, then feeling like I couldn't back out without looking like an idiot and losing thousands of dollars. Which, you know, is pretty much the same thing.

The glass of wine has gone straight to my head after not eating all day and being jet-lagged. I lean back on the sofa, enjoying the warm buzz as it spreads through my body. Then a thought occurs to me and I sit up with alarm. "Where's your dog?"

Cat laughs. "You mean Stevie?"

"Stevie?"

"Yeah." She grins. "Stevie Nicks. She's with Mark, my ex. We share custody." She makes a face.

"Oh." I relax back onto the sofa with a chuckle. "I was worried for a moment."

Cat ponders me over her wine glass. "You're really nice. I feel awful about how shitty I was to you earlier. Will you let me take you out, to make it up to you?"

"You're letting me stay here for the night. You don't have to make it up to me," I say. Her face falls and I feel bad. "But I'd love to go out," I add, even though I'm still exhausted.

Her eyes light up. "Great!"

I groan inwardly at all the effort it will require, but my mouth twitches into a smile. My first night in New York and we're going out! Maybe it will be fun.

Now I just have to find something to wear and wash twenty hours of travel off me.

5

_____

"My brother owns Bounce," Cat says, locking the front door behind us. "It's kind of a dive, but we get cheap drinks." She drops her keys into her bag, turning to me. "You want to walk? It's only twenty minutes."

"Sure."

Big mistake. I'd forgotten how fast she walks, and by the end of the block I'm nearly breathless from trying to keep up with her. Fuck, I'm going to have to get much fitter to survive this city.

We stride along Waverly Place and my head is spinning in the evening light, taking in everything: the clink of cutlery from restaurants that open out onto the sidewalk, the smell of pizza cooking in a stone-oven, the conversations from people passing by, the multitude of yellow cabs honking in the evening traffic. All around me the city feels alive, like it is living and breathing on its own beneath my feet, and I feel a thrill that I'm here, part of this.

We stop quickly at Washington Square Park and I stare up at the arch in wonder, before Cat hurries me along. As we head across Broadway, Lafayette and Bowery, I notice how the rows of residential brick buildings give way to bigger, more commercial buildings, and the narrow avenues open out onto big, busy intersections. It's not long until we're in the East Village, where the buildings are similar to the West Village but not as tidy, not quite as fancy. It has a funky vibe and, despite my jet-lag, I'm excited to be out, the pulse of the city filling me with renewed energy.

"I'll grab us drinks," Cat says over the music as we push into Bounce. "You find a table."

I check out the crowded room, waiting for my eyes to adjust to the low lighting. The place is packed three-deep to the bar, which runs down the left hand side. The right wall is exposed brick, lined with tables and red vinyl booths—not one of which is free.

"Where?" I ask, turning back towards Cat, but she's already making her way to the bar.

Right, okay. Find a seat somewhere. I can do that.

But as I glance around, that prickly feeling of self-consciousness crawls over me again, like it did in Starbucks. I feel as if everyone can sense I don't belong here. I know this isn't a classy bar, but the women just *look* different from the women back home—more cool, more comfortable with themselves, more at ease. I have the strong urge to turn and run back to the apartment.

No, I tell myself. This is my first night in New York, and I'm not going to run away just because I feel stupid. I flew all the way over here on my own, navigating the bloody Houston airport during my layover and dealing with a delayed flight. I caught a taxi on my own, I handled the whole apartment debacle. Well, I didn't exactly *handle* it but I got through it, for now. In the past twenty-four hours I've done more things that scare me than I have in the past five *years.* I can manage a little drink in a bar. I just have to hold my head up and pretend I belong.

I spy a booth opening up down the back. Taking a deep breath, I push my way through the crowd, elbowing a few guys out the way, and slide in as my soles tingle with relief. Why did I wear heels? My feet are killing me after walking here at Cat's breakneck pace.

A cute guy emerges from the crowd and his eyes swivel in my direction, his face breaking into a grin. I glance behind me to see who he's grinning at, then I realize it's me.

Oh.

"Hey," he says, sliding into the booth next to me. He has messy, dirty-blond hair, brown eyes, and a very cheeky smile. I'm instantly drawn to him, but that sets my internal alarm bells off. The last man I was drawn to dumped me in a parking lot on my birthday.

"Uh, hi."

"I'm Cory." He extends his hand and I shake it.

"Alex. Nice to meet you."

He cocks his head as I speak. "Where are you from?"

"New Zealand." There's a glimmer of pride in my chest as I say that. I might feel like a dork with my accent, but I know New Zealand as a country holds up pretty well overseas, what with the gorgeous scenery and Peter Jackson and the All Blacks and everything.

"That's awesome," he says, and I swoon at his deep American accent. I'm a sucker for it, actually. I don't know how I'm not going to jump into bed with every American man that pays me attention. Maybe moving here was a terrible idea.

I run my eyes over him. He's tall and in good shape—I can see that through his fitted T-shirt. I'm pretty sure he's flirting with me, with that look in his eye, and I'm not going to lie—I could use a little boost right now.

Look, I'm not hideous, I know that. I've got caramel-brown shoulder-length hair that has a natural wave to it, hazel eyes, and a heart-shaped face with a peaches and cream complexion. I've been told many times that I'm pretty, even if I wish I was a bit skinnier. I'm tallish—five foot seven —with an hourglass figure, carrying my weight on my hips and bust. I've mostly made my peace with my curves, but getting dumped has a way of making a girl feel a bit down on herself. And moving to this city hasn't helped.

Cory grins, leaning closer, and I blush under his flirtatious gaze. It's been a while since I've gotten this kind of attention and I'd forgotten how fun it is. And even though I know better, I lean closer too.

"Cory! Get away from her!" Cat appears at the table, clutching two drinks. "Is *this* where you've been? I had to wait at the bar for ages." She scowls as she slides into the other side of the booth.

Oh. Shit.

Realization rolls over me and my face warms. I quickly slide away from him.

"This is my brother. I see you've already met," Cat says, glaring at Cory.

"I didn't know she was your friend," he mumbles.

I laugh, raising my hands. "It's okay. No harm done." I lean closer to Cat, speaking under my breath. "Fuck, I'm sorry. I had no idea he was your brother."

That was close. One minute I tell Cat I'm not interested in meeting anyone, the next I'm nearly shacking up with her brother. I need to get a grip.

"It's okay. He can't help himself." She throws Cory a look of exasperation. "Don't you have some *work* to do?"

He shrinks, sliding out of the booth. "I'll catch you later, Alex."

I give him a nod and reach for my wine, while Cat waves to someone across the bar.

"Hey, Geoff," she says as a slightly pudgy, dark-haired guy joins our booth. "This is my new friend, Alex."

He extends his hand and smiles warmly. He's got a kind face and green eyes that sparkle behind his black-rimmed glasses, and I think I pick up a bit of a gay vibe but I can't be sure. Either way, I immediately like him.

"You two get to know each other," Cat says, pushing to her feet. "I'll go get you a drink, Geoff." She swivels towards the bar, and this time she heads straight for Cory.

Geoff turns to me with a smile. "So, how do you know Cat?"

"She's friends with a friend of mine from back home. She rescued me today when I got stuck," I say. I'm not sure I want to go around telling everyone what an idiot I was to get sucked in by an internet scam because I made a major life decision while blackout drunk.

He nods. "She's good like that."

"She didn't seem very impressed when we met," I confess. "Something about her ex ruining her day."

"Yeah, Mark is a total dick." Geoff raises his eyes to the ceiling. "He makes her life a nightmare. But it's okay, because she's going to meet Mr. Right soon."

"Oh?"

"She's on a dating kick. Didn't date much for a couple years after her divorce, but now she's ready to meet someone new."

I give him a puzzled look. "That's weird. Earlier she said men are the worst."

"Oh, they are. Just last week I had a drink with a guy

who wanted me to go home with him after he called me fat."
Geoff laughs bitterly. "The dating scene here is rough. Cat's
met loads of guys but, you know, you have to kiss a lot of
frogs and all that." He folds his hands on the table. "So, what
are you doing in New York?"

I tell him about coming to write, leaving out the details
about my ex and my parents. When I do that, it makes it
sound more like an adventure born out of a restless free
spirit rather than a desperate attempt to reroute my disappointing life.

He listens intently, genuinely interested, and I notice I
feel very comfortable with him.

"I love your necklace."

I touch the book charm. "Thanks! It was a gift."

"I should sell them. I run a bookstore in the West Village
called Between the Lines."

"Oh, I love books! I was assistant manager at a bookstore
back home." I decide not to tell him that romance novels
have always been my preferred genre. I don't need another
person making me feel stupid right now. "Do you have any
job openings?" I ask hopefully. I know I didn't come here to
do the same thing as back home, but I'll need to find something to survive on until I start making money from my writing. I picture myself in a charming little bookstore in the
Village, with worn leather armchairs and jazz music playing
softly, while rain beats against the pavement outside and—

"No, sorry." Geoff gives me an apologetic smile, pushing
his glasses up his nose. "We're fully staffed and I have
people coming in to apply for jobs all the time."

"Oh." The image vanishes from my head and I nod. "Of
course." As if it would be that easy for me to even *get* a job,
let alone one in a lovely bookstore where I could meet other

writers and maybe even mingle with New York's literary crowd.

No. I'll probably end up stuffed into a shrimp costume, waddling through Times Square and handing out fliers to a local restaurant for three dollars an hour. And that's if I'm lucky. I don't even want to contemplate the alternative.

I look down into my wine glass with a heavy sigh. Cat and Geoff are friendly but that doesn't help with the fact that I'm homeless and jobless—and now, thanks to that apartment scam, nearly broke. If I don't find a job soon, I won't have any choice but to go home with my tail between my legs.

6

I'm dreading today. Apartment hunting in Manhattan is not for the faint of heart. Well, that's what I've heard. I've never tried it, and given the choice I wouldn't be. But I'm determined to find my new home in this big city. So, I've lined up a few apartments to check out.

The first is only a few blocks from Cat's place and I walk over mid-morning. I let myself wander slowly, taking in the neighborhood. The streets are cute, with small gardens and trees, beautiful brick facades and arched doorways. In the distance I hear the ever-present soundtrack of sirens and car horns, but most of them aren't nearby. In fact, this area is sort of quiet. It really does feel like its own village.

I turn down a pretty street, lined with golden Gingko trees, and find the building I'm looking for. Pressing the buzzer, I wait nervously.

"Hello?" a voice says behind me, and I turn to see a middle-aged man.

"Oh, hi. I'm here to view the apartment?"

He nods and gestures for me to follow him through a

gate, down from the street level. We enter through a heavy door into a small space. No, it's not small. It's tiny.

"So, this is the living room," he says with a grand sweeping gesture, as if he's showing me a suite at The Ritz and not what is, essentially, a basement.

I nod, trying not to grimace. What is that smell?

He takes a few steps and cracks open a door. "And this would be your room. My room is down the back."

"Oh," I say, surprised. I didn't realize it was a shared apartment. Still, beggars can't be choosers and all that. And he seems nice enough, I suppose.

I poke my head into the room and my jaw drops. It's not a room—it's basically a broom closet with a window.

He smiles at me and I notice he has food in his teeth. I give him a polite smile in return, willing myself to stay positive. Maybe this will have to do until I can find something better.

"What is the rent, again?" I ask. "Twelve hundred a month?"

He shakes his head. "No. Two thousand."

My eyes widen in shock. Two thousand a month to live in a closet? Jesus, I couldn't afford to live here even if I *wanted* to.

I quickly thank him and leave, desperate to get away from the odor lingering in that place. Once outside on the street, I gulp in a breath of fresh air, then release it in a frustrated sigh.

Oh well, maybe the next one won't be so bad. I know they can't all be winners. Good thing I got the worst one out of the way first, I guess.

But it only gets worse: apartments so teeny I can barely get in the door let alone put my books or clothes anywhere;

creepy roommates that make me feel like I'd need to sleep with one eye open.

By the afternoon I'm practically despondent. I trudge along West 8th Street towards the Village, holding back tears. No apartment, and I haven't even *begun* to think about searching for a job.

One thing is painfully clear, though. There's no way the apartment package I purchased online could ever have been real. It's almost laughable that I thought it was. Because now that I know what your money can actually buy you in terms of Manhattan apartments, well. I was an idiot.

Mum said it was insane to come here and I'm starting to think she was right, because—

Huh. That's weird.

Across the street I see a flash of something—or rather, *someone*—familiar, and I freeze, trying to figure out how I could possibly know someone around here.

Oh, wait.

Broad shoulders. Expensive suit. Beard...

It's the guy from Starbucks that I showered in coffee.

Shit, I hope he doesn't see me. He may very well march over here and demand I fork out for a new shirt.

What's he doing around here in the middle of the day, anyway? Shouldn't he be down on Wall Street or something? He's clearly a businessman, and as I watch him from across the street, my mind fills in a few other details about what sort of guy I think he is: single, probably a bit of a womanizer with that physique, living in a penthouse or other fancy apartment with views of the park. He seems like the type to get up early and hit the gym before work, which I imagine to be the kind of job where people shout into phones all day and only care about the bottom line.

I mean, okay, I could be wrong. Everything I know about

men like him I've learned from films like *The Wolf of Wall Street*. But he just *looks* like a typical New York businessman.

He turns to cross the road and before I can even register what's happening, I've ducked behind a lamppost to hide. For some reason my heart is thumping, and I get a flashback to his scowling face in Starbucks. He was so pissed off, and if he does expect me to stump up the cash now, I'd be royally fucked.

I brave a peek around the post and notice he's heading down the street, away from me.

Thank God.

My head slumps forward in relief, and that's when I notice the paper tacked to the post. It's a "help wanted" advert. No mention of what the job is, but it specifies women. There's no experience required, and it pays in cash. That's all I need to know.

I whip my phone out and dial the number as fast as I can, and it's not until it starts ringing that it occurs to me it could be something really shady. Shit, I could be ringing a pimp right now. I'm not *that* desperate.

Am I?

No, don't be silly, I tell myself. I'm sure it's something perfectly reasonable. Besides, I don't have many options. As long as it's not prostitution—or something else illegal—I'll do it.

I cross my fingers as the call connects.

WELL, the good news is that I'm not selling my body or dealing drugs. The bad news is that I have to wear a wedding dress and hand out fliers up and down West 8th to advertise a bridal boutique.

It's been three days now and I have to admit, it's a *little* humiliating. Especially the dress; it's polyester and taffeta and just plain unflattering. It smells like it's been worn by *many* people before me, and it itches, so I have to wear a white tank top and leggings underneath. But it's not just that. The irony of wearing a wedding dress every day when I'm feeling ready to give up on love is not lost on me.

I'm trying to be positive, though, because it has some unexpected perks. I mean, with all that walking up and down the street I'm getting in a lot of steps, so that has to be good for me. And it gives me several hours to just think.

Today, I thought about my writing. I used to write a blog a few years ago—mostly about dating and how shit it was—and I was thinking I might try writing on there again, just to warm up. That's my plan for tonight: write a blog post about moving to the city.

But first, dinner. I spot a pizza place on the walk home to Cat's apartment after work. After popping back to change out of my white leggings and tank (thankfully, I don't have to walk home in the hideous wedding dress), I head out to grab one.

I take the massive pizza box from the counter with an embarrassed smile. Apparently ordering a whole pizza for one was a mistake. It's *huge*. In New Zealand a pizza is about the size of a dinner plate. This pizza is bigger than a manhole cover. By the time I get back to the building my arms are starting to ache with the effort of carrying the damn thing.

I'm about to step into the apartment when I hear an odd noise coming from upstairs. It almost sounds like crying, but I can't be sure. With the pizza box hot in my hands, I climb a couple of steps until I can peek onto the next floor. Sitting in the hall, clutching a book and backpack, is a boy, around ten years old. His legs are crossed and he's sitting with his back leaning against a door, like he's waiting for someone.

I climb another step and clear my throat so he knows I'm there. He glances up, quickly wiping his face with the back of his sleeve.

"Hi. Are you okay?"

He nods, looking down at his hands. I think he's embarrassed I've caught him crying, so I try to say something reassuring.

"It's okay to cry if you're upset. I cried not that long ago because my boyfriend wanted to break up, so then I decided to move to New York and—" I break off with a cringe. Probably best to leave it there.

He gives me a peculiar look.

Okay, so that wasn't the right approach. He must think I'm some kind of maniac, cornering him in the hallway and bleating on about crying.

My gaze drops to the book in his hands. It's Bill Bryson's *A Short History of Nearly Everything*. "Are you reading that?"

"Yes."

"Woah," I say, impressed. "That's difficult reading for someone so young."

He shrugs. "We read a lot in my family."

I take another step up. "Yeah, well, reading is awesome. Where are you up to?"

"Um, I've just started. It's taking me a while."

"You know, I think there's a kids' version of that book."

"I know." He frowns. "But it was too easy."

I chuckle. This kid likes a challenge.

"Where are you from?" he asks, finally looking at me properly. He has chocolate-colored eyes and a brown fringe

—sorry, *bangs* is what they call them here—slanting across his forehead.

"New Zealand. Do you know where that is?"

He frowns again. "Of course."

I raise my eyebrows in surprise. I don't imagine American kids learn much about New Zealand.

We lapse into awkward silence, me standing halfway up the staircase holding a pizza box, him sitting in the hall with his book and backpack.

"So, why are you sitting out here?" I ask eventually. I want to ask why he was crying but don't want to embarrass him again.

"I'm waiting for Dad to get home. He's running late."

I feel a pang of sympathy. It's nearly eight o'clock. He must be hungry. "Did you have dinner?"

He shakes his head.

"Well, if you want, I have way too much pizza here. Would you like some?"

His eyes drift to the box and he bites his lip. "I... shouldn't."

Well, I guess I am a random stranger offering him food in a hallway. Probably the right answer. But I can tell he desperately wants a piece and *I* know it's safe for him to eat.

"When is your dad getting home?"

He shrugs.

"Hmm. Okay, I'll be right back." I pop down the stairs and into the apartment, putting a few slices of pizza on a plate for myself, then take the rest up in the box. I set it down next to him, pausing. "You're not allergic to dairy or gluten or anything, are you?"

He shakes his head and I relax.

"Okay, cool. Well, I've taken all I want, so if you feel like eating some you can, and if you don't that's okay too." I smile gently.

He looks at me, examining my face like he's trying to figure me out. "What's your name?"

"Alex."

"I'm Henry."

"It's nice to meet you, Henry. I'm staying downstairs. I'm going to go and eat my pizza now." I turn to go, then glance back. "Will you be okay here?"

His gaze wanders over to the pizza box and he nods. "Dad should be home soon."

"Okay. I hope you feel better."

He gives me a little smile, revealing a cute dimple in his cheek. "Thanks."

I head down the stairs, wait for a moment, then peek back up over the top step. He's devouring a slice of pizza and I grin to myself as I head back inside.

7

Americans are obsessed with Halloween. So many stoops on the walk back to Cat's place tonight are crowded with pumpkins or plastic skeletons. Some even have masses of white cobwebs over the railing. But it's fun.

I wish I could say the same about work. Well, today wasn't so bad. Being Halloween, fewer people noticed the crazy woman on the street in a wedding dress. But otherwise, it's pretty demeaning. It's cold out and when I asked my manager if I could wear a jacket, she told me to "toughen the fuck up" or she'd find someone else. And a few days ago, someone threw a soda can at me as they drove past. It didn't hit me, thankfully—their aim was shit—but it gave me a hell of a fright. I didn't spend four years at university to do *this*.

I wander through the Village, crossing over 7th Ave and heading along Charles Street, crunching through the carpet of orange and yellow leaves. They smell sweet and musky in that way that fallen leaves do, and I let out a heavy sigh. I'm loving being in the city, but it's been two weeks and I'm still sleeping on Cat's sofa. And while I'm enjoying the cuddles with her tiny pug Stevie, I want my own place. I'm trying, believe me, but it just feels impossible. Every place I've looked at is either absurdly expensive or impossible to get because there are so many people looking. It's a nightmare.

I know writing will make me feel better, but I haven't been doing it. I wrote one blog post a week ago and that's it. Between apartment hunting and surviving at work, I just have no inspiration.

I shake my head firmly, deciding that tonight, I'm going to write. Just the thought of that lifts my spirits.

My phone buzzes in my bag and I pull it out to see a missed call from Mum. Guilt nudges me in the chest and I pause on the sidewalk, my finger hovering over the call button. I haven't spoken to my parents since arriving in the city. I've texted them, so they know I'm alive, but I know that if I talk to Mum she'll ask a million questions—or worse, she'll remind me what a mistake I've made. And given I'm working in a shitty job and still technically homeless, I'm worried I might just end up agreeing with her.

No. I can't face her right now.

I jam my phone back in my bag and continue, shivering in the early evening air. I'm only wearing my white leggings and tank top under a thin jacket and it's quite cold. The sky has turned a dark, slate gray, the air cool and thick with the promise of rain. Just as I turn down our street, the sky completely opens upon me, turning the streets to rivers in seconds. My jacket is soaked through, my clothes drenched as I dash along the pavement, dodging people in dripping Halloween costumes. Finally, I reach the building and push the front door open. I can't wait to get inside, take a long hot shower, and settle down with my laptop.

"Hold the door!" I hear behind me as I duck in out of the rain.

I hold it with one hand, using the other to peel off my soggy jacket. I can feel my clothes sticking to me all over, my hair dripping down the sides of my head.

"Hi, Alex!" I look up to see Henry in a raincoat, giving me a bright smile.

"Hi, Henry." I return his smile, rummaging in my bag for my keys, trying not to create a puddle in the foyer.

"Dad! This is my friend, Alex."

A figure steps through the door behind Henry, obscured behind an umbrella, shaking water off onto the doormat. I offer a smile just as the umbrella is lowered, but my brain short-circuits when I see who's in front of me.

Broad shoulders. Expensive suit. Beard.

Gah, not again!

I grimace, praying he doesn't recognize me, but when his deep brown eyes collide with mine, his features harden.

"Oh. Hi."

I should be slinking away but I can't move, I can't take my eyes off him. His dark hair is wet and water is dripping down one side of his face, his short beard damp with rain-drops. He's brushing water off his suit jacket impatiently.

Fuck, he's *hot*. Was he this good-looking the last time I saw him?

I glance between him and Henry, putting the pieces together. So he's Henry's dad, and... he lives in the building? I didn't see that coming, although it explains why I keep seeing him around the Village.

Unease pinches my gut, and I realize I'm intimidated by him. Maybe it's the business attire, or because he's older, or the fact that he could demand money from me at any second.

Okay, I did ruin his shirt, but it's not like I *wanted* to spill my coffee all over him. He was rushing me, making me flustered. I think back to how impatient he was, how he spoke to the barista like I wasn't even there. I bet he's one of those men who has no respect for women, especially if he is a womanizer.

It's then that I remember what I'm wearing, and I look down at my clothes in horror. My tank top is already low-cut —it has to be, so you don't see it above the wedding dress— and now the thin white cotton is practically transparent. The black lace of my bra is clear as day, and when I notice my cleavage glistening with rain, I shudder with mortification. Of all the times to run into this guy and I look like I've entered a wet T-shirt contest.

"Hi," I squeak, glancing up again.

"Alex, is it?" He places his umbrella in the stand by the door then turns back, his gaze sweeping over me.

I half nod, half cringe, clutching my jacket to my chest in an attempt to regain some dignity.

He extends a wet hand. "Michael."

I take it in mine, giving him a meek smile.

"Where are you from, Alex?" Michael asks politely as he waits for Henry to check the mailbox. Every word in that rich, deep American accent slides over my skin like silk and I struggle to find my words.

"She's from New Zealand, Dad." Henry turns back to us with a grin. "She moved here because her boyfriend wanted to break up, and—"

"Thanks, Henry," I say hastily, my face glowing red. I hazard a glance at Michael and there's a glimmer of amusement in his eyes.

"It was Alex who gave me the pizza last week," Henry explains, wandering over to the stairs.

Michael stiffens. He turns to me as Henry heads up the steps. "Oh. That was you? You didn't need to do that."

I shrug. "He was upset and said he hadn't eaten, so—"

"Yeah, well, I was on my way with dinner." He rakes a hand through his wet hair, irritation flickering across his features.

I raise my eyebrows, taken aback. "Okay. Sorry." I'm not sure what else to say. If anything, I thought I had been kind when Henry was obviously upset and alone, but apparently not. "I didn't mean to interfere, I was just—"

"It doesn't matter," he interrupts, his brows drawing together.

"Dad!" Henry calls from up the stairs.

"Anyway," Michael grumbles. Then without even saying goodbye, he turns and heads up the steps, his expensive shoes squeaking on the wet floor.

I stand in the foyer, dripping and cold, gaping after him.

What the hell was that? One minute he's being, well, not exactly friendly but at least polite, then the next he's looking at me like I'd offered his son crack instead of pizza.

I shake my head in disbelief and slide the key into the lock, squelching into the apartment. The sooner I can get out of these soggy clothes and into something warm and dry, the better.

8

"I've got a surprise for you!"

Cat wanders into the living room as I'm wringing water from my hair into a towel. I've had a lovely hot shower and was just about to sit down with my laptop, but the excited look on Cat's face tells me I won't be doing that.

"Okay," I say warily. "What is it?"

"I made us costumes!" She grins, pulling two hangers out from behind her back.

I stare at the hangers. "You *made* me a Halloween costume?"

She nods. "I know you've been having a hard time with apartment hunting, and work sucks. But it's your first Halloween in America and I thought we could dress up and go out, have some fun!"

"Oh," I say, touched. "That's so sweet." I wasn't planning to go out tonight, but after that weird run-in with Michael, I'm not sure I'm in the mood to write. Drinking and dancing, on the other hand, sounds quite appealing.

"This one is yours," Cat says, passing me a rather small amount of fabric. "It's Snow White."

I reach tentatively for the costume and hold it up. There's a blue bodice with puffy sleeves and a big red bow at the middle of the low-cut neckline. A tiny yellow skirt flares out from the waist. I can see that it's definitely Snow White themed, but only if she was moonlighting as a stripper.

"And I'm going as the Evil Queen!"

My gaze shifts to the purple and black outfit Cat's holding up.

"What do you think?" she asks, looking at me expectantly.

I glance back down at the costume, unsure what to say. She's put a lot of work into it, which is very thoughtful, but can I really *wear* this?

"Try it on!"

I scan my brain for some kind of excuse—for any reason as to why I can't possibly put this tiny shred of fabric on my body and go out in public—but my mind is blank. And when I look at Cat's hopeful face, I feel a stab of guilt.

"Okay," I hear myself saying. I take the costume into the bathroom and wedge myself into it. It's a bit tight and the skirt is short, but my boobs steal the show as they threaten to spill out. Seriously, where did she get the pattern for this costume? This is *not* the Snow White I remember from childhood.

"Come out!" Cat calls from the living room.

I take a deep breath and wander out, feeling ludicrous. She has changed into her Queen costume, which is equally revealing.

"Wow!" Cat says, beaming. "You look great."

"Yours looks good too. But..." I run my eyes over her costume, confused. "These outfits are quite sexy. I thought Halloween was about dressing scary." Although, given the amount of my flesh that's exposed in this outfit, maybe it *is* a bit scary.

"No one dresses scary. Haven't you seen *Mean Girls*?"

A laugh escapes me. I have, but I didn't realize that was real.

"So will you come out? I need Snow White to complete the look."

I glance down at my costume again, thinking of all the time she spent making this for me. She's only known me for a couple of weeks, but she's gone to the trouble of custom-making me a Halloween costume so I can have a fun night out? That might be the nicest thing anyone has ever done for me.

"Alright," I say with a smile. Besides, Halloween in New York could be fun, right? "But I'm going to need a drink."

We open a bottle of wine while we get ready. I spend extra time on my appearance (since "sexy" is apparently the theme of the evening), curling my short hair into loose waves before putting a red bow in, and borrowing some dark red lipstick from Cat. Instead of my usual comfortable ballet flats, I opt for heels so my bare legs look longer. We'd just come out of winter back home, so my legs are paler than I'd like. But then I guess Snow White isn't exactly a bronzed goddess, is she?

By the time we're getting into an Uber to head to the East Village, I'm feeling excited and, dare I admit it, a little sexy.

It's nice, actually. Work has been awful and I'm stuck sleeping on a friend's couch, but tonight I can go out with some friends and pretend my life isn't a total mess. Isn't that what Halloween is all about, anyway? Dressing up and pretending?

As we push through the crowd at Bounce and find a

table, I see that Cat wasn't wrong about the sexy thing—
almost no one is dressed scary. But I find myself feeling self-
conscious again. The women in this city are something else,
and every time I think I'm looking good, I go out and
remember I'm not from this world.

"Thanks for making me a costume," I say as we slide into
the booth. "That was sweet."

"I nailed it, too. Got your measurements pretty much
spot on."

"Yeah, how'd you do that?"

She takes a sip of her vodka soda, assessing my costume.
"I have a good eye for this stuff. I've been sewing forever."

I nod. It's well-made, with lots of details. I glance down
at my cleavage on full display and giggle. "It's a bit tight,
but—"

"It's supposed to be tight. You look hot."

My face warms as I sip my wine, and Cat gives me a
funny look.

"You know that, right? I'd kill to have curves like yours."

I straighten, smiling modestly. "Thanks. It's been a
culture shock, coming from a small town to this glamorous
city. And, I don't know, I've been feeling a bit bad about
myself since my ex..."

She waves a hand. "That's normal. But trust me, he's an
idiot."

"Who's an idiot?" Geoff drops onto the vinyl seat beside
me. I turn to take in his costume: a red and black plaid shirt
with black suspenders, over jeans. In his hand he's holding a
plastic ax.

"Oh, hey! You look great!" Cat grins and Geoff gives a
half-bow in his seat. "Very lumbersexual."

A little snort-laugh comes from my mouth and for a
second I'm horrified, thinking Geoff might be offended.

But he just shrugs. "I figured if I came as a lumberjack I might attract a bear."

He and Cat share a laugh, then turn to look at my mystified expression when I don't join in.

"A bear?"

Geoff chuckles, patting me on the arm. "It's a gay term for a guy who's big and hairy. You know, like a bear."

"Oh! That's cute."

He wiggles his eyebrows playfully. "You two look fantastic. Now," he says, adjusting his glasses and taking a sip of merlot, "who's an idiot?"

"Alex's ex."

Geoff raises his eyebrows. "Ex? Do tell."

So I fill him in on the details of Travis dumping me on my birthday behind the Italian restaurant to go travel the world. In truth, I haven't thought about Travis all that much since I've arrived in the city, mostly because I've been in survival mode, too worried I'll have to go crawling back home.

But as I recount the whole sorry story—how we weren't together for long but I'd kind of thought it was going somewhere—a strange sensation creeps over me. With every sympathetic head nod from Geoff, I feel increasingly foolish. Geoff and Cat are older than I am—mid-thirties, I think —and clearly a lot more worldly than me. I bet they'd never be so stupid as to believe there's such a thing as happily ever after.

I give them a strained smile as I wrap up my sad little tale. "But it led me here, where I'm starting a new life. So, it all turned out okay in the end." I decide not to mention that it doesn't *feel* okay right now. No point in killing the mood.

Cat pushes out of the booth. "I'll get us more drinks. Same again?"

We both nod, and I drain my wineglass with a heavy heart. Thank God Cat gets cheap drinks, otherwise I'd be drinking water. I'm not paying rent at the moment, thanks to her generosity, but I'm saving every spare penny I can for an apartment deposit, when the time comes. *If* the time comes.

"Well, I'm glad things are working out here," Geoff says with a warm smile. "I was going to ask if you still needed a job, but you're obviously all set."

My hand stills on my glass. "What?"

"I had someone quit yesterday, and I figured if you were still looking for work you might be interested. But if—"

"Yes!" I cry, setting my glass down with a thud. "I am interested!" It takes all my self-control not to grab Geoff by the collar and beg him to hire me.

He eyes me with amusement. "But don't you have a job?"

"Geoff—" I take a breath, trying to keep the hysteria out of my voice. "My job is awful. I get treated like shit, and I have to do things I *never* thought I'd do."

Geoff's expression shifts from amusement to outright horror. "What are you doing?" He leans closer, lowering his voice. "Are you stripping, or something?"

"What?!" I shriek, aghast. "*No.* I have to wear a wedding dress up and down West 8th for a bridal boutique." I give a hollow laugh. "Stripping might actually be better. Fewer people would see me and I'm sure it would pay more."

"Jesus." Geoff shakes his head. "Okay, well there's a job up for grabs if you want it."

"Yes! Please!" Relief crashes through me. "What are the hours?"

"It's full time, but the hours vary from week to week. I know you said you were assistant manager back home, but this won't be management. So—"

"Geoff, if you have a job open where I don't have to

publicly humiliate myself, I'll do whatever you ask." He laughs and I observe him over my glass of wine. "You said you get applications all the time. Why do you want to hire *me*?"

"You're a friend of Cat's, so I'm happy to help you out. Plus..." He hesitates, as if considering how much to share, then releases a long sigh, letting his gaze float across the bar. "I was once young and fresh-faced, new to the city with just the clothes on my back and the dreams in my heart..."

I bite my lip to repress a laugh at the dramatic and faraway look in his eye. He catches my expression and chuckles.

"Okay, fine. I had a U-Haul crammed with my things and an apartment my parents got for me. But the point is, I know what it's like to arrive here and not know anyone—to feel like you don't even know *yourself*."

A rueful laugh slips from me and I glance down at my wineglass. I'm not sure if he realizes how close to home his words have hit.

"So if I can help you out, then I will. Besides, I've got a good feeling about you."

"I can't thank you enough. This is..." I feel my throat closing with grateful tears and I swallow. "I won't let you down."

Geoff gives my arm a squeeze. "I know you won't."

Cat returns with our drinks and I hold mine up in a toast. "To Geoff, my savior."

Cat cocks her head. "Okay, what did I miss?"

"Geoff just gave me a job."

"Oh! That's awesome."

I nod happily. "No more wedding dress."

"I still can't believe you wear a wedding dress on the

street." Geoff sips his merlot with a chuckle. "The things we do to stay in the city."

Cat laughs, and begins telling us a horror story about a job she had once, years ago. Geoff counters with his own horror story, which no one can top. As we sip our drinks, chatting and laughing, I find myself feeling lighter for the first time since arriving in New York. It's not just the wine, or my new friends—it's knowing I won't have to endure that hideous job anymore.

Now I just have to find somewhere to live.

Geoff leaves after a while in search of his "bear," which he insists he won't find at Bounce. I give him a huge hug, overwhelmed with gratitude for my new job. I knew I liked him.

Cat and I share another drink in the booth as I fill her in on my fruitless apartment hunt. Just talking about it is killing my buzz. I'm about to tell her I'm considering looking in—*gulp*—New Jersey, when she waves across the bar.

"There's Mel!"

I look at the throng of people but I can't see who she's talking about. Then, a tall, slim woman pushes her way out of the crowd. She's dressed as Wonder Woman, with the red and gold corset-style top, knee-high red boots and the tiny blue skirt barely covering her long, slender thighs. Her full red lips curl into a smile when she spots us. She's older—I'm guessing around forty—and despite all of Cat's kind words earlier, I shrivel a little as she approaches.

"Hey!" Cat grins, gesturing to me. "This is Alex."

I give Mel a meek smile as she slides into the booth gracefully. Even in a freaking Halloween costume she is the most sophisticated and chic woman I've ever met in real life.

"So," Mel says, her dark eyes sparkling as she glances at me, "you're staying with Cat?"

I nod, sipping my drink. I'll need a *lot* more booze if I'm going to co-exist in the same time and space as this movie-star woman.

"What brings you to New York?" She raises her martini to her lips. God, even her choice in drink is cool.

"Oh, uh," I say, flustered. I don't know what it is, but I feel very intimidated by her. "I decided to move here after..." I flounder, unsure of how to say it without sounding like a loser.

"After her idiot ex made a big mistake," Cat offers, and I shoot her a grateful look.

"Idiot ex? I've got one of those." Mel gives a heavy eye-roll, flicking a wave of mahogany hair over a bronzed shoulder. "Aren't men just total assholes?"

"Mm," I say, refusing to let myself think about Travis again.

"Anyway." She shakes her head, twirling her martini glass. "What do you do?"

An hour ago this question would have had me wilting with shame, but now I can't contain the grin that spreads across my face. "I've just got a new job at a bookstore in the West Village."

Cat nudges me. "She's also a writer. That's why she moved here: to write."

"I'm not really a writer," I say quickly. "I want to be."

Mel nods. "What do you write?"

"Um..." I glance down, feeling silly. All that talk about coming to New York to be a writer and I've only written one measly blog post. "I write a blog," I say at last. "Well, I used to. I've been lacking direction lately. I feel like I need a project or something to guide me, because I'd like to write more."

"What did you blog about in the past?"

For some reason I feel my cheeks color. "Just dating, mostly. And how shit it was."

"Sounds interesting. I'll have to have a read. I work for a women's website and we're always looking for new writers."

"Of course!" Cat rolls her eyes to herself. "Why didn't I think of that?" She turns to me with a grin. "Mel should check out your blog."

"Oh." I wave a hand. "It's mostly posts from a few years ago."

Mel offers me a benevolent smile. "It doesn't matter how old it is if it's well-written and there's truth to it."

I contemplate Mel's sincere face. I don't know why I was intimidated; she seems like a lovely person. I guess she's one of those people that we all love to hate: beautiful, successful, intelligent and also nice. You know the ones I mean. It's like they're perfect and you can't help but hope that there must be something secretly wrong with them, like maybe they have an extra toe or a hideous scar somewhere or something.

But gazing at Mel's friendly face, I can't hate her. She's just too nice.

"Anyway," she adds, sipping her martini, "if you want to be a writer, you need to be writing. Find something you love to write about, and do it."

I sigh, sagging against the booth. She's right—I need to be writing. It's pretty damn simple, isn't it?

9

A couple of hours—and *many* drinks later—Mel and Cat want to head to another bar downtown, but I decide to call it a night. Even though I've been here for two weeks now, my body still feels like it hasn't quite adjusted to New York time.

Plus, I'm in a weird mood. I might have found a way out of the job from hell thanks to Geoff, but Mel's words about writing brought me down from that temporary high. Because now that I'm not trapped in a soul-sucking job, I have no excuses.

I get an Uber back to Cat's place alone and wobble up the front steps. Probably a good thing I called it a night when I did, because I can feel myself sliding into sad drunk territory.

I key in the code for the front door and let myself into the lobby, looking forward to getting into my PJs. Searching in my bag for my keys, a hiccup escapes me, followed by a giggle. I did have a fun night. And I'm pretty sure I caught Cory checking me out at one point, which was a nice confidence boost. It's this Snow White dress, I'm sure. I giggle again as I glance down at the skimpy costume I'm wearing. I wouldn't have been caught dead wearing this back home, but here, on Halloween, I fit right in. And, just quietly, my boobs look *great* in it.

But... oh, shit. My keys are not in my bag, I realize, as I dump the contents out onto the table under the mailboxes. A million things tumble out—wallet, phone, EpiPen, tissues, pens, lip-gloss, earphones—but no keys. Even in my tipsy state I can see they aren't there.

"Fuck," I mutter, dropping my empty bag and rubbing my face. I must have left my keys on the kitchen counter.

I grab my phone with a sigh. Cat's going to hate me asking her to come home now, but what else can I do? It's already close to midnight and I don't fancy sleeping on the lobby floor. But when I call her it goes straight to voicemail, so I leave a message. Then I scoop the contents back into my bag and trudge over to the stairs, slumping onto the bottom step.

I'm just about to attempt a sexy selfie when the front door to the building opens and I look up expectantly. But it's not Cat, it's—fuck, not *again*—him. My heart jumps and I silently curse Cat for making me wear this preposterous costume. I, once again, look like an idiot, while he's still wearing his suit, his gaze focused down on his phone as he strides across the lobby.

From where I'm perched on the bottom step he looks taller, his shoulders broader than I remember. Each time I see him it's like he's gotten a bit more handsome—and a bit more grumpy.

He pauses at the bottom of the stairs, lifting his gaze to meet mine. His brow furrows into its default frown and he heaves out a breath. "You know, I'm trying to think of a time recently when I looked up and you weren't there."

Okay, a *lot* more grumpy.

I raise my eyebrows, huffing in disbelief. What is he implying, that I'm loitering out in the lobby, desperate to run into him? It's hardly my fault he happens to live in the building where I'm staying. And I'm getting pretty sick of his disagreeable attitude, if I'm honest. Maybe, I think, as the alcohol courses through my veins, it's time to give him a piece of my mind.

I push to my feet, ready to say something scathing, but as I do his expression shifts. I watch as his gaze dips down my dress, lingering on my bare legs before returning to my face. His espresso-dark eyes lock onto mine and I feel a flicker of heat low in my belly. I mean, what the hell was that? Did he just—was he checking me *out*?

No, that can't be right. He's possibly one of the sexiest men I've ever seen in real life, and I'm quite sure I'm not in his league. Gorgeous, successful New York businessmen don't tend to find themselves interested in women like me. Jesus, I must be pretty drunk if I'm imagining that.

But drunk I am indeed, because next thing I find myself imagining is him lifting me up onto that table over by the mailboxes and sliding one of his big hands up my thigh. I shiver at the thought of it, my whole body flushing with heat.

Oh God. Drunk and horny is *not* a good combination.

I clear my throat, hoping my little fantasy is not evident on my face. And now we are standing, staring at each other in silence, and I can feel the tension gathering around us, thick and heavy.

Shit, say something.

"You, uh, don't take Henry trick-or-treating?"

He shakes his head, pocketing his phone. "He goes with

his uncle. They do a whole"—he gestures vaguely and scrunches his nose—"*Star Wars* thing."

"Oh." I can't help but smile, picturing Henry dressed up as Yoda or something. How cute.

Michael narrows his eyes at me. "What are you doing lurking in the hallway at this time of night, anyway?"

I smirk. "Hoping to run into *you*, obviously."

There's a little twitch in his lip, a spark dancing in his eyes as they explore my face. For one crazy moment I actually think he's going to laugh. But, no—he manages to suppress what is clearly a foreign and unnatural urge for him, his expression returning to neutral.

"I'm locked out." I smooth my hands down over the tiny skirt of my costume, watching as his gaze follows them. It was sweet of Cat to make this for me, but I've had about enough of dressing up since arriving in this city. I smile to myself at the thought that I'll never have to wear that hideous wedding dress again. Geoff is a lifesaver.

Michael cocks his head. "What are you so happy about?"

"Nothing. I just... I got a new job tonight. At a bookstore," I add proudly.

He raises his eyebrows. "Oh yeah? Which one?"

"Between the Lines."

He nods, scrubbing a hand over his beard. His gaze lingers on me and I feel a spike of self-consciousness again. I attempt a casual laugh to cover it.

"And what have you been up to? Hot date?" I say, then immediately cringe. I don't know why I'm trying to banter with him when the two interactions we've had have been nothing but awkward and unpleasant. Maybe I was trying to see if he could crack a smile. I'm sure he was close a moment ago.

Anyway, I'm quite certain he was at the office again,

closing on a deal or something, given he's still in his suit. That delicious suit.

"Something like that," he mutters.

Oh.

I feel an unusual twinge in my chest, and it takes me a second to recognize it as envy. He might be grumpy as fuck, but lucky bloody woman.

"And you're coming home alone?" I joke awkwardly. "Shouldn't you be bringing her—" *Shit! Abort! Abort!* What the hell am I saying?

I stare at the ceiling, grimacing. It's like I've forgotten how to be a normal person all of a sudden. When I risk a glance at Michael's face, he's regarding me with that same look of amusement in his eyes.

"She wasn't really my type," he says at last, loosening the button on his suit jacket. He drags a hand through his hair, messing it up. It's longer on top, I notice, and God, it looks even better all tousled like that. What I wouldn't give to thread my hands up into it.

Fuck. I should not be out in this corridor alone with him after drinking. I'm going to say something stupid and embarrass myself. Wait, I already have.

I force myself to clamp my lips together and just shut the hell up. My phone buzzes in my hand and I glance down to see a message from Cat saying she's on her way home.

Good. Okay. Michael will leave in a second and until then I need to just zip it.

But he doesn't leave. He's still studying me, apparently debating whether or not to say anything more. Eventually, he lets out a long sigh. "It was a set-up. I don't know why I bothered."

I suppress an eye-roll. Honestly, this guy. First he makes someone else take his kid trick-or-treating so he can go on a date, and then she's not good enough for him? No doubt he's got exceedingly high standards and this poor—probably quite attractive—woman had no chance of meeting them. I feel indignant on her behalf.

"What was wrong with her? She wasn't beautiful enough?"

"Oh, she was beautiful," he says. "But that's the problem. You women all think that if you're beautiful you can get away with anything."

A dart of irritation shoots through me, quickly chased by confusion. "*Us* women? Why am *I* being brought into this?"

"Because—" He rakes his eyes over me with a smirk, and I shrivel a little under his glare. I *knew* he was one of those men that didn't respect women. It was clear from the start.

"You're all the same," he mutters, shaking his head. And before I can say anything in response, he steps past me, taking the stairs two at a time, until he's out of sight.

And I'm left, for the second time this evening, staring after him in shock.

10

R omance.

Mel said I should find something I enjoy writing and do it. I've been lacking direction in my writing, feeling like I need something to help me focus, and a romance novel might be a good place to start.

I've wanted to write one for years—hell, I've read enough of them—but I've never had a good reason to finally sit down and do it. Now, maybe I do. Because I suddenly find myself overcome with inspiration. Inspiration that has come from an unlikely source: my rude neighbor.

Well, okay. A good portion of my inspiration has come from my fantasies about him, which are based entirely on his good looks and have nothing to do with his personality. I'm pretty sure *that's* non-existent.

But I've also been thinking about what he said, about how he shouldn't bother dating because women are all the same, or some crap like that. He's clearly a cynical, misogynistic asshat, and that further inspired me. Because while the men in real life are always disappointing, the men in romance novels are not.

Okay, I know. These books are full of mush that isn't realistic, or whatever it was my mother said. But isn't that the point? It's escapism. There's only an issue if I believe that it could be *real*.

I'm thinking about this as I dress for my first day of work at the bookstore a few days after Halloween, Stevie watching me from her spot on the sofa. She's come to like curling up at my feet when I sleep and it's adorable. I might not have a man right now, but her tiny, furry body keeps me company. I can see why Cat loves her so much.

Grabbing my bag, I give her a quick cuddle, then slip out into the cool morning air. An elderly lady is slowly coming up the front steps. She looks to be in her eighties, in slim-fitting navy pants with a finely-knitted shawl sweeping down over her shoulders. Her long gray hair is pulled back with a shell hair clip and long earrings dangle from her ears. She has an air of elegance about her, even if she is slightly stooped.

"Good morning," I say as I pass.

She stops and glances at me, a smile warming her creased face. "Well, good morning." She pauses as if thinking, before adding, "No one says good morning anymore."

"You're right. Not here in New York, anyway."

"Oh, you're from out of town!"

I nod. I guess you could say New Zealand is "out of town."

"Have you moved into the building?" She raises one gnarled hand to gesture to the apartment building behind me.

"I'm staying with a friend. Do you live here?"

"For thirty-seven years now." A light breeze blows past, loosening a few wisps of hair around her face. She turns and, clutching the handrail, begins to take another careful step up.

"Um... would you like some help?"

"Oh, thank you." She lets me take her arm and I guide her up the stairs. "You're a lovely young lady," she says. We reach the top and she turns to me. "I'm Agnes."

"Nice to meet you, Agnes. I'm Alex."

"Well, I hope you enjoy your stay. If there is anything you need, let me know. It's an odd bunch in there, but I'm always happy for visitors." Her gray eyes light with a smile.

I grin in return, pleased that I stopped to talk to her. See, this is what neighbors should be like: friendly and kind, ready to lend you a cup of sugar and all that. Not grumbling because you offered their son pizza or, you know, dared to wait in the lobby.

And then a thought occurs to me. If she's lived here for so long, maybe she knows Michael. Maybe she knows why he's so, er, unpleasant.

"Thank you, Agnes. I wonder—" I hesitate, glancing into the building to make sure we are alone, then turn back to her, lowering my voice. "Do you know the man who lives on the second floor, Michael?"

"Michael." The wrinkles around her eyes deepen. "Oh yes. Wonderful man."

I frown. We must be talking about two different men.

"No. The man with the son, Henry?"

"Yes, Michael. He's a very nice man. And Henry is a sweet boy."

Wow.

"He's had a rough time of it," she continues. "Went through a divorce a few years back. I never did care for his wife."

I stare at her.

"It's a shame," Agnes says with a shake of her head. "A lovely man like that without a wife."

I'm speechless. A *lovely* man? How is it possible we are talking about the same guy? A thousand questions flood into my brain and I'm desperate to ask more but I don't know where to begin. After a moment I realize that I'm just gaping at Agnes, and I quickly pin on a smile.

"Well, I should probably get to work. It was nice to meet you."

"And you, dear."

I head back down the steps, processing what I've learned as I walk the few blocks to work, my head a cloud of confusion.

I LOVE MY NEW JOB! Well, in my previous job I had to brave the elements in a wedding dress that smelled like B.O. while dodging garbage thrown at me from passing cars, so the bar was pretty low.

But it's more than that. It's a bookstore, which at the very least is *related* to writing. And yes, I know this is what I did back home, but it's not the same. For one, it's in the West Village in *New freaking York*, so that makes it a million times cooler. And two, Geoff is *awesome*. I haven't sorted out a working visa yet, and when Geoff brought it up I thought my chance at the job was gone. Instead, he agreed to pay me in cash until I get it sorted. How nice is that?

The more I get to know Geoff, the more I like him. He's friendly and kind, intelligent and quick-witted, with a dry sense of humor. I can see why his shop does so well. People love him.

The store isn't huge, but it has a great selection of both new and secondhand books. It's at street level, with windows where the sun streams in for a couple of hours around midday, and narrow aisles where shelves of books stretch up to the high ceilings.

But the thing I love most is the atmosphere of the store. It's cozy and welcoming, with that indescribable smell of books, and soft music playing—Sinatra, I think. Even if Geoff didn't hire me I'd be happy to hang out here all day.

I spend most of the morning learning about the cash register, how they organize and shelve books, as well as how to add new inventory into the system. Geoff talks me through locking up and gives me a set of keys. Then I putter around the counter, tidying and rearranging the bookmarks we have stacked next to the register, greeting customers and generally loving every moment. Not just because I'm warm, in my own clothes, and no one is shouting obscenities at me from a car window—but also because, for the first time in ages, I'm feeling inspired to write.

The afternoon is quiet, and Geoff tells me to take some time to browse the store and get familiar with everything. He says that I'm welcome to borrow books if I see anything I like, and I decide that's the perfect invitation for me to check out the writing section, to see if I can find some books on how to write a romance novel. I'm delighted to find we have a few, which I flip through eagerly. There's lots of information about structuring a novel and creating the characters, and while some of the books are geared towards writing tender, sweet romances, there are also some that show how to write the naughty bits. Perfect.

I grab one of each and just as I'm about to go and pop them behind the counter, I spy a small section of erotica. Come to think of it, some erotica could be helpful. Not for *me*, of course—for my writing. I'm going to need to be able to write sex scenes without using words like "throbbing manhood" and "lovestick" and all that, right?

With a quick glance over my shoulder—Geoff, thankfully, is pricing stock a few aisles away—I tiptoe over and pull a few titles off the shelves.

Wow. These things are hot and heavy, and while I don't think I'll be writing with such graphic detail, I could learn a thing or two. I should probably borrow them. For research purposes, obviously. No other reason.

I add a couple to my pile, then head back down the aisle towards the counter. A familiar voice stops me in my tracks, and my pulse skips when I realize who it is.

"Yes. Yes. I'll be home when we agreed. Yes, drop him off then."

I pop my head between the shelves and spy Michael with his phone pressed to his ear, his face creased into its usual frown. What is *he* doing here? He's the last person I feel like running into in the middle of my first day at work.

I slink back behind a stand of Moleskine notebooks and hold my breath, as if he'll hear breathing and somehow realize it's me. No doubt he'll be up in arms about running into me again and I'll end up feeling stupid, somehow. Maybe I should just hide here, until—

Actually, no. This is my place of work, for crying out loud. I even *told* him that a few days ago. He can hardly get annoyed at me for being here.

I square my shoulders, lifting my head high. I'm just about to stride past him to the counter when I remember what I'm holding. I glance down at the stack of books in my arms and despite myself, I feel my cheeks color.

Shit.

Somehow I can't see Michael, with his disdain for everything female, perusing my reading material with any kind of admiration. Who knows what nasty remark he'll have up his sleeve?

His frustrated voice drifts down the aisle to where I'm hovering. "Look, I said I'll be there, okay?"

I can't stop myself; I peek around the stand at him. I haven't seen him in a few days, and I notice his usually perfect suit jacket is a bit rumpled. He looks tired, almost worn-out, and for the first time I see a flash of something real beyond his chiseled, expensive, brooding exterior. Maybe he is human, after all. I feel a whisper of compassion for him after what Agnes told me this morning. Is it possible she's right and he is a nice guy?

He lifts a hand to loosen the collar of his shirt, revealing a hint of dark chest hair. My eyes linger on it and heat uncurls deep inside me. A little fantasy begins to play out in my head; one involving him taking me on the floor of the book aisle when no one else is around.

He hangs up the call and stuffs the phone into his pocket, glancing up. Instinctively, I whip back behind the stand of Moleskines, my heart slamming into my ribs. It's like I've been caught in the act; watching him, imagining him touching me, and—*fuck*—I'm still holding these damn books...

Panic tears through me as his footsteps approach, and I thrust the books onto a stepladder behind me.

"Hello, Alex."

I spin back to face him, my cheeks warm. "Michael," I say with as nonchalant an air as I can muster. "What a surprise, seeing you in here."

"Uh, yes." His gaze slides to the right. "I forgot you work here."

I falter for a second, thrown. He *forgot*? Really?

He glances back at me and adds, "I come here all the time anyway, so..." he trails off, slipping his hands into his pockets, and his shoulders flex through his suit jacket. I swallow hard, noticing my mouth feels dry. I wonder what he looks like without that jacket.

Shit, pull yourself together.

I tear my eyes away, attempting to fold my arms across my chest in a casual manner. But all it does is press my breasts up, as if I'm *trying* to draw his attention to them. Oh, the curse of an ample bosom.

I let my arms drop with a cringe. Why do I find it so impossible to be normal around this guy? And more to the point, why do I care? He's been nothing but a jerk to me.

He peers at me strangely. "Are you okay?"

I plaster a smile on my face, reminding myself where I am; the first day of a new job that I do *not* want to mess up.

"I'm fine! I'm just..." What am I doing again? Not shopping for erotica when I should be working. *Be professional!* "I was just enjoying the large selection of books we stock. For example, this"—I gesture with a vague motion to the bookshelf in front of me—"is my favorite section."

He follows my gaze to the shelves and frowns, leaning closer to inspect the titles. "You're interested in military history?"

God, no. But better that, than the books I was just carrying.

"Oh, yes." I nod emphatically. "I find it *so* thrilling."

"Really?"

"Of course. It's fascinating, all of the, er, history." I wince as I hear myself. Jesus, I sound like some kind of simpleton.

"How... interesting." His brow knits as he gazes at me, like he's trying to make sense of me. The longer he stares, the more I start to sweat. Any minute now he's going to make some sweeping generalization about women and it's making me nervous.

I give an awkward laugh and lean against the stepladder behind me, inadvertently dislodging my stack of erotica and romance books. They slide out at our feet with a thud.

Oh fuck.

We both glance down at the stack. The cover on top has a bare-chested gentleman with a suggestive bulge in his pants, a crown dangling from one hand, and the title *The Prince of Pleasure* across the front in red script.

Oh my God.

My face is on fire as I glance back up to see Michael biting his lip, attempting to hold back a smirk.

"Just a little light reading there?"

"Um..." Mortification washes over me. I wish the ground would swallow me up and end this bloody nightmare right now.

He bends to collect the books, handing the pile to me. I hold them to my chest, against my hammering heart.

"Is this your usual reading material?" His eyebrows are raised and there's a tug at the corner of his mouth.

I clear my throat, trying to think of something witty to say, but I'm drawing a blank. First he sees me in a slutty Snow White costume and now he catches me with an armload of erotica. He must think I'm a sex-crazed lunatic.

"It's..." I start, but I can't think of anything to say. I'm perspiring with embarrassment now. From the corner of my eye I see Geoff wander past and I'm struck by a flash of brilliance. "Oh, these aren't *mine*. I'm just reshelving them." I lean forward, lowering my voice in a conspiratorial manner. "It's amazing what some people read." I give what I hope is a carefree laugh and turn to jam the books onto the military history shelf, before focusing my attention back on Michael. "Now, is there something I can help you with?"

Michael glances from the shelf to me, amusement gleaming in his eye. "Sure. Where's your travel section?"

I turn to show him, then pause. "I thought you came in here all the time?"

"Uh—" His gaze flicks down the aisle then back to me. "I do. I'm just... testing to see if *you* know. You haven't worked here very long."

My jaw tightens. "Of course. This way." I lead the way to the next aisle and indicate the travel section. Someone has shoved a few books in the wrong place and I quickly set about straightening them up.

Then, before I can step out of the way, Michael leans past me to grab a book. The buttons of his shirt strain across his broad chest as he reaches to the shelf, and when his hand brushes over the back of mine, there's a shock through me. All the tiny hairs on my arms stand on end and I feel almost light-headed.

But Michael, oblivious, just takes the book and scans the back cover. "Do you know if this is any good?"

I try to formulate a response but I'm still reeling from his brief touch. And he's close enough that I can smell him—an intoxicating combination of woodsy cologne and the faintest hint of sweat that's doing something wicked to me. It's just so *manly*. It's been ages since I've smelled something like this and I just want to huff it all in until I'm dizzy.

"Alex?" Michael prompts, a V forming between his brows.

I catch Geoff watching me quizzically from behind a stack of books the next aisle over. Shit.

"Er... yes?"

"This book. Is it any good?"

I glance down at the book in his hands. It's new, I think, because we were going to be getting it at the store back home but it hadn't arrived before I left. It's supposed to be the new *Wild*, or something. "I haven't read it, sorry."

"Why not?" Tiny, almost imperceptible crinkles form around his eyes. "Because there's nobody naked on the cover?"

Heat rises up my neck. I knew he hadn't bought that little performance back there. My teeth grit in irritation but I force myself to stay calm. It's time to show him I'm an intelligent woman with a wide breadth of knowledge—to put him in his place, once and for all.

Ignoring his comment, I turn to the shelf and pull out a slimmer book—one I actually have read and loved for years. "I'd recommend this, instead," I say with an air of expertise.

He takes it and reads the back cover, running a hand over his short beard, his brow wrinkled in thought. I try not to stare but I can't help myself. I know Agnes said he was lovely, but where is she getting that from? To me he's been nothing but rude and obnoxious. But... *God*, he's easy on the eyes. Up close I notice his beard has flecks of gray in it, which only makes him sexier. I'm guessing he's a good decade older than me, at least. And he must be nearly a foot taller than I am—definitely over six feet...

He glances up to catch me staring and gives me an odd look. Flustered, I turn back to the shelf and yank out a bunch of books.

"Or you could try these." I thrust the pile into his hands.

He shuffles through the titles and pulls one out on top. "What about this one?"

I tilt my head to look at the cover. Oops. I should have chosen more carefully because that book—*Three Months on the Appalachian Trail*—isn't good. Well, I don't know for certain because I haven't read it, but I do remember a customer back home saying something about it being disappointing for some reason. And I can't very well have him buy it and then think I don't know what I'm talking about, so I just carry on as if I'd read it last week.

"Oh, there are much better books. I'd definitely recommend the other one over that."

He lifts his eyebrows. "Really? Why's that?"

"Well, er... this one has some good points, but it doesn't give very detailed information about the, uh"—I scramble for the right words, my face hot—"topography... and all that."

"The topography?"

"Yes... of the mountain ranges and the terrain and—" I break off with a vague gesture. "*You know.*" I give him a meaningful look, as if we are both experienced hikers who have a shared knowledge of such things and therefore they don't need to be spoken aloud.

He cocks his head to one side, his brow furrowed. Somehow, I don't think he's buying my spiel.

Dammit.

For good measure, I throw in a few more details. "I also think it had bad reviews. Plus, er, the author isn't very well-known or respected." I give him a smug smile. *See, I know my stuff.*

But he narrows his eyes at me. "Really?"

Shit. I don't know.

"Well, the last thing I want is for you to buy something that's only going to disappoint."

He gives an indignant huff, but I can't for the life of me figure out why. I open my mouth to say something more and he cuts me off.

"Never mind." He leans past me to place the books back. Before I can stop myself, I inhale his scent again and my breath catches in my throat.

"Sorry I can't be more helpful," I mumble, my cheeks burning.

He rubs the back of his neck, gazing at me with that deep frown etched on his face, then sighs. "It's fine. Thanks." Then he strides towards the door before I can say anything more.

Geoff appears beside me out of nowhere, wide-eyed. "Who was *that*?"

I hesitate. I'm hardly going to tell Geoff he's Cat's neighbor, in case it gets back to Cat that I'm—for reasons I can't quite fathom—pissing him off and causing tension in the building. I mean, Agnes loves him, so Cat probably thinks he's the bee's knees too. It's just *me* who can't seem to get along with him.

"Just... a guy I accidentally spilled coffee on a few weeks ago. He was impatient and rude and... I don't know. He was a bit of a jerk."

Geoff rolls his eyes. "Ugh, I know the type. Too busy thinking about himself to worry about anyone else. And I bet that's an expensive suit."

I nod. "He's the kind of person I imagine when I think of New Yorkers: rude, impatient, career-obsessed."

Geoff pretends to look hurt and I laugh, shaking my head at him. Because that's what I like about Cat and Geoff. They're nothing like that.

"Well," Geoff says, patting me on the arm reassuringly,

"I'm sure the nonsense you were spouting about that book put him off coming back."

I cringe. God, he heard that? I bet I've lost the job now. I open my mouth to apologize, but Geoff just laughs.

"It's okay. We don't want him here anyway," he says. Then adds quietly, "Even if he is gorgeous."

11

Not a brilliant first day at work. Well, the morning was great but seeing Michael just kind of killed the afternoon. I don't know what that guy's problem is.

Anyway, I've got bigger issues right now. Cat texted me just as I was leaving work to say that we need to discuss our living situation, and I'm pretty sure she's going to tell me she wants her living room back. I can't blame her, right? I've been on her sofa for two and half weeks, which she probably wasn't counting on when she offered me a place to crash. I wasn't *planning* on staying there that long.

I try to think happy thoughts on the walk back from work—new job, yay! Geoff is lovely, yay!—but by the time I'm entering the apartment, my stomach is turning like a corkscrew. Because if Cat kicks me out, none of that will matter.

She's standing on a step-ladder in the living room, hanging some curtains in the corner when I enter. Stevie bounds over to me, jumping up my leg and demanding a pat as I close the door. I stoop to pet her head with a sigh. I'm going to miss this pup.

Cat glances over as I place my bag on the counter. "Oh good, you're home."

"Hey." I pick Stevie up to cuddle, taking a deep breath to prepare for what's coming. "You wanted to talk about the apartment, yeah?"

"Yes!" She grins as she climbs down the ladder.

"I haven't found a place yet, but I can hopefully get out of your hair in the next couple days. Would that be okay? I just need to—"

"Wait. You think I'm asking you to leave?"

"Er..." I scratch my nose. "Well, yeah."

"No! I had an idea that could work for both of us." She pauses, chewing her lip. "Would you consider living here? I can't offer you a room, but there's that area over there." She gestures to the corner of the living room where she was hanging the curtains. I notice her sewing stuff is gone, and there's a bed and dresser tucked behind the partition wall. "I know it's not ideal, but I won't charge you anywhere near what an apartment would cost."

"Oh," I say, taken aback. It had never occurred to me that Cat would want me to stay here. It is a lovely apartment, but I was kind of hoping for my own room, or even my own place. Still, I haven't found a single apartment that meets the criteria of being somewhere I'd actually want to live, available now and—perhaps most crucially—within my budget.

Cat gestures to the corner. "Come and have a look."

I set Stevie down and wander over, stepping into the nook behind the partition. She's sewed some thick, dark curtains and hung them from the ceiling, with big ties to hold them back when I want to open them up. She's made up a double bed with fresh linen, put a dresser and lamp in the corner and even put up a rail to hang my clothes. And while it's not quite where I imagined myself living in all my fantasies of New York, it's a cozy space with a roommate I know and like.

"Are you sure?"

She smiles. "Of course. We can come to an agreement on the rent."

I cast my gaze around the nook, feeling relief sink into my bones. I can't believe she went to all this trouble to set this up for me, after everything I've been through. Grateful tears prick my eyes and I quickly blink them away. "Why are you doing this?"

She looks down at her hands, lifting her shoulders in a light shrug. "I know you've had a hard time finding a place. And the more I thought about you leaving, the more I realized I've been enjoying the company. So, if you want to stay, you're welcome."

"I'd love to stay, Cat. Thank you so much." I drag my suitcases into the nook with a happy sigh. Stevie jumps up onto the bed and watches as I begin to unpack.

"Oh shit, is that the time?" Cat's glancing down at her phone with a frown. "I've got to get ready!" She disappears into the bathroom and I hear the shower turn on.

I put away all my clothes, taking my time to fold and hang everything neatly. Once all my things are in their new home, I slide my suitcases under the bed, glancing around. Cat appears in the living room, giving me a fright. I'd forgotten she was home, she's been in there so long. But I can see why; she looks stunning.

"Hot date?"

"Sort of," she says, reaching over to stroke Stevie's back where she's curled up on my bed. "Mel and I are going on this group date thing. They can be fun, but the guys are a little..." She rolls her hand, searching for the right word.

"Disappointing?"

"Exactly. But it's fun going out with Mel, at least. Ooh!" Her eyes brighten. "You should come with us!"

"Oh..." I sink down onto my new bed beside Stevie. "I don't think so. Thanks, though."

"Are you sure?"

I nod. "I might take a break from men, focus on my writing for a bit."

"Because of your ex?"

I think of Travis and how jaded I've been feeling about love recently. "Something like that," I mumble. "Anyway, I came all the way over here to write, so I need to work on that. If I could just figure out what to write about." This morning I was excited to begin my romance novel, but after seeing the amusement in Michael's eyes when he caught me with my stack of books, the thought of doing that now makes me feel deflated.

"Why not write about not dating?" Cat suggests.

"What?"

"You said you wanted a project to help you focus. You could blog about all that—about moving here and not looking for a man. Write about what it's like to be single in the city." She shrugs as she grabs her purse off the counter. "Could be interesting."

I rub Stevie's back, thinking. I guess I could blog about that. It's similar to what I used to blog about, after all. But when I sit with the idea, something is missing. It doesn't excite me in the same way my romance novel does—or, at least, it did this morning. Still, it's the best idea I've got right now.

Cat turns to me, smoothing her hands down her dress. "Okay, how do I look?"

I give her a once-over as she fusses with her purse and reapplies her lipstick. Instead of her jeans and combat boots —the funky style I've gotten used to—she's wearing a slinky black dress and heels, her lips now a deep shade of red. It's sexy, but it's kind of jarring after the way she's looked since I met her. It's like she doesn't quite look like herself. But then I guess I've only known her for a couple of weeks.

"You look amazing," I say truthfully. I'm not sure I could pull off a dress like that.

Cat gives a humble smile, putting her lipstick into her purse and snapping it shut. "Thanks. So, what are you going to do this evening?"

"Write. I'm going to write." I wave as she heads out. "Have fun!" The door closes behind her and I pull my laptop out, powering it on. Silence rings through the apartment, my fingers hovering over the keys.

Great. Time to write. Here we go.

I stare at the glowing screen, willing the words to come. But they don't. Instead, all I can think about is Michael, in his suit, taking me on the floor of the book aisle.

12

Ugh, this is stupid. Why on earth am I thinking about that asshole? He was *nothing* but rude to me.

I stuff the thought of him back into that dirty little box in my head, and pad into the kitchen to make myself a cup of tea. As the kettle boils, I look around the apartment—officially my New York home, now—and feel a smile creep onto my lips. Between this and my new job, it's finally starting to feel like things could work out for me here in the city.

Now if I could just get myself to write something.

I take my tea and settle onto my new bed beside Stevie, determined to get some words down. Picking up my laptop again, I mull over Cat's idea to blog about being single in the city. It could work, I suppose.

I'm about to open up my browser and sign into my blog when I notice that Emily is on Skype. We've been texting but I haven't spoken to her properly since that first day in Starbucks. I click on the icon to call her and a second later her face lights up my screen.

"Hi!" Her cobalt-blue eyes are bright, her shiny blond

hair pulled up in its usual ponytail. Just seeing her face makes me miss her.

I adjust my screen so the camera catches me properly. "Hey."

"Are you having a blast over there? How's it going?"

"Good," I say, unable to contain the grin pulling at my mouth. I grab Stevie and hold her up to the camera. "Meet my new roommate. Cat asked me to move in."

"Oh!" Emily's smile widens. "That's fantastic. She's great, isn't she? And Stevie is so cute."

I nod happily, setting Stevie back down. She curls her tiny body into a warm ball against my leg.

"So tell me everything. What's been happening?"

I fill her in on the past few weeks: the wedding dress ordeal, Geoff giving me the job at the bookstore, meeting Mel and getting inspired for my writing. But I pause at this point as Michael's mocking face flashes into my mind again.

"What is it?" Emily asks, narrowing her eyes.

"Nothing. I just..." I let out a sigh as I reach for my cup of tea on the nightstand. "There's this guy—"

"Ooh!"

"No." I hold my hand up. "No 'ooh.' Because he's a total dick."

She scrunches her pretty button nose. "That sucks."

"Yeah. I mean, he's *gorgeous*."

Emily raises her eyebrows, smiling playfully.

"But he's rude and arrogant and cynical," I add, before she gets any ideas. "And the worst part is, he lives upstairs from me, so I keep running into him." My mind drifts to him showing up at the bookstore today, and how he claimed he'd forgotten I worked there. What was that about? Did he actually forget, or did he seek me out just to taunt me? I shake my head to clear the thought and focus my attention back on Emily. "Anyway. How are you?"

"Oh, you know, same old." She laughs, but it sounds hollow.

"What's going on?"

"I got passed over for a promotion that I was pretty sure I was going to get."

Emily has been working in marketing for years. I'm not entirely sure what she does, but it's something to do with sports or athletic gear... I think.

"Oh that sucks, I'm so sorry." I make a face. "Did they say why?"

"Nah. But it might be time for me to move on from this company soon anyway. I'm over all the politics." She's quiet for a moment. "So... did you, um, hear about Travis?"

"No. What happened?"

"Oh, it's nothing," she says, glancing away from the screen.

I roll my eyes as I take a sip of tea. She's hopeless. "Come on, Em. What is it?"

"Okay. He has a new girlfriend."

I lower my tea, feeling a strange sting. I haven't been thinking about him much since I've arrived in the city but this is kind of a surprise. A new girlfriend, already? It's only been a month! Must be some exotic woman he's met while on his travels.

"Oh," I say eventually. "Well... good for him." I take another sip of my tea, ignoring the tightness in my chest. Here I was thinking I'd mostly moved on from Travis, but the mention of him with someone else has me feeling a bit ruffled.

"Yeah," Emily says. "She lives here, though."

"How's that going to work?"

Emily clears her throat, chewing her nail. "Well, he's not going overseas anymore."

"Wait. I thought he'd already gone?"

"Er, no. And now he's not going at all."

"What?" I rub my forehead. "How do you know all this?"

"Your mum told me. Apparently she was talking to his mum, and he said he fell in love with this chick really quickly and can't leave her now, or some bullshit."

"You're kidding."

"No." She cringes. "Sorry, hon."

"I can't fucking believe this," I say through gritted teeth. "He dumped me because he wanted to travel and live this amazing life, then a month later he falls in love with someone else and *isn't going*?"

"I know," Emily says, nodding vigorously. "What a dick."

I nod too. And then, to my surprise, I hear myself laughing. This is kind of funny. Maybe not in an obvious way, but it is. I moved all the way over here because he told me I was living a small life. Well, I've certainly proved him wrong, haven't I? And the irony of this whole thing is that he's still there, living a small life. Just with someone else now.

The laughter dies in my throat as hurt settles over me. He said he was leaving me because he wanted a bigger life, but now he's staying there. And that means it wasn't our life that wasn't enough for him—it was *me*.

I look down at my tea, feeling stupid. If I wasn't enough for Travis, then there's no way I could ever be like the chic women of New York. I come from a tiny town that no one has ever heard of, in a country that most people assume is part of Australia. I wear clothes from discount chain stores, or thrift stores when I find them in my size. I only own one pair of heels. I don't get Brazilian waxes or manicures. I don't go to spin classes or Bikram yoga or pilates. I only, just the other day, learned that Fendi is a designer and not a car manufacturer. I'd never thought much about these things before, but after being dumped and then thrust into the glamor of New York, I just feel like a dork with my funny accent and lack of sophistication.

And that just makes everything crystal clear. Because I don't think I could find romance over here even if I *wanted* to.

Still, that's not why I'm here, I remind myself. I'm here to write. Except that's not really happening either, is it?

I sag against my pillow with a weighted sigh.

"You okay?" Emily asks, leaning closer to the screen.

"I don't know. I'm so grateful for Cat and Geoff. But... I've hardly written anything. What if moving here was a mistake?"

"What? No way." She shakes her head. "You just need to give it some time. It's only been a few weeks! Of course you haven't written anything. You're probably still dealing with the culture shock and getting settled in. Once you're more settled, you'll write. But I think moving there was such a good thing for you."

"My mother doesn't think so," I mutter, sipping my tea. She's been calling non-stop and I haven't answered. I've texted her vague updates, but with everything up in the air regarding my living situation I just couldn't face talking to her.

Emily snorts. "I know. She's been calling me to check in."

"Really?"

"Yeah. She wanted to see if I'd heard from you because you haven't called her—which I totally get. You're doing your own thing and she doesn't understand that."

"No, she doesn't."

"She asked me to try and convince you to come home," Emily admits. "She said you're living in a fantasy world."

"Seriously? What did you say?"

"I told her it was your choice and we shouldn't interfere."

I think back to the conversation I overheard the morning after my birthday, but instead of feeling upset, irritation shoots through me. I've moved all the way over here and got a job, made new friends—and now, thankfully, I have somewhere nice to live. How can she keep saying I'm living in a fantasy when I'm here, making it a reality?

Determination solidifies in my chest. Emily's right; I was getting settled in and adjusting to everything. But now, I can commit to my writing. I might not be reeling in the men over here, but that's fine. In fact, I think Cat's suggestion was good. Being single is the thing I need to help me find my writing focus, at least for now. Maybe in the future I can date again, but right now the idea makes me want to scream.

I wrap up the call with Emily and sign into my blog, scrolling back through my old posts. They're from a few years ago, and as I reread them, I can see the optimism in old Alex—the belief that Prince Charming was out there. And I think again of Travis, of how I'd convinced myself that he and I had a future, and how he's with someone else now.

Before I can talk myself out of it, I delete all my old posts and give my blog a new name: *Single in the City*.

Then I open up a spreadsheet and start making a list of every online magazine, website and blog that I want to contribute to, so I can contact them. It's time to put in the work and start taking this seriously.

I'm here to write, and I'm not going to let anything stop me.

13

My finger hovers over the "unfollow" button and, despite myself, I hesitate. I should have unfollowed Travis when we broke up, but because he never posts anything it didn't occur to me. Well, he started posting, alright. That's the problem with people getting all bloody loved-up—they want to share every sordid detail with the world. And if I have to look at one more picture of Travis with the new "love of his life," I'm going to vomit.

With a deep sigh, I tap "unfollow" and toss my phone onto the kitchen counter. I don't love how this whole thing played out, but I think it was the push I needed. After learning about Travis a week ago, I've been writing my ass off and reaching out to websites that I think would appreciate my writing. I considered asking Cat to give me Mel's number, since she said she worked for a women's website, but it seemed a bit forward to be asking her for favors, especially after everything Cat and Geoff have already done for me. Anyway, it feels good to be taking control of this and doing it on my own—even if no one has replied yet.

I pull the fridge open, contemplating my dinner options, and there's a clatter out in the foyer. When I look through the peephole, Agnes is coming in out of the cold November air. She has a black and white hounds-tooth coat over her slightly stooped shoulders. I step into the lobby and my eyes land on a bag of groceries spilled across the floor.

"Hello, dear."

I gesture to the groceries. "Can I help?"

She gives me an appreciative smile. "If you don't mind."

I gather her things into her carry bag and wander with her towards the stairs. She reaches a thin arm out for the bag and I'm about to hand it to her, then stop. "I'll carry them up, if you like?"

"That would be lovely. Thank you."

I sling her groceries over my arm and we begin to climb slowly, me helping her as we go.

"So, how are you liking New York?"

"I love it." It's true: after everything I've been through getting settled in over here, I do love the city itself. Sure, it can be smelly and dirty, it can be noisy and overwhelming. But it just has this energy, this life that pulses beneath my feet. And even though it's starting to feel familiar I also, paradoxically, don't think I'll ever get used to the feeling of living in such a magical place.

"That's good," Agnes says as we step onto the second floor landing and turn up the next set of stairs. "I do love it here. This building has been my home for thirty-seven years now and I wouldn't live anywhere else."

I'm overcome with questions, wanting to know more about Agnes and her life over the past thirty-seven years. "What did you do?"

"Do?"

"For work, what did you do?"

"Oh, I didn't work," she says as we step onto the third floor landing and amble towards her apartment. "That was my husband. He was a good man—very loving, always looked after me." She fumbles in her bag for her keys then raises a weathered hand to unlock the door.

I step into the apartment behind Agnes, taking in my surroundings. It's like our apartment but it's stuck in time a few decades ago. The kitchen is old, with bare wooden cupboards, tiles with stained grout, and a refrigerator so ancient I can't believe it's still working. In her living room she has a mustard-yellow velour sofa that is so old it's fashionable again, and the whole apartment has a slightly musty smell.

Agnes heads into the kitchen, gesturing to the counter for me to place her groceries. "Would you like to stay for a cup of tea? It's the least I can do to thank you for your help."

"You don't have to thank me, Agnes, I'm happy to help. But actually, a cup of tea would be nice."

She motions to the sofa for me to take a seat. "And what about you, dear?" she asks from the kitchen, taking out cups and saucers.

"Sorry?"

She smiles as she pours boiling water onto the teabags. "Have you got a boyfriend?"

"Er, no." Well I did, but then he dumped me to travel the world, only to end up staying home with someone else instead. I swallow back the bitter taste in my mouth at the thought.

Agnes balances two delicate china tea cups on saucers as she walks over to the sofa, the cups trembling slightly in her hands. She places mine down on the wooden table in front of me, and steam swirls up from the cup. "No one taken your fancy?" she asks, easing herself onto the sofa beside me.

Michael's face flashes into my mind. I haven't seen him since that afternoon at work a week ago, so it's been easy to forget how awful his personality is and just remember the way his suit fit his shoulders, how good he smelled up close. And the more I thought about that, the more inspired I got for my romance novel again.

I borrowed those books from work, figuring that since I won't be having any real romance in my life I may as well write about it. I'm going to miss all that stuff, if I'm honest. Wondering if things could go somewhere, the anticipation and excitement of seeing each other. And—I'm not going to lie—I'll miss the sex. I already do. Sure, I own several battery-operated devices designed to help me in that area on my own, but come on—my bedroom doesn't have *walls*, for crying out loud. And when I do get time alone, well... it's not nearly the same as the real thing.

Anyway, it was fun writing a scene inspired by Michael at the bookstore. I rewrote what happened between us, took back some of the power. Instead of him catching me with an armload of erotica and smirking, he pinned me against the bookshelves and, well, I'm sure you can guess the rest. I changed the names of the characters, so it wasn't about Michael and I at all, but instead about a couple called Matthew and Annie. Which is *totally* different.

Well, of course it's different. Matthew has a decent personality, unlike the bastard I keep running into. Although, Agnes did mention...

"You know Michael, downstairs?" I say without thinking.

She raises her eyebrows. "Oh? You're interested in Michael?"

Shit.

Heat flares up my face. "Oh, no, that's not what I meant. He just, well, you said he was a nice guy, but..." I spread my hands, unsure how to explain the unpleasant encounters I've had with him.

Agnes gives me a warm smile. "Yes, he is a lovely man, comes up here for tea often. I do wish he would get out and meet a nice lady, but he doesn't seem up for it."

I suppress a snort. He doesn't seem up for it? More like he doesn't actually *like* women. That guy has got womanizer written all over him. One proper date on Halloween and he ran for the hills. He probably prefers them in and out of his bed quickly, that way he doesn't have to deal with complicated things, like their thoughts and feelings.

"He has been under some stress lately," Agnes continues. "I can't quite remember what it was, but he did mention something."

"Something at the office, maybe?" I reach for my cup and saucer and take a careful sip.

"Office?"

"At his job?"

She frowns. "He doesn't work in an office, dear."

What? What about the suits? What about the board meetings and the buying and selling stocks and the bottom line?

Agnes catches my perplexed expression and continues as she sips her tea. "He's a writer, I believe. Written quite a few books. Even has things published in *The New York Times*," she adds proudly, as if he were her own son.

"A writer," I repeat, baffled. We can't be talking about the same guy. "We are talking about Michael, on the second floor. Henry's father?"

She nods. "Yes, that's him."

My eyebrows shoot up as I raise my tea to my lips, my mind whirling. I cannot believe this. A writer! This is bad news indeed, because it just makes him sexier. Even if he does seem to be incapable of smiling.

I mean, take the last time I saw him. I was trying *so* hard to be helpful with those travel books and he couldn't have been any more ungrateful if he tried.

I replay the moment where he got annoyed as I rambled on about that Appalachian Trail book, and something clicks in my brain.

No. It couldn't be... could it?

I set my teacup down, turning to Agnes. "Thank you so much for the tea, Agnes, but I've just realized something and I have to run. I'm sorry."

She smiles. "That's okay, dear. It was lovely chatting with you."

"And you. Thank you," I say again, and I dash out the door and down the steps. I pause only to grab my bag from the apartment, then walk as quickly as I can to work, my mind in overdrive.

Geoff is cashing up the register when I arrive at the store, breathless.

"Alex!" He looks up, concerned. "Everything okay?"

"Just a second," I call over my shoulder as I stride down the aisle to the travel section. I stop right at the spot where Michael leaned across me, the first time I smelled his scent and my heart skipped a beat. My eyes search the shelf and land on the book, the one I told him was terrible. I grab the spine and pull it out, reading the cover: *Three Months on the Appalachian Trail by Michael Hawkins*. My pulse is racing as I flip to the inside of the back cover. And there he is, staring right back at me: a slightly younger—but still insanely sexy —Michael.

Oh my God.

Geoff has appeared beside me, his face lined with worry. "What's going on?"

I turn to him, wide-eyed, and hold up the back inside cover to show him.

"Wait..." His brows draw together in confusion. "Is that the hot guy who was in here a while back?"

I nod dumbly.

Geoff leans in closer to inspect the picture and his shoulders start to shake.

"I can't believe it," I mutter as Geoff howls with laughter. "I told him all kinds of crap about how this book had bad reviews and the author wasn't well-respected." I grimace, thinking of the awful things I said.

Geoff is wiping tears from his eyes with exaggerated mirth. "This is brilliant. You told him his book was shit, right to his face."

I nod again. Fuck, I'm an idiot.

"I haven't even read it," I mumble, feeling a wash of shame. No wonder he was so annoyed with me.

Eventually Geoff calms down and takes a deep breath. "So, read it."

"I think I will." I owe him that much, I guess.

Geoff takes the book and examines the photo in the back. "Michael Hawkins. God, he's sexy. Sexy Michael." Geoff gets hearts in his eyes and I roll my own.

"Well, he might be sexy but he's been an ass to me. Seriously, every time I see him—"

"What? How many times have you seen him?"

Whoops.

Geoff lowers the book, narrowing his eyes at me, and I release a long breath.

"He's my neighbor, Geoff. He lives upstairs from Cat."

"Really? Why didn't you say anything?"

I shrug, feeling my cheeks warm. "I don't know. He and I haven't exactly seen eye to eye. I was worried you might tell Cat and she might get annoyed, or something."

"Oh. Well, I won't say anything." Geoff hands me the book, and I think about what Agnes said.

"There's this sweet old lady in our building called Agnes, and she told me he's divorced. She also said he's a lovely man, even though I've never seen it."

Geoff raises his eyebrows and I shrug again.

"Maybe he's one of those guys who's not normally nice, but is nice to little old ladies."

Geoff practically melts. "That's still kind of endearing."

"I guess." I turn and we wander back down the aisle. "But would it hurt him to be kind to others, too?"

"Did she say anything about the divorce?" Geoff inquires as he steps back behind the register. "Like maybe it turns out he's gay?"

I smother a smile. "No. She didn't *out* him to me, Geoff."

"Oh well. There's still hope."

I tuck the book inside my bag and Geoff gives me a funny smile.

"He is a dark horse, this Sexy Michael. A writer who is nice to little old ladies, but not to young, cute ones."

I laugh as I head out the door and turn towards home. Geoff's words linger in my head, and for the first time, I start to wonder if maybe I've misread Michael.

14

I stay up most of the night reading Michael's book. I'm not lying when I say I can't put it down. I don't know what the customer back home was carrying on about. It's so good. And I'm not just saying that because I sort of like him.

Because I think I do like him.

Maybe.

I mean, beyond the physical attraction, which is undeniable. But reading his book, I realize he's nothing like I thought. The book is about a lot more than his time on the trail; it's about him and his life. He's funny and caring and really smart. He's passionate about nature and travel and history, about his son, and he was completely ripped apart by his divorce, which surprises me. In person, he's come across as so rude and cynical, but I wonder if he's still just dealing with the fallout of his marriage. He doesn't go into any detail about what happened—hell, he doesn't even name his ex-wife—but it's clear that it's scarred him. That's the reason he gives for going to walk the trail in the first place.

And he is a brilliant writer. He writes with such openness and honesty and emotion. More than once I'm moved to tears by his writing.

I owe him a massive apology. I can't believe I told him this book was bad.

I read for hours, curled up with Stevie. Eventually, I fall asleep, Michael's book in bed with me. I'm not sure what time it is that I doze off, but when I wake there's sun coming in through the living room windows and Cat is in the kitchen, making coffee. I was so engrossed in the book I didn't even close the curtains to my nook last night.

"Morning," Cat calls from the kitchen. She wanders over to my bed with a travel coffee cup in her hand, and pats Stevie on the head. "She looks so cozy. Do you mind if I leave her here with you today?"

I yawn and sit up on my elbows. I don't have work today. I was planning to stay in and keep reading Michael's book, maybe write later. It will be nice to have Stevie's warm little body for company.

"Sure." I reach over to scratch behind her ear.

"Thanks. Just take her out in a few hours, then again later."

I nod, snuggling back under the covers. I doze off again as I hear the door click shut behind Cat.

A few hours later, I wake and take Stevie out for a walk to get a coffee. When I get back to the apartment, I settle onto the sofa to continue with Michael's book, Stevie stretched out beside me. It only takes me another hour before I finish it. The first thing I want to do after that is go online and see what else he's written, but when I glance up I notice Stevie is gone.

I peel myself from the sofa and stretch, scanning the room for her. Maybe she needs to go out again. But she's not over by the door. Instead, her bum is up in the air wiggling, her face buried in my bag.

"Stevie!"

I pull her out of my bag, but she's got my EpiPen in her mouth like it's a chew toy.

"Stevie, no!"

I'm not sure what will happen to her if she breaks and ingests it, but I'm sure it won't be good. I manage to carefully wrestle it from her tiny jaws and put it back in my bag, placing it up on the counter out of her reach.

"Right." I raise my hands to my hips and look down at her. She cowers as if she knows she's been bad, and I reach down to pat her head. "It's okay, little pup. Let's take you out again."

After I've taken her around the block, I remove her leash in the lobby, opening the door to our apartment. At that moment, Michael comes down the stairs. He has a gym bag slung over one shoulder and is focused on his phone, his face creased in concentration.

I hover in the doorway, watching him. He's in a hooded sweatshirt, gray sweatpants and sneakers. It's the first time I've seen him out of his suit, and he looks nothing like the man I thought he was when I first met him. Knowing what I know now, I'm not even sure how I came to all those conclusions about him. Well, okay, he said some things about women that weren't great, but Agnes did say he'd been having a hard time recently.

Either way, I owe him an apology for insulting his book.

"Um, hi," I say tentatively.

He glances up from his phone and stops in front of me. "Oh. Hello."

God, now I don't know what to say. I can't just launch

straight into "I'm sorry I said your book was crap even though I hadn't read it."

I clear my throat. "I, er, was wondering if you have a moment?"

His eyes flit to the front door then back to me. "I'm on my way to the gym."

"Right. Okay." I try to ignore the strange sense of disappointment that rolls through me.

He wanders across the foyer, grasping the door handle and pulling it half open before turning back to me. "Is it urgent?"

I shake my head.

Stevie appears at my feet and Michael looks down at her, his face softening. He reaches a hand out to her but before either of us can do anything, she dashes out through the open front door, down onto the street.

"No!" I cry.

Michael's eyes widen and his gym bag slips to the floor. "Shit!"

All my thoughts of apologizing to him are replaced by the much more urgent realization that if anything happens to Stevie, Cat will *kill* me.

I push past Michael and race down the front steps, but I can't see her. My heart is juddering as I scan the street.

Shit, shit, shit.

Michael appears beside me, worry lining his face. "I'm so sorry, Alex."

I turn to him, fuming. "She's not even my dog!"

"I know."

I dig my nails into my palms as panic rises in my chest. "Fuck! What am I going to do?"

"Okay," he says confidently, taking charge. "You go that

way, I'll go this way. Walk around the block to look for her and we can meet back here in five minutes."

I nod, inhaling a shaky breath. We peel off in opposite directions.

"Stevie! Stevie girl, where are you?" God, if anything happens to her I'll never forgive myself. I know Cat loves her more than anything.

I quickly round the block and end up back on the front doorstep. Michael strides towards me, empty-handed.

"Any luck?"

I shake my head, resisting the urge to say something scathing.

"Okay," he says again. "This time go down a block that way."

We head out again and walk a block around and back, but still nothing. We meet up on the front steps of our building and I begin to pace back and forward, my gut clenched tight like a fist.

"I can't believe this is happening," I mutter, wringing my hands. Cat's been so good to me and after everything she's done I let this happen. I feel on the verge of tears.

Michael catches my expression and puts a hand on my arm, halting my frantic pacing. "We'll find her," he says gently.

"How do you know?" I wail. "She's probably crushed under a truck by now." Tears spring to my eyes and I turn away. I do *not* want to cry in front of him.

"No, don't be silly. She won't have gone far."

I don't know why, but that makes me snap. All the frustration I've felt towards him for being such a dick comes rushing back, and I wheel around to face him. "I can't believe you! You've been nothing but a total jerk to me from the very beginning. I know I made some mistakes but you've been awful. You act all superior, like I'm just some idiot, but this is *your* fault." I stab a finger at him accusingly.

His mouth opens in shock and for a second I think he's going to yell at me. I feel a flicker of uncertainty and draw in a breath, willing myself to stand my ground. Because I mean every word, whether he likes it or not. He has been a jerk and he has made me feel like an idiot, but *this* is totally on him. He's the one that let Stevie out the door.

Oh God. Stevie. I rub my face, glancing up and down the street again before turning back to Michael. Just as I think he's going to say something nasty, his face crumples and he looks down at his hands.

I feel a flash of surprise. This is the first time I've seen him like this: uncertain, wrong-footed. He's not scowling, he's not trying to place the blame on me. He knows he's in the wrong.

He opens his mouth to say something, then closes it again, dragging the heel of his hand over his forehead.

I tear my eyes away from him and look back down the street, gnawing on a fingernail. There's still no sign of Stevie and I feel desperate. There has to be someone I can call, something I can do.

"I'm going to go searching again," I say.

"Okay." Michael nods. "I'll go too."

We head out again in opposite directions, but this time I don't stop at one block. I go around the next block and the next, calling Stevie's name. Fear clutches at me as I pound the pavement, getting further and further from the apartment. The cold air bites through my thin sweater, but I'm so anxious about Stevie I don't even care.

Please Stevie, I beg silently, *where are you?*

My phone buzzes in my pocket and I ignore it. It's probably Cat checking in on Stevie and I can't face her yet.

"Stevie," I call, over and over, my voice hoarse. But it's no use; she's not here. I don't know where she is or what's happened to her, and tears prick my eyes again. I'm the worst roommate—the worst friend—ever. Cat will never forgive me and I'll have to move out. I'll have to leave the city and it's all Michael's bloody fault.

My phone buzzes again and I pull it out with a weary sigh. Probably best to just get this over with.

But it's a number I don't recognize.

"Hello?"

"Hey," Michael says on the other end, breathless. "We've got her."

"Oh, thank God!" I'm so overcome with relief I want to sob. I sag against a lamppost, forcing myself to take a deep breath. "Okay, I'm heading back." I practically skip the few blocks back to the building and happiness sweeps through me when I see Agnes and Michael on the front steps, Stevie curled up on Michael's lap. "Stevie!" I cry, scooping her up and kissing her little pug face. "Thank God you're okay." I hold her tight, waiting for my heart to stop racing.

"She was here with Agnes when I came back," Michael says, relief etched on his face.

"Thank you, Agnes. Thank you." I give her a grateful smile, cradling Stevie in my arms. "I thought she was gone. I thought—" I break off, unable to say my worst fear out loud.

Agnes smiles. "I don't think she got very far. Came sniffing up to me a few moments ago. She's such a sweet dog."

Michael pushes to his feet. "She is a cutie." He reaches forward to tickle her under the chin and she melts in my arms.

I glance up at Michael, feeling a spasm of regret for the things I said. I know it was all true, but I didn't mean to be so blunt. And, I realize, I still haven't apologized for the whole book misunderstanding. But now doesn't seem like the right time.

"I'm so sorry, Alex," Michael says earnestly. "I should have been more careful."

I survey his sincere face, realizing once again how wrong I was about him, wanting to make things better. "It's okay. I'm sorry too, all the things I said..." I shake my head. "I was just so worried."

He nods in understanding and something occurs to me.

"How did you have my number?"

"You gave it to me in Starbucks, remember?"

"Yeah," I say, frowning. "But I wrote it on a napkin. And that was like a month ago, and you never did call me about your shirt."

He looks momentarily caught off-guard. "Oh, well, I kept it in my phone... just in case."

I stroke Stevie's head, studying him. Is it my imagination or is he blushing a little?

Agnes starts up the steps and Michael immediately takes her arm, helping her up. It looks so natural, as if he's done this a hundred times before, and I remember her saying at length what a lovely man he is. I'm starting to wonder if, just maybe, she could be right.

"Thanks for your help, Agnes," I say as I climb up behind them. I squeeze Stevie again just to reassure myself that she's still safe in my arms.

"Oh, I didn't do anything, dear." Agnes turns at the top of the steps, her eyes sparkling as she looks between Michael and I. "It was all you two."

15

I've found my favorite coffee shop.

A bold claim, I know. Admittedly, I haven't tried *every* coffee shop in Manhattan, but there's something about this tiny place—called Beanie—that I love. It's warm and cozy, the smell of sweet, buttery treats mingling with the powerful spice of espresso. There are only a few small tables, but the baristas are so nice; they've already memorized my order and they don't mind if I sit for hours and write. Oh, and best of all—it's on our street!

A few days after the close-call with Stevie, I wake early and head to Beanie to write for a couple of hours before work. I'm getting into a bit of a groove with my life in the city now—working at the bookstore, writing before or after work, going for a drink with Cat. My romance novel is coming along nicely, and my blog is doing well. I've even got a few followers—beyond Cat, Geoff, Emily, and Harriet, I mean. And I've been pleasantly surprised by the fact that people are enjoying what I have to say about being single in New York. Every time I get a comment on one of my posts, I'm inspired to write more.

I slip the door of Beanie closed and take a seat at my favorite spot; a stool at a bar in the window, looking out over our street. Pulling out my laptop, I take a sip of coffee then get to work on another blog post. It doesn't take long until I'm in that sweet spot where I can write easily for ages, without having to think or try too hard. Flow, I think they call it. It's so good to get into this space, because—

"Any more runaway dogs?" I hear from behind me.

I flinch. God, there are some real lunatics in this city. I lean in closer to my laptop, avoiding the presence I can feel hovering nearby.

A throat is cleared. "I, ah, saw you through the window and thought I'd come say hi."

Oh. I think that voice is talking to me.

I look up from my laptop to see Michael gazing at me. He gestures to the empty seat beside mine. "May I?"

Oh, right. He was talking about Stevie.

I give him a small nod, taking in the playful expression on his face. He might find it amusing, but losing Stevie was terrifying. And I'm still a bit anxious after everything I said to him, everything that has happened between us.

He sits on the stool, placing his coffee on the table, and stares out the window in front of us, not saying anything.

I shift awkwardly, my fingers poised over the keys. I can't keep writing with him right there. I glance at him from the corner of my eye, wondering if he has anything more to say or if he's just going to sit there, making me uncomfortable. Despite myself, I notice he's looking very nice in a wool coat, sweater and jeans.

After a while he turns to me. "So, I think I owe you an apology."

I let my gaze slide back to my laptop and run my finger along the space bar. This should be interesting.

"I think maybe I've been kind of rude to you."

I raise my eyebrows, still avoiding his gaze. I guess I can't disagree.

"Look, we didn't exactly meet under the best circumstances," he points out, and I cringe, thinking of the coffee soaking into his fancy shirt. "But, besides that..." He softens. "I think I've been kind of a jerk."

I twist in my seat to look at him, concealing a little smile behind my hand. "And why was that, exactly?"

He's quiet, fiddling with his coffee cup as he stares out the window again. "I've been in court the past couple of months, dealing with... something."

I narrow my eyes. "What did you do?"

He snorts as he looks back to me. "Why do you assume it was something *I* did?"

I open my mouth, then close it again, feeling a bit sheepish. I don't know why I assumed that, but he does have a point. "You're right. Sorry."

He releases a long breath. "My ex has been trying to get full custody of Henry, if you must know. It's been a stressful few months."

I feel a rush of compassion. After reading about him and his son, about how cut-up he was in his divorce, I can understand why he's struggled with that so much. No wonder he's been feeling so resentful and angry towards women. I guess being in court explains why I kept seeing him in suits.

"Anyway. It's all over now and she didn't win, which is a relief. But it was a nasty ordeal, especially for Henry." He runs a hand over his beard, his eyes distant, then he fastens his gaze back on me. "The other day when Stevie escaped, I felt really bad. Afterward, I thought a lot about what you said. You're right; I've been an asshole. You caught me at a bad time, but I shouldn't have taken it out on you, and I'm sorry. I hope you can forgive me."

I suck my bottom lip into my mouth, letting my eyes roam over his handsome face. "It's okay. I don't blame you for being mad about the coffee. And that's awful about your ex. I'm sorry you had to go through that." We sit in silence for a while as I try to find the courage to say what I really want to say. Eventually, I take a deep breath. "I, er, might owe you an apology too." I reach down into my bag and pull out my copy of his book, placing it on the table between us.

His eyebrows shoot up, then his face breaks into a smile, then—I can't quite believe it—he *laughs*. It's the first time I've ever seen him smile, let alone laugh, and my lips part in surprise. The deep chuckle that rumbles from his chest is so delightful it's as if sunlight has burst in through the window, lighting up his face and warming me through until my whole body is humming.

Whoa.

I pull my gaze down to the book in my hands, remembering the awful things I said. "I'm so sorry. All that stuff I said—"

"It's okay." He holds his hands up, giving me a wry smile. "I know it's not my best work. I've made my peace with it."

I shake my head. "I loved it, I really did. When I said all that stuff, well, I hadn't actually *read* it."

He chuckles again. "Yeah I kind of figured, based on your comments regarding—what was it?—the topography and mountain ranges."

My cheeks warm. "Yes, well. I'm sorry."

"It's okay." He takes a sip of coffee, not lifting his gaze from me. "So you're from New Zealand, right?"

I nod.

"And Henry said something about breaking up with your boyfriend?"

I grimace, recalling how I spilled my guts to Henry in the hallway when I was trying to cheer him up. But how was I to know Michael was his dad? "Er... yeah. Just before I came over here."

"Is that why you moved?"

"Yes." I run my finger around the rim of my coffee cup, thinking, and realize there was more to it than that. "And no."

Michael tilts his head, eying me curiously. For some reason I feel the urge to go on.

"Have you ever just stopped to look around at your life and realized nothing is how you want it?"

"Yes," he says without hesitation, and for some reason this surprises me. "So what was wrong? What did you have that you didn't want?"

I think again, recalling that moment I sat in my old flat with my parents, taking stock of my life and feeling empty. "Nothing. I didn't really have *anything*. That was the problem. I just..." I pause, wondering how much to share. Strangely, I find that I want to share more, that I feel comfortable talking to him. Maybe it's because I read his book—because I read about some of his personal experiences. And even though it was only through a book, I feel a sort of connection to him now—like I know him, in a way. It makes me feel like I can talk to him.

I let out a long sigh. "I guess I just realized that I'm thirty —that I've gone through my whole twenties without taking my dreams seriously. It's like I have nothing to show for my twenties. And now... I don't know. I sort of feel like it's now or never."

He gives a slow, thoughtful nod. "I get that. I was about thirty when I finally started going after what I want, too."

I rub my forehead. "I always thought that by thirty I would have my shit together a bit more, you know? I should have figured this out by now."

"Says who? I'm in my forties and I still don't feel like I have my shit together." He gives me a kind smile. "Don't be too hard on yourself."

I gesture to his book. "Well, you're a lot more successful than me."

"Sure, my career is going well." He shrugs. "But that's not everything. It's only one area of my life."

I think back to the jaded man I saw on Halloween after a date, and feel a wave of sympathy. I know what he said at the time wasn't very nice, but after reading his book I have a much greater understanding of why he felt that way.

His mouth lifts into a small smile, and for a second I think maybe he knows what I'm thinking about.

"So what were you doing, then?" I ask over my coffee. "Before you were thirty, I mean."

"I worked in finance."

I raise my eyebrows, the image of him in his suit flashing into my mind. No wonder that look worked so well on him. "And you didn't enjoy it?"

"No. My folks pushed me into it, thought it was a good career. But I wanted to write. Always have."

I breathe a disbelieving laugh. My parents might not have pushed me into finance—thank *God*—but they sure have their own ideas for my life that do not align with mine. And as for always wanting to write... Well. I get that too. Big time.

"So what made you decide to leave finance and write?"

He thinks for a moment, raising his cup to his lips.

"Same as you. I turned thirty and took a good look at my life and realized that I didn't want it to stay the same. I wasn't taking my dreams seriously, either. So I started to do that."

Warmth spreads out through my chest as I absorb his words. I'm not crazy, I realize. I'm not the only one who's felt this way. He understands.

He sets his coffee down and fixes his attention on me. "So what are *your* dreams, then?"

I give him a shy smile. "To write, as well. That's what I'm passionate about."

"Yeah?" There's a little spark in his eyes as they linger on my face.

"Yeah."

He motions to my laptop. "What are you working on?"

"Oh, just... a blog post." For some reason I feel a bit silly, thinking about my tiny blog in the context of this conversation.

"What about?"

I glance at my laptop, hesitating. He's a real writer, with books and everything. The last thing I want to do is tell him I write a blog about being single. It's hardly the dream writing life we were just talking about.

"You know, er, various topics. What do *you* write about?" I ask, to take the spotlight off me. "I know you write books about the Appalachian Trail, but—"

"You mean *terrible* books about the Appalachian Trail," he interjects, a smile peeking over his lips.

I groan. "I'm never going to live that down, am I?"

"I'll make a deal with you." His eyes dance as he leans closer to me. "Tell me what you write about and I'll forgive you for pretending you read my book."

He's got me backed into a corner now, but for some reason I'm reluctant to tell him. I don't know why. It's not like I need to impress him. And as much as I might be starting to like him, I know nothing will happen. I'm so much younger than him and he's a successful New York writer. I don't think he'd ever look twice at someone like me.

And what was Agnes saying? Something about how he's not up for meeting women—something that was quite evident in his book, despite all my previous assumptions about him being a womanizer.

None of that matters, anyway. Because my twenties didn't just teach me to take my writing seriously, they also taught me to stop believing in fairy tales. I know better than to go looking for happily ever after now, especially with someone so far out of my league.

I move my eyes over his friendly face, so different from the man I first met. He has crinkles at the corners of his eyes when he smiles, and there's a dimple in his cheek, hiding under his dark beard. It's adorable. My heart gives an involuntary kick when his smile quirks up a little on one side, and I can't ignore the desire simmering inside me, threatening to boil over.

Shit, I need to get a hold of myself.

I force the air out of my lungs, closing the lid on my laptop. "Maybe another time. I should get to work." I drain the cold dregs of my coffee and slip my laptop into my bag.

We head out onto the sidewalk together, and a few feet away there's a guy shaking a cup with change in it. I'm guessing he must be homeless, or close to it, and it's cold out. I haven't seen many homeless people in the city. Compassion nudges me closer, and I stuff a $5 bill into his cup. It's not a lot but it's all I can part with right now.

"God bless," he says gratefully.

I turn back to see Michael watching with interest.

"What?"

"You're sweet. Most people would just ignore him."

I sling my bag onto my shoulder. "Hopefully it helps. It's not much."

"Yeah. He'll probably just use it for drugs or something, though."

"You're so cynical!"

Michael gives a light shrug. "Well, it's true."

"You don't know that," I say as we start to wander down the street. "That's totally making an assumption based on the way he looks. It's like, someone could look at you and say, 'he's just a dumb jock. He probably spends all his time in the gym and is as thick as two planks.'" I think of all the assumptions I made about Michael when I first met him and how wrong I was.

He stops walking and turns to me. "You think I look super fit?"

I blush furiously. Jesus, why did I say that?

"I didn't say *super fit*," I mumble.

"But you *did* suggest that I look fit." His mouth tilts into a teasing grin.

"Ugh, whatever." I roll my eyes and turn to walk away, more because I'm embarrassed and don't want him to see me blush again than anything else.

"Hey, Alex." He falls into step beside me. "Why don't you give me some of your writing to read?"

I stop again and glance at him. He's looking at me warmly, his eyes twinkling, a smile on his mouth. It's like now that I've cracked that frowny exterior he can't stop smiling. I'm not used to this new, friendly, smiley Michael. If I thought he was sexy before, this is something else.

"Because," he continues, his lip twitching, "if it's anything like your other reading material, it's got to be good."

"Other reading material?"

"Yeah. What was it, *The Prince of Pleasure*?"

Oh my God. Somehow, during the course of this perfectly pleasant conversation, I'd let myself forget about our interlude at work. I press my eyes shut in mortification, feeling heat creep up my neck. Because some of my writing *is* like those books, but I'm certainly not going to be telling —or showing—him any of *that*.

I brave a glance at him. There's a playful light in his eyes and his mouth is cocked in a sly grin. It sends a little thrill through me and I bite my lip, trying to make sense of what's going on here. It almost feels like he's flirting with me, which is weird. I'm *quite* certain I'm imagining that. My cheeks burn under his gaze and I look away.

"No, it's *not* like that. That was just... something else," I mutter, feeling silly again. Why do I feel like this around him? He always reduces me to this blushing, mumbling mess, and I can't stand it. "I should get to work. I'll... see you around." I spin on my heel and stalk off, pretending I don't hear him calling out after me.

16

The fluorescent lights flicker on as I step into the laundry room, and I smile, relieved to be alone with my dirty laundry.

I guess this isn't how one is supposed to spend their evening on Thanksgiving, but I haven't completely opted out of the whole American holiday thing. I wrote a blog post a few days ago about dealing with invasive questions from your family over Thanksgiving dinner (you know the kind: "when are you going to settle down with a nice guy?" and "you're not getting any younger, don't you want children?") and I watched the parade on TV.

But, you know. When you're running out of clean clothes to wear—so much so that you have to wear your pink bunny pajama pants to the laundry room—it becomes a bit of an emergency.

I place my basket on top of a machine. Even though it's a cold and dank room, it still has that nice smell of laundry powder and dryer sheets, which is oddly comforting. But— bugger. I've forgotten my coins.

I dash back up to the apartment and when I return, I'm

surprised to see Henry, clad in dinosaur pajamas, glancing around at the machines.

"Hi, Henry." I wander over to my machine, pretending not to be on the lookout for Michael. I haven't seen him since we shared a coffee at Beanie almost two weeks ago, and I've been avoiding the hall in case I run into him. I felt so awkward after the last time.

Of course, it would be just my bloody luck that he'd come down here the one time I'm doing laundry in my pajama bottoms.

Henry turns to me, clutching a towel in his hand. Concern is etched on his cute face.

"You okay?" I ask.

He holds up the towel. "I need to wash this, real quick." His voice trembles with panic.

"Okay. Do you want some help?"

He glances around at the machines before looking back at me. "Yes, please."

I take the towel. It's cream colored and covered in some kind of tomato-based sauce. "What happened?"

"Promise you won't tell my dad?"

I nod.

"I dropped a jar of sauce and I didn't know how else to clean it up, so I used this."

"Where is your dad?"

Henry's eyes are wide with worry. "He's in the shower but he'll be out real soon."

I glance down at the towel, forcing myself not to picture Michael in the shower. I might have been avoiding him, but I can't say I've been avoiding thinking about him. It's making for some great romance writing, though. All that pent-up sexual frustration has to go somewhere.

"You didn't want to tell him?" I ask, turning towards a machine.

"It's one of my mom's towels. I thought he might get mad."

I freeze at Henry's mention of his mother. Michael made some oblique references to her in his book, and he mentioned she was trying to get full custody, but beyond that I know nothing about her. She was just this kind of abstract idea in Michael's past.

But now, holding her towel in my hands, she becomes a concrete, real person. In my mind a picture of her appears: a tall, slim goddess, stunningly gorgeous, elegant and sexy. He's pretty damn easy on the eyes, I'm sure he wouldn't marry a troll. But maybe—

"Can you help?" Henry pleads.

Shit.

I take a breath, trying to focus on the problem at hand. Poor Henry looks on the verge of tears.

"Yes, of course. Sorry." I open a machine and stuff the towel inside.

"Oh! I don't have any quarters," he says, his voice rising in panic again.

"It's okay, I've got lots." I give him a reassuring smile as I put some of my powder into the machine and push a coin into the slot. "Everything will be okay, Henry."

He doesn't look convinced.

"You know, I'm sure your dad wouldn't be mad if it was an accident."

He shakes his head, his brow knitting. "I think Mom wants the towel back. And if I've ruined it then Dad will be mad, because Mom will yell at him." He glances over my shoulder at the washing machine. "How long will it take?"

"Probably a while. If you want, I can keep an eye on it for

you. Why don't you go back upstairs? I'll put it in the dryer once it's washed."

"Are you sure?" His eyes dart between me and the door.

"Of course. I've got to stay to do my laundry too. I'll take care of it. I'll leave it over here when it's done." I gesture to an empty shelf.

"Okay. Thanks, Alex." He dashes out of the laundry room.

I smile to myself, absently loading my clothes into the washer. He's a sweet kid. But his mom sounds... Well. It's not my place to comment.

Knowing I've got a good hour to kill, I pop back up to the apartment and grab my laptop to keep me company. Unsurprisingly, I find myself in the mood to write some romance. The mention of Michael in the shower got the creative juices flowing, and it's not long before my fingers are flying over the keys.

I've been writing so much of this romance stuff lately and I think I'm getting pretty good at it. I'm enjoying it more than my blog about being single, if I'm honest. I don't know what it is, but it just feels more *me*.

Still, I want to actually *do* something with my writing, and I'm not sure if I'll ever be comfortable showing my romance novel to anyone. At least with my blog I've got readers—two dozen, now—who can relate to my posts. And that's cool.

After a while, I put my laundry and Henry's towel into the dryer and return to my laptop. I'm halfway through describing a naughty scene with Michael and I—uh, I mean Matthew and Annie—and it's pretty good, if I say so myself.

"The water cascades over Matthew's hard—" I hear from behind me and I snap my laptop shut, turning to see Michael peering over my shoulder.

"Stop it," I say, feeling my cheeks color. When I hear it out loud like that it sounds ludicrous. I haven't shown him any writing and the *last* thing I want him to read is this. I take in the cheeky grin on his face and, despite myself, a smile slides onto my lips.

"Cute PJ's." He gestures to my bunny pants.

I grimace as I remember what I'm wearing. Still, nothing I can do about that now, and what difference would it make? I could be here in a ball gown and I'm sure he would be unaffected.

My eyes wander up and down his body before I can stop them. "Right back at you." He's wearing dark green and blue plaid pajama pants with a white T-shirt, his hair damp from the shower, looking gorgeous as usual. I swallow, trying not to look at his shoulders, clearly defined in the snug-fitting T-shirt.

He wanders around, surveying the washers. "Where's the towel?"

"What do you mean?" I push to my feet, feigning innocence.

"Oh, come on." He gives me a knowing smile. "There was sauce smeared all over the kitchen cabinets and the linen closet was open. It's not exactly a job for Sherlock Holmes."

I giggle. "He was very worried you would be mad at him." I motion to the dryer behind me. "It's in there."

"Thanks." He flashes me a grin, then his smile fades away. "Have you been avoiding me?"

"Um. Maybe."

"I knew it! What have I done now?"

"Nothing..." An awkward laugh slips out. "Not really."

He raises his hands to his hips, gaze pinned on me.

"It's... I don't know." I lift a shoulder in a shrug. "I just feel weird around you." Whoops. I hadn't planned on being so honest but that just came out.

He raises his eyebrows. "Why?"

"Why? Because I have a huge crush on you, and every spare second I get I'm thinking up dirty things I want to do to you, then writing about it in a romance novel while trying to convince myself I'm not *really* writing about us, but rather two fictional characters who just happen to have similar names to us."

Well, that's what I should have said. But I can't be *that* honest. Instead I say, "I don't know."

A smile plays on his lips, his eyes lit with amusement as he watches me.

I frown as that familiar feeling of embarrassment creeps up my spine. "Stop that," I say, gesturing to his expression. "You're always doing that. Always laughing at me."

His smile vanishes. "I'm not."

"Yes, you are. You're smirking. You're always mocking me, like you think I'm just some hilarious joke."

His eyes soften and his mouth curves into a gentle smile. "I'm not laughing at you, Alex. You make me smile and you make me laugh, but I'm not laughing *at* you."

"Well, just stop it."

He chuckles, crossing his arms defiantly. "Stop what? Enjoying your company?"

"Yes," I mutter, but I give him a wry smile anyway.

He chuckles again, then stands there with his arms folded, gazing at me.

"So." I shift my weight. "Er, happy Thanksgiving."

"Thanks, and you. What have you been doing?"

"Nothing. I spent the day reading."

His brows furrows. "You spent the day alone?"

I nod.

"That sucks. I didn't realize. You could have had dinner with us, we had way too much turkey."

"Oh, it was fine," I say, trying to ignore the fizzle of pleasure I feel at the thought of having dinner with him and Henry. "Thanksgiving doesn't mean much to me."

"Still... no one should spend Thanksgiving by themselves."

I fight against a smile and lose. He's being really sweet. I think back to our conversation at Beanie, when he listened to me talk about turning thirty and wanting to go after my dreams—when he made me feel like I wasn't crazy.

Shit, why does he have to be such a nice guy? Things were a *lot* easier when I thought he was a misogynistic jerk.

His gaze shifts to my laptop on the table. "What were you writing?"

"Oh..." Warmth spreads over my neck. "Nothing."

"Didn't seem like nothing." He leans against one of the machines, arms still crossed, expression playful. "Seemed quite interesting."

I dig my teeth into my lower lip, running my eyes over him. I can't help but wish I wasn't having this conversation in our basement laundry room, in my pajamas. And then I notice, part of me *wants* to tell him about my novel. Not about the characters, or the oddly familiar scenarios or anything in any detail, but just the fact that I'm writing a novel. I'm excited about my writing, and after our last conversation, I know he'll understand that.

But then what? He'll realize what a dreamy, romantic sap I am and lose all respect for me. And no doubt he'll think my choice in genre is silly, because it's not high-brow or literary or any of that meaningful stuff.

Or worse—he'll want to read it.

"I'd love to read some of your writing."

Fuck.

"Really?" I choke on a laugh. "Now?"

He shrugs. "Why not?"

I think of the scene I was just writing about him in the shower and heat streaks across my cheeks. Jesus. The last thing I need is for him to read that. He'll think I'm a horny maniac. *And potentially a bit of a stalker.*

"Er, I don't think so. It's... I'm not ready to share it. It's a work in progress."

He studies me for a second then gives a small nod. "Okay, I get it. But when you're ready, I'd love to read it. I might be able to offer some advice."

Actually, that's a good point. For example, he might say, "we'd never have sex in that position," and then offer some helpful alternatives. Hopefully with a practical, hands-on demonstration. I swallow hard at the thought, because *God*, I want him right now. Maybe on one of the machines, during the spin cycle...

I shake my head to clear the thought. *Pull it together, you horndog.*

"Thanks. Yes. I'll keep that in mind."

An awkward silence settles over us, punctuated only by the sound of the dryer spinning behind me. I wait for him to say goodnight and leave, but he doesn't.

"So how long have you been in New York now?"

I think for a moment. "Um, like a month and a half?"

"And you've done all the tourist stuff?"

"Well, no." I give him a sheepish smile. "I've hardly left the West Village. I did take a cab up to Times Square but it was so full-on that I came back home. I want to go see more of the sights, but I've been so busy settling in and working and stuff. And, I don't know. The city... it's a bit intimidating." I look down at my hands, feeling stupid. I wanted to move to New York and now that I'm here, I spend most of my time within the same ten-block radius. Which, come to think of it, is probably about the same size as my hometown.

I glance up, expecting Michael to be regarding me with another of his amused expressions, but he's not. He's sawing his teeth across his bottom lip, his face thoughtful. "What are you doing next week?"

"Er..." I hesitate, taken aback. "I'm not sure. Working probably, and writing. Why?"

He shrugs, a smile quirking one corner of his mouth. "If you have some time free, why don't you let me show you some of the sights? I'd take you sooner but I have to work. So if you don't mind waiting until next week... what do you say, a native New Yorker showing you around?"

There's a flutter in my stomach as his words sink in. He's asking me out for a day of sight-seeing. Well, he's not *asking me out*, obviously, but he's offering to show me around. For a whole day. The two of us.

"Um... are you sure you don't mind?" I manage at last, attempting to sound as nonchalant as possible. Because I'm not nonchalant. I'm cartwheeling inside.

He gives me a strange look. "Of course I don't mind. It will be fun."

"Okay, sounds good." I try my best to contain my silly grin. "What will we do?"

"We can do whatever you want." Something kindles in his eyes as he holds my gaze, and I wonder, just for a tiny nanosecond, if we are actually talking about sight-seeing at all. My breathing quickens as I imagine him stepping closer and pressing his mouth to mine.

Then the dryer beeps behind me, breaking the spell.

Of course we're only talking about sight-seeing. I'm a delusional moron with a bad habit of slipping into romantic daydreams in the presence of delicious men. Well, this one, anyway.

With a sigh, I turn and pull out his towel. It's warm in my hands and as I pass it to him, our fingers brush. This sends a zap of electricity right through me. If he feels it too, he doesn't show it.

"Well, I'll text you and we'll organize it. I'm looking forward to it." He gazes at me for a moment longer, then drags his eyes from mine. "Goodnight."

And even though I know I shouldn't, I watch his butt as he walks out of the laundry room.

17

We're almost a week into December now and it's cold. I'm having to get used to dressing in layers. Back home winter was pretty uneventful, so it's a bit of a shock to the system. And I'm sure it's only going to get colder.

I inspect my outfit in the mirror: a violet-colored long-sleeved dress that hugs my curves and sits mid-thigh, over black wool tights and leather knee-high boots I found in a thrift store back home. I know this day out with Michael doesn't mean anything, but I still made an effort. It's cute, if not exactly sexy. But honestly? It's too damn cold to be sexy.

There's a knock on the front door at 9 o'clock sharp. I'm trying to play it cool, but my mouth has a mind of its own, pushing into a grin when I turn the handle and see Michael on the other side.

Fuck, he looks *good*.

He's in dark jeans over brown boots, a navy-blue knitted sweater under a black cashmere coat. But the best thing of all is his smile. His mouth is tilted into the sexiest grin and his brown eyes are sparkling. With that expression, you'd think he was picking up Scarlett Johansson for a night of torrid sex rather than just plain old me for a tour of the city.

But hell, I'll take it.

"Hey." He links his hands and leans against the door frame. "You ready?"

I nod, trying to ignore the little flip in my belly as I pull on my coat and follow him out onto the street. I'm kind of nervous, which is absurd. This isn't a date. And I know that. But my body is getting all ahead of itself, like it knows something I don't.

Just bloody rein it in, I mentally chastise myself. I should know better than to turn this into some fantasy day out in town together.

There's a cab waiting for us on the street and Michael opens my door. I lower myself onto the seat, then slide all the way over, expecting him to climb in after me. But he closes the door like a gentleman and wanders around to the other side, so I hastily slide back, hoping he didn't see.

God, I've already embarrassed myself and it's only been five seconds.

He climbs into the cab and leans forward to say something to the driver I don't quite catch, then turns back to me with a grin. "I've planned just a few places. I hope that's okay? We can do the rest another time."

Another time? Cue another belly flip.

"Sure," I say casually, attempting to flatten the smile pulling at my mouth. "So where are we going?"

"I thought we could do Grand Central Terminal, then Times Square, then head over to Rockefeller Plaza. What do you think?"

"Oh. No Empire State Building?" I try not to sound disappointed, but I guess I assumed that one would be a no-brainer.

He shakes his head with a mischievous smile. "No. We could do that another time if you like, but Top of the Rock in Rockefeller Plaza is better. Trust me."

Anticipation ripples through me. Because I do trust Michael, and I think this is going to be fun—beyond hanging out with him, that is. I spent the past week thinking about the fact that I was going to be spending the day with Michael, and I didn't actually stop to think about the sight-seeing part. But we are going out to see the city, and that's exciting.

I turn and watch the streets around us change as we leave the Village and head uptown. Slowly, the low, residential buildings give way to more skyscrapers and office blocks, more glass and steel, until eventually, we pull up outside the beautiful facade of Grand Central Terminal.

I rummage in my bag for money to pay the driver, but Michael just hands over his credit card with a smile.

"I've got it," he says, and my stupid brain adds a point to the mental "date" column it seems to be running.

Stop it, now.

We step out onto the sidewalk and have to cross the road and walk back to take in the facade, it's so huge. It's like something out of ancient Rome, with its massive stone columns and arched windows, completely at odds with the modern buildings surrounding it. Above the main entrance is the clock and winged statue; beautiful and iconic.

"Will you think I'm a total dork if I take pictures?"

Michael laughs, slipping his hands into his coat pockets. "Not at all."

I pull my phone out and snap some photos of the facade. Then I turn around to take a selfie in front of the building and Michael reaches for my phone.

"Here, I'll take it."

"Oh," I say, feeling a blush spread over my cheeks despite the cold air. "Okay." I pose in front of the building, trying not to feel like a fool with him watching me.

He hands the phone back with a smile. "You want to go in? It's really cool."

I nod and follow him back across the road and in through the glass doors onto the concourse. It takes me a second to adjust to everything—the echo of footsteps and voices, the cavernous ceiling above us, the dim lighting—but when I do I just gape around in awe.

This place is *spectacular*. The curved ceiling stretches what feels like miles above us, painted in the most intense green-blue, overlaid with intricate gold detailing of the zodiac. At each end of the marble concourse is a stone staircase leading up to a balcony, and there are huge arched windows along the walls. All around me, people are milling from doorways to corridors leading off to different tracks, and an announcement comes on over the loudspeaker which makes it feel like I'm in the middle of some grand airport.

"Wow," I breathe, wide-eyed. Even though people are weaving past me, hurrying to get to important places, I'm rooted to the spot, trying to absorb everything.

"I know, isn't it beautiful?" Michael watches me for a moment, then gives me a gentle nudge. "I'll go grab us a coffee. What do you want?"

I break out of my trance and turn to him. "That's okay, I can—"

"No, you wander around and take it in. I'll grab something from over there"—he gestures to a coffee stand—"and be right back."

"Okay. Um, just a cappuccino, thanks. Here." I reach into my bag for cash but he shakes his head.

"I've got it. You go look around, I'll come find you." And he wanders off to the coffee stand while my mind does another mental tally in the "date" column.

Still, it's hardly a date if he's running off at the first chance, is it?

With a sigh I turn and wander, trying to absorb everything around me. Everywhere I look there's someone doing something interesting, or some beautiful detail in the marble and stone. I climb the stairs at one end and snap a few photos overlooking the concourse, trying to capture the magic I feel at being here.

A few moments later Michael appears at my side, handing me a coffee. "I got you a muffin too. I hope you like chocolate."

I take the muffin and coffee with a surprised smile. "Thank you. That's really sweet."

He gives a little chuckle. "I'm a sweet guy once you get to know me."

I let my eyes linger on him. He *is* sweet, I'm coming to see, and it's killing me.

Fixing my gaze back on the concourse below, I sip my coffee, watching the people milling about. "I love to people-watch," I say after a while.

"Yeah?"

I nod. "I like to imagine who people are and what their lives are like. I wonder about where they're going and what they're thinking."

Michael scrubs a hand over his beard, watching the people below. "Most of them are on their phones with their earphones in. They're probably all zoned out."

"Maybe. Or maybe they're texting someone they love to tell them they miss them, or they're checking their dating app to see if anyone has connected with them, or they're putting on their favorite song to cheer themselves up after something bad has happened..." I trail off, and when Michael doesn't say anything, I look down at my coffee with a grimace.

Way to get carried away, Alex.

But Michael angles his body towards mine. "Maybe," he murmurs. There's a warmth in his eyes, a tiny line between his brows as he contemplates me, like he's trying to figure something out.

"I know it's silly," I mumble. "But—"

"It's not."

I feel his gaze on me while I sip my coffee, and when I finally glance back at him, he huffs a laugh, looking down at his cup with a funny little smile. My heart stumbles and I force myself to look away before I put any more scores in my mental "date" column.

I focus back on the beautiful architecture around us, trying to ignore Michael's presence right beside me, trying to pretend I'm not desperately wishing he would lean over and kiss me under the ceiling of stars.

18

W ell, Times Square was just as chaotic and crazy as it was the first time I attempted to visit. But somehow, with Michael there, I felt fine. Mostly it was just crowded with tourists and people peddling souvenirs, but it was fun to see the lights and everything.

And Michael was even cool with getting a big pretzel from one of those street vendors, which surprised me. He's a real New Yorker and I thought he might turn his nose up at something so cliché, but when I said I was going to get one, he grinned and bought one for himself, too.

The highlight, so far, has to be Top of the Rock. And I can see why he chose it over the Empire State Building. Because when you go up Top of the Rock, you get to see the whole skyline, *including* the Empire State Building.

And it's breathtaking.

I knew there was a reason I chose New York, but while I was busy running around the West Village I'd let myself forget about the rest of the place. This city, though, it's something else. It's alive, it's buzzing with life and possibility. God, I know it's so cheesy, but it does feel like the place where dreams can come true.

By the early afternoon we're down at Rockefeller Plaza, watching the ice-skaters on the rink below. Across the rink stands a huge Christmas tree, lit from head to toe in a rainbow of sparkling lights, above the famous gold statue. The whole place feels like something out of a film, but I find myself thinking I'm not going to get the happy ending I've always wanted. I hate to admit it, but it's true. Just because I've realized happily ever afters are only for romance novels, doesn't mean a tiny part of me isn't still wishing for it.

I sneak a glance at Michael. He's leaning on the railing watching the skaters below, his eyes creased at the corners in that little smile of his. I know I've been pretty obsessed with his looks since I first laid eyes on him, but with every passing moment I'm learning more and more about the kind of man that he is, and I can't help but like him—the *real* him, underneath his handsome exterior. It's kind of freaking me out. He's so oblivious to my feelings, even though I'm quite sure they're all over my face every time I look at him.

Either that or he's just politely ignoring them. Perhaps that's closer to the truth.

He turns to me now, catching me staring. The crinkles around his eyes deepen and I turn away as heat spreads across my neck.

Fuck, I'm just mooning over him like a schoolgirl with a crush on a teacher or something. This is *exactly* what I was trying to avoid—slipping into fantasies and daydreams. All it takes is a few hours in the company of a hot guy and I turn right back into my old self. I spent all morning pretending we were on a date, for Christ's sake. What is wrong with me?

"You all good?" Michael asks, bumping his shoulder

against mine. His breath comes out in a white cloud in front of us.

I force a bright smile. "Of course." I pull my phone out and take a few pictures of the ice rink. When I turn the phone around for a selfie, he reaches for it. I try my best to look normal as he takes my picture, but I'm not sure I quite pull it off.

Then he stands beside me, switching to the front camera and leaning close. And there on the screen of my phone is the pair of us, side-by-side, in front of the ice rink. Michael grins into the camera, and I watch as my own face lights up, gazing at the two of us together. We'd make a cute couple. Before I can stop myself, I'm imagining what it might be like if he was my boyfriend, taking a picture of us for a holiday card or a photo frame to put on the mantelpiece.

He smiles as he hands the phone back. "Send me those."

"Oh. Sure." I flick through the pictures and he leans over my shoulder, looking too. My breathing goes shallow with him so close, with his warmth pressing against my back. It takes all my strength to keep my eyes on my phone—to not turn around and slip my arms inside his coat and snuggle into the heat of him.

"That one." He points to one of the selfies of the two of us. Then he reaches over and flicks back through the photos until we get to the ones he took of me. And I definitely do *not* look normal—I look manic. But Michael adds, "And that one."

Confusion swirls through me as I forward both the pictures. I don't know what he wants with a picture of me posing like an idiot. Maybe he thinks it's funny, like all the other things about me he finds so amusing.

I pocket my phone and lean forward on the railing,

gazing across the rink. "The tree is beautiful. It must look amazing at night."

"Yeah." Michael leans back beside me. "It's stunning in the dark."

I feel myself wilt a little. I'd love to see it, but I'm not sure I'll come back uptown alone at night just for that.

My gaze lands on the skaters below and I turn to Michael hopefully. I might not get to see the tree sparkle in the dark, but there's something else we could do.

"You want to skate?"

He raises his eyebrows. "What, now?"

"Sure. It would be magical, ice-skating here."

He chuckles. "You'll need gloves. Do you have gloves?"

I nod, gesturing to my bag. "Do you?"

He taps his coat pocket with a smile.

"Can we?"

"Well, we could." A self-conscious laugh chuffs out of him. "I'm not very good. My balance is terrible. It's hard to skate when you're this tall."

I trail my eyes over him. He *is* tall—I'm guessing six foot four, or so. But still, he's pretty built and he goes to the gym, so I know he's fit. Much fitter than me, that's for sure.

"Seriously?" I give him a teasing smile. "I thought you were really athletic. You can handle it."

"How do you know I'm athletic?"

"I don't know." I shrug. "You just look—"

"Super fit?"

"Shut up," I mumble, glancing away.

He shuffles closer on the rail, nudging his shoulder against mine. "Let's do it."

I turn to him, and there's a flutter behind my ribcage because he's so close. "Really?"

"Yeah. It's your first winter in New York. Let's ice skate at Rockefeller Center."

A thrill runs through me and I push away from the railing, looking around for the entrance to the rink.

"But no laughing at me," he adds, attempting a serious face.

I shove him with a giggle. "Oh, I'm not promising that."

19

If ever there was a perfect scenario in which I would make a dick of myself in front of Michael, it would probably be on ice. The rink looked so magical from up on the Plaza, but now that we've got our skates on, I'm seriously questioning this decision. I haven't been ice-skating since I was a kid.

But I'm pleasantly surprised to find that it only takes me a few goes around, holding the railing, to find some confidence. Turns out it's kind of like riding a bike, and it's not long before I can push away from the side and glide across the ice, even if I am a bit wobbly. I barely notice the cold anymore as I look around, trying to take in the fact that I'm here, ice skating in New York City.

Michael, however, wasn't kidding when he said he couldn't skate. I didn't realize how difficult his height would make this, but he can't find his balance properly and he sticks close to the sides. It's odd to see him so out of his depth—this big guy, afraid of falling on his ass. Everything is turned on its head and *I'm* the one who's capable, who's watching as *he* flounders. I can't say that I don't enjoy the shift in the power dynamic.

Still, after a while I start to feel bad. Every time I glance over he sends me a weak smile, and I can tell he isn't having a good time.

I skate across and lean against the railing beside him. "We can go now if you want."

"What? No way. I'm having fun."

I look at his hands as they grip onto the railing for dear life, and stifle a laugh.

He follows my gaze. "Yeah, okay," he says with a chuckle, loosening his grip. "I'm not great. I warned you about that. You're a natural, though."

I flash him a grin, doing a little twirl on the ice, my coat swirling out around me. His cheeks dimple and he pushes off the railing towards me. My heart almost stops as his gloved hand slides into mine, and we tentatively set off to do a loop together.

Together.

Wow. It's like I'm in a dream, ice skating at Rockefeller rink, hand-in-hand with him. Any minute I'm going to wake up on the sofa in my old flat, with drool down my face and the imprint of the TV remote on my forehead.

But that doesn't happen. Instead, I try to keep Michael steady as we make our way around, loving the way his big hand feels in mine, the way he tightens his grip when he feels like he's going to fall.

We make it around the rink without touching the sides, Michael beaming at me the whole time. I giggle at his expression, at how proud he is of something so silly.

He squeezes my hand. "Thanks for making me do this, Alex." His whole face is alive in a way I've never seen and I squeeze back, my heart somersaulting in my chest. It would be so easy to pull him towards me, to reach up and press my lips to his. I practically have him captive, after all. He could hardly make a getaway on those unsteady legs.

I give in to the daydream edging its way into my mind: Michael's strong arms tightening around me and pulling me close, the warmth from his touch rushing over me despite the ice. I imagine what the brush of his lips might feel like over mine, how his eyes would crinkle in that sweet way as he gazes down at me, so gorgeous that I can't see anything else. My stomach fills with butterflies at the thought and a little ache tugs at me.

But Michael drops my hand and I swallow, forcing myself to push the image away. I've spent *way* too much time writing my romance novel.

I watch as he carefully skates a few feet away from me, testing his legs. Then he turns, his eyes bright as they meet mine. He goes to push off and skate back to me, but something happens and he loses his balance. I watch in horror as he wobbles, his arms windmilling at his sides, his skates slipping out in front of him as he tries to stop his fall.

But it's inevitable. His legs shoot out from under him and he lands on his back with a huge thump.

"Michael!" I skate over and drop to my knees beside him, my pulse whipping through me.

He's gasping for breath and I realize he's winded from the fall. I grab his arm, helping to pull him up to a sitting position. People whiz past us, and I can feel the wet from the ice seeping through my tights, but I don't care. I'm too worried about him.

He manages to suck in a breath, and I feel him squeeze my hand again. That's when I realize I'm holding his hand and clutching his arm in concern. I try to loosen my grip but my hands won't listen.

"Whoops," he says with an embarrassed smile. He attempts a laugh but it turns into a wince.

"Have you hurt yourself?"

He rotates his left shoulder and nods.

"Fuck," I mutter, glancing around. There's no way I can pull him to his feet by myself.

"It's okay. I can get up." He drops my hand and winces again as he awkwardly clambers to his feet.

I push up to stand and take his arm, helping him over to the exit where we climb out. He takes a seat at a table, but I'm too worried to sit. I hover beside him, wanting to rub his back and soothe him, but not wanting to hurt him more.

He tests his shoulder again, grimacing in pain, and guilt chews through me.

"I'm so sorry," I say, wringing my hands. This is all my fault. He said he didn't want to go and I forced him.

He looks up at me. "What? Why?"

"Because I made you skate. And, shit, now you're going to have to go to the hospital and it's going to cost you a *fortune* in medical bills because you have no bloody public health care over here." I rub my forehead. He has every right to be mad at me—I couldn't blame him.

But Michael's eyes just glitter in that amused way they do when he thinks I'm being silly. "I have insurance," he says, rotating his shoulder again. "But I don't think it's that bad. Maybe just get me some ice?"

"Erm..." I glance at the ice rink and back at him, and he laughs, then winces. "Okay, okay," I say, looking around for one of the skate-rink attendants. At that moment a guy in a blazer comes running over to us. There's a lanyard around his neck with his name—Barnaby.

"That was quite a tumble!" he says jovially, but there's an air of nervousness about him.

"Yes." I place a tentative hand on Michael's shoulder. "He's hurt his shoulder, so can we—"

"Oh dear. Please remove your skates and you can come with us."

"Come with..." I begin but Barnaby dashes off and leans close to speak to another attendant. I glance at Michael in confusion and he rolls his eyes.

"They're probably worried we're going to sue."

A disbelieving laugh slides from my lips as I unlace and remove my boots. "Seriously?"

He nods, reaching down for his boots and flinching again. I wave his hand away and crouch at his feet, unlacing his boots for him.

"Try to look pissed off and we'll get season passes or something," Michael says with a pained grin.

I glance up at him. "Do you actually *want* season passes?"

But he doesn't say anything. He's just watching as I undo his boots and slip them off, one after the other. Something shimmers in his eyes, and I can't help but wonder if he likes having me down here, on my knees in front of him. I'm not going to say I mind it, although I'd prefer that we weren't surrounded by throngs of tourists and that it wasn't freezing. No, I'd rather we were indoors, with Michael reclining on a huge bed, and instead of a winter coat I'd be wearing a lacy—

"Okay!" Barnaby appears again, wrenching me from my daydream. Probably just as well.

We grab our shoes, following after him. He leads us inside to the underground concourse and over to a door marked "staff." We head through and down a corridor and into a tiny room with some chairs, and he disappears again.

It's not until then that I realize I've been clutching

Michael's hand in worry this whole time, as if my touch is somehow going to make him feel better.

I give him an awkward smile, dropping his hand as we take a seat. "Sorry," I mumble, but he doesn't say anything. It's insanely warm in here after being out on the ice, and I stand, shrugging my coat off. "What would we even sue them for, anyway?"

Michael's gaze travels down over my dress before returning to my face. It reminds me of that evening when he saw me in my Snow White costume, and I blush.

"I don't know," he murmurs, locking his gaze with mine. He has the same look in his eye as when I was down on my knees and it makes my heart thump a little harder.

"Righty! Okay, here we are." Barnaby is back with an ice-pack and a clipboard, and he thrusts both into my hands. "You'll need to complete this."

He vanishes again and I glance down at the clipboard with a sigh. It's all kinds of legal stuff about how they're not responsible, blah blah blah. "You want me to fill this out?" I offer, handing the ice-pack to Michael.

"If you don't mind."

"You're not going to sue?" I ask, half-kidding. I'll never understand the American legal system.

Michael shakes his head. "It's not that bad. Besides," he adds, his face darkening ever so slightly, "I've spent enough time in court lately."

I settle down on the seat and fill in the form. It only takes a few minutes and I can feel Michael's gaze on me the whole time. He must be worried I'm going to do it wrong, or something.

Setting the clipboard aside, I turn to him with a frown. "Aren't you going to..." I gesture to the ice-pack.

He gives me a sheepish look. "Would you mind? I can't quite reach."

"Oh! Right, of course." I spring to my feet.

He gingerly slips his coat off and I step behind him, ready to put the ice-pack on his shoulder. But before I can do that, he grabs the hem of his sweater with his right hand and peels it off, until he's just sitting there in a black tank top.

And—holy *shit*.

Saliva pools in my mouth as my eyes track over his gorgeous, sculpted shoulders and the muscular curve of his biceps. And when he glances back at me with those espresso-colored eyes, heat races up my body.

"Alex?" he prompts, and I blink.

"Yes. Sorry." I shake my head, trying to stop the unfolding of a million dirty fantasies in my mind, and press the ice-pack against his shoulder. Believe me when I say it takes every ounce of strength in my body not to lean forward and run my tongue over his smooth, hot skin.

He flinches at the touch of the ice-pack, and I place my left hand on his bicep to hold him steady. That's the only reason, I swear, because he keeps pulling away. There's a painful little groaning sound from his mouth as the ice numbs his shoulder, but my twisted mind just hears a sexy groan.

That does it. I imagine myself down on my knees again, but this time I'm reaching for his zipper and making him groan again and again until he's so overcome with pleasure that he forgets all about his shoulder—that he forgets his own damn name.

Jesus. How on earth have I ended up here, alone in this tiny room with half of Michael's clothes off? And—*for fuck's sake*—how am I supposed to keep it together now?

I feel his arm flex under my fingertips and my breathing goes haywire, molten heat pooling between my thighs. This man is so undeniably sexy and I'm losing it. It's like I'm caught in a spell as I slide my palm over his bicep, the feel of hard muscle under silky skin making me quiver.

He turns to glance up at me again from under his thick lashes and suddenly the whole room is crackling with electricity. His eyes pin me in place as a flush creeps onto his cheeks, and if I didn't know any better, I'd think—

"How are we getting on in here?"

We both turn to the door as Barnaby comes sashaying back in, bright-eyed. He snatches up the form, nodding in our direction when he's satisfied we aren't heading straight for the lawyer's. Then he spins on his heel and exits before either of us can say anything.

I suck in a breath, taking a step back from Michael. That was close. God knows what I might have done if Barnaby hadn't come in right then. I think I was about three milliseconds away from climbing onto Michael's lap.

I need to get a grip, before I do something to utterly humiliate myself.

MICHAEL IS quiet in the cab on the way home. I'm not sure if it's because he's in pain, or because I weirded him out with my creepy sexual vibes back at the rink. Either way, I feel bad because he went to so much trouble to show me the city and I just ruined it by getting him injured and then lusting all over him when he was vulnerable. Poor guy.

I clear my throat and he turns to look at me. "Sorry again about your shoulder."

He shakes his head. "It wasn't your fault. I haven't been

on an ice rink in at least a decade. I should have known it wouldn't end well." He lets out a grim laugh.

"You don't take Henry skating?"

He thinks for a second, then frowns. "No, I don't. Do you think he'd like that?"

"Um..." I hesitate, feeling like I've wandered onto fragile terrain.

"He would, wouldn't he?" Michael rubs at his jaw, his brow pulled low. "Why haven't I thought of that?"

Whoops. I didn't mean to make him feel like a crap father. I cringe, glancing away. When I finally look back, Michael is still lost in thought.

"Well, thanks, anyway," I say. "I really appreciate everything today."

He gives me a funny look. "What?"

"You know, taking the time out to show me around."

"This isn't a public service, Alex," he says, amusement tugging at his mouth. "I enjoy hanging out with you."

"Oh." Pleasure weaves through my chest.

"It's hard moving to a new place," he continues with a compassionate smile. "It's always nice to have a friend show you around, help you feel more comfortable."

Right. Of course, he just sees me as a friend. I know that. It's only in my overactive imagination that anything more is happening.

Still, I think, casting my gaze out the window at the passing streets, I'm glad to have him as a friend. If that's all I'm going to get, then I'll take it.

20

Being single over the holidays doesn't have to be depressing! Just follow my five tips to make the festive season spectacular as a single gal.

I pause my typing to lie back on my bed and scratch my head. Five tips to enjoy the holidays being single... I can do this. Although, I'm not sure I even *have* five tips.

Well, there's drinking. That's got to be one, right? I know *I'll* be drinking.

I'm not exactly looking forward to the holidays. I'm miles away from my family in a new city, and lusting after a guy I can't have. I guess I could always write an *honest* blog post about all that, but who wants to hear me moan? Everyone moans about being single and it's depressing. I've tried to keep the whole theme of my blog positive and upbeat, to focus on the *good* things about living the single life. I figure if I do that enough, I might actually start to believe it myself.

I also thought that keeping it light and happy might be more likely to get me a guest-spot on one of the sites I've been applying to. Not that anyone has gotten back to me. Okay, that's not true; I got auto-replies from five of them and a brief "thanks but no thanks" from a few more. Given I've contacted thirty-six websites, blogs and online magazines, that's not a brilliant outcome.

My phone buzzes on the bed and when I see Mum's name on the screen, guilt floods me. I still haven't spoken to my parents, choosing instead to preserve my sanity. Harriet's been great, though, sending texts of encouragement and asking how it's all going. Even though we never spent much time together back home, I've been surprised to find I miss her over here.

No, it's not just her—I miss them all. Maybe it's knowing Christmas is around the corner and I'll be away from my family, or maybe it's just that I've gotten the space I needed, but I do kind of want to talk to my folks, to tell them how my writing is going and how much I'm loving the city. I'm sure that once they hear how things are going over here they'll be supportive and happy for me.

I set my laptop aside and, taking a deep breath, I press the talk button. "Hi, Mum." There's silence on the other end, and I pull the phone away to check the call is connected. "Are you there?"

"Oh, hello darling," Mum says, surprise in her voice. "I didn't think you were going to answer."

There's another wave of guilt and I grimace. "Yes, sorry. I've been busy. But I do have time to chat now if you'd like?"

"That would be lovely!"

More guilt.

"So, how are you getting on in The Big Apple?"

"Good," I say, deciding to focus on the positive and not mention the apartment scam that set me back thousands or the ill-advised crush I've developed on my neighbor. "I've been writing my blog, which is going well."

"Your blog?"

I falter. Surely she knows what I'm referring to? I shared the link on Facebook when I started writing it. I'd kind of assumed she would be *reading* it, but come to think of it she never did mention anything in her emails. "Yes, Mum. I'm writing a blog. I put it on Facebook, didn't you see?"

"Oh, yes. There was something," she says vacantly.

I let out a sigh. "Well, anyway, I've got over fifty followers now."

"Oh. That's... nice."

I roll my eyes. This is about the level of enthusiasm I should expect from her. Just because I've been away for a couple of months working on my writing career doesn't mean she's now started to understand it. I instinctively touch the book charm around my neck, thinking of how baffled my parents were by my choice to move over here, to leave "everything" behind back home. "Yes. It is good, Mum."

There's a pause, then I hear her rustling about on the other end. "Okay, just a minute," she says.

"What?"

"I'm at the computer now. I'm going to have a look at your website."

"It's a blog. That's—"

"Oh, wait. Something isn't working. Hang on." The phone crashes down and I hear her call out to Dad. "Clark! Why isn't the computer working?"

In the background I hear Dad's exasperated voice. "Calm down, Audrey. I'm sure it's nothing."

There's more rustling and I hear the sound of their ancient computer boot to life. For a few minutes I simply pick at a nail, waiting.

"Okay, I'm back," Mum says at last. "*Single in the City*? Is that right?"

"Yes."

"*My life as a single girl in New York City,*" Mum reads aloud. "*Who needs men when you can live a fabulous life alone?*"

I cringe as I hear my own words read back to me. Something about them grates at me, doesn't sit right. I guess after developing this silly little crush on Michael, I've been slipping back into my old ways a bit.

It's been a week since we went on our non-date around the city, and I smile whenever I think of it. I'm not sure how else to explain it, but it's like Michael kind of woke something in me. I'd forgotten what it's like to really like a guy. I haven't felt this feeling for ages—not even with Travis. In fact, the more distance I get from that whole thing, the more I realize it wasn't quite the romantic comedy I thought it was. It was definitely a lot more *com* than *rom*, that's for sure. And now, I barely think of him.

Michael, on the other hand, I *cannot* get out of my mind. After our day out, I've been letting myself imagine how nice it would be if some of my fantasies weren't just in my head. I know it's silly, that I should know better now, and I've been trying to fight it—without much success. It's making for some great romance writing, at least.

But that does make me feel a bit weird about my single blog. Because even though there are some great things about being single, it kind of blows when you've got a crush on someone.

"Is this right, Alexis? You're swearing off men?"

"Yes. Well—no, not forever. Just for... a while."

"Hmm."

"What?"

"Are you sure that's wise, darling, avoiding men? You're not getting any younger. Don't you want to have a family?"

I suppress a groan, rolling onto my back to contemplate

the ceiling. I probably should have seen this coming. "It's not forever, Mum. I just don't feel like being with anyone right now." Though as I say this, I feel a little twinge in my stomach. I promptly ignore it.

"Hmm," she says again, and I have to bite my tongue. I know she doesn't give Harriet this much of a hard time about settling down. But then, she is a few years younger, and Mum and Dad have never been as hard on her as they are on me. She doesn't exactly give them much to complain about.

"I don't mean to be discouraging, sweetheart," Mum says. "But surely there are other things you could write about, without having to sign up for some crazy project like this?"

"It's not crazy," I say, feeling defensive. "I'm choosing to focus on my writing and that means not dating for a while. It's not like I've had my uterus removed."

"Don't be so *sensitive*, darling."

A frustrated breath gusts out of me. My parents have always complained that I'm too sensitive, and the minute I get even the tiniest bit annoyed or defensive, Mum whips out that line. I have to hand it to her, though—it works. Because what am I supposed to say to that?

"I'm surprised you're even wanting to write about this," she continues. "I assumed you'd be writing one of those ridiculous romance novels you love so much. Always dreaming of Prince Charming."

My cheeks heat with shame. Good thing I didn't mention my novel, then. She'd just see that as concrete proof that I'm living in a fantasy.

And then I think of how much I've been enjoying writing about Matthew and Annie. Except, it's not really about *them*, is it? We all know who it's really about. Which would be fine, but I don't just *write* about Michael, I *think* about him. All the time. Like a bloody lovesick teenager.

I swallow back the acidic taste of disgust in my mouth. What is *wrong* with me? How did I let myself end up back here again?

"Yes, well," I mumble, resolving to sort myself the fuck out. "Don't worry about that, Mum."

An uncomfortable silence stretches between us and I'm about to end the call when Mum speaks.

"Have you given any thought to when you might come home?"

I frown. "What? No."

"We're going to miss you at Christmas. And then it's Harriet's birthday later in January, so if you're back by then, we could—"

"Jesus," I mutter, staring at the ceiling and wishing it would cave in on me. "I won't be home in January. You know I've *moved* here, right? I *live* here now."

"Well, yes. I know you wanted to move to the big city and do your writing, and the blog is very nice. But you did give up an awful lot just to write a few words on a little website."

Irritation fizzles in my gut and I make myself take a deep breath. "Mum—"

"I just think that maybe it's time you grew up and got back to the real world. If you came home, darling, I'm sure I could talk to Julie about getting you another job at the bookstore. It probably wouldn't be assistant manager again, but—"

"Mum, stop," I snap, sitting up on the bed. I press my balled fist into my eye, willing myself to stay calm. I should have known this is exactly how this conversation would go. "I like living here. I like writing my blog. And I'm not coming home."

There's silence on the other end and I grind my jaw, knowing this is going nowhere.

"I have to go," I mutter. "I'll... speak to you soon." I hang up the call and toss my phone aside. My eyes land on my laptop and I reach for it, determined to get this blog post finished.

Determined not to indulge any more fantasies of Prince Charming.

21

There's something about being drunk at midday that feels kind of naughty, like sneaking into the copy-room to have sex at an office party, knowing you might get caught.

Not that I've ever worked in an office. Or had sex in a copy room.

I don't make a habit of drinking in the middle of the day, but according to Cat, "boozy brunches" are a thing in New York. Basically, you go to brunch and eat as normal, but you also get bottomless cocktails. *Bottomless cocktails.*

It's bloody brilliant.

Cat decides that I'm not a proper New Yorker until I've had a boozy brunch, so she takes me to a restaurant in Chelsea on Friday.

We meet Mel outside the restaurant and I immediately shrink when she approaches us. I'd forgotten how stunning Mel is. Today she's wearing a charcoal wool minidress with tan, suede over-the-knee boots, her long dark hair pulled back into a sleek ponytail. Next to her I feel like a teenager in my jeans, knitted sweater and ballet flats.

We sit at a tiny table and order. It's not long before a huge pitcher of margaritas is placed on the table and I pour a generous glass, taking a big swig. Ooh, this is delicious. Another big swig. I could get used to this life.

"So." Mel fixes her attention on me, margarita in hand. "I've read your blog."

My eyebrows shoot up. "My blog? Really?"

Cat elbows me. "I hope you don't mind—I showed it to her. It's so good."

I give Cat a bewildered smile. I knew she was reading along, but I figured it was just a moral support thing.

"Shit." She reaches into her purse to retrieve her phone and frowns at the screen. "It's Hayley at the store. I'd better take this." She pushes to her feet and wanders down the back of the restaurant, leaning against a wall as she talks.

Mel turns back to me. "Cat's right, your writing is good. I love the way you explore being single here in New York. It's hilarious."

"Oh. Well, uh, thank you." I'm not sure I was going for "hilarious," but that's okay.

"Are you happy being single?"

"Er... yes." I raise my drink to my lips, ignoring the dart of disappointment I feel.

Mel nods, not saying anything more, and for some reason I feel the urge to ask her about her own love life. A sophisticated, chic New York woman like her could have her pick of men. She probably dates handsome billionaires. Exclusively.

"What about you?" I ask, slurping back my margarita. "Do you like being single?"

She gives me a tight-lipped smile. "It beats being married to an asshole."

"You were married?"

A shadow falls across her beautiful features. "Years ago," she says, gazing off into the middle distance. "He cheated on me. Said he was bored with our life together and that I wasn't enough for him, after I caught him in bed with someone else. I was *heartbroken*."

"Wow." I shake my head in disbelief. "That's terrible." I can't believe that someone would cheat on Mel. She's the woman you cheat with when you're bored with your old wife, not the one you're *bored* with.

She straightens her shoulders and clasps her perfectly manicured hands together, forcing a stoic expression. "Anyway." Her lips twist into a secret smile. "I've met someone new."

"Oh!" I lean forward, grinning. "Tell me more."

"Ah—" Mel's gaze flicks over my shoulder then back to me as Cat joins us at the table again. "Another time. So, what are your plans for your writing, going forward?"

"Um, I'm not sure." I take a long sip of my margarita as I turn this question over. I'm chugging along with the blog, despite still hearing nothing from the sites I've been contacting. But it's important that I keep focusing on this single topic, because right now it feels like the only way to keep my head on straight.

After talking to Mum a couple of days ago, I've been trying to dial down the Michael fantasies. This wasn't helped by him texting to ask when I want to go sightseeing again, but somehow I managed to keep my wits about me and reply with a vague, "Sometime soon."

Instead of daydreaming about Michael, I've been throwing myself into my blog to remind myself why I'm choosing to be single right now. And as for my novel, well, I'm just working on that on the side. Mostly.

The problem was that my fantasies were getting out of

hand. I wasn't just writing my novel, I was letting myself imagine Michael with, well, *me*. So I've been rounding out the Annie character, developing her so we are polar opposites. For example, she's got red hair. And she's an inch shorter than me. And she's from a *totally* different part of New Zealand than I am.

Okay, I'm clutching at straws here. I know. But it *is* helping, because yesterday I hardly thought about Michael at all, after working on my novel for six straight hours.

A smile sneaks onto my lips as I recall a really juicy scene I wrote between Matthew and Annie, inspired by the ice-skating shoulder injury thing. It starts with her putting the ice-pack on his bare shoulder, but then he turns around and pulls her onto his lap. He tosses the ice-pack aside and unbuttons her dress, a slow grin spreading across his face as he—

"So, what do you think?" Mel is looking at me intently and I feel a spasm of alarm.

Shit. What did she say?

"Er, absolutely." I nod as if I'd been listening the whole time.

"Great. I think you're going to like Justin."

Justin?

"Okay," I say, taking a big slurp of margarita to hide my confusion.

Mel waves across the restaurant. "Justin, over here."

I watch as an older man with salt and pepper hair and an earring in each ear strides over and shakes hands with Mel and Cat.

"This is the friend I was telling you about," Mel says, gesturing to me. "*Alex*."

Justin takes a seat at the table, extending his hand. "Nice to meet you, Alex."

"You too."

We pause while Justin flags down a waiter and orders. Meanwhile, I've had two margaritas and the room is starting to get fuzzy. And it's only midday! This is fun.

"So, Alex." Justin turns to me when our food arrives. "I'm not sure how much Melanie has told you..." he trails off, lifting his eyebrows.

Told me what? Is *this* her new man? He doesn't seem her type. Sure, he's not bad-looking, but I actually thought he was gay.

I glance at Mel, who's grinning. Even Cat is giving me a sly smile. What am I missing here?

"Uh, well," I begin, refilling my margarita from the pitcher on the table, stalling for time.

Mel was saying something earlier. What was it? Something about... Nope. I'm drawing a blank.

I study their expectant faces. Maybe they're engaged, and that's why she was waiting for Cat to get back to the table. Or maybe she's pregnant!

But Justin and Mel aren't holding hands or looking even slightly romantic. In fact, all of Justin's attention seems to be focused on me.

Oh. *Oh.*

I think I know what's going on here. They're trying to set me up with him. That must be what Mel was going on about earlier. She read my blog about how *happy* I am being single and could obviously see through the ruse. God, they must really pity me if they feel the need to find a man and ambush me at brunch.

"Well, you know Mel," I say eventually. I fiddle with my glass, unsure what else to say. Justin is nice enough, but he's much too old for me—even though I do seem to be attracted to older men lately. Well, one in particular.

Still, I can't bear to hurt Justin's feelings, or let Mel and Cat down after they've gone to all this trouble. They probably think they're helping me out and I don't want to appear ungrateful. I'll have to let them down easy.

I smile politely. "You, er, seem very nice, Justin."

"Oh. Thank you. I've been looking forward to meeting you after everything Mel has told me."

I nod, sipping my drink, trying to ignore the sense of unease snaking up my spine. How am I going to get out of this?

"So how long have you been writing?" he asks.

Right, so Mel told him I'm a writer. Did she show him my blog too? I wonder if he also found it "hilarious." I bet they were all sitting around, roaring with laughter over the poor girl who moved to New York after being dumped and now can't get a man.

Or—oh God—maybe he thinks I'm easy, that I'm desperate for a shag, assuming that since there's no one else around I'm going to just jump into bed with the first guy to come along. I can't believe Mel and Cat thought this was a good idea.

"Uh, since I was a teenager." I shift in my seat, willing the room to stop spinning around me. I shouldn't have had that third margarita.

His mouth hooks into a devilish smile. "Wow. So you've got a lot of experience. Mel told me you were eager." He winks and my stomach tightens in trepidation.

Are we still talking about writing?

I glance at Mel, starting to feel panicked. This guy is kind of a creep. Why on earth would she think I'd be into this? But she just grins back at me and sweat prickles along my brow.

"I guess you and I have a few things to discuss, then,"

Justin continues, leaning towards me. "Shall we go somewhere more private?"

My heart lurches and the room swims out of focus. That's it. I'm putting a stop to this, right now. "I'm not going to sleep with you, Justin," I blurt.

His smile disappears. "What?"

I suck in a breath, reaching for a glass of water. This would be a lot easier if I wasn't three sheets to the wind. "I'm sorry. I don't know what Mel has told you, but I'm not looking for a man."

All three of them stare at me, wide-eyed. I don't know why they're so shocked.

"I know I write about being single, but I'm not desperate. And I *don't* need to be set up." I glance pointedly at Mel and Cat.

Justin shakes his head, looking bewildered. "I have no idea what you're talking about, Alex. We're offering you a chance to write for us."

What?

I glance at Mel, her arms folded across her perky chest, her head cocked to one side in mild amusement.

"*Write* for you?" I echo.

Justin nods.

"About what?"

He gives an odd laugh. "Being single!"

Mel rolls her eyes, leaning forward. "Were you not listening before? I showed your blog to some of our editors and they loved it. They want you to submit a piece for our website. Justin is my *boss*."

I place my glass of water down carefully. "What website?"

"Bliss Edition."

"Wait—" I remember Mel said she works for a women's website, but not *this* one. "You work for Bliss Edition?"

Justin nods, mirth skimming across his features.

"And... you want me to write something for you?"

"Yes!" All three of them say in unison.

There's a burst of excitement in my chest. Bliss Edition is one of the online magazines I've been trying to contact for ages!

Mel sits back in her seat, exasperated. Justin exhales and takes a sip from his cocktail, chuckling to himself.

"What was that you were saying about sleeping with Justin?" Cat asks.

"Nothing." I flap a hand, feeling my face redden. "I can't believe this! I've been wanting to submit something to your site. This is amazing."

"You have an interesting take on single life here in the city," Justin says. "We've been toying with the idea of creating a specific column on our site to connect with the eighty thousand single women in your age bracket, because we haven't targeted them from this angle. Your blog is just like the sort of thing we're looking to create." He takes a leisurely sip of his drink, as if I'm not holding my breath and hanging on his every word. "And I thought, if you're interested, you could submit a few sample articles. If we like them, there's the chance it could lead to a permanent feature."

My jaw slackens in shock. Holy shit.

"There are a few other people we're considering," Justin adds, "but you're definitely in the running. Whatever you send us will be published on the site whether you get the regular feature or not, so it will be good exposure for your blog. But the sooner you can send me a few pieces the better, because we're hoping to launch the column in the new year."

A thrill runs through me. I can't believe this! What an insane opportunity.

"Okay," I say breathlessly, beaming. "That's... thank you so much. I'll get started right away."

"Great!" Justin grins. "Send me something exactly like what you've been doing; single life here in New York, through a light, upbeat, positive lens. Can you do that?"

I feel my smile slip ever so slightly, but I quickly pin it back in place. Because I can do that, of course I can. Sure, I've been feeling a bit less than positive about being single lately, but I'm working on that.

I nod at Justin, raising my glass to his. "Absolutely."

22

B y the time I get back to the apartment I'm practically giddy with excitement. Well, that and the margaritas. What a great day this is turning out to be.

I settle in on my bed with my laptop, ready to start writing my first official piece for Bliss Edition. But I'm so amped up I can't focus. After everything, I've finally got my foot in the door. I know I might not get the permanent column, but if I write my butt off, there's every chance I *could* get it. This is the start, the first rung on the ladder to my success. I can just feel it.

I set my laptop aside, unable to sit still. I want to celebrate, to share this news with someone. Cat and Mel already know, of course, and I'll tell Geoff when I see him at work tomorrow. I'll call Emily later after she finishes work, and probably text Harriet. And, well, there's no point in telling my parents, at least not right now.

My gaze lands on Michael's book on my nightstand and I smile. It's been a week and half since our day out in the city. We've exchanged a couple of texts and that's been fine, but now I'm itching to see him. I want to share—maybe even celebrate—this small victory with him. I'm sure, as a fellow writer, he'll be excited for me.

I grab my phone and twirl it in my hand. I could see him, right? I know I'm trying to douse the flames of my crush, but what am I going to do, avoid him forever? I can keep it together enough to see him without losing the plot. It's fine.

Before I can talk myself out of it, I fire off a text.

Alex: Hey! Are you free sometime soon? I got some cool news about my writing.

I toss my phone casually aside, telling myself I don't care if he even replies. But as soon as it hits the bed, regret washes through me. What am I *doing*? Why on earth would he care?

My phone vibrates and I look at it in surprise. He's texting back already? That can't be right. But I see it is, and my heart cartwheels at his words, my regret vanishing.

Michael: Good to hear from you! Sure, what are you up to today? I'm just at home working, so stop by if you're around? Or we could go for coffee?

I glance up at the ceiling above me, as if I'll somehow be able to see through to his apartment. He's up there, right now? Would it be too crazy to go up now? There's a shiver of anticipation through me at the thought and I realize I really, really want to see him. Just to share my news, of course.

I check my appearance in the mirror, adding a fresh coat of mascara and smoothing my hair, then climb the stairs to Michael's apartment. As I knock, there's a funny little flutter of nerves in my belly. And when he opens the door and his face breaks into a grin, my heart bounces against my ribs.

"Hey!" he says, stepping aside so I can enter. "Come in."

"I hope it's okay I just came up. I figured it was easier than texting back and forth."

"Of course. It's a nice surprise." He closes the door behind me. "Sorry I haven't been in contact much. I'm just on this deadline with my editor breathing down my neck. It's been crazy."

I smile, taken aback. "That's okay. How's it going?"

"Almost done, thank God."

He heads into the kitchen and despite my best intentions, my eyes help themselves to the view as he reaches into the cabinet. He's in jeans and a black T-shirt—nothing fancy —but he looks delicious as always. For the briefest moment I consider wandering up behind him and slipping my arms around his waist, pressing my face into the warmth of his back, sliding my hands down to his—

"Do you want a drink or something?" He turns to catch me staring and I blush, quickly glancing away.

Shit. I've been here five seconds and I've already regressed. *Get it together.*

"Er, yes, please."

"Herbal tea okay?"

"Sure."

I let my gaze wander around his place while he fills the kettle. It's similar to our place in terms of layout, but bigger. The walls of the living room are dark red, lined with chunky wooden bookshelves, books spilling out everywhere. There's a worn tan leather sofa in the middle of the room and a wooden dining table between the kitchen and the living room, instead of a breakfast bar like we have. In the spot that I'm pretty sure is right above my bedroom nook, he has a desk with a computer and leather desk chair. I smile to myself, picturing him writing in that spot at night while I'm in my nook below, thinking of him.

I can't believe I'm in Michael's home. It feels strangely familiar, like I've already been here a hundred times, but then I also want to go around and look at everything, turn every item over, search for more clues about this man and who he is.

"Sorry the place is so messy," he says, watching me as I take it all in.

"Don't be silly." I lean back against the counter with a grin. "It's the right amount of cozy. Besides, books don't count as mess."

He chuckles as he places teabags into the mugs.

"How's the shoulder?"

"Good. I went to see a physical therapist and he gave me a few exercises to do. It should be fine in a week or so."

I take the mug of tea from his outstretched hand. "I'm so sorry. I should never have made you—"

"Hey, come on. You didn't make me do anything. I had a great time out with you."

"Except for when you nearly broke your back on the ice."

"Well... that part wasn't great." He turns to lean back against the counter opposite me, his eyes animated as they move over my face. "But the rest of it was. Even the bit after."

I look down at my tea and press my lips together in an attempt to contain my smile. Is he referring to the part where he took half his clothes off and I had to use super-human strength to resist him?

My eyes drift back up to his. He's sinking his teeth into his bottom lip, his gaze resting on me, and for a second I wonder if he felt what I felt, in that tiny room when I was icing his shoulder. Because there was a moment when I thought maybe he did, but that's unlikely. I'm prone to imagining these sorts of things.

I clear my throat, forcing the image from my mind. I'm

going to have to work a lot harder on not getting caught up in Michael fantasies with this new writing opportunity.

"So, um, I got some good news about my writing today."

"Yeah?"

"An online magazine wants me to write a few articles for them." I try to hold back my grin but I can't. "And if the articles do well, it could become a regular thing, like a column on their site."

"No way!" His mouth curves into a broad smile. "That's awesome."

"I know." I do a happy hop on the spot and Michael laughs.

"When will you find out?"

I think back to what Justin said. "They're launching the column in the new year, so probably in a couple of weeks."

"And what's it about?"

Bugger. I was kind of hoping we wouldn't have to get into all that.

"Oh, you know." I dip my teabag up and down, avoiding his gaze. "Just... things." It's excruciating hearing myself sometimes, I tell you. I don't know what I was expecting—of *course* he was going to ask what it's about.

I hazard a glance at him and he's leaning against the counter, cradling his steaming cup of tea as he regards me with amusement. "Look," he says after a pause. "I get that it can be hard to show someone a work in progress, or whatever. But you won't even tell me *what* you write about. It's almost starting to feel like, I don't know... you don't want me to know."

He's right. I haven't wanted to tell him. I think mainly it's because it doesn't feel like, well, a very impressive topic. He wrote this stunning, moving memoir about walking the Appalachian Trail after his divorce. I write posts about wearing comfortable underwear because no one is going to see it. Will he even *get* it?

"Okay," I say, rubbing my nose. "Just... don't judge me, okay?"

"I won't. I promise."

I raise my eyes to the ceiling, unable to look at him as I speak. "I write a blog about being single."

He's quiet for a beat. "Okay. And what is the *column* going to be about, then?"

"Being single and... how great it is."

There's another beat of silence. When I finally make myself look at him, he's just staring at me.

"You write about being single? Seriously?"

"Er... yes?"

"Right." His gaze slides to the floor and his brow furrows in thought. "Why didn't you tell me *this* is what you write about?"

I cringe. "I don't know."

I wait for him to say something, but he's still frowning, scrubbing a hand over his beard. Eventually, he blows out a breath and lifts his gaze to mine, then his mouth softens into a sheepish little smile. "Sorry. I just... I kind of thought there was something happening here."

I look around in confusion. "Where?"

"Between us." He gestures to me, then him.

Us.

Wait. What?

What?!

"Are you—" I swallow hard, trying to process this. "Are you serious?"

"Yeah. At the ice rink, I thought..." he trails off, then huffs a laugh, glancing away. "I was going to ask you out."

I gape at him as his words slot into place in my brain.

Michael was going to ask me out. Michael. Asking me out. Is this for real or am I fantasizing again?

"Because...?" I prompt, wanting to make one hundred percent sure that I am understanding him correctly.

"Because I like you."

I give a slow, mute nod, absorbing this information. My heart has taken off at a gallop and I'm desperately trying to rein it in. Of all the things I thought he was going to say when I came up here, this was *not* one of them.

He rakes a hand through his hair as an awkward chuckle slips from him. "Shit. I feel kind of stupid, actually."

Oh God.

I shake my head. "No—"

"I'm sorry, Alex. I don't know what I was thinking."

"No, really—"

"Can you just forget I said anything?"

Forget Michael said he was going to ask me out? Holy Moses. Of course I can't bloody forget that.

I give a frustrated groan, dragging the heel of my hand over my forehead. "This complicates things."

He grimaces. "I'm sorry. I've freaked you out, haven't I? Please—forget I said anything."

"Michael—" I open and close my mouth, hesitating. It's on the tip of my tongue to tell him that I like him too. But... what will that mean? Will he ask me out?

My pulse ticks up at the thought—at going out to dinner, maybe, somewhere nice. He'd be the perfect gentleman, we'd have a lovely time, he might even kiss me...

Fuck.

I drag my gaze away from him, my mind in free fall. I want that. I want all that.

But I *shouldn't* want that. I know better than to fall for it again, to give in to my romantic side. Harriet pointed it out:

the definition of insanity is doing the same thing and expecting different results. And what did Mum say, that I'm always dreaming of Prince Charming?

No. I don't want to be that person anymore. I know better than to hope for a fairy-tale ending again.

Besides, what would that mean for this opportunity with my writing? Justin never said I had to *be* single, but how the hell would I write a column championing the single life if I wasn't? They wouldn't offer it to me, would they?

I shake my head, clearing away the jumble of thoughts. There's too much at stake to give in to what I ultimately know is a bad idea.

"It's fine, don't be silly. You haven't freaked me out."

He eyes me uncertainly. "Are you sure? I don't want to lose you as a friend."

God, he looks so adorable, like he's actually worried I'm going to walk away from him.

"I'm sure," I say, resisting the urge to reach over and cuddle him. "I want us to stay friends."

"Okay. Good." He straightens up, giving me a smile that doesn't quite reach his eyes. "Well, that's great news about your writing."

I raise my cup of tea to my lips, nodding absently.

"You must be excited," he adds.

"Yeah," I mumble. And I sip my luke-warm tea, wondering why the excitement I felt earlier has all but evaporated.

23

I straighten the Christmas tree in the window display, smiling faintly as a customer passes. The whole store has a festive feel to it, with the tinsel and the music. There's no escaping the holiday season around here, no matter how much I might want to.

I still cannot believe Michael said he wanted to ask me out. This whole time I had a crush on him, and he liked me too. I have to keep reminding myself that I actually didn't imagine that part. And it's... well, it's bittersweet.

I know I'm doing the right thing by focusing on my writing, even if some of the shine has gone from it. At the end of the day, it's not even about choosing my career over a guy. It's about the fact that I'm choosing to go against that inner urge—the one that is telling me to throw caution to the wind and to, most likely, throw my heart under a bus. The one that has steered me wrong so many times before.

"It has to be a guy." Geoff taps a finger against his lip, eyes narrowed at me as I wander over.

"What?"

"The reason you've been moping around all morning."

I shake my head, attempting to paint on a smile.

"Oh, come on!" He's rearranging the Staff Picks shelf without paying much attention. He's much more interested in talking to me.

I release a long, resigned sigh. "Okay. Fine. It is."

He pushes his glasses up his nose, his eyes growing wide. "Yes?"

Despite my crappy mood, a laugh tickles my throat. He's going to love this. "You know my neighbor—"

"Sexy Michael," he says, his eyes wider still.

"It's him."

"I knew it!" he exclaims, startling a customer. We both shoot her an apologetic smile then Geoff turns back to me, lowering his voice. "So, what's happening then?"

"Nothing," I say, waving a hand. "Well, he told me he wanted to ask me out."

Geoff manages to suppress his squeal, but only just. It squeaks out the side of his mouth like a balloon slowly deflating.

I snort a laugh. "Nothing is going to happen."

"What? Why not?"

"I—" I stop, wondering how to explain my newfound cynicism when it comes to love. Then I just shake my head, settling on the easiest explanation. I told Geoff about the articles I'm writing—and the possibility of getting a permanent column—as soon as I arrived at the store this morning. So I know he'll understand. "If I want to write this single column, I won't be able to date, so..." I lift a shoulder, as if all of this is no big deal and I don't kind of feel like I'm dying inside.

"Do you like him?"

"He's... okay."

Geoff lifts his eyebrows and I feel a smile push at my lips.

"Alright. Yes. I like him." Understatement of the freaking century.

"And you think it's worth choosing your writing over him?"

I let my gaze slide down to the display, straightening a copy of *The Great Gatsby*. "It's the whole reason I came to the city. And this is a huge opportunity for me. I still can't believe that I'm going to get my writing published on Bliss Edition, and that I could even become one of their writers. It's crazy."

"It's great," Geoff says with a grin. "And I'm not at all surprised. You're a fantastic writer."

"Aw, thanks." I pause, wondering if I should tell him about my romance novel. He saw me borrow those books a while back, so I'm sure he won't be surprised. "I've also been working on a romance novel, just for myself. It's fun."

Geoff's grin widens. "I bet."

"Yeah. I had to do something with all the—" I break off with a vague gesture, looking at my boss's expectant face. He might be my boss, but I've come to see Geoff more as a friend. No reason to censor myself. "Repressed sexual energy," I say at last.

Geoff's biting his lip to keep from snickering. "Wow. So you *really* like Michael."

I nod, feeling my smile waver. I do. And while I want *so* much more than to be friends with him, I'm also trying to make my peace with things as they stand.

"I think you should just go for it," Geoff says, placing a copy of *War and Peace* under my name on the Staff Picks list. I roll my eyes and reach for it, placing *Fifty Shades of Grey* there instead.

"Geoff, are you not listening to me? I *can't*. The chance to write this column is important to me and that's what the whole bloody thing is about: being single and loving it."

Geoff eyes me. "And are you loving it?"

I shrug.

"I see." He's quiet for a moment. "Well, surely you can just be friends with him? If you can manage that," he adds with an exaggerated wink.

"I think I can. At least, I want to try." And I've been mulling this over. Surely one of the things about being single is having platonic relationships with the opposite sex, including dealing with the intense urge to jump into bed with them when it's a bad idea. This is an issue I could explore in my writing. I tell Geoff my thoughts and he nods in agreement.

"Yes. I think you're right. So really," he says, a wicked grin spreading across his face, "you're going to *have* to spend time with him, for research. Your writing depends on it."

I giggle. "I don't think I have a choice."

Geoff picks up a duster and starts working around the front display. "Hey, what are you doing for New Year's Eve?"

"I have no idea."

"Maybe we should throw a party."

"What, here?" I glance around the store.

"No. We could hire a bar."

"It's like two weeks away! Everything will be booked. Plus it would cost a fortune."

He adjusts his glasses, considering this. "Yeah, you're probably right."

"We could have the party at our place," I suggest, and his face brightens. "I'd have to ask Cat, though. And it might not work, because there are other people in our building."

Geoff's eyes glint with mischief. "Perhaps the *other people* in the building should be invited."

"You mean Michael?" I say wryly.

He gives an innocent shrug, as if the thought hadn't even occurred to him. "Well, you know," he says, focusing his attention on the display in front of him, "if Michael is there, and you are there, and neither of you have someone to kiss at midnight..." He wiggles his eyebrows playfully and a laugh bubbles in my chest.

Fuck, that sounds delicious, but what a disastrous idea that would be. I'm quite certain that if I let myself kiss Michael, I wouldn't be able to stop. I'd be tearing his clothes off and dragging him into bed to give him the happiest fucking new year of his life.

Still, a New Year's Eve party does sound fun—a lot more fun than spending the night at home alone.

"Fine," I relent. "I'll ask Cat."

CAT'S SITTING at the breakfast bar when I get home.

"Hey." I drop my bag and kick off my shoes. "What are you doing for New Year's? Geoff and I thought maybe we could throw a party here."

Her eyes light up. "That's a great idea! We should totally do that."

I grin, firing off a text to Geoff. He sends back a row of salsa dancer emojis that makes me laugh.

"What are you up to tonight?" I pad into the kitchen, surveying the takeout bag on the counter.

"I have a date."

"Ooh! Who with?"

"Someone I matched with on Tinder." She stuffs some fries in her mouth. "His name's Kyle."

I pull a half-full bottle of wine from the fridge. "Why do you do all this? Like, why not just wait and see if you meet someone? Why all the dating apps and that?"

"Because I want a relationship. It's not like it's a biological clock thing, or anything—I don't want kids. But... it would be nice to meet a good guy."

I nod as I slide onto a seat at the breakfast bar beside her.

"It's hard work, though," she continues around a mouthful of burger. "All the dressing up, all the effort of putting your best foot forward, not letting them see your faults and all that. It's like going on a job interview."

I take a long sip of wine. "Why not just be yourself?"

"Dating is like a sport, here. There are all these unspoken rules and it just feels like a test, the whole time. But... you have to play the game if you want to win." She shrugs, taking a big bite of her burger and chewing thoughtfully. "It's not like I'm not picky," she says after a while. "I know what I want, and that's someone who's nothing like my ex."

"What's your ex like?"

"Ugh. Mark's a dick." Cat makes a face, flicking through her phone and showing me a picture. On the screen is a guy with dark mussed hair and gray-blue eyes. He's holding a leather jacket over one shoulder, hooked on his finger like guys do when they think they're cool, and there's a silver chain around his neck. I can't quite put my finger on what it is, but there's something kind of slimy about him.

"He thinks he's so cool with his tattoos and his ripped jeans. And he flirts with women *constantly*—he even did it when we were together. He just drives me nuts. So basically anyone who is the opposite of him has a chance." She picks up her burger, taking another bite. I reach for a fry but she bats my hand away.

"Why are you eating now? You're not going to dinner?"

"No, we are. But I usually order a salad on a date, so the guy doesn't think I'm a pig. Then I end up starving like an hour later."

I snort, pushing off the stool and wandering over to my bedroom nook. "Is Mel going out with you tonight?"

"No." Cat stands and tosses the takeout bag in the garbage. "I think she's started seeing someone, but she won't tell me anything about him."

"Yeah, she mentioned something at brunch, but she wouldn't tell me much. Do you think she's waiting to see if it becomes serious first?"

Cat leans against the kitchen counter. "I'm not sure. Usually she's pretty open when she's dating someone. But for some reason she has been quiet about this one." She shrugs, then wanders into the bathroom and runs the shower.

I recline on my bed, my phone vibrating with a text. When I see it's from Michael, pleasure sings through my bloodstream.

Michael: Hey! What are you up to tomorrow afternoon? I thought of another classic New York place you need to see.

Well, that sounds interesting. And what a great opportunity for me to test my we-can-just-be-friends theory.

Alex: I'm free, what were you thinking?

Michael: It's a surprise. Pick you up at 3 p.m.

A surprise? My stupid heart skitters about with excitement, and I make myself inhale deeply. *We're just friends, for God's sake.* My body isn't listening, but it's fine.

Alex: Sounds good :)

I set my phone down and reach for my laptop, determined to get started on an article for Justin. But as I stare at the flashing cursor, my mind keeps straying to Michael, to what this little surprise of his could be.

No, I tell myself firmly. I'm not going to keep daydreaming about him, about the things he said, about how vulnerable he looked when he told me he liked me...

Shit, this is harder than I thought.

The blinking cursor is mocking me from the screen, so I force myself to get some words down. Any words.

How to be just friends with someone when you have a huge crush on them and want nothing more than to rip their clothes off...

There. That's a start.

I stare at the words, willing my fingers to write more, but they're frozen. I still can't believe Michael likes me. And now he's taking me somewhere as a surprise, and that's really sweet. Because he's sweet, isn't he? And now I might get to spend New Year's Eve with him, and if I do...

Cat comes back into the living room and I jump, slamming my laptop shut. Jesus, I've been sitting here in a Michael-induced daze for forty minutes. How the hell did that happen?

"I shouldn't have eaten that burger," Cat says as she wanders to the kitchen. "Now I feel bloated."

I take in her sexy fitted black dress, her perfectly styled hair, her flawless makeup. She looks fantastic, but I notice again that she doesn't look like her normal self.

"You look great! Besides, at least you won't be hungry now."

"I guess," she mutters, grabbing her purse. Then she stops, forcing the air from her lungs. "Wouldn't it be great if we could just be ourselves around men without having to play all these stupid games?"

"Yeah," I answer automatically. Then I pause, thinking of the way I behave when I'm around Michael. For the most part, I think, I've just been myself. Okay, sure—I haven't told him I've been picturing him naked, or that I'm writing a romance novel based on what I want him to do to me, but I'm not putting on an act or trying to impress him. Am I?

Cat pulls on her coat and gives me a weary smile. "I'll catch you later. Hopefully I'll have a wonderful story to tell you about how I've met a rich and sexy guy. Wish me luck!"

I give her a big grin, holding up crossed fingers as she leaves. I wish she would see how fun she is when she's simply being herself, and not try to impress men so much.

As the door closes behind her, I turn back to my laptop, feeling an idea blossom in my mind. I open a new document and start an article for Justin. This time, I'm inspired by Cat —by what she said about playing games and putting on an act and feeling like you can't be yourself. Because when you're single, you're free of all that.

The words flow quickly, and it's not long before I have a rough draft. I'm smiling as I set my laptop aside, imagining my words on Bliss Edition. Then I lie back on the bed, wondering where on earth Michael could be taking me tomorrow.

24

I look at the corner building across the street, wide-eyed. There's a red canopy running around the ground level displaying the words "Strand Bookstore," and several matching banners above.

"What is this place?" I ask Michael. I have a feeling I'm going to like the answer.

He grins as the crosswalk signal goes and we step out onto the street. "It's the biggest bookstore in the city. Eighteen miles of books."

I stop in the middle of the road, turning to him in disbelief. "Eighteen *miles*?" I might not have quite mastered the conversion of kilometers to miles, but I do know that's an awful lot of books.

Michael grabs my arm and drags me across to the curb with a chuckle. Then, we enter through the doors into what I can only describe as my idea of heaven. There are books everywhere I turn, and the space is *huge*. It's not just some cute nook in the Village, like Between the Lines; it's the whole ground floor of this building. It's not just books, either; there are bags and bookmarks and mugs and socks and buttons and every conceivable item a book lover could want.

Sweet Jesus. How did I not know this place existed? I should have come straight here from the airport! Why have I been wasting my time on the rest of the city?

"This is amazing," I breathe.

"I thought you'd like it. There are three more floors too."

"More floors?!" I spy a stack of shopping baskets by the door and lunge on one, giddy with excitement.

Michael laughs. "Maybe you should get a cart."

"Oh, yes!" I glance around and his eyes crinkle in amusement.

"I was kidding."

"Oh." Heat warms my cheeks and I shrink. Who gets this excited about books?

You know what? *I* do.

I straighten my shoulders, thinking back to the conversation with Cat yesterday. I don't need to impress Michael—in fact, if I'm going to be his friend, I should just be myself.

He reaches for another basket with a smile, apparently not at all disturbed by my display of enthusiasm. "Here. I'll carry an extra basket in case you need it."

I stare at him for a second, fighting the urge to get down on one knee and propose. He's carrying an extra basket for all my books. I just... can't. This is game over.

He gestures for me to explore and I shoot him a huge grin, turning back to the stacks of books. The first thing I do is find the writing section, and we spend a good chunk of time looking through the different writing books. Michael checks out a few, then says he's going to have a look upstairs.

After the writing section I find the romance section and, well, let's just say I could die right here and I'd be happy. I've never seen so many romance novels in one place—and not just new, but secondhand, too. We have a decent selection at Between the Lines, and we had a handful in the shop back home, but most of the time I bought the titles I wanted online. This is the first time I've seen so many in one place, begging to be bought and read and treasured.

I'm about to reach for one when an uncomfortable feeling prickles across my skin, making me hesitate. I know I'm writing my own romance novel—and I borrowed those books from work—but I haven't actually *bought* a new romance novel in a few months. Every time I wanted to, I've resisted, remembering Mum's heartless words. I've been mocked for reading them for years, so they've always felt like a guilty pleasure, but for some reason her words the morning after my birthday hurt so much more.

It's not just that, though. Ever since things ended with Travis, I've felt so jaded. It's like I've just given up on the idea of true love. In a way, I almost feel like romance novels have betrayed me. Mum's right—they've given me this ideal view of the world, this hope that I could meet my soul-mate and live happily ever after. And that's just left me disappointed.

But... as much I hate to admit it, I miss them. It's almost like a part of myself disappeared when I let go of the thing I loved.

I run a finger over the beautiful spines, feeling a pang in my chest. I'm here in this paradise and I'm denying myself the thing that has always brought me happiness. Maybe it wouldn't hurt to indulge myself.

With a quick glance over my shoulder to check Michael isn't around, I grab a stack of novels and carry them over to a chair. As soon as I sit down and start looking through the vibrant, candy-colored covers, I feel my heart piece itself back together a little bit.

Then, before I know what I'm doing, I go back for more,

pulling one after another off the shelf and hoping I have enough self-control not to buy them all. I feel like I've just been offered a feast after nearly starving to death.

In the end I manage to cull my selection down to just five novels, which I think we can all agree shows extreme self-control. Combined with the four writing books I found, I'm only buying nine books in total. The old credit card is going to take a bit of a beating, but I haven't treated myself like this for ages.

I heave my basket down the aisles, wandering for a while, looking for Michael. Eventually, I find him down a small, narrow aisle, tucked against the back wall. It's a section with poetry, and there are a bunch of old, antique books. I run a finger along their ancient spines, inhaling their musty smell and smiling to myself.

Michael grins when he sees me.

"Hey," I say, setting my basket down. I've done my best to arrange the books so that the romance novels are tucked behind the writing books. I don't want a repeat of what happened when he caught me at work.

His eyes flick to my basket then back to me, and there's a twitch in his lip. "Just a few books there?"

I giggle. "I know. I have no *shelf* control."

"Did you just make a book pun?"

"I did," I say, grinning. "Because, look!" I pull a book out of my basket and hold it up. It's a collection of jokes for writers, which of course I absolutely *must* have.

A smile hints at Michael's mouth as he eyes the cover.

I flip it open and scan for something to read aloud. "Ha ha, listen to this: *The past, the present and the future all walked into a bar.*" I pause, glancing up at him, then add, "*It was tense.*"

A laugh rumbles from his chest and I giggle again,

looking back down at the book.

"Oh, here's another one: *I'll never date another apostrophe. The last one was too possessive.*" I chortle again as I place the book back into my basket.

Michael is quiet and I feel a spasm of self-consciousness, glancing up at him. His eyes are sparkling as he gazes at me, deep creases around the corners. For a second I think he's amused by me like he always seems to be, that he's going to say something about how silly these puns are—how silly *I* am.

But he doesn't. Instead, the corner of his mouth lifts into a smile as he says, "You're so cute."

My heart stumbles, tripping over itself at his words. He thinks I'm *cute*? He doesn't think I'm silly—he thinks I'm *cute*.

I stare at him breathlessly. What am I doing? This man thinks I'm cute and I'm choosing not to be with him? Why am I—

"Well, this looks interesting." Michael pulls a book from my basket—one of my romance titles.

Instinctively, I grimace, feeling embarrassed. But then I remember what I decided: I'm not trying to impress him. I'm just being myself. I've been denying my love of romance but holding these books in my hands has made me feel better than I have in a long time.

"Yes." I lift my chin, taking a deep breath. "I read romance novels. And I'm writing one too."

"Hmm," he says, and I can tell he's struggling not to smile by the way his lower lip is trembling.

"You can judge me all you like, but—"

"Alex," he says, his face softening as he places the book back in my basket, "why would I judge you for liking romance novels?"

I falter, surprised by his response. "Well... you thought it was hilarious when you saw me with them at work."

"Did I?"

"You were making fun of me."

"No. I wasn't making fun of you. I was actually..." He rubs the back of his neck, and his cheeks turn crimson as his gaze falls to his feet. "I was trying to flirt with you. Not very well, obviously."

"Oh," I murmur, processing this. I think back to that day when he showed up at work. "Did you really forget that I worked there?"

"No," he says sheepishly. "I... wanted to see you."

Delight sweeps through me, and when he glances up with a shy smile, my heartbeat wobbles. For a second I forget all about the fact that I'm not supposed to be interested in him, and contemplate stepping forward to kiss him.

Shit. *Snap out of it.*

"And then I told you your book was crap," I say, attempting to lighten the mood. "So you thought, *fuck her, she's a bitch.*" I give a strained laugh, but Michael doesn't join in.

"I never once thought that."

He's staring at me so intensely that my pulse is rushing. I swallow, suddenly aware that we're alone down this narrow aisle, and he's standing very close to me. It's the bloody injured shoulder ordeal all over again. How do I keep ending up in these enclosed spaces with him? At least this time he's fully clothed, though it wouldn't be hard to remedy that...

I shake my head, willing myself to pull it together. I need to get out of this bookstore and get some fresh air. I need to take a cold shower.

I go to reach for my basket, but Michael stops me. "Is

that why you didn't want to tell me you're writing a romance novel? Because you thought I'd make fun of you?"

"I don't know." I lean against the bookshelf behind me with a weary sigh. "They're a bit of a guilty pleasure, I guess."

"What is there to feel guilty about?"

I think of Mum's words and cringe. "They give you unrealistic expectations, make you want things you can't have."

"Like what?"

The word "love" almost tumbles out of my mouth, but I catch myself just in time. Because that's crazy—I can't tell Michael that. But when I glance at him, I can tell he knows exactly what I'm thinking.

I look down at my hands. "Do you remember at Beanie, when I told you I felt like I had nothing to show for my twenties?"

"Of course."

"Well... I wasn't just talking about my career." I may as well be honest. He probably deserves an explanation for everything, anyway. I mean, he told me he liked me and I just... didn't respond. I didn't tell him any of the things I was thinking. I just let him believe I didn't like him at all.

"Okay, this is embarrassing, but—" I glance up and down the aisle, checking we're alone. "I got dumped on my birthday, and it... made me really bitter."

"Some guy dumped you on your birthday?"

I look back at Michael, expecting to see pity in his eyes, but there is none. If anything, he looks almost shocked.

"Alex, that's... that's fucking awful."

"Yeah." A humorless laugh breaks from me. "At the time, I thought he and I had something special. It's pretty obvious now that we didn't, but it was humiliating."

Michael gives a slow nod. "And that made you stop

believing in love."

I nod too, unable to meet his gaze. "And, you know. I'm thirty and I'm still single, after dating for years. Lately I've felt like maybe these books"—I gesture to my basket —"aren't realistic. Like maybe love really is a fantasy." I scratch my arm, trying to ignore the sadness tugging at me. "For years I wanted to meet someone and fall in love. And the more I wanted it, the crazier I felt. So I just... stopped." Well, I tried. But looking at Michael's handsome, understanding face, I realize it hasn't worked one bit. "I just wanted to grow up and stop believing in fairy tales."

"Is that what you think growing up is? No longer being optimistic?"

"Well, you're older than me and you're..." I motion towards him vaguely, searching for the right word.

Amusement pulls Michael's mouth into a smile. He raises his eyebrows, waiting for me to finish.

"Well, you're kind of cynical."

He nods. "I am, and it's the thing I dislike the most about myself. I'd never realized that until I met you. Why do you think I'm drawn to you, Alex?"

I shrug, because honestly? I don't have the faintest clue.

"*Because* you're optimistic. You have a way of seeing the world that makes me want to be more positive. But what you're saying about love..." His brow knits, and something flickers in his eyes. "There's nothing crazy about believing in love."

I gaze at him, feeling a wry smile creep onto my lips. "Well, I never thought I'd hear that from the same guy I ran into on Halloween."

Michael grimaces. "Yeah. That guy was a dick." I chuckle and he shakes his head. "I didn't think I'd feel that way again either, but... things change. Sometimes people come into your life who make you question things you'd always assumed were the truth." His eyes crinkle into a tender smile, and my heart swoops. Because I'm quite certain he's talking about me.

I rub my chest, feeling an ache building behind my ribcage. I can't believe this guy, standing here in the poetry aisle of the most amazing bookstore I've ever seen, telling me to believe in love. *I'm* supposed to be the romantic here —he's supposed to be the cynic. But it almost feels like, right now, he knows me better than I know myself.

Fuck. I can't keep doing this. I can't keep telling myself I don't want him.

Without stopping to think, I take a step closer, stand up on my tip-toes and press my lips to his. He's caught off-guard and stumbles a little against the shelf behind him. It takes a fraction of a second for him to respond, but when he does...

Oh my *God*.

His warm lips brush over mine in a soft, gentle kiss, and his hands settle lightly on my waist. There's a zing through me, a thrill at kissing him finally, at how lovely it is.

And then my thoughts come piling in and I step back, embarrassed.

What the hell is wrong with me? One minute we're having a perfectly nice conversation then the next I'm throwing myself at him. I cringe as heat sweeps over my cheeks.

"Shit." I touch my fingertips to my tingling lips, studying the carpet. "I'm so sorry."

But when I force myself to meet his gaze, he's looking at me with dark eyes and a sexy smile, shaking his head. "No. Don't apologize." His gaze drops to my mouth. "Kiss me again."

25

Oh God. I know I shouldn't kiss him again, but fuck—I'm only human.

I slide my tongue over my bottom lip, ready to press him up against the bookshelves, when I hear a sound beside us.

"Excuse me, could I just..."

My eyes swivel to see a young woman, gesturing down the aisle beyond us, and I resist the urge to scream. "Oh, yes. Sorry."

We both turn awkwardly to let her pass, and I take a second to get some air into my lungs. I want so badly to kiss him again, but this woman is hovering nearby now, and—well, I guess we are in public. I can hardly blame her for wanting to browse books in a bookstore. But still.

Michael and I stare at each other for a moment, then he reaches for my basket and hauls it up onto his arm, not taking his eyes off me.

"Come on." He nods towards the front of the store. "I want to show you something."

We make our way to the register, my heart still tumbling

about in my chest. As Michael heaves my basket up onto the counter, I can barely get my wallet out, I'm buzzing so much from our kiss. I hand my credit card over in a daze as the clerk scans my items.

"Oh, you're a writer?" She places my writing books into the bag.

"Er, yes," I mumble, acutely aware of Michael beside me.

"That's so awesome. I've always dreamed of being a writer but never really gotten around to it." She slides the bag across the counter to me. "Have a great night."

I take the bag with a faint smile, feeling myself droop. What a timely reminder that I too used to only dream of writing and now I'm making it a reality. And kissing Michael is a sure-fire way to crush that dream, to see it dissolve into dust and scatter into the wind, until I'm right back where I started.

He turns to me as we step back out into the chilly air, pulling his beanie down onto his head and winding a scarf around his neck. While we were in there—for *three* hours, I now realize—it's gotten dark, and quite a bit colder. I attempt to pull my coat tighter but I'm struggling with the massive bag of books.

I'm just about to tell Michael I should go when he takes my bag of books to carry it for me—and my heart melts.

Shit. I am in so much trouble.

"You wanted to show me something?" I hear myself ask.

"Yeah, if you're not in a hurry to leave?" His eyes are bright and excited, and I nod, powerless to walk away.

With my books tucked under his arm, he flags down a passing cab and we climb inside. And I realize too late that it was *not* a good idea for me to get into a cab with him. The backseat is an even smaller space than the book aisle. I can smell his woodsy cologne and he's within easy kissing distance. If he says anything even remotely sweet, I'll lunge at him.

And if he tries to kiss me, I'm done for. I'll be yanking my dress up my thighs faster than he can pay the driver.

I lean against the window, pressing my warm cheek against the cool glass, praying for strength as we head uptown. We sit in traffic for a while, but Michael doesn't say anything—and he doesn't touch me, which is both a relief and an overwhelming disappointment. He just gazes out the window in thought.

When we finally come to a stop, I stumble out of the cab, my head a cyclone of confusion.

No, I'm not confused, I tell myself firmly. I know what I'm doing: being friends with Michael, focusing on my writing, not wishing for another happy ending. We shared one little kiss but it's over now. Everything is fine.

He gestures down the street with a secret smile. "This way."

I follow him, intrigued. We turn a corner and that's when I recognize we're at Rockefeller Plaza. And as Michael leads me across the Plaza, weaving between tourists who are out despite the cold night air, I see why he's taken me here. You can't miss it: the Christmas tree, lit from top to bottom in a dazzling display of twinkling lights, right behind the ice rink.

"Wow," I breathe as we reach the rink, gazing across at the tree. "It's stunning."

Michael sets the bag of books down at his feet and leans on the railing. "Yeah. I thought you might like to see it at night."

I glance at him, watching as he shivers in the cold air, pulling his beanie down over his ears. He turns to me with a big, boyish smile, his dimple deep in his cheek, and my breath stutters. I can't believe he remembered. My heart squeezes at how unbelievably sweet that is—at how sweet *he* is.

I can't stop myself; I reach a hand up to his face, needing to touch him, to show him what this means to me. I run my thumb over the smooth skin of his cheek to his beard and keep it there, feeling the roughness of his beard against my palm. His eyes flutter closed as I touch him, and when I don't remove my hand, he steps closer, slipping his arms around my waist and drawing my body to his.

Yep. I'm done for.

He gazes down at me, his eyes black and penetrating. His mouth opens, then closes, before he finally asks, "Can I kiss you?"

I nod breathlessly. Fuck, if he doesn't kiss me I'm going to die.

But he does; he lowers his mouth to mine in a slow, sweet kiss that sends a shower of sparks through me. I circle my arms around his neck and tilt my head, melting into the warmth and softness of his lips. I've never kissed a guy with a beard before and there's the most delicious tickle against my cheek. Something about that sends fire shooting down through my center, makes need bloom hot between my thighs.

Jesus Christ. I'm trying to keep it together, but it's a losing battle. I let out a little moan against his lips and I feel him smile, tightening his arms around me. When his tongue dips into my mouth, seeking mine, my knees buckle and he has to hold me against him.

"Get a room!" a passer-by calls and we both laugh, drawing apart. But not too far; he rests his forehead against mine, gazing at me with dark eyes, his breath warm and sweet on my lips.

"I thought you just wanted to be friends," he murmurs, and I giggle.

We stare at each other for a few moments, both of us grinning, figuring out our next move. Quite frankly, I just want to get him into bed, but...

I glance down at my stack of books at his feet with a heavy sigh. I hear the words from the clerk at Strand again —*I've always dreamed of being a writer but never gotten around to it*—and, with all my strength, I pull away. When I see the light dim in Michael's eyes, I take a deep breath, letting the freezing air fill my lungs.

"Michael, I haven't been entirely honest with you."

He lifts his eyebrows. "Does this have something to do with all the kissing?"

"Yes. I should have told you this the other day, but I... I like you too. A lot."

The corner of his mouth twitches into a smile. "Yeah?"

I nod. "I'm sorry I didn't tell you. I've been trying to fight it."

"Why? Because of the stuff we just talked about?"

"Yeah," I mumble. I look over at the Christmas tree, at the picture-perfect scene in front of me. "I promised myself I wasn't going to do that anymore—keep hoping for some- thing that would never happen. So I tried to convince myself that I wasn't feeling anything. But—" I cut myself off with a hollow laugh, thinking of Geoff's words. "I was kidding myself."

I let my gaze slide back to him, and before I know what I'm doing I step up onto my toes and brush my lips over his, stealing a kiss. When I pull away he's gazing at me affection- ately, and he laces his fingers through mine.

"The thing is," I say, looking down at our joined hands, "these articles I'm writing—this column..." I glance back up at him, feeling a little stab at the patience on his face. "This is the best opportunity I've had in a long time. I really want this. And because of the topic—"

"I know. You don't have to explain." He gives me a soft smile, squeezing my hand. "You're writing about being single. You'll probably have to be single to write it."

I shrug. "Yeah. I mean, they never actually said that, but... I don't see them giving it to me if I'm not."

"I get it." He lets out a heavy breath and it's a white mist between us. "Alex... I'll do what you want to do. I like you a lot, but I don't want to get in the way of your career."

I groan, tugging on his hand. "Saying that makes me want you more."

"I want you, too." A half-smile lifts his mouth, then drops away. "But if we want to be together, we need to do this right. I don't want you to regret ruining this opportunity for me. You'll know in a few weeks if you've got the column, why don't we wait and see what happens?"

I swallow hard, looking down at the ice-rink below. A few weeks, knowing that he wants me as much as I want him, knowing what those lips taste like now... "I'm not sure I can," I mutter.

When I glance back at him, he's giving me a woeful little smile, and he releases my hand. "I think you should take some time to think about what you want."

I nod, trying to ignore the feeling of despair that's settled over me.

We gaze at each other for another moment, then Michael picks up the bag of books and we wander out of the Plaza, finding a cab home.

In the cab we don't talk. I turn his words over in my mind: *take some time to think about what you want.* I know he means well, but that's not going to help me in the slightest.

Because it's not that I don't know what I want. I do, and it's crystal clear.

I really want to write for Bliss Edition and, if I get the chance, to become one of their featured writers. I want to be paid to write, to make something of myself, to show my parents it's *not* ridiculous—and I want to prove to myself that I can do it.

But I also *really* want Michael.

Shit.

26

*A*nnie *runs her hands down Matthew's firm, sculpted torso, biting her lip as she admires the impressive bulge in his pants. She knows what's in there and she wants it all.*

Her hands are quivering as she—

Wait, should that be *quivering* or *quavering*? I halt my frantic typing to double-check.

Writing a romance novel isn't how I'd usually spend Christmas Day, but it feels like it's the only thing keeping me sane right now. It's been five days since Michael kissed me under the Christmas tree at Rockefeller Plaza—five days since I told him I needed time to figure out what I wanted to do—and he's been nothing but patient and understanding. He's texted once to ask how I am, but he hasn't asked what's going on and why I can't just sort myself the fuck out—a question I've been asking myself repeatedly.

Since meeting with Justin I've worked my butt off on two articles, which I sent through yesterday. They're some of my best work, I think, and I'm super excited to see them published on Bliss Edition. Every time I think about what this could mean for my career, I get a rush unlike anything else.

Well, except the rush I get when I think of Michael: his lips brushing over mine, his hands on my waist, the desire in his eyes. That feeling is intoxicating, and it's making it a *lot* harder to figure this out.

I thought I'd decided, to be honest. I sent my articles off to Justin, proud of what I'd done, but ultimately knowing my heart wasn't soaring in quite the same way it did when Michael kissed me. But then I got an email from Justin. He said the pieces were "funny and relatable—just what we're looking for," and that he'd be in touch soon. Reading that, my heart picked itself up and did a happy dance, and I realized that no, I wasn't quite as certain as I'd thought.

There's a ding from my browser and I turn back to my laptop with a sigh. The chat box pops up in Facebook and I smile when I see it's Harriet. I've been so pleased to get some space from my family these past few months, but Christmas Day without them has been a bit of a bummer. Despite my last discouraging phone call with Mum, I've spent the whole day under a strange cloud of homesickness. Even Matthew and Annie couldn't distract me from that.

Harriet: Merry Christmas!

Alex: Merry Christmas. Miss you!

Harriet: Miss you too. Christmas hasn't been the same without you here. How's the writing? Have you heard any more about that job?

Guilt gnaws at me. Harriet has been so encouraging ever since I told her about the meeting with Justin, texting to check in, and I haven't replied. I've been... distracted.

Alex: I sent through a few articles and they loved them, said they'd be in touch.

Harriet: That sounds promising! See? Mum and Dad

don't know anything. You're not living in a fantasy world —you're making things happen!

She's right. Mum was on at me about "getting back to the real world," but this *is* the real world—my writing, the possibility of working with Justin.

Alex: Thanks :)

I'm going to make more of an effort with Harriet, I decide. She's been so supportive since I moved over here. I never knew how much I needed that from my sister, but I do.

I'm about to ask her how things are back home when there's a knock at the door.

Alex: Sorry, got to go. Chat soon x

When I look through the peephole, Michael's face is on the other side. Joy zips through me like an electrical current, lighting me from head to toe. I just want to pull him inside and kiss him senseless.

Instead, with inexplicable restraint, I swing the door open and offer a casual, "Hey."

His cheeks dimple into a smile. "Merry Christmas!"

"You too," I say, grinning like an idiot and immediately losing my cool. Shit, I know it's only been a few days but I've missed him. Is that crazy?

Well, I don't care. Because looking into those gorgeous eyes right now, I realize I *have* missed him. A lot.

Fuck.

He leans against the door frame. "What are you up to for Christmas dinner?"

"Not much. It's dinner for one, I'm afraid."

"Oh, come on. Your first Christmas in America and you're spending it alone?"

"Yep." Cat invited me to join her family lunch, but I didn't want to spend the day with people I don't know. I figured she'd be home tonight, but apparently she's seeing Kyle again.

Michael's brow knits. "I was worried about that. You spent Thanksgiving alone as well."

He was worried about me being down here alone? Of course he was. He's the sweet guy who took me to the greatest bookstore on earth, who remembered how much I wanted to see the Rockefeller tree at night. My heart swells at the thought and a smile springs to my lips.

"Henry and I made too much food. He made the gravy and he's very proud." Michael gives a chuckle. "If you're not doing anything, would you like to join us?"

My smile falters. "I... don't know." I glance down at my hands, shifting my weight. "I haven't, er, figured out, um..." I grimace, unsure how to phrase it. Our kiss now feels like a long time ago and, given how relaxed Michael seems to be right now, I find myself wondering if he's just moved on from the whole thing.

But when I glance up he gives me an understanding smile. "It's okay. That's not why I'm asking. I'm not expecting anything, Alex. Just come and have a nice meal with us, as friends. Agnes will be there too."

A cocktail of relief and disappointment swirls inside me. Because as much as he's absolutely saying the right thing, apparently part of me is wishing he wasn't.

"Okay," I say at last. "I'll just change and be up."

He grins, pushing away from the door frame and heading back upstairs.

I pad into my bedroom nook with a smile. I was worried that seeing Michael again might be weird, given this state of limbo we seem to be in. But maybe dinner will be okay. And I can't deny I'd rather spend the evening with friends than by myself.

I refresh my makeup and tidy up my hair, pinning some of it back from my face. Then I slip on a cute navy dress with gold details around the neckline and put some gold studs in my ears. A little lipgloss, then I head up the stairs.

When I knock on the door, Michael greets me with a dishtowel over one shoulder. The side of his mouth kicks up into a grin as he closes the door behind me. "You look beautiful."

"Thank you," I murmur, trying not to swoon into his arms. I let my eyes wander over his dark jeans and olive green button-down shirt, the sleeves rolled to the elbows. He's changed since he came knocking on my door and looks rather nice himself. But I can't quite find the words to say it —at least not in any appropriate way—so I just stand in the entranceway to his apartment, clutching my hands together in front of me. It occurs to me that I should have brought a bottle of wine or something.

Michael heads back to the kitchen. "Come in, make yourself at home."

I wander into the living room, smiling as I'm enveloped by the cozy feeling of his apartment. It's warm, and there are Christmas carols playing quietly in the background, a small tree in one corner with assorted baubles. But the best thing is the rich, savory smell of roast turkey. I haven't had a home-cooked meal like this for ages and I'm only now realizing I've missed it. There's a feeling in here, something both familiar and new, something I can't quite put my finger on. But it feels... good. Really good.

I cast my eyes over Michael's bookshelves. There's a lot you can tell about a person from their books, and his collection is fascinating. A lot of non-fiction books on history, nature, anthropology, architecture, travel... but also a lot of fiction. An interesting combination, which makes me smile. That's one of the things I love about him. He's not only easy on the eyes—he's intelligent and interesting, too.

In one corner I notice a whole stack by the same author: Ken Follett, historical fiction. We stock his books at work, and while I haven't read any of them, I'm pretty sure Harriet has.

"Would you like a glass of wine?" Michael asks from the kitchen.

"Yes, please."

He brings two glasses into the living room, handing one to me. "It's a sauvignon blanc from New Zealand." The grin he gives me is all boyish charm and I can't help but laugh as I take the glass, wondering if he's always bought New Zealand wine or if this is a new thing.

"Thanks." I gesture to his bookshelf with a teasing smile. "Bit of a Ken Follett fan, I see."

"Yeah, well." A self-effacing laugh slips from him. "Consider it research."

"For what?"

He hesitates, then releases a breath. "I have an idea for a series I want to write. Historical fiction, similar to that."

"That sounds great." I grin at him over my wine. "You should totally do that."

"I don't know. It's commercial fiction, quite different from anything else I've written. I don't know if people will take it seriously. I mentioned it to my agent and she wasn't very encouraging."

"Why not?"

"I think she's just worried that I won't be able to transition into fiction."

I feel a prickle of defensiveness for him. I know all too well what it's like to have people not support your writing.

"I'm sure you could, you're a great writer. Have you written any of it?"

"Not yet. I've taken notes, but it seems kind of pointless to get started on something that's not going to go anywhere."

I frown, thinking of my romance novel. I'm quite certain it's not going to go anywhere, and yet, I love writing it. I'm even getting close to finishing it, I think. "You wouldn't do it just for the fun of it? Surely that's reward enough in itself, right?"

He scrubs a hand over his beard. "Yeah. I guess you're right." His gaze lingers on me, his expression thoughtful, and there's a little frisson through me. "What about that romance novel of yours? What are your plans with that?"

"Oh." I twirl my wineglass. "I'm not sure. Probably nothing."

"I'd like to read it." There's an undeniable spark in his eyes now, and my heartbeat quickens. I just want to push him back against his bookshelves and drop to my knees in front of him.

Gah! Don't think about that!

"Why historical fiction?" I blurt.

Despite my abrupt subject change, he gives a sincere smile, unable to resist answering my question. "I love history, learning about the way people used to live, what their lives were like. You know, there's a universality to it—to being human. We all struggle with the same things, even thousands of years ago. I thought with fiction, I could create these characters who live in a different time, and…"

As he speaks, his whole face lights up and his eyes come alive like that time at the skating-rink. There's so much passion in his voice, in the way that he's gesturing with his hands, talking about his ideas with unguarded excitement now, and my heart feels like it could burst.

This man, he's just... he's so gorgeous, so smart, so passionate.

I stare at his mouth as he speaks, mesmerized by the fullness of his bottom lip, the way it curves up slightly higher on one side, the way it looks so soft beside the coarseness of his dark beard. And, *fuck*, that beard. I don't know what it is, but it's so manly, so—

"You okay?"

Shit. I was so busy obsessing over his mouth I didn't even notice he'd stopped speaking.

I meet his gaze with a nervous laugh. "What? Yes, I'm fine. I was just..." *Thinking about your mouth, what it tastes like, how it would feel all over my body.* I shiver forcefully at the thought and Michael's eyes flash, a seductive smile slanting his lips.

Jesus. Am I that bloody transparent?

"Hi, Alex!"

I leap back from Michael as Henry appears in the hall-way. "Hi, Henry," I mumble, sinking down onto the leather sofa and trying to ignore the amused look from Michael. My face heats as I mentally scold myself. What am I doing, thinking these thoughts about Michael? This is Christmas Day—with his *son*, for Christ's sake. I need to behave *appropriately*.

Henry flops down on a chair and I turn to him with a smile. "Thanks for letting me crash your Christmas dinner."

"I'm glad you could come."

"I'm glad you could come too," Michael murmurs as he heads back to the kitchen, his gaze briefly meeting mine. That sexy smile is still dancing on his mouth, and it makes my heart kick against my ribs as I raise my glass to my own smiling lips.

"Could you get that?" he calls when there's a knock at the door. "It will be Agnes."

"Hello, dear," Agnes says as I open the door. "Merry Christmas."

"Merry Christmas." I take in her outfit—a festive red sweater, slim black pants, and tiny glass Christmas tree ornaments dangling from her ears. As I close the door behind her, gratitude swells inside me to be spending this evening with her and Michael and Henry when I could have been alone. I reach out to hug her and she squeezes me tight.

"Merry Christmas, Agnes," Michael says affectionately when we enter the living room. He gives Agnes a kiss on the cheek before she lowers herself onto the sofa beside me.

"What a lovely man," she murmurs, and I have to smile. I can see exactly why she sings his praises so much.

My gaze drifts over to watch as Michael sets a huge turkey down on the table. There's something incredibly sexy about a man who can cook, which I'd never realized until this very moment. He turns to catch me staring and I blush. When I glance at Agnes, she's watching me curiously.

"So, what's new with you, Agnes?" I ask, throwing back the rest of my drink.

"Not a lot I'm afraid, dear." She smiles as Michael hands her a glass of wine. "What about you?"

Michael holds out the bottle to offer me a refill, and I nod, avoiding his gaze. "Er, nothing. Nothing at all."

"That's not true," he says. "You got some good news with your writing."

Oh, right. My writing. Shit, since being in Michael's presence I'd all but forgotten about that. It's like seeing him has erased my mind of everything else. And that's not good, is it? What a train wreck.

"Well, yes. There was something with my writing."

"Wonderful," Agnes says. "What happened?"

"I got asked to write some articles for a website, and if they do well then I might be offered a permanent job, writing a column for them." I think back to my chat with Harriet, attempting to remind myself how important this is to me.

"How exciting!" Agnes says. "And what are you writing about?"

Michael sets a dish of green beans down on the table and pauses, listening. It's like an elephant has barged into the apartment and sat down between us, sucking all the oxygen out of the room, and I feel myself wilt.

"It's about being single," I mumble. "And how it can be fun and fulfilling to live without a man."

Her face lights up. "That's fabulous! I've been without a man for years and I'm just fine."

I give a half-hearted smile, glancing at Michael. His gaze slides from mine as he turns his attention back to the table, and I suddenly feel guilty talking about this with Agnes when I haven't even given Michael an answer about what I want. Is he feeling as tortured as I am by this whole situation?

Or—fuck—is all this weird tension in my head?

"But you know," Agnes continues philosophically, "being a single lady is only fun when there isn't anyone special. Because if you meet someone special, that's a whole lot more fun." She winks at me and I look down at my glass, feeling my cheeks color.

She's right, of course. Ever since Michael and I talked at Strand, I've been replaying his words—*there's nothing crazy about believing in love*—and as much as my past experience tells me otherwise, I want to believe him. Which makes writing about being single harder, despite the fact that I desperately want this job. And that's why I'm in this damn predicament.

"Is it ready yet, Dad?" Henry asks, wandering over to survey the dining table.

"Sure is, bud. Let's eat."

As we sit at the table, Michael carves the turkey. We share a smile and I feel myself relax. Of course Michael isn't finding this as torturous as I am. I need to get out of my head and just enjoy the meal with my friends.

"So, Henry, what did you get for Christmas?" Agnes asks as we eat.

He beams. "Dad got me a bike."

"Woah, what an awesome Christmas present," I say, and Michael looks pleased.

"It's super cool. Mom said I couldn't have it, but Dad said I could."

"Well, we have to make sure she's okay with it too," Michael says.

Henry screws up his face. "She's so mean sometimes."

"She just worries about your safety, bud. She's not trying to be mean."

Henry shrugs and stuffs a forkful of turkey into his mouth.

"Ugh. That woman," Agnes mutters, and Michael and I both turn to look at her in surprise. She's too busy loading turkey onto her fork to notice.

I glance from her to Henry and Michael, feeling the air around us thicken. Michael's gaze drops to his plate and his shoulders fall almost imperceptibly. What am I missing here?

I'm about to open my mouth and ask, but decide against it. It's not my business, and I don't want to ruin

Christmas by dredging up some long-buried family history.

Silence stretches between us as we eat, and I remember our New Year's party. That will lighten the mood.

"What is everyone doing for New Year's Eve?"

Michael shrugs. "Not much. Henry and I usually watch a movie."

"We are going to have a little party in our apartment if you'd like to join us."

"Can I come?" Henry asks.

"Of course. If it's okay with your dad." I glance at Michael.

"That could be fun. I'm sure it will be better than sitting at home with your old man," he says with a wry chuckle, and Henry grins.

"What about you, Agnes? Do you have plans?"

She shakes her head. "Not in ten years."

"Well, we'd love for you to come to our party."

A smile stretches across her creased face. "That sounds lovely, dear. I'm not sure I'll last until midnight, but I will certainly stop by."

I grin, thinking about New Year's Eve as I finish my meal.

After dinner, Henry puts a movie on and settles onto the sofa while Agnes rises with a yawn and makes to leave.

"Are you sure you don't want to stay and watch a movie or something?" Michael asks, walking her to the door.

She squeezes his arm. "Thank you, Michael, but I'm tired and ready for bed. It was a delicious meal, thank you very much." She leans closer and murmurs something else to him, her voice low, and as much as I strain my ears from the table, I can't make out what she says.

"Oh." He chuckles, his cheeks pink. "We'll see." He kisses her goodbye again and offers to help her up the stairs but she insists she can manage. The door closes softly behind her and he comes back over, beginning to clear the table.

I stand to help him clear the plates, and as I look around at the table where I shared a meal with my friends, warmth rushes through me. It's that same feeling I felt when I arrived this evening, and I realize that whatever happens with Michael and my writing and everything else weighing on me, I'll be okay. I've got friends who care about me here in New York, miles away from home. I feel like I belong here a lot more than I did back there, and that's worth more than anything.

27

"Let me help with the dishes."

Michael places a stack of dirty plates beside the sink. "It's okay, this won't take long."

I stare at the counters dubiously. The kitchen looks like a bomb has hit it.

"Please," I insist, suppressing the urge to laugh. "Let me help."

He hesitates, then gives me a grateful look. "Okay. Thanks."

Running the hot water, I hunt around for the dish soap and find a bottle under the sink. Michael grabs a dishtowel as I slide some plates into the soapy water.

"Do you miss your family today?" he asks.

I turn his question over in my mind as I scrub. I spent all day thinking I felt homesick, but now that I'm here in Michael's apartment I realize it wasn't so much homesickness as loneliness. Because I haven't felt it once since stepping through Michael's door.

"Not really."

"You're not close with them?"

I shake my head. "I'm probably closest with my younger sister, Harriet." Saying this makes me smile. We've never been close before, but somehow, it feels different since I left New Zealand. "Do you have siblings?"

"Yeah, a brother. He's five years younger, but we've always been pretty close. He's out of town at the moment but if he was here we'd probably be spending the day together." Michael dries a plate, then sets it down. "What about your folks? What are they like?"

I glance down at the book charm around my neck, wondering how much to share. I don't often talk to others about my relationship with my parents, and I can't help but wonder what he'll think of me. But when I look back at Michael's compassionate face, I feel the urge to tell him everything.

"My parents... we're very different. They don't understand me and they think me living over here is crazy. Last time I spoke to Mum, she wanted to know when I was coming home—back to the 'real world.' They think me pursuing writing is stupid. They always have. You know what my mother said when I first told her I wanted to be an author? She said, 'oh, that's cute.'"

Michael chuckles. "Well, that's what most adults say to kids when they tell them what they want to be when they grow up."

"Sure. But I was twenty-five."

"Oh." He grimaces.

"Exactly. I'd always known they'd never really taken me seriously, but one morning I overheard them speaking, and it—" I break off, surprised to feel a lump form in my throat.

"What did they say?" Michael asks gently.

I draw an unsteady breath. "They said I need to get my head on straight and stop dreaming of things I can't have.

They said I read too many romance novels—that they're just full of nonsense and they've given me unrealistic ideas about life. They said I live my whole life in a fantasy. I mean... they aren't totally wrong. I do have my head in the clouds a bit, I know that. I spend a lot of time daydreaming." I huff an uncomfortable laugh, fiddling with the dish brush and staring into the bubbles. "Anyway. When you hear stuff like this from your parents, it's kind of shit."

Michael sighs beside me. "They made you feel ashamed about who you are."

I give a small nod, remembering the cold, prickly feeling that washed over me at my parents' words, at the disgust in Mum's tone as she spoke to Dad. I try to push the memory away but it won't go.

"Have you tried talking to them about it?"

"No. There's no point. Every time I do, I end up getting upset and they tell me I'm too sensitive." I shrug, picking up another dirty plate and dumping it into the water. Rehashing all this is making me feel a bit morose, actually. I swallow against the emotion welling in my chest. "Maybe they're right," I mutter.

"And you think that's a bad thing?"

I let my gaze slide back to Michael. He's studying me intently.

"Alex..." He reaches a hand towards me, then stops himself. "It's not a bad thing at all. And as for dreaming too much..." he trails off with a little laugh. "You're a writer, that's part of the job. But it's not just that." He sets the dish-towel down, gazing at me fondly. "It's who you are. And there's nothing wrong with any part of it—with any part of *you*."

I stare at him, my throat so tight I can barely breathe. Then he reaches his arms around my shoulders and pulls me into a hug. My hands are still in the sink, but I twist towards him and rest my head against his chest, closing my eyes, wondering what that warm feeling is rushing through me, filling me up, making me want to sob.

And then I realize what it is. It's the feeling of being seen, for who I am, and being accepted anyway. It's the feeling of being understood.

"Don't let anyone make you feel ashamed for who you are or what you want," he murmurs into my hair. He presses a kiss to the top of my head and I squeeze my eyes shut, letting a tear escape down my cheek, overcome with the strangest sense of peace. Somehow, in the space of five minutes, he's watched me fall apart and put me back together again in a way that no one ever has before. And I don't know what to do with that.

When he finally releases me, he smiles softly, dragging his thumb under my eye and wiping my tears away.

I give him a watery smile, attempting a laugh. "See? Too sensitive."

"No." He shakes his head, gazing at me. "It just means you feel deeply—you care. I learned that about you the second you gave change to that homeless guy outside Beanie." He picks up the dishtowel again, smiling to himself.

I look down into the sink, trying to quell my smile. I can't believe he remembers that.

"Thanks for listening," I say after a pause. "I don't often talk to people about this. You probably think it's pathetic, still worrying about what your parents think at my age, but—"

"Not at all. I understand, probably better than most. I don't think you ever grow out of wanting your parents to be proud of you." A shadow passes over his face as I hand him a clean plate, and I remember him telling me his parents pushed him into finance instead of letting him write. My heart squeezes.

"You think your parents aren't proud of you?"

"Not really. Well, not my father. He's—how do I put this? He's a difficult man. Hard to please. Never been all that impressed with my choice to be a writer, annoyed that I gave up my 'real job'. And when I got divorced, he was just so disappointed in me." He focuses on drying the plate. "Anyway. I'm closer with my mom, but because of Dad I don't see them all that much. I'm much closer with my grandmother. She lives in Vermont, otherwise we'd be spending Christmas with her."

I feel my eyes widen. "Your grandmother is still *alive*?" Whoops. That might have sounded a bit rude.

"Yes, she's still alive." Michael cocks his head to one side, sending me an amused look. "Just how *old* do you think I am?"

"Shit, sorry." I cringe. "I didn't mean..."

His mouth twists into a smile. "You think I'm really, really old, don't you?"

A laugh escapes me. "No. It's just, well, my grandparents all died when I was little. And I know I'm younger than you, so I figured..." I shrug.

"Yeah, yeah," he teases.

"So... how old are you?"

"I'm forty-one."

I nod, turning back to the dishes. That's about what I thought.

"Does that bother you?"

I glance back at Michael, surprised. "Why would that bother me?"

He lifts a shoulder but he doesn't say anything more, and for a second he looks a tiny bit vulnerable.

"No," I murmur, forcing my attention back to the sink. "It doesn't bother me at all."

We do the dishes in silence, both of us lost in thought. After a while, Michael asks, "So what do you think of life in the city?"

My mouth pulls into a grin. "I love it."

"Must be different from home?"

"God, yes. I come from a town of seven thousand people. They couldn't be any more different."

"You don't miss it?"

I shrug. "I love the energy here, but it has been full-on over the holidays." New York does Christmas on a grand scale—big displays, bright lights, Santas on every corner. And I've loved it, mostly, but I can't deny it would be nice to get away from the frenzy of the crowds for a while. "I don't miss home but I miss the quiet, sometimes."

He thinks for a moment. "If you want a break from the city, I have a cabin you could use."

"A cabin?"

"Yeah. It's a family cabin, but hardly anyone else uses it. Mostly just me and Henry, sometimes my brother. It's at Indian Lake."

I mull this over as I scrub. Maybe I should get away. Some time out could help me sort my head out with everything.

"Where is Indian Lake?"

"In the Adirondacks."

I let out a disappointed sigh. "Thanks for the offer. It's a nice idea, but I have no way of getting there."

Michael takes a few dishes and stacks them in a cupboard. "When would you go? I'm driving up to see Nana in the new year. I could drop you there on the way."

"Henry wouldn't mind?"

"He'll be with his mom for the week."

"He didn't want to see your Nana?"

"Oh, he did." Michael twists the dishtowel in his hands. "But that's the week he's supposed to be with his mom and she wouldn't let him come."

"She wouldn't *let* him?" I ask, handing him a glass.

He sighs. "It's easier to go along with her than cause drama."

I think back to the way he shrank at the dinner table, to the fact that he was battling for custody recently, and a question works its way to the tip of my tongue. "What... um, if it's okay to ask, what happened with you and her?"

His hand stills on the glass, his brow pulling low. He opens and closes his mouth a couple of times before finally saying, "I'm not sure if I want to get into all that right now. I will explain it to you, but... not today. Not at Christmas." His brow remains furrowed as he meets my gaze. "Is that okay?"

I nod, examining his face. Clearly I've hit a nerve here, and I'm not sure I want to press any further. I turn back to the sink, dumping some cutlery into the water. It wasn't my place to ask, really. I'm about to apologize when he speaks again.

"Anyway, if you want a ride to the cabin, I'm happy to take you. It's pretty remote—no cell service, no wifi. But it's a good place to just get away."

I smile at the thought. "Yeah, okay. That would be great. Thanks."

Henry has fallen asleep on the sofa and Michael goes into the living room. He flicks the movie off and pulls a blanket up over him, kissing him on the head. It's such a tiny thing, but it's so tender it immediately endears him to me. He picks up the dishtowel again as I finish off the dishes and drain the sink.

"You're a good dad," I say.

Michael smiles modestly. "Thanks. I try, but I feel like I'm constantly screwing up."

I root around in a drawer looking for cling film to cover some of the leftovers.

"You kind of helped me to see that I've not been the best dad, though."

I pause, turning to him. "I have?"

"Yeah. You kept pointing out all these things I wasn't doing, and I started to think—"

"Wait." I straighten up, confused. "What are you talking about?"

He laughs. "I don't think you meant to, but you made me see what I'd been forgetting. Like, I never gave Henry pizza, or took him trick-or-treating. And the ice-skating... Anyway, I realized that I'd been kind of uptight, too worried about doing the *right* things, that I forgot the fun things are important too."

"Oh," I murmur. "Shit, I'm sorry. I never meant to—"

"I know." He puts a hand on my arm. "But I'm glad. I'd been so stressed, so, I don't know... pissed off at the world. And then I met you, and you reminded me that it's good to laugh and to have fun."

I think back to the grumpy guy I met in Starbucks, the man who was unpleasant to me in the hallway on Halloween. He *was* damn uptight when I met him.

But he's not that guy at all anymore. Now, he's playful and cheeky and fun. If I think of our day out in the city, or the visit to Strand, or even just this evening, he's a far cry from the guy I met. Is that really because of *me*? Happiness flows through me, warm and bright, at the thought. And— God, I know I shouldn't—I place my hand over his and squeeze, holding his gaze.

We stand there for a long moment in his kitchen, staring at each other, neither of us wanting to move. My blood is pumping hard, fast, and I try to ignore it, but when Michael draws his hand away, the intensity of my disappointment shocks me. It doesn't matter what I tell myself. My body knows the truth.

He finds the cling film and I wrap up some turkey in silence, mentally berating myself. It's my fault I'm in this position—*I'm* the one who can't sort their shit out here. And with every passing second, I feel the weight of my indecision pressing in on me, crowding out the kitchen, suffocating the air from my lungs.

"I'm sorry," I blurt.

"For what?"

"For this whole thing." I gesture vaguely and he looks puzzled. "For my writing, for us, for not..." I scan his face for a sign of understanding, when it occurs to me that maybe he's not suffering in the same way that I am. This whole evening I've been torturing myself about it, but maybe he's already moved on and all of this awkwardness is in my head.

"Alex, it's okay." He softens, taking a step closer. "You don't have to apologize."

"But am I imagining that things are weird? They feel weird."

"Well, yeah. A little."

I look up at him. "Why?"

"Because we like each other," he says simply.

I bite my lip. "Do you... you know, do you still..."

"Of course. I can't switch my feelings off. I'm just not acting on them."

I let out a tormented groan. "What am I doing?" I mutter, more to myself than him. I rub my forehead in agitation and he reaches for my hand.

"Hey, it's okay. We talked about waiting until you find out what's happening with this job, and that's the right thing to do." He takes my other hand, and now he's holding them both, giving me a gentle smile. My whole body is humming at his touch, and I gaze up at him, swallowing hard.

"You think so?"

He nods. "Do you remember our conversation in Beanie? You told me you spent your twenties not going after what you want, and now you are. I admire that."

"And what if I *get* it?"

"Well..." A line forms along his brow. "Then we'll cross that bridge when we come to it. But I want to support you, Alex, and if that means... I don't know, waiting until we can figure out how to make this work, then so be it." His eyes fix on mine, serious and fiery. "Because when we finally do this, we are going to do it right."

Oh *God*.

My heart rate skyrockets at the heat in his gaze, the promise in his words. I'm so breathless I can't even bring myself to respond.

He stares at me for another second, then drops my hands with a chuckle. "Until then we will just be weird friends. Okay?"

I glance down at my hands, still tingling from being held in his. "Okay," I murmur. He's right; my writing is important to me. Why do I keep forgetting that? I sigh, stepping away from him. "I should probably go."

Disappointment flits briefly across his face and he nods. "Yeah. Okay."

"Thanks for inviting me tonight." I wander to the front door and pull it open. "I had a great time."

"You're welcome. I'm glad you came."

I turn back to say goodbye and it feels awkward. I'm not

sure if I should lean in to hug him, or maybe I should shake his hand? No, that would be too formal. Perhaps a high-five? No, that would be silly. A wave?

But before I can do anything, he leans in and kisses me on the cheek. I feel the whisper of his beard against my skin and I'm immediately transported back to Rockefeller Center, when he pulled me close and kissed me underneath the Christmas tree. It's so lovely I almost moan, and it takes all my strength not to throw myself against him and pin him to the wall.

Just friends? Come on Michael, you're killing me here.

"Goodnight, Alex," he says with a playful little smile, and I get the sense he's well aware of the effect that kiss had on me.

I shake my head in disapproval, but I can't curb the insistent smile on my mouth. "Goodnight, weird friend."

I hear him laugh as I turn and head down the steps home.

28

"Alex, this isn't a pre-schooler's birthday party," Geoff says, pouring himself a piña colada slushie from the machine.

I look down at the cardboard party hats in my hand. "Hey. You put me in charge of decorations, Geoff, so you're wearing it." I thrust a hat into his hand.

"Fine." He rolls his eyes as he slips it onto his head, pulling the elastic under his chin.

I grin, handing one to Cat. At least they are fancy party hats: black with gold lettering that says "Happy New Year" and a gold pom-pom on top. They match the color scheme for the party: gold and black streamers, balloons and a banner. I also organized two slushie machines for cocktails and a cute little selfie corner with props like fake mustaches, wigs, silly glasses and speech bubbles that Cat made.

"I kind of wish I could stay now," Cat says with a sigh. Turns out things have been going well enough with this Kyle guy that he invited her to some exclusive New Year's party downtown. She didn't want to abandon our party, but Geoff insisted she go.

"Don't be silly," he says, elbowing her. "You've got a hot date on New Year's Eve! At least you know you'll get a kiss."

She raises her eyebrows dubiously, taking a sip from her margarita slushie.

"Did you invite Mel?" I ask.

Cat shakes her head. "She's out with her new man for the night." She gives me a tight-lipped smile as I hang some balloons, turning to check the room.

We've pushed the sofa back against one wall, got a few folding chairs and cleared a small dance floor area. Geoff put some music on the stereo through his phone and switched off the main lights, so the room is only dimly lit by some twinkle lights. We are ready to go.

Agnes is the first to arrive, dressed in a black turtleneck and slim-fitting black pants. There's a string of pearls around her neck, and her long silver hair spills down her back behind a black headband. She's the epitome of sophistication. I want to be her when I get old.

We show her to a comfy spot and get her a cocktail, then Geoff peppers her with questions while Cat and I greet some other guests. There's a couple of people from the bookstore, some people Cat knows through her shop, a few others from the building and some of Geoff's friends.

By nine o'clock Michael and Henry still haven't arrived. I haven't seen Michael since Christmas, distracting myself with my romance novel and consoling myself with the knowledge that I'd see him tonight. But now I'm thinking he might not even come, and I find myself feeling quite deflated.

I knock back a couple of shots and dance with Geoff and Cat to take my mind off him. I don't need Michael here to have a good time. In fact, it's probably better that he's *not* here, given how much I've had to drink. I get way too flirty when I'm drunk.

I'm just about to grab another drink and flop down beside Agnes, when Michael and Henry appear in the doorway. Elation swoops through me and I'm beaming as I bounce over to greet them. "Hi, guys!"

"Hi, Alex." Henry stands in the doorway shyly.

"Hey." Michael gives me an apologetic smile. "Sorry we're late. We have a tradition of watching a movie together on New Year's Eve and it went later than I'd expected."

"That's okay, I'm glad you came. Henry, there's soda in the kitchen and snacks over there. Help yourself. Oh, but—" I reach for a couple of party hats and hand them over, my face deadly serious. "You *must* wear these."

Henry pulls his hat on, then wanders over to check out the food.

I turn back, noticing Michael's wide grin as he pulls his party hat on. His gaze travels over me and, I swear, I can *feel* his eyes sweeping across my skin, around my curves. I splurged a little for tonight on a gold sparkly dress that hugs my hourglass figure and shows off my cleavage. New heels, too—black, patent, higher than I'd normally wear.

"Alex, you look..." he trails off, shaking his head.

Shit, that can't be good. I frown, adjusting my dress.

"Nice, I mean," he says quickly. "You look really nice."

Oh.

"Thanks." I blush, even though "nice" is how you would describe your mother looking.

He surveys the room and I let my eyes climb his frame, admiring his dark jeans and button-down shirt the color of red wine, sleeves rolled to the elbows, exposing his forearms. God, he's lovely. Maybe we could sneak off upstairs while—

Whoops. Perhaps I need to dial back the tequila for a bit.

He turns back to me, slipping his hands into his jeans pockets. I'm just about to get him a drink, when Cat appears beside us on her way out. I smile, but she narrows her eyes to slits.

"Hello, Michael."

He nods. "Catherine."

So formal. So icy, I almost shiver. My brow knits in confusion as Cat's gaze cuts to me.

"Alex, can I have a word, please?" She drags me towards the kitchen before I can protest. "Why did you invite *him*?"

"What? I invited everyone in the building." I scrutinize her murderous face as she shoots daggers across the room to Michael. "Why are you so annoyed? You weren't this bothered when Agnes showed up."

She gives a furious huff. "Yeah, but Agnes isn't—"

"Cat?" I turn to see a tall, handsome guy weaving across the room towards us.

"Kyle!" A grin breaks across Cat's face, all signs of animosity gone. As he reaches her side, she mutters to me under her breath, "We'll talk about this later." Then she beams up at Kyle as if the sun is shining out of his ass, and I watch in bewilderment as she gives me a carefree wave goodbye and sails out the door.

Well, that was bizarre. First the icy reception towards Michael, then what was all that fake cheer with Kyle?

I shake my head, wandering back to Michael, still standing awkwardly by the door. "Sorry about her."

He wipes a hand down his face. "Why does she hate me so much?"

"I have no idea." I analyze his features, searching for clues. Maybe she only knows the Michael I met months ago

—the grumpy guy in the hallway who didn't have a pleasant thing to say to anyone.

He clears his throat and I remember my manners.

"Let's get you a drink." I grab his arm, trying not to notice how strong and firm it feels as I pull him over to the drinks table. I let my hand rest on it longer than necessary, enjoying the warmth of his skin under my fingertips.

He gives me a teasing laugh. "It seems I'm a few behind you."

I nod, pouring two tequila shots and placing both in front of him with a slice of lemon.

"You're kidding." A smile flits over his mouth as he eyes the shots. "You do realize I'm not as young as you. The hangovers are a lot worse at my age."

"Come on." I giggle and push the glasses closer to him. "It's New Year's Eve. Let's have some fun."

My words hang in the air and he gazes at me for a moment, his eyes dancing. There's a thrill down my spine as the space between us hums with possibility. Then Michael grabs the shots and knocks them back in quick succession, biting the lemon. Fuck, I would do anything to take that out of his mouth with my own right now.

Geoff appears beside me with a mischievous grin. "Alex, who is your *friend*?"

Oh God, Geoff, I attempt to transmit telepathically. *Do not embarrass me.*

"Geoff, this is Michael. Michael, this is my boss at the bookstore, Geoff."

Geoff puts a hand to his chest, pretending to look hurt.

I roll my eyes, adding, "And he's also a *dear* friend."

"Good to meet you," Michael says, extending his hand. Geoff pounces on it with a hearty shake.

"And you, Michael. I've heard a *lot* about you."

My cheeks grow hot, even though they're already rosy from drinking. I elbow Geoff in the ribs, and Michael laughs while Geoff backs away, wiggling his eyebrows up and down suggestively.

Jesus Christ.

"Sorry about him," I mumble, handing Michael a piña colada slushie and feeling slightly mortified.

But he just grins as I rest against the wall, watching people dance. He leans beside me, his gaze on Henry, chatting to one of our other neighbors.

After a while, Michael leans closer to talk to me over the music. His breath is hot on my ear, sending goosebumps scattering across my skin. "How's the romance writing coming along?"

Heat creeps up my neck. It's coming along quite nicely, thanks to me channeling all the lust I've felt for him onto the page. In fact, it's been an *extremely* productive writing week. "It's, uh, good."

"I don't suppose you'd let me read it?"

"God, *no*."

His eyes glint as he appraises me, like he's enjoying winding me up. "Why not?"

"Because..." I search for a reason I can actually say out loud. Because it's literally a blow by blow—pun intended—account of everything I want to do to him. Because it's the only way I can think of right now to not go crazy with desire for him. "It's embarrassing," I say at last.

"It can't be that bad."

I smirk. Yes, it can.

"Come on," he urges, flashing me a flirtatious grin. "I might like it."

My cheeks glow. "You might," I mutter, turning back to look across the room, and beside me I hear him chuckle.

We stand side-by-side, drinking and watching the others dance. And I decide if Michael can needle me relentlessly about my romance writing, I can give him a hard time too.

"How's the historical novel coming?"

He takes a long sip from his cup, avoiding my gaze. "It's not."

"Why not?"

"I told you why. My agent doesn't want me to write it."

I face him squarely, the alcohol giving me confidence. "And I told you to write it anyway."

His eyes swing to me. "You did."

"So do it. Just for fun. For you."

He scrubs a hand over his beard, a smile peeking around his mouth. "And since when are you telling me what to do?"

"I—" I bite my lip, trying to ignore the electricity crackling between us, trying not to say something I shouldn't. If I thought I was having fun at this party before he arrived, I was wrong. Since he got here I've felt alive, buzzing, drawn to him by a magnetic pull that's impossible to fight. It's not the alcohol, it's *him*. It's always him.

I open my mouth to tell him exactly this, when I spot Geoff and Agnes peering at us from across the room. Geoff leans close to whisper something to Agnes, and the spark inside me fizzles out.

What am I doing? I shouldn't be over here, flirting with Michael. We agreed to be friends and I'm behaving like this. Drinking or not, there's no excuse.

"Um, I'm just going to mingle for a bit," I mumble to Michael. I weave across the room to where Agnes is nestled on the sofa with Geoff perched beside her. "You two okay?"

Geoff grins over his drink. "How's Sexy Michael?"

"What?" I glance at Agnes but she just sips her drink as

if she hasn't heard. "Geoff," I mutter, giving him a subtle cut-it-out motion.

But not subtle enough, apparently, because Agnes says, "Don't worry about me, dear. Your friend Geoffrey has already filled me in on everything."

"Everything?" I repeat, my gaze darting back to Geoff. I told him about the kiss at Rockefeller, and the fact that Michael was prepared to wait until I found out what was happening with this job opportunity. I *thought* I'd told him all that in confidence, but trust Geoff to make a beeline for Agnes and spill his guts.

Geoff shrugs innocently. "I was just making conversation. Besides, you two looked pretty cozy over there."

I glance back to where Michael is still leaning against the wall, watching us with interest. My heart does an involuntary flip and I turn back to the others, forcing a neutral expression. "We're just chatting," I say with as much disinterest as I can muster. "That's all. Nothing is going on."

Agnes frowns. "You could do a lot worse than Michael, you know."

I let out a sigh, gazing down into my slushie. "I know. He's... really great." As I say this now, I realize I can't think of a single thing I don't like about him. It's amazing how kind and genuine Michael is, given how attractive he is. Most guys with looks like his think they're God's gift and are absolute shitheads.

Come to think of it, that in itself feels like a bit of a red flag. What do they say, that if something seems too good to be true, it probably is? I remember my mother telling me that I'm always dreaming of Prince Charming and feel a ripple of unease.

No. I straighten up, pushing the thought from my head. It's New Year's Eve. I don't want to think about the shit my parents have said to me, the career I'm trying so hard to build, the questions Agnes and Geoff are asking. I just want to party and have fun, maybe flirt a little—not worry about these tiny inconvenient details.

"Can I get anyone another drink?" I ask, giving Agnes and Geoff a sunny smile. And when they shake their heads, I turn and stride back towards Michael, determined to enjoy myself for the rest of the evening.

29

"That's the most fun I've had in ages," Michael says as we lean against the wall, catching our breath.

I suck back some slushie, pressing a cool hand to my warm cheek. Michael took Henry up to bed a while ago, then Agnes went up, offering to keep an eye on him until Michael was ready to go home. I was on the dance floor when Michael returned, and I managed to convince him to join me. I didn't expect much out of him, but all it took was one song before he completely let loose.

"Thanks for making me dance." He angles his body towards me, grinning. "You always do this."

"Do what?"

"Make me do these things I think I don't want to do. And then I'm always glad I did."

I smile, remembering his words on Christmas. I like the thought of him having fun because of me.

His gaze rests on me for a moment, then slides across the room. He watches the dance floor, sipping his piña colada, then asks casually, "What are your plans for midnight?"

I give a baffled laugh. "Um, I'll count down, I guess.

That's the usual tradition, isn't it?"

"Yes. It is." He chuckles self-consciously, raking a hand through his hair. "Any other traditions you might be interested in?"

I scan the room for clues, wondering what on earth he's talking about. Then it hits me. Surely he can't be referring to the midnight kiss? But when I dare to glance at him, I know that's *exactly* what he means. He's looking at me almost hopefully, and butterflies swarm in my stomach.

I pull in a breath, trying to regain control of my escalating pulse. I know I wanted to have fun tonight, but I didn't mean *that* much fun. "Is that something friends do?"

The side of his mouth lifts into a smile. "I don't know. I've never had a friend like you before. But I figure it's New Year's Eve and it's a tradition to kiss at midnight. Maybe tonight"—he gives a little shrug—"the usual rules don't apply."

I raise my eyebrows, battling a smile, half wanting to laugh at his hopefulness and half wanting to tell him off for putting ideas in my head. My heart is thundering now at the prospect of kissing him again, even if it's a terrible idea. I try to find some words but all I manage to do is gurgle out an incomprehensible, "Uhhrm." I tear my gaze away as my body flushes with heat, and when I glance back at him he's still gazing at me, his mouth tilted up in a suggestive smile.

Holy *hell*.

But... let's be rational here. Is he right? Of course the usual rules don't apply on New Year's Eve. I *could* kiss him, it wouldn't be the end of the world. It would just be one little kiss. One delicious little kiss.

But as I take in his playful expression and the way it makes my whole body tingle, I realize that while his logic is sound, I don't have the kind of self control required for it.

Because if I kissed him tonight, it would be game over. I'd wake up tangled in his sheets, and I don't see myself coming back from *that* to write about how blissful it is to be single.

No. Best to put that idea out of his mind right now.

I lean forward, so that my mouth is right by his ear, and before I can stop myself I inhale a lungful of his woodsy cologne. It makes me dizzy with lust and I have to grip onto his arm to keep myself steady. All the alcohol isn't helping, either. It's such a powerful combination that I'm too light-headed to think straight, too intoxicated to prevent the next words from leaving my mouth.

"Michael," I say, my voice low and husky, "there is no way I would be able to stop at just a kiss."

He turns his head towards me ever so slightly, so that his beard scratches against my cheek, and gives a grunt in my ear. All of a sudden I'm imagining what that beard would feel like against my thigh, if he had his head buried between my legs, and I feel a throb right where I want him so badly. At this point I have to physically pull myself away from him, and I suck my whole slushie back in one gulp, giving myself an ice headache so bad that all the heat drains from my body.

Just as bloody well.

I notice Geoff waving to me across the room and with an exasperated sigh, I excuse myself.

"Are you going to kiss Sexy Michael at midnight?" Geoff asks when I approach.

"Why?" I say wryly. "Because if I don't, you will?"

He licks his lips, eying Michael across the room. "It's worth a shot."

I give a faint laugh and look down at my drink, feeling myself sag. I'd give anything to kiss Michael tonight, but I know it's not a good idea.

Geoff tilts his head. "You okay?"

"He did kind of suggest we kiss."

Geoff's eyes widen and he almost squeals. I have to whack him on the arm to keep him in line.

"I'm not *going* to. God, I want to, so badly. But I can't."

"Oh, just *live* a little!" Geoff cries, and I give a melancholy little chuckle.

"I will, one day. But not tonight. Please keep me away from him at midnight."

"Really?" Geoff's shoulders slump. "Are you sure?"

"Yes," I say resolutely. I take a long slurp from my drink. Michael is across the room chatting to one of our neighbors, and longing tugs at me as I watch him.

I wrestle my gaze away and turn back to Geoff, begging him to distract me. We down some tequila shots and talk for a bit, but I can't quite follow what he's saying because I still have one eye on Michael, and I'm struggling to focus on anything at this point with all the booze in my system. Then before I know what's happening, we're counting down. The room spins around me as we count, as everyone hugs and cheers and, as if on a timer, Auld Lang Syne plays through the speakers.

I catch Michael's eye across the room and he tilts his head to one side, smiling, raising his glass to me.

But I can't bring myself to respond. Instead, I feel a surge of misery.

This fucking sucks. All I want is to kiss him but I've quarantined myself on the other side of the room, for reasons I'm struggling to even recall. This isn't a happy new year. This is a crappy new year.

I push my way past a few people and stumble into my bedroom nook, yanking the curtain closed behind me, frantically trying to remind myself why I shouldn't kiss him.

"Hey." He pokes his head in through the curtain, his face drawn with concern. "Are you okay?"

I pull off my party hat and slump onto the bed. "Not really."

He hesitates, then slips in through the curtain and pulls it closed behind him, removing his own hat as he sits beside me. "So this is your room," he says, looking around in the dim light. "I like it. Very cozy."

I can feel the heat from his body next to me. It takes all my strength not to lunge at him, not to tell him that I'll give up everything if I can have him. Somehow, I manage to keep it together, staring at the floor and trying to make it stop spinning.

Michael heaves out a sigh and pushes to his feet. "I should go." He rubs the back of his neck, a deep frown etching itself across his brow. "I don't think you want me here."

"I do," I say hastily. I stand and put my hand on his chest, meeting his gaze. I can feel the thrum of his heartbeat against my palm and it's hypnotizing. His eyes are dark and fierce, almost dangerous in the way they pierce through everything, straight into me. I let out a helpless little whimper, sliding my hand up around the back of his neck and stroking my fingertips over the soft, warm skin at his nape. He swallows visibly, the muscles in his neck flexing beneath my hand, and heat races up my body.

Fuck.

I give him a pained look. "I'm trying to stay away from you. We agreed to just be friends, but you're making it impossible."

"I know. I'm sorry." He grimaces, staring down at the floor. "This is harder than I thought it would be. I just... it's New Year's Eve and I wanted to kiss you." He pulls in a raspy breath, taking a step back, and my hand falls to my side. "But you're right. It wasn't fair of me to ask, and if you don't want to—"

"You think I don't *want* to kiss you?!" I say incredulously. I wobble on my heels and steady myself against my dresser. "Of *course* I want to kiss you. Fuck, Michael, I want to get down on my knees in front of you right now and..." I trail off, my eyes dropping to the obvious arousal behind his zipper. Saliva pools in my mouth at the sight and I let out another little whimper.

"Jesus, Alex." He grinds his jaw. "You can't say shit like that to me."

I lift my gaze to his. My face is flushed from more than just drinking now, but I don't care about keeping it together anymore. "Why not?"

"Because you're driving me fucking *crazy*," he growls, reaching to adjust the bulge in his jeans. A muscle ticks in his neck and I can tell he's physically restraining himself from reaching for me.

I stare at him, wide-eyed, breathing hard. This is a side of him I haven't seen—this charged-up, hulk of a man who looks like he's about to wreck me. And, oh *God*, how I want him to.

I run my tongue out and over my bottom lip. "Come here."

He doesn't hesitate to close the distance between us. I'm backed up hard against my dresser now, and he places his arms on either side of me, caging me in. His dark eyes bore into mine but he doesn't try to kiss me. Impatience burns hot between my thighs, melting away every single one of my vows to stay away from him, and I know I've lost the battle. Hell, I've lost the whole war.

"Michael," I say hoarsely. "Kiss me. Now."

His mouth lands on mine before I can even take a breath, but the relief is overwhelming. And it's nothing like the kiss at Rockefeller, which was tentative and gentle. No; this time he takes charge, pushing his hands up into my hair, tilting my head back so my mouth opens for him. Then his tongue slides over mine in a dirty, wet kiss, and my hands fist in the front of his shirt. I moan right into his mouth and he sinks against me, molding the length of his body to mine. Lust blazes through me in hot, blinding waves when I feel how hard he is.

Holy fuck, I knew it. I knew as soon as I kissed him, I'd be done for. But I don't even care anymore. All I want is his naked body on mine—at whatever cost.

I break the kiss, grabbing his hand and tugging him towards my bed. I want to taste his salty, musky taste, to feel the weight of him pin me down against the mattress.

But he follows my gaze and laughs. "Alex, we can't. You don't have any walls."

Dammit to hell, this stupid bedroom nook with no walls. What was I *thinking*?

I look at him desperately. "Could we... do you think Henry is asleep yet?"

He groans, pressing me back against the dresser and lowering his mouth to drag it over my neck. "I *really* want to take you to bed right now, believe me."

Oh, I do believe him. The proof is in the bulge digging into my belly, making me tremble with need.

"But, honestly—" He draws away from me with a little growl. "I just wanted a kiss."

"I warned you," I say, stabbing a finger at him.

"I know." He gives me a rueful smile. "But, come on. I don't want to fuck you on New Year's Eve because we're drunk. I want to do this right."

I can't even begin to imagine what doing this right looks like anymore. I just shake my head, pulling him back to me until his mouth is on mine again, until all I can taste is the pineapple and coconut on his tongue.

I hop up onto my dresser behind me, wrapping my legs around him. He responds by grinding his hips against me and kissing me hard, his tongue sweeping over mine in long, hungry strokes, and I lose it. I paw at him wildly, my fingers clawing down his shirt and scrabbling for his belt buckle.

"Oh God," he says in a rough, shaky voice, as if he doesn't quite trust himself to stay in control. His big hands wrap around mine. "We can't. I want to, so badly, but I'm not going to do it like this."

I'm about to start begging, when I hear Geoff's voice.

"Alex? Are you in there?"

Michael draws back to look at me, and when I give one final, half-hearted tug on his buckle, he bites back a smile.

"Yeah," I call to Geoff as disappointment settles over me. "I'll be out in a second." I sigh, dropping my hands from Michael's belt.

He steps away and adjusts his pants, smoothing his hands over the shirt I nearly shredded in my fervor. He considers me for a second, then reaches out to tuck a strand of hair behind my ear. "You're so beautiful, Alex."

I close my eyes, letting those words float through the drunken haze into my brain, hoping I remember so I can replay them over and over again later. When I open my eyes, he's still gazing at me.

"If you want to do this—*us*—then I want to do it the right way. And that's not tonight."

I nod, blowing out a long, resigned breath.

"Can we talk about this when we're sober?"

"Yeah." I hop down off the dresser, stumbling and

steadying myself against him. I hiccup loudly and clap a hand over my mouth in horror, but it's too late—he heard. We stare at each other then both dissolve into laughter.

"Shit." I rub my forehead. "I'm really drunk."

"I know," he says, somehow both affectionately and teasingly. He hooks an arm around my shoulders and plants a kiss on my temple. "I'm going to get you some water, then I'll go home. Okay?"

"Okay." I sink down onto my bed against the pillows. My drunk buzz is quickly giving way to exhaustion.

Michael appears with a glass of water and watches while I drink it, then he lowers himself onto the bed beside me. He smooths a hand over my forehead, gazing at me tenderly, and something in my chest breaks.

"I like you so mush," I say, hearing my words slur as I reach for his hand and lace my fingers through his. "I feel good around you, like I can be myself and you understand me. You like me anywhere. I mean, whoops—" I giggle. "Any*way*." I squeeze his hand as the next words tumble out my mouth. "I don't care about writing this column if it means I get to be with you."

A tiny, hopeful smile lifts one corner of his mouth. "Yeah?"

"Yeah." I reach to pull him closer, and he brushes his mouth over mine in a soft, delicate kiss, letting out a little sigh as he pulls away.

"I like you a lot too, beautiful girl," he murmurs, raising my hand to press his lips to the back of it. "But you're very drunk. Let's talk tomorrow, okay?"

I nod, snuggling back against the pillow as Michael's hand caresses my arm. I feel my eyelids grow heavy and I drift off to sleep with a smile on my face.

30

I 'm dead. That's what this feeling is. It's a familiar feeling, too.

I crack one eye open and wait for the pain to subside, but it doesn't. I need painkillers and water, fast.

Peeling myself from the bed, I stand and wobble to the bathroom, stepping between discarded cups and party hats. Geoff has passed out on the couch, still wearing his party hat, snoring.

My head is pounding so hard I can barely stand. In the bathroom I manage to down a few painkillers, then I lower my mouth and drink straight from the faucet, trying to piece together the events of last night.

I know Michael was there. And Henry, I think. And I talked to Michael—well, of course I did. It would be weird if I hadn't. What did we talk about? Something about... writing, maybe?

I stumble back through the living room and collapse onto my bed again, willing the painkillers to work faster.

There was dancing too, I think. Did Michael dance? Even in my hungover state, the thought of that makes me smile. I try to reach further back in my brain, to find another scrap of memory I can pull out into the light, but my thoughts fade away as I slip back into sleep.

Somehow, I sleep through until the afternoon. By the time I wake, I feel a bit better. I've still got a headache but it's dialed down from a ten to a four. I'm going to need to eat something soon, though.

I roll over in bed and reach for my phone to check the time, surprised to find a text from several hours ago.

Michael: Good morning. How's the head?

I stare at the screen for a second, waiting for my brain to catch me up. Last night... Michael...

But nothing is coming. Ugh, I'll text him later. I need coffee.

Yawning, I toss my phone aside and climb out of bed. When I push the curtains to my nook open, I see that Geoff has attempted a quick tidy of the living room before leaving, bless him. Cat's not home either, I notice as I pad down the hall. Maybe her and Geoff went out. Or maybe her date with Kyle went a *lot* better than she'd planned.

I manage to shower and get dressed, then head out for a coffee and something delicious to eat. I slide into my favorite table in the window at Beanie, with a massive latte and chocolate muffin in front of me. Perfect.

Nibbling on my muffin, I pull my phone out to see if I got any photos of last night. There's loads of pictures I don't remember taking, and I stop on an especially cute picture of Michael and I at the selfie corner with some of the silly props. I've got one of the mustaches on a stick and he's wearing huge glasses. I smile at how happy we look, and as I flick through more pictures of us, fragments of last night start to piece themselves together in my brain.

Yes, Michael and I *did* dance together. It was fun, I recall with a giggle. And we flirted... yes, we flirted a lot. We talked about... kissing? I think we did. I might've even told him I wanted to kiss him. But I didn't *do* it, of course, because—

Oh. Fuck.

A memory comes back to me, clear as day: the taste of pineapple and coconut, the slide of Michael's tongue over mine. It's so vivid, so visceral that I can *taste* it, and it sends a violent shiver through me.

More memories chase that one and my face heats with shame. Because I didn't just kiss him, I *threw* myself at him. Oh God... I think I even tried to rip his clothes off. The poor guy! I was like a rabid dog, frothing at the mouth for him. I'm surprised he made it out alive.

Actually, that's a good point... What happened? I know for certain we didn't sleep together, so how did it end? Did he push me off him? Did *I* walk away?

Ha. That doesn't seem likely. My self-control was clearly at an all-time low and I'm sure that, if he let me, I would've done every dirty thing I could imagine.

So *what* happened?

I scan the depths of my brain, groping about for clues, but come up empty-handed.

It doesn't matter, anyway—there's no excuse for me mauling him like that. As humiliating as it is, I need to apologize. And maybe, if I'm lucky, he'll volunteer the rest of the information. Then we can have a good laugh at drunk old Alex and put it behind us.

I consider going up to his place now to apologize, but as I polish off my muffin, nausea climbs the back of my throat. I'm getting serious morning-after-my-birthday flashbacks and I think I need to lie down again. I greatly overestimated my ability to be up and at 'em today.

Abandoning my half-drunk coffee, I rise to my feet and

hurry back home along the street. My head is pounding again by the time I push through the door, and I'm relieved to see Cat is still out and the apartment is quiet. I slump onto my bed and crawl under the covers, typing out a text to Michael. He's supposed to be driving me up to the cabin tomorrow, so an apology right now might be a good idea.

Alex: I'm so sorry about last night, I was wasted. Can you forgive me?

Michael: You don't need to apologize.

Alex: No, seriously, I'm sorry. Can we just forget everything?

I watch the screen, waiting for his reply. Apprehension squeezes my gut as the little dots appear, then disappear, then appear again. After what feels like forever, his reply comes through.

Michael: Fine.

I exhale in relief. Thank God, I haven't destroyed our friendship with my crazy antics.

Alex: Cool. Is it still okay to get a ride to the cabin tomorrow?

Michael: I'll pick you up at 7 a.m.

TRUE TO HIS WORD, Michael pulls up outside the building at seven sharp in an old, beat-up 4x4 truck. He leaps out, taking the front steps two at a time.

"Hey!" I grin as he enters the lobby.

"Hey," he says, not meeting my gaze. He grabs my bags, heading straight back out onto the street, and I feel my smile slip as I follow him out. Then he dumps my bags on the back seat and opens my door, not saying anything.

"Thanks," I mumble, hopping in.

We don't speak as we weave through the streets, out of the Village and up along the Hudson River towards the George Washington Bridge. When I sneak a glance at him, his line of sight is fixed on the road, his brow furrowed slightly. Something seems a bit off with him, but I'm not sure what. Well, it is early. Maybe he hasn't had his coffee yet.

I twist in my seat to gaze back at the city as we cross the bridge. I see the Empire State Building and Chrysler Building silhouetted against the slate-gray sky, and a smile slides onto my lips. I still can't believe I live in this city—the city I'd dreamed of for years, the city I'd seen in movies, that always felt more like a dream than a real place. And now, I call this city home.

With a happy sigh, I sit back and stare ahead through the windshield. "Thanks for letting me tag along," I say after a while.

Michael grunts and I look at him with a frown. Jeez, what is going on with him today?

He glances at me and I smile, hoping it might somehow make him lighten up, but the V between his brows deepens and his gaze cuts back to the road.

Bloody hell, he's in a bad mood. I haven't seen this guy for a while. This is Starbucks Michael, Halloween Michael —the first Michael I knew. I wonder why he's back all of a sudden?

"Um, is everything okay?"

He looks at me again and sighs. "Yeah. Fine."

I study him for a second, then cross my arms and turn to stare out the window at the gloomy sky. Dark clouds are gathering fast, which seems to match Michael's mood perfectly. This is going to be a long trip.

I DON'T KNOW how long I sleep for, but when I wake the first thing I notice is that everything is white. Like, *everything*.

Michael is leaning forward in his seat, squinting his eyes to make out the road as we inch along.

I sit up, taking in the frosty surroundings. "It's snowing," I say in wonder.

Michael grunts. "Yes."

"Are we nearly there?"

"Yes."

I can barely see five feet out the window. I glance at Michael, worried. "Are you okay? Can you see?"

"Enough."

"It's a lot of snow," I murmur, snuggling into my seat. I don't know what I've gotten myself into. I've never been in so much snow and don't know the first thing about it. I can't even build a fire. I'll probably freeze to death in his cabin and Michael will have to tell people how pathetic I was. I shiver at the thought.

"I thought it would pass," he says, concentrating on the road. "But it seems to be getting worse."

"Should we be driving in this?"

"You want to sleep in the car?" he snaps. "We'll freeze to death."

I shrink down in my seat. "Sorry."

He glances at me, softening a little. "I hate driving in this weather. We're nearly there."

I try to figure out where we are, but I can hardly see anything beyond the white. Eventually, we pull up a driveway and through the frosty haze I can just make out a log cabin.

"Okay, stay here."

"You want me to freeze to death?" I joke, but Michael doesn't laugh.

"I'm going to clear some of the snow so we can get in." He jumps out of the car and I see him battling with a shovel to clear the path to the doorway. After a few minutes he comes back to the car and grabs my bags, then comes back to grab some groceries we stopped for on the way. Finally, he opens my door and tells me to follow him. I step out into the snowy wonderland, my breath coming out in a cloud around me. It's like a scene from a fairy tale: snow-flakes falling in front of a log cabin surrounded by trees.

Wow.

"Alex! Get in here!"

I walk carefully, my boots sinking into the snow as I make my way up the path. Michael closes the door behind me and I peel my coat off, taking in my surroundings. It's a typical log cabin, with the big round log walls, high peaked ceilings, stone fireplace, and a big, worn sofa with two armchairs. To the right is a small kitchen with wooden cabinetry and simple wooden bench tops. Several doors lead off the living room.

"Okay, I'll show you around and explain everything before I head off."

I turn to Michael, concerned. "You're going back out again, into that?" I gesture to the window and the white abyss beyond.

He shrugs, slipping his hands into his jeans pockets. "I said you could have the place to yourself."

"You also said you hate driving in this weather."

He stares at the floor, quiet.

"I think you should stay, at least until the snow clears. It's not safe to drive in this."

He puffs out a frustrated breath. "Fine. I'll go get my

bags from the car and make sure the water and everything is working. Can you make a fire?"

I cast my gaze over the massive stone fireplace, the stack of logs and the box of kindling. I've never made a fire before, but I watched Dad do it a lot as a kid. How hard can it be? Besides, the last thing I want to do is make Michael any grumpier than he is. And I don't want him to think I'm some useless woman who's worried about chipping her nail polish, or something.

"Absolutely," I say, striding towards the fireplace with confidence. He disappears out the door and I start stacking kindling like I've seen Dad do in the past. I find a box of matches on the mantle-piece and light the pile, waiting expectantly. Not much happens, so I heap on some more twigs and thin branches from the basket beside the fireplace. But all that does is make smoke pour into the living room.

Fuck.

This isn't like the fireplace we had back home, which was a box where you could close the front door. This is wide open and the smoke is billowing into the room, up to the ceiling. Where are the damn flames?

I stand, glancing around in panic. I know putting logs on it won't help, but if I try to put it out we might not get another one going.

Gah! Why did I tell him I could do this?

"What the hell are you doing?" Michael appears back inside, slamming the front door and yanking off his coat. He waves his arms through the air as he strides over.

I shrivel. "I'm sorry, I was trying to—"

"Forget it." He nudges me aside and kneels in front of the fireplace, fussing about with the kindling.

I stand rigid, my arms folded as I watch him, not daring

to move. Eventually, once he has coaxed flames onto the wood, he stands and turns to me.

"I'll show you your room." He takes my bags through one of the doors, into a tiny bedroom with a single bed. "Leave the door open so it heats up," he instructs. Then he shows me the bathroom and the kitchen, before unpacking my groceries into the pantry.

I perch on the sofa in front of the fire, slowly warming up. Even though it's only early afternoon, it's almost dark with the storm. Michael turns on a couple of lamps, and a warm yellow glow falls over the room.

"You want some lunch?" he asks, rooting about in the pantry. He pulls out some dried pasta and canned sauce, holding them up.

I smile gratefully. "Sure, if you don't mind."

While he cooks and I sit in front of the fire, it dawns on me that we are going to be staying here, in this house together, tonight. This is exactly the sort of situation I should be avoiding, but we don't have a choice now. At least he's back to being Grumpy Michael, for whatever reason. He's a lot less appealing as Grumpy Michael.

Although, that brooding look is sexy...

No. Being trapped alone with him here is *not* a good excuse to throw caution to the wind and jump him. I need to be vigilant.

After we eat, I do the dishes, hoping it might improve his mood. But when I come back into the living room, there's a scowl gathered around Michael's eyes as he stokes the fire.

"I'll have to sleep out here tonight so I can keep this going," he says as I ease myself back onto the sofa.

"You don't have a fireplace in your room?"

"Yes, but you'll need this one to keep warm."

I picture sliding into bed with him in front of a blazing

fire and shiver with longing. That is, until I glance at his thunderous face. He must be irritated that he has to give up sleeping in his own bed to keep the fire going for me.

"Um, I can do it."

He snorts. And as I watch the yellow firelight lick over his glowering features, I suddenly snap.

"Jesus, Michael! What the fuck is your problem?"

He glances at me, eyes wide with shock.

"Okay, look. I know I messed up the fire and I shouldn't have told you I knew what I was doing. But that doesn't explain why you've been angry with me *all* morning."

He turns to stare into the flames, stroking a hand over his beard in thought. "I'm annoyed about what happened on New Year's, Alex."

"Oh God." Shame slaps my cheeks and I raise a hand to hide. "I know, I'm so sorry. I shouldn't have kissed you like that."

"What?" He gives me an odd look. "No, I *wanted* you to kiss me. That's... that's not it."

"Then what?"

"I—" He hesitates. "It was what you said, before I left."

Shit. Who knows what I said, blind drunk?

And then a horrible thought occurs to me. What if I was a total bitch to him? I don't even want to consider it, but sometimes when I drink... That would certainly explain why he's so mad. Or, fuck, maybe he stopped the kissing and I got angry, which is quite possible. And *mortifying.*

I rub my forehead vigorously, as if that might dislodge a memory, and Michael frowns at my bemused expression.

"How much of New Year's do you remember?"

I grimace. "Not much. I'd had a lot to drink."

"So had I, and I still remember it."

"Well excuse me, Mr. Perfect Memory." I make a face.

His eyes track over me for another moment, then he exhales. "I guess it's not fair to be mad at you if you don't remember."

"What... happened?"

"You said something..." He lets his gaze slide from mine. "Something I really wanted to hear."

My heart jumps. What does *that* mean?

"Then why were you angry?"

"Because the next day you texted me and told me to forget it."

"Oh." I want to ask him what I said, but honestly? I'm terrified of the answer. Instead, I take a breath to ask something else I desperately want to know—something that's been eating away at me since yesterday. "Michael, why, um... why didn't we sleep together?"

He lifts his eyebrows. "You don't remember that, either?"

"No," I mumble. "I just thought, you know, we were kissing, and... did I stop it?"

"No, Alex." There's a flash of amusement in his eyes. "You did *not* stop it. I did."

"But... you said you wanted to kiss me. So why stop it?"

"Because we were drunk! I didn't want it—*us*—to be that; drunk sex on New Year's."

"Oh," I murmur. He was being a gentleman, not taking advantage of what I, apparently, was eagerly offering. "That's... that's really sweet."

His eyes linger on my face and his mouth softens into a smile. "I'm sorry for being a jerk."

I smile too, relieved to see him coming around. "It sounds like I wasn't that nice to you on New Year's Eve. Sorry I can't remember."

There's a twitch in his cheek. "I never said you weren't nice."

Right, that's it. I have to know.

"Are you going to tell me what I said?"

He sinks his teeth into his bottom lip, playfulness lighting his eyes, and shakes his head.

"Come on!"

"Nope." His gaze remains locked on mine as a slow smile spreads across his face, and desire ignites in my bones. God, that's all it takes—one provocative smile from him and I start to unravel.

With a low chuckle he pushes to his feet, raising his arms above his head to stretch. His sweater lifts, exposing half his abdomen, and my eyes fix on the bare skin. There's a trail of dark hair from his navel down to the top of his belt buckle—a path to his treasure. My fingertips tingle with the need to touch it, to follow and see where it leads. And when he catches me shamelessly feasting on him, his eyes spark with a hunger of his own.

Holy fuck.

Heat rockets through me, settling in an ache between my thighs. Suddenly I'm gasping for breath and I have to look away or I don't know what I'll do. No wonder I was behaving so inappropriately on New Year's Eve after a boat-load of booze. I'm barely holding it together now, stone-cold sober.

I need to get away from him. Fast.

"Right." I dig deep into my reserves of self-restraint as I rise from the chair, knowing there's only one way to get this out of my system. "I'll be in my room, writing."

"You might be more comfortable at the table. Plus it's warmer out here."

"No, thank you," I say stiffly, walking straight to my room and closing the door, even if that means being cold. The further I am away from him, the better.

I sink down onto the bed and flip my laptop open, desperate to dive into my romance novel. I should be working on another article for Justin, but I'll be honest—I'm scraping the bottom of the barrel for upbeat angles on being single. What Agnes said at Christmas keeps coming back to me: *being a single lady is only fun when there isn't anyone special.* And Michael—the guy who wouldn't have sex with me when I was drunk, who went out of his way to bring me up here even though he was mad—he's pretty fucking special, I think.

But it's not just that. I've sent through three, feature-length articles now, and while Justin has been encouraging, they haven't even been published yet. It's already the second of January, and he said the column would be launched in the new year. After everything, I'm beginning to wonder if I'm even in the running for it after all.

I push the thought from my head as my laptop powers on. Because right now, there's only one thing I want to write about, and that's *not* being single.

It's an hour later when I look up from my laptop and my neck is stiff. Michael was right, I should work at the table. I crack open the door to the living room and I'm relieved to see he's not there. He must have lit the fire in his room, after all.

I wander out and set my laptop down on the dining table, then pop into the bathroom. The wooden floor is cool under my feet and I shiver, gazing at the bathtub longingly. I could have a quick bath to warm up before getting back into my writing. That would be nice.

Michael has left some fluffy towels out for me, so I run the bath and slip my clothes off, sliding into the deliciously warm water. I sit in the tub, watching the steam swirl up into the air. It's amazing that I'm here in this warmth while the world outside is freezing. The weather here is crazy. In a way, I'm relieved Michael is here with me, because if I were snowed in by myself I'm sure I'd panic, or freeze to death. At least with him here I know I'll be okay. Of course, the idea of him helping to keep me safe only makes me want him more.

With a sigh, I drain the tub and dry off, slipping my clothes back on. The last thing I'm going to do is walk across the living room in nothing but a towel in case Michael is out there.

But the bath did the trick, I think. With a serene smile, I head back out into the living room, feeling warm and snuggly, ready to dive back into my writing.

I find Michael sitting at the table with my laptop open in front of him. He stands slowly and turns to me, his eyes wide.

I tilt my head. "What?"

His cheeks are flushed and he looks a little shaken. No, actually, he looks—well, almost turned on. What was he reading on there? Oh...

No.

He huffs out a breath. "I, uh, read some of your romance writing."

Fuck.

31

"What?"

A smile nudges his lips. "It's *really* good."

Heat rises up my neck and colors my cheeks. If he read it, surely he's figured out that I'm writing about us. And if that is the case, then... I'm going to die.

"Uh, well," I begin, groping for some kind of reasonable explanation and grasping nothing. I reach over and slam my laptop shut.

"You left it open. I just caught some of it, then I couldn't stop reading." He shrugs helplessly. "I'm sorry."

I glance at the front door. I don't care if the snow is up to my neck—I'd rather be out there right now.

"Alex." His voice is a low, husky rumble as he says my name. "Wow."

My gaze flits back to him and I realize I've lost the ability to speak. Why on earth didn't I close my laptop? How could I have been so *stupid*?

"You know," he murmurs, taking a step closer, "I couldn't help but notice the names you've chosen for your characters."

Shit. Shit, shit, shit.

I stare down at the carpet, my face glowing. This can't be happening. *Please, God, I'll do anything to make this stop.*

"Matthew and Annie. They're *very* similar to Michael and Alex." He steps closer still. "And some of the scenes you've chosen seem familiar. There was this one scene in a bookstore, one in a hallway on Halloween, and another in a cabin..."

Fuck. He's figured it out.

Humiliation crashes over me in hot waves and I close my eyes, wanting to die.

"You've been writing about us."

I feel him step closer, then he places a finger under my chin and tilts my face up to his. My eyes flutter open involuntarily to find him gazing at me. But he's not laughing or mocking me. Instead, there's fire in his eyes and his mouth is slowly curling into a grin that sends my heart rate through the roof.

I swallow hard. "I know it's stupid, but—"

"No. It's not stupid. It's *hot.*"

I hesitate, certain I'm misunderstanding. "What?"

"Yeah. Reading that—" He stops on a heavy breath, his eyes hazy as they roam my face. "It was like reading my own fantasies."

I feel my jaw unhinge. He's not appalled or disgusted. He's *turned on.*

Fucking hell.

He trails his finger down my neck and along my collarbone. Goosebumps erupt over my skin, each one a tiny proof of the effect he has on me, of how much I want him. I'm breathless, staring at his mouth, wondering what his teeth would feel like skating over my skin. And God, those lips—so full and soft and delicious. I think of the pineapple taste of his kiss, the way his tongue felt sliding over mine, and molten lust shoots down through my center. Kissing him felt like the best thing in the world.

He must be thinking the same thing, because he lifts his hand to my face and drags his thumb over my bottom lip, swallowing visibly. Our eyes meet again, and when I see the raw, burning desire reflected back at me, my whole body feels like it will combust.

I pry my gaze away and Michael drops his hand. We stand in a thick cloud of tension, and when I finally risk glancing back at him, he's staring at me hard.

"I don't want to push you, Alex. But—fuck. You can't say you're okay being friends and then write stuff like this." He forces out a lungful of air as a frown drags his eyebrows together. "You want to know what you said to me on New Year's?"

"Yes. *Please.*"

"You said you didn't care about your column if you could be with me."

I want to be shocked by this, but I'm not. Because part of me had been thinking it all New Year's Eve. Hell, that thought has been coming to me since he told me he liked me, three weeks ago. I thought I'd done a better job of fighting it off, but apparently, with enough alcohol in my system, I finally broke down and admitted what I want.

And that's Michael. It's always been Michael.

His gaze slides away and his jaw tightens. "I don't know if I can keep doing this with you. It's fucking killing me."

"I know," I whisper. "It's not just you."

"So what do you want me to do, then?" His voice has a gruff edge to it, and when his eyes meet mine again they're dark, smoldering with frustration.

My blood rushes under my skin as I take a step closer. "I want you to kiss me."

There's a flicker of surprise on his face, quickly chased by relief. I expect him to pounce on me, but he doesn't; he takes my face, sliding his fingers into my hair and stroking his thumb over my cheek. Every atom in my body zings with anticipation as he lowers his mouth, brushing his warm lips over mine in the most soft, spine-tingling kiss of my life.

Then he draws away, still holding me as his eyes search mine. "Are you sure?"

I push up onto my toes and kiss him again, harder. "I want you," I murmur against his lips. "You have no idea how much I want you."

His mouth tugs into a disbelieving smile, and he drops his hands to my waist, drawing me close. "I want you too, beautiful girl."

Beautiful girl. His words hit me straight in the core and I shudder out a breath. I'm instantly hot all over, months of desire compressed into this one moment, ready to explode like a stick of dynamite at the slightest touch. But Michael is patient and gentle, his fingertips on my waist urging me closer as his lips graze my jaw and tease the corners of my mouth, then land on mine in another feather-soft kiss.

"Fuck, Alex," he murmurs, "I can't believe this is finally happening."

"Me either," I breathe, giddy. It's like he's flicked a switch and now my body is a live wire. Urgency pulses through my veins and I push him back against the table. My hands slide down to reach for his belt buckle, but he catches them in his own and I get a strange sense of déjà vu. I draw back to find his mouth quirked in amusement.

"This reminds me of New Year's."

"Oh God," I mutter, pulling away. But he tugs me back by

my hands, pressing a kiss to my mouth. "I'm not complaining. But I want to do this right." He slips his hand into mine and leads me across the living room. And just as he does, a thought occurs to me.

You see, the thing about being a single girl, in the middle of winter, with no prospects on the horizon, is this: you don't spend a lot of time tending to your overgrown nether regions. It was all fine and good when it was just me, without a man in sight. But now, with Michael leading me towards his bedroom, I cry out in fear.

"Wait!"

He stops abruptly, his forehead scrunching as he turns to me. "Are you okay?"

Right. I am just going to be straightforward, no matter how embarrassing it may be.

"Look. I know this is stupid, but... when it's winter and you're single, you don't always... maintain the highest standards of... personal grooming." Oh shit, that sounds even worse than it is—like I don't shower, or something. "I haven't shaved my bikini line in ages," I blurt, and heat streaks across my cheeks.

"Is that it?" He gives a little chuckle. "Alex, I don't care. I want you as you are, warts and all."

"I don't have warts!"

He laughs again. "I was kidding. But, listen. While we are making disclaimers..." His expression turns serious and he rubs the back of his neck, his gaze falling to his feet. "I, uh, haven't had sex in a long time."

I feel a flash of surprise. "Seriously?"

"Seriously."

"Wait." I narrow my eyes. Men have a habit of distorting this sort of thing. I bet it's been, like, three weeks or something. "How long is a long time?"

"Um, over a year." He glances up at me sheepishly, and I can't stop the delighted smile that breaks across my face. When I first met him I was convinced he was a womanizer, but instead, he's been off the market completely.

"You don't have to look so pleased about it," he says dryly.

"It's a good thing."

"Yeah, well, you might not think so once we get down to it."

"Why not?"

"Because..." Pink stains his cheeks. "It just, uh, the first time... it might not last very long."

"Oh." I give him a gentle smile. "I don't care."

"I don't want you to be disappointed." He looks worried and my heart squeezes. I've never wanted him more.

"Michael, I could *never* be disappointed."

His expression relaxes and he cups my face, lowering his lips to kiss me. His tongue dips into my mouth, licking against mine. It's tame, but I can sense the wild appetite underneath. When he sucks my bottom lip into his mouth and drags his teeth across it, my legs shake with need.

Fuck.

This man... he can do whatever he wants with me. I'm ruined. I let out a whimper of surrender, knowing I've crossed the line now and there's no going back.

32

I lower myself to the edge of Michael's bed. When I look up, he's gazing at me with dark eyes, flushed cheeks and parted lips. He almost looks a bit stunned, like he can't believe I'm here. Hell, I can barely believe it.

"You okay?"

"Yes," he says, his voice scraping up his throat as he takes a step closer. "Fuck yes."

Shit, my hands are trembling. It's like I'm nervous or something, which doesn't make any sense. I've had sex before—loads. But this feels different, somehow. This feels significant. Like once we do this, things will be forever changed—*I'll* be forever changed.

And I want that, I realize. I want him to change me.

I reach for him and he takes my hand, dropping to his knees on the floor in front of me. His hands slide around my waist and slip under my sweater, warm against my back. When I lean in to touch my lips to his, I see a hint of vulnerability in his eyes, completely at odds with his huge frame and strong hands. I try to reassure it with my kiss.

My lips move across his cheek and down, so I can tuck

my nose into his neck, under his ear, breathing in the scent of his cologne. It's a woodsy smell, like cedar. And then there's the smell of *him*. It's just him—his skin, or something. Fuck, it's amazing. I want to buy it in bottles and spray it all over my sheets.

"You smell so good," he murmurs into my hair.

"I was just thinking the same thing." I press my mouth to the soft skin of his neck, sliding my tongue out to taste him, biting gently. He sucks in a ragged breath, his pulse quickening against my lips.

I'm trying to be patient, but it's not working. My hands snake their way down again, twisting in the hem of his shirt. When I give it a little tug, he raises his arms obediently, watching me take in every inch of his gorgeous body with thirsty eyes as I slip it over his head.

Holy hell. I can't stop looking at him. He has such a man's body; not flawless or overly chiseled, but real and solid and firm. My fantasy self spent a lot of time constructing a mental image of what was under his clothes, but what a joke that was. I couldn't have imagined the scar down the side of his stomach, a tiny puckered line that I trail my fingertip over with a smile. I couldn't have imagined the way the dark hair on his chest, peppered with a few grays, spans from one nipple to the other and tapers down to his waistband. And I couldn't have imagined the gentle dip in his lower back, which I discover as I slide my palms around his waist and down over his hot skin, skating onto the curve of his firm, denim-clad ass.

A small moan escapes his mouth as I lean in to kiss his strong shoulders. The shoulders I've looked at over and over again, the ones that almost made me lose the plot when he injured himself at the ice-rink. I'm breathing heavily as I mold my hand to the hard swell of muscle.

"Michael, God… you're so perfect."

"I'm not perfect," he mumbles, but I ignore him.

"You're gorgeous." My lips graze his neck, fingers stroking his cheek, his beard. I'm delirious with the thought that this is actually happening, trying not to smother him with my hands. "I could touch you forever." My mouth is running away from me but I don't care.

His fingertips curl tighter into my waist, like he's holding on for dear life. "I'd like that," he murmurs in response, and fireworks burst inside my chest.

I shuffle back on the bed and he crawls up beside me, positioning himself against my side, tucking his body in against mine. His kisses are lingering and lazy, like we have all the time in the world, but when I feel his tongue slide over mine, my body lights up like the Rockefeller tree. My hands reach for his belt buckle again, and again he catches them, this time chuckling against my lips.

"Not yet. You need to remove some clothes now."

He kisses me with teasing strokes of his tongue as he slides his fingertip under the hem of my sweater, nudging it up. I'm electric, heat. Every part of me is on fire, feeling like I'm about to boil over just from the way he's slowly peeling my clothes off. Each brush of his fingertips over my skin leaves a trail of hot embers in its wake. I'm not sure how I haven't self-combusted yet.

"Michael," I plead, urging him to hurry up, to strip me and take me.

But he just shakes his head as he pulls my sweater off, tossing it aside. He lets out a little sigh as he gazes at me, dipping down to press a kiss in the valley between my breasts. He's painstakingly slow as he removes my bra, my jeans—as if he's unwrapping a precious gift. Then he runs his eyes up and down my frame, drinking me in, and self-consciousness crawls up my spine. He's firm and sculpted; a model of physical strength. I'm soft curves and squishy bits. Why haven't I spent more—I mean, *any*—time in the gym?

But he doesn't care. It's obvious in the way he drags his nose over my shoulder, along my collarbone, inhaling my scent, exhaling his satisfaction. His hands slide down the sides of my breasts, over my stomach, palms flat as they smooth across my skin, and I realize I'm being savored, treasured. And just like that, I've never felt more beautiful.

"Alex…" His voice is husky, like it's a chore to speak. "You're all I've wanted for so long. I—fuck." He climbs on top of me now, caging me inside his arms as he stares down at me. But he's not touching me at all and I'm dying.

I slide my hands onto his butt and pull him down between my parted legs. His weight settles over me—heavy, solid, pressing me into the mattress—and I sigh at the feeling of his warm skin against mine, his bulk pinning me to the spot. I'm not small, but he's bigger than any guy I've ever been in bed with—a solid wall of muscle and man. Beneath him I feel almost delicate, and this delights me.

"Am I too heavy? I don't want—"

"You're fucking perfect," I breathe. "You're all I want."

His eyes crinkle into a smile, then his lips are on mine, taking my mouth in a hard, passionate kiss. His hands are shaking as he lowers them to undo his belt buckle, and when I slip my greedy hands inside and take hold of him, he groans, pressing himself against my palm. I can't believe I'm finally touching him and—*fuck*—I am not disappointed. That's another thing my fantasy self could never have adequately imagined: the thickness of him, the firm and silky feeling of him, the way he grows even harder in my hand.

Every stroke draws a low growl from his throat, an involuntary thrust from his hips, until he reaches for my hand and pulls it off him. "Stop. Or this will all be over right now."

I giggle, dizzy with the knowledge that I'm making him as crazy as he's making me. I can't help but feel a twinge of disappointment, though, because my next plan was to use my mouth.

He stands and shucks his jeans, his boxer-briefs, and I gape at him naked before me. Fucking hell. He's *glorious*. I have the brief thought that he's ruined me, now; I'll never be able to look at another man with desire. But I don't care. I don't want another man again.

He points to my underwear with a sexy grin. "Off. Now." His tone has a bossy edge to it and I give a huff of arousal as I kick my panties off.

He lies back beside me and when his hand snakes down below my waist, I quiver against him.

"Oh God, Alex," he murmurs as his fingers slide over the wet heat between my thighs.

He kisses me roughly, his fingers moving over me in slow, deliberate strokes, dipping inside, teasing. It only takes a few seconds of this for me to know that sex with him is going to be better than anything I've had before. This isn't some sloppy fumble with one eye on the TV, some half-hearted prod below the waist before he can move onto the good stuff. But then, he's not some twenty-something guy I met at the pub. He's a *man*—a man who's been married and had a kid and come out the other side, wiser for it. He's taking his time, relishing the way my body responds, eager to learn the things I like. And it's working.

I arch into his hand, begging for more with my hips, and I feel him smile against my mouth. He's taunting me, holding off, and impatience tears through me.

"Michael," I whine. "You're killing me."

He laughs. "Yeah. Okay." He pushes back with a playful grin, running his hands down my thighs. Then the grin completely drops off his face. "Shit. I don't think I have a condom." He leans over and rifles through the nightstand, then turns back to me, wide-eyed.

"You don't have one in your wallet?"

He shakes his head. It's ironic, but the fact that he doesn't carry them makes me want him even more.

I prop myself up on my elbows, glancing at the window and remembering the snow. We can't even dash out to the store. Disappointment crushes my ribcage as I look back at Michael, naked and more than ready to have sex with me.

Have we really come this close only to stop?

33

And then something occurs to me.

"Wait!" I say, leaping up and darting into my room for my bag. I rummage through it, searching for the stash I kept in there for Travis and I. He hated to carry them. I know it was a while ago now, but... *please tell me I didn't throw them out.* I dump the contents of my bag onto the bed and paw through it frantically.

And then I remember: the zip compartment in the back! I rip it open and inside is a whole strip of them.

Yes! I send up a silent prayer of thanks as I race back into Michael's room and hold them up triumphantly.

Shit. This makes me look a bit slutty, proudly brandishing twelve condoms in the air. As if I'm always walking around with this many in my pocket, ready to drop my pants for anyone, anytime.

"I've had these for ages," I mumble, my neck hot. "I don't always... well, you know, my ex and I—"

"It's okay." Michael's lip twitches. "You don't have to explain. It's your business."

"I know, but I want you to know. I don't just jump into bed—I mean, I haven't—"

"Alex, I know." His mouth softens into a smile as he reaches for me from the bed.

I climb on beside him, handing the condoms over. I know I should look away, but I can't. My eyes are glued to the deft movement of his fingertips rolling the condom down his length, desire throbbing hot and heavy between my legs. How did I end up here, about to have sex with this man?

He looks up to catch me watching and a slow, wide grin stretches across his face. Then he nudges me back onto the mattress, his eyes intense as he lowers his weight back onto me, settles himself between my thighs. The heat of him— the smell of him—rushes over me, and I sigh. I love the pressure of him against me, heavy and reassuring, his mouth so close we are breathing the same air.

He lies there for a moment, gazing at me, and raises a hand to brush my hair out of my eyes. My heart is drumming as I look up at him, drunk with desire.

Carefully, he pushes inside me. I gasp at the thickness of him, waiting for my body to adjust, to soften and allow all of him in. He doesn't rush, doesn't start jackhammering away; he waits too, and it's his patience that allows me to relax. When he can tell I'm comfortable, he gives a gentle roll of his hips, and pleasure radiates through me, into every corner of my body.

"Uhhhh," is all I manage, digging my fingernails into his shoulders and trying not to fall apart. We haven't even started and I'm almost finished. I get the sense that if he's not careful, he could destroy me. But that's exactly what I want.

He grins at my incoherent response and crushes his lips

to mine, moving inside me. "Fuck," he murmurs, kissing along my jaw, his beard scratching against the sensitive skin on my neck. "You feel amazing. I knew you would."

I want to say something back, something to communicate the sensation of bliss sweeping through me, but I can't find the words. All I can do is thread my hands up into his hair and bring his mouth back to mine, kissing him with such intensity that he'll know how I feel without me saying a thing.

He sinks into the kiss as we move together, our bodies learning the feel of each other, the shape of each other. Even in bed he's a gentleman; focused on me, making sure I feel good, watching to see how I respond and adjusting accordingly. So attentive, so thoughtful.

But I can tell he's holding back, and all I want is for him to let his body take over. I've waited months, hungry for this man and his touch, and I don't want him to be careful and measured with me. I want *all* of him, including the urges he's trying to suppress. I want it reckless, I want it raw.

"Michael," I breathe. "You don't have to be so gentle."

"I'm just—" he rasps against the skin of my neck, his voice shaking. "I don't want to rush." His lips press, then suck, and I clench with how badly I want him to let loose on me.

"Please," I beg. "I want—I *need* you to give me everything. I want you to wreck me." Christ, I can't believe the words coming out of my mouth. I've never asked for what I want in bed like this, but with him... I can't not.

His movements still, and he draws away enough to meet my gaze. I feel a pinprick of uncertainty, but his eyes darken to black and he gives a grunt of approval. He pushes back, sliding his left hand down behind my knee and lifting my leg up onto his shoulder. Using his other hand to brace himself, he changes the angle and gives another thrust, watching for my response. I nod and his hips roll forward again, and again. He's deeper now, but his movements are still constrained and I can't stand it.

I need to push him, make him lose control. I lift a hand to my breast and his gaze drops to it. He's breathing hard as he watches the way my fingertips pinch my nipple. I don't even know who I am right now, but I can't stop. When I reach for his hand and place it on my breast, guiding his thumb over the hard peak, an inhuman growl tears from his mouth. His eyes flame with lust and he forces my leg up higher, sending a thrill through me as he increases his pace. I puff out a hot breath, my heart rate doubling as he takes control, takes what he wants.

"*Fuck*, Alex." His voice is rough, almost angry. His brow is pulled low, his jaw set hard, and I get a flashback to the Michael I met in Starbucks, the guy I ran into on Halloween. Finally—here's the gruff man I wanted to ravage me. He's brutal passion, intensity; his mouth set in a determined line as he drives into me again and again, all measure of self-control gone. It's the most delicious sensation, the force of him slamming into me, the power in his hips as he shows me no mercy.

He's giving me exactly what I want and it's driving me wild—like, actually wild: I claw at him like an animal and bite into his arm beside me, making broken, mewling sounds. I seem to have lost all inhibitions because the only thing that matters right now is the feel of him inside me and the need blazing in his eyes.

It takes me entirely by surprise, my own release. I feel the pressure building, I know I'm winding up like a jack-in-the-box—but most of the time it never pops, not during sex, not unless I pry the lid open myself. But Michael is relentless and he knows exactly which spot to hit.

I gasp as I realize what's happening, bucking against the mattress, my eyes pressing closed. He holds me down, grunting with exertion. I know he's watching everything, but I'm too far gone to care. I'm splintering apart, scattering into the ether, riding the sensations ripping through me. A whimper escapes my lips and he lowers his mouth to capture it, to capture me as I give myself over to him.

Just as I think I've wrung every drop of pleasure from my body, it hits me again: another explosion of ecstasy, shattering me into a million pieces. Michael's hand is tugging at my hair now, his mouth devouring mine, his hips still pumping forward, and I'm not sure how much more of this exquisite annihilation I can take. But he's reached his limit too. He lets out a primal groan, throwing his body down onto me. I hold him close as he shudders against me, all of him mine in that moment. Then he goes still, his skin hot against mine, our breaths coming in ragged gasps.

We lie like that for a while, with him still inside me, his body still pressed against me, and I can't help but wish he would never move.

34

Eventually, Michael peels himself off me and ducks into the bathroom. I stand to grab my underwear from the floor, but my legs buckle beneath me. Jesus. I can't even *stand* after that, it was so good.

With a delirious giggle I push onto my wobbly legs and reach for my underwear, clumsily yanking them on. Michael returns a moment later with a chunky knitted blanket over one arm and a lazy smile on his mouth. He pulls on his boxer-briefs then hops back onto the bed, patting the spot next to him. I crawl up his side and he slips an arm around me, draping the blanket over us both. Then he dips his head to plant a long, lingering kiss on my lips, and I hum contentedly against his mouth.

"Just so you know," I murmur, snuggling into his warm chest, "that was *not* disappointing."

He chuckles and I feel it reverberate through my body as he tightens his arms around me. "Are you sure?"

I pull back, giving him a dead serious expression. "Are you kidding me? It wasn't even on the borderline of disappointing. In fact," I say, snuggling back in and inhaling his intoxicating, masculine scent, "I was not disappointed *twice*."

"Oh." He chuckles again, burying his face in my hair. "Good. You have no idea how long I've wanted to not disappoint you. Ever since I saw you dressed up on Halloween..." he trails off and when I draw back to look at him, he's biting hard into his bottom lip.

"Seriously?" I gape at him in disbelief. "You *were* checking me out as Snow White?"

"Fuck yes. You looked so damn hot in that costume." He shakes his head and makes a sexy grunting sound, his eyes glinting. "You want to know what I did as soon as I got upstairs after seeing you in that?"

I give a little huff, feeling hot all over as I picture him at home, touching himself and thinking of me. And *God*, if I had a dollar for every time I'd done the same and thought of him, I'd be a bloody millionaire.

"I actually—" He breathes a laugh, as if he can't quite believe what he's about to admit. "I liked you the moment you spilled coffee on me in Starbucks."

"Really?"

"Yeah. Why do you think I held onto your number?"

I twist in his arms to face him properly. "But you were so angry!"

"Yeah, I was. Look, it wasn't great being scalded by hot coffee." He nudges me playfully in the arm. "But I was more mad at myself for being attracted to you."

I bite back a grin, because that's... that's fucking adorable. "But why were you such a dick to me after that?"

"I don't know." He grimaces. "I was dealing with all that shit in court, and you just kept showing up, refusing to let me forget who you were."

"It wasn't intentional!"

"I know," he says, a smile hinting at his mouth. "When I saw you on Halloween... I know I wasn't nice. I was just *so sick* of women playing games and trying to manipulate me. My ex is a master at it and it drives me crazy. I'd been dealing with all that in court, and then my date had been a nightmare... Then I saw you and it was like you were the same. Another beautiful woman just messing me around."

"What? How?"

He lifts a shoulder. "You were just there in the lobby, looking so fucking sexy but being so cold. It felt like you were taunting me. I wanted you and I couldn't have you."

"I wanted you too." I glance away, feeling my cheeks color as I add, "I started writing my romance novel after that night."

He gives another grunt. "Fuck, Alex. We should have just gotten together then."

"Yeah. We've wasted a lot of time, haven't we?"

He strokes his beard, thinking, then says, "No. I'm glad we did this the long way. Because we didn't rush into something before we were ready. I've done that before and it never works out." He repositions himself to gaze at me. "You're not like most of the women I've met. A lot of the women in New York are—" He cuts himself off with a heavy exhalation. "Look, I know not all women are like this, but it just feels like the ones I've been meeting lately are man-eaters. They have these insanely high standards and they want perfection. They treat dating like a sport and everything is so fake. It's exhausting."

I think of Cat and her dating spree the past few months: the way she compared it to a job interview and the amount of work she puts into looking and behaving a certain way when she goes on a date. I guess he's not wrong.

"But you—you're just yourself and you don't try to

impress me. You're so caring, so sweet. You see the good in the world, you're optimistic and hopeful." His eyes are tender, lit with affection. "I know those are the things you don't like about yourself, but they're the things that make you who you are."

Warmth rushes along my skin, down my limbs, sinking into my bones. I think of Christmas Day in his kitchen, when he held me and made me feel understood, and I realize I feel the same way now. I always do around him.

"And I'm sorry I was such a jerk earlier," he adds quietly. "After Christmas, I felt so connected to you. And then on New Year's... I don't know. You've been so hot and cold with me. It felt like you were playing games and I am so over that shit. I'm not going to do that."

"Oh," I murmur. "I'd never thought of it like that. Shit, I'm sorry. I wasn't trying to play games."

"I know." He takes my hand, sliding his fingers between mine and squeezing. "It's okay, I know. That's not who you are."

"It's not. I could never do that to you, Michael. You're such a good guy. When I'm with you I just feel like myself. You listen to me and I feel like... I don't know. You understand me and accept me in a way that no one else does." I pause, then add, "And you're a great dad. I know you worry that you're not, but you are."

He gazes at me with a sad smile and I wonder when someone last said these things to him. He needs someone to tell him he's a good guy and a good dad. I feel a sting in my heart at the thought that maybe he's been a bit lonely. I don't ever want him to feel that again.

Regret seeps into me as I think about the past couple of months, the time I've let slip away. "I'm the one who should be saying sorry. I shouldn't have fought this so hard."

He raises my hand to his lips and kisses the back of it. "It's okay. I know you had your reasons."

I look down at our hands with a sigh. "Yeah," I mumble, wondering how to explain that after Travis dumped me, I was beginning to believe the problem wasn't men—it was *me*. I always find it too easy to imagine—or hope for—things that aren't there. I still feel like I can't quite trust my ability to distinguish between reality and fantasy.

But when I look at myself through Michael's eyes, I see things differently. I see myself the way he sees me—and that's why it feels like this time, it's different. I really want to trust that feeling.

Still, I'd be lying if I said there wasn't another thought nagging at me. Because if I'm not careful, I could lose the writing career I've only just started to build—the thing I've dreamed of my whole life, the thing I gave up on back home, the thing my parents have told me over and over is not going to happen. Since I've been writing, I've rediscovered my passion and it's helped me find a sense of inner strength I didn't know I had. And I can't lose that now.

That thought scares me more than anything.

35

I don't want to think about that now.

I push all thoughts of my writing from my head, tracing my fingertip through the patch of hair on Michael's chest. The feel of his warm skin beside me, the smell of him filling my lungs... There's a flutter between my legs as my eyes track up and down his body. Is it crazy that I want him again, so soon?

He shuffles up the bed slightly so he's sitting back against the headboard, then reaches for me, and there's a zing of anticipation down my center.

Maybe it's not just me.

Feeling bold, I turn and swing one leg over him, straddling him. He slides his hands around my waist and onto my back, and I tilt my head down, pressing my mouth to his. His tongue is the most delicious thing I've ever had in my mouth. Well, so far.

We kiss leisurely, nibbling on each other, tasting each other, and it's not long before I can feel his growing desire pressing against me. Inching back on his lap, I slip my hands inside his underwear, sighing in his ear when I feel how much he wants me again.

And this time, I'm going to do this my way. I climb off his lap, crawling down between his knees. His eyes darken as he watches me slide my hand around his hard length and moisten my lips. I'm aching to have him in my mouth, to taste him. Hell, I've imagined it enough times.

"Alex," he says, his voice rough like sandpaper. "You don't have to do that."

I gaze up at him hungrily. "I know I don't have to. I *want* to." Then I lean forward and swipe my tongue over the tip of him, savoring his salty taste.

"Ohhh," he growls, threading a hand into my hair. "Do you know how many times I've pictured you doing this?"

I giggle, heat blossoming low in my belly as I stroke my hand up and down, admiring the impressive shape and size of him.

"Especially after what you told me at New Year's."

"What?" I lift my hand off him and lean back. "What did I tell you at New Year's?"

A low laugh rumbles from his chest. "That's right, you don't remember." His eyes glitter as he reaches down and wraps a big hand around himself, stroking gently, his gaze still fixed on me. I let out a pant at the sight of it, feeling my thighs quiver.

"You told me you wanted to get down on your knees in front of me." His mouth tips into a sexy grin. "You didn't finish the sentence, but when you stared at my crotch and licked your lips, it was pretty obvious."

"Oh God." I raise a hand to my hot face, grimacing. "Did I really say that? Shit, and then I didn't do it, did I? No wonder you were angry."

He barks out a laugh. "That's not why I was angry. I'm

pretty sure you would have done it if I'd let you."

I glance away in shame, but he reaches out and takes my chin, tilting my face back towards his.

"I was angry because I liked you and the next day you pushed me away. I just wanted to be with you."

I smile, reaching forward to slide my hand around him again. His head drops back against the headboard and he groans on an exhale.

"Did that turn you on?" I murmur.

"What?"

"Me saying that to you, on New Year's."

"Uh, yes. Do you know how hard it was to walk away from you that night? It nearly killed me. As soon as I got home, I had no choice..." He shrugs, like it's no big deal and he did this often. Well, apparently he did—and *fuck*. Heat shoots through me, burning intense at the meeting of my thighs.

"Maybe this will make up for it."

I lean down, lowering my mouth over his thick length, and all the air rushes out of his lungs. He drops his hands to my head, but not to push me—just to feel me move up and down over him. I draw him into my mouth, one hand wrapped around the base, sliding my tongue up and down. I take my time, savoring everything: the taste of him, the shape and feel of him, the way he keeps breathing my name, the way I can tell he's trying to hold back. And that little grunting, panting sound he's making, the way he's tugging on my hair—God, I want him again.

I stop, leaning back to glance up at him. And before I can do anything, he swings a leg over me, breathing hard as he tucks himself back into his underwear. He hauls me against him, crushing his lips to mine before pushing me up the bed, against the headboard.

"Your turn, dirty girl."

I give a self-conscious giggle. "Dirty girl?"

"Mm-hm." He leans over me, lowering his lips to my ear, rubbing his beard against my cheek. "The way you asked me to fuck you earlier? You're nothing like the sweet girl I thought you were."

Color floods my cheeks. "Well, I'm still—"

"Alex, I'm just teasing," he says with a grin. "I loved it." He lowers himself to his elbows in front of me, sliding his hands up my thighs. "But I want to taste *you*, now."

"Oh." I clamp my legs together. "No, not now."

His brow furrows in confusion. "Are you serious? I didn't expect you to be shy."

"No, it's not that."

"You don't like it?"

I snort. "God, no. It's not that either. It's just... can we wait until we're back home and I've had a chance to, er, tidy up?"

"Oh." He chuckles, moving to sit beside me at the headboard. "You know I don't care."

"I know. But I feel kind of self-conscious."

His shoulders slump with disappointment. "Are you sure?"

I nod.

"Okay. But as soon as we're home, you're putting those legs over my shoulders."

I give a grunt at the thought, skating my palm up his muscular thigh. He leans over to kiss me again, and I inch my hand closer to the bulge threatening the cotton of his boxer-briefs.

"But, um," I say, feeling a bit uncertain, "can we—you know, are you still in the mood to..."

"What? Have sex again?"

I give him a little nod.

"Fuck yes." He looks at me like I'm crazy. "Don't ever ask me again. I can assure you, the answer will always be yes."

I kick my underwear off, giggling, drunk on lust—on *him*. I wait as he rolls on a condom, then I climb onto his lap and ease him inside me again. We both moan at how good it feels.

"Alex," he murmurs into my shoulder, his teeth nipping at my skin. "You know I'm crazy about you, right? I haven't been crazy about anybody in a long time."

Elation rolls through my chest in a wave, lifting my heart, making it float. I caress a thumb across his cheek and over his delicious beard. "I'm crazy about you too."

"It's not just sex. It's... it's *us*." There's the tiniest line on his forehead that makes him look vulnerable as he speaks. "I feel better when I'm around you. I want you around me all the time. I need to know—"

"I know." I press a kiss to his brow, smoothing the line away. "I want to be with you, Michael. I want to be yours, I want you to be mine. More than I've ever wanted anything."

He lets out a relieved breath. "Good," he murmurs, tightening his grip on me. He takes my mouth, his tongue claiming mine as he presses himself up deep inside me.

This time it's slower, like a smoldering fire on the brink of bursting into flames. We gaze at each other, moving together as I rock on his lap, relishing every sign of pleasure on the other's face. Our mouths communicate wordlessly, our tongues merging as we both tip over the edge, clutching one another, becoming one.

We sit there, holding each other close as our breathing returns to normal, and I realize something that makes my heart race more than anything we've done so far.

I'm not just crazy about him. I'm *falling* for him. Hard.

36

I wake to the feeling of a strong arm across my waist. It takes me a moment to remember where I am, and when I do, happiness bubbles through me.

I'm in Michael's bed. In *Michael's bed*.

Sweet Jesus, I have died and gone to heaven.

We've been snowed in at the cabin for five nights now, and each morning that I've woken up in this spot I've had to remind myself where I am—and that I'm not dreaming.

The past five days have been bliss. There's no other word for it. Michael is so affectionate, so smitten, and I just feel cherished in a way I never have. And the sex—*fuck*. The sex is like nothing else; raw and dirty, sweet and tender. Everything I need it to be.

We've barely left the bedroom but when we have, I've been hard at work on my romance novel. After several days of Michael's undivided attention, my lips bruised from his kiss, my skin worn smooth by the path of his hands, I let myself write the part I'd been hesitating on for so long. I wrote the happy ending.

It's terrifying letting myself free-fall like this, back into that place where I'm daring to believe that I might get a happily ever after. But it's also exhilarating. Because if I do... that will be everything.

I roll over to gaze at Michael, his head heavy against the pillow, his eyes still closed, the thick lashes dark against the creamy-white of his cheek. Before I can stop myself, I reach a hand up to that cheek, just wanting to touch him. His sleepy eyes flutter open and crease into his gorgeous smile.

"Good morning, beautiful." In one swift move, his arm spins me and pulls me hard up against him, so we are spooning.

Oh God. I never want to leave this exact spot. I could die right here and I'd be happy.

I feel an unmistakable hardness pressing against my butt and I wiggle playfully against him. A sexy grunt comes from his mouth as he kisses along my shoulder, into my neck, over my earlobe. All the nerve endings in my body tingle and I twist around to face him. He gropes about on the nightstand for a condom before we give in again to the ache we have for each other, the ache that never seems to go away, no matter how many times we make love.

When we finally lie still, our limbs tangled in the sheets and our breathing heavy, our lust satiated for now, I gaze at the ceiling dreamily. I still cannot believe I'm here, in Michael's arms.

After a while he says, "I think we can probably go home today."

A knot forms in my stomach and I pull the sheets up to my armpits, anxious at the thought of going back to the city. Sure, I'm ready to leave the house, believe me, but I am a bit worried about what will happen with us back home. I've tried not to let my mind go there, but what if Justin *does* end up offering me the job? Then what will I do?

I force the thought from my head. I can't think about all that. I don't want to think about it.

Michael shifts onto his side and props his head up on his hand, gazing at me. "If it were up to me, we'd never leave," he murmurs, reaching across and trailing his finger along my arm. "But I have to get back to Henry."

I roll my head to the side and give Michael a tentative smile. Is he worried about going back to the city too? Is he worried about how our new relationship will hold up in the real world?

He scans my face. "You okay?"

Of course everything will be fine, I tell myself. The problem with my fantasy self is that it's just as skilled at imagining disasters as it is the good stuff.

I lean over to kiss the tip of his nose. "I'm more than okay. Shall I make us some coffee?"

He nods, settling back against the pillows with a happy sigh.

I slip out of the covers and pull on my underwear, glancing around the room for my clothes. My eyes land on Michael's hooded sweater and I reach for it, pulling it on. I bury my face in the fabric, inhaling the scent of his woodsy cologne and soap, feeling all snuggly.

"Hey," he protests mildly, but when I turn to him, his mouth hooks into grin. "Shit, you look sexy. Come back here."

I giggle. "In a minute. Let me get coffee."

See? Everything will be fine.

MICHAEL IS quiet on the ride home. His hand is resting on my leg, and my own hand is up on the back of his neck, stroking his hair—it seems neither one of us wants to stop touching the other—but I can't shake the feeling that he has something on his mind.

"You okay?" I ask, thinking back to the tense drive up here.

He glances at me, his mouth curving into a smile. "Yeah, beautiful. I am. I just—" He pauses, and apprehension pinches his brow. "I have to ask. What are you going to do about this column if you get offered it?"

Oh. Right.

I pull my hand away and turn to gaze out the window, watching the passing landscape. I've been trying not to think about this, because... I have no idea.

"What about your romance novel?" Michael tries again when I don't answer. "Have you thought about what you'll do with it when you finish it?"

"Not really."

"I thought it was good."

I blush, glancing at him from under my lashes.

"I don't know the genre, so I can't comment on that." He shoots me a flirtatious grin. "But it certainly, uh, had the desired effect."

"That's only because you thought it was about you and me," I say with a wry smile.

"It *was* about you and me."

My blush deepens. He's got me there.

"And I loved it." He takes my hand and lifts it to his mouth, pressing a kiss to the back of it. "Why do you think I made you give me a copy?"

A laugh tickles my throat. Yesterday Michael said he wanted to read it properly, since I'd finished the draft. I was nervous but then I figured, what the hell? The cat's out of the bag—he knows it's about us—and just quietly, if he reads the whole thing, we might even get to act out some of my favorite scenes.

He grins. "I can't wait to read it all."

"Just... don't show it to anyone, okay? It's not polished yet, and—"

"Of course. It's for my reading pleasure only." He emphasizes the word "pleasure," wiggling his eyebrows up and down, and I laugh again. "But seriously. Which do you enjoy writing more? The articles or the novel?"

"The novel," I admit.

"Yeah?"

I nod. "It's fun, and I have total control over how I write it."

"If that's what you love the most, maybe focus on that."

"Well... I don't know if I want to publish that."

"Why not? There's a huge market for it."

That's true. But it's not really that. What would my parents say about me publishing a romance novel? It would just confirm their belief that I don't live in the real world, spending so much time "dreaming of Prince Charming," to use my mother's words. I know Michael said I shouldn't be ashamed of who I am, and I'm trying not to be, but I had never intended to share my romance novel with anyone. It was just a side-project to let off steam over Michael. And while the thought of publishing it does give me a thrill, I don't want to give my parents more ammunition.

But if I got a paid writing job on a big platform like Bliss Edition, that's a bit more respectable. I'd have the reputation of the whole organization behind me, and maybe they'd finally take my writing seriously.

"Do you *want* to write the other stuff?" Michael asks. His gaze slides over and when it meets mine, he can read the answer on my face. "Right. Well, there you go."

I heave out a sigh. "Yeah, but it's not that simple. I'm not like you. I don't already have loads of things published. This could be my only chance."

"No. This would be your *first* chance. You're a good writer and you'll get plenty of opportunities. But maybe this whole single column..." he trails off and exhales, drumming his fingers on the steering wheel in thought. Eventually, he sighs. "If you write about something you don't want to write about, Alex, it will show. Trust me, I know about this stuff."

I contemplate his profile as he drives. "What do you mean?"

"You know that book of mine you criticized?"

"*Three Months on the Appalachian Trail*?"

He nods. "You know why that book got terrible reviews? Because it was crap. I didn't spend three months on the Appalachian Trail."

"Honestly, the things I said about your book weren't true," I protest, but he shakes his head.

"You might not have known it at the time, but they were."

I cast my mind back to the moment in the bookstore when he got so irritated by my comments. No wonder he was so sensitive about it. But—once I'd read it—I truly did love it.

"So, what happened? You didn't walk the trail?"

"I walked it for like a week then went back to my cabin. I didn't enjoy it and I didn't want to write the book. But I had to."

"Why?"

"I'd already spent the advance, a lot of it on expensive hiking gear. I had this idea of who I could be; some sort of outdoors man. And I lasted one week." He chuffs an ashamed laugh.

I look down at my hands. Maybe he's right. I don't want to sign up for something that I'll end up hating and make a mess of it. And if I'm honest, I am *not* excited at the prospect of writing a column about the single life, not since spending the week with Michael. Because this past week I've felt happier than I have in ages. And by that, I mean *years*. It's not only the sex—which, frankly, is so good I can hardly walk—it's being with someone who just gets me, who laughs at my silliness and makes me laugh too. It's being comfortable with someone and knowing they like you just as you are. Warts and all. How can I tell people I'd rather be single when I feel like this? I can't.

Still... if Justin were to call me and tell me I'd got the job, I'd struggle to turn it down. After all, this is what I've been working towards since I arrived in the city. I guess I'd have to tell him that I'm not single anymore, and hope he could give me something else to write about. That's possible, right?

With a sigh, I push it all from my mind. I haven't even been offered the job and I'm not sure I will be. If I am, well... I'll figure this all out then.

"Your brother looks so much like you," I say, changing the subject. I'd stumbled across some family photo albums at the cabin, and I couldn't keep my cool when Michael let me look through them. These two boys with dark hair and cheeky grins, playing down at the lake, rolling in orange leaves, opening Christmas presents together... It was adorable. And even though Michael is five years older, they were clearly the best of friends. How could I *not* fall for him after that?

"Yeah, we still look pretty similar."

"He must be one good-looking guy."

Michael glances at me sideways, his lip twitching. "You think you might like the look of him, then?"

I know he's winding me up and I'm relieved to feel the atmosphere in the car lighten, so I play along. "Well... does he have a beard?"

Michael strokes a hand over his short beard, lines of amusement fanning around his eyes. "He doesn't. You like the beard, huh?"

I bite my lip and lean forward to run my fingertips over the coarse bristles. I never knew I would like a beard, but I can't deny how much it turns me on. "It's pretty hot."

"Oh yeah?" He sends me another glance, one eyebrow raised. I love this playful side to him.

"Well, it's *alright*," I tease.

He pretends to look hurt. "Only alright?"

I lean over so my lips are on his ear, and slide a hand slowly up his thigh. "No. Not only alright. It's fucking sexy. *You're* fucking sexy. Why do you think I was forced to write all those dirty things in my novel? I couldn't stand how much I wanted you, how much I wanted to do dirty things to you." I squeeze his upper thigh, tempted to take my hand higher.

He groans, his eyelids briefly fluttering closed and his knuckles whitening as his grip on the steering wheel tightens. I hear his breathing get heavy and a quick glance down at his lap tells me I've got to him. My whole body feels hot at the sight and I want nothing more than to tell him to pull over into a rest stop so I can have him again. I can't help myself; I kiss his neck and nibble his ear, palming the bulge in his jeans until he tells me to stop or he's going to unwittingly drive us into a ditch.

I grin and lean back against my seat, watching his flushed face as he tries to concentrate on the road, feeling deliriously happy.

We ride the rest of the trip in comfortable silence. And

when I think about my writing I get a strange sense of peace, knowing that whatever happens, I'll be able to make it work.

As we finally head back over the George Washington Bridge, the city comes into view; the unmistakable, iconic Empire State Building, the classic silhouette of the Chrysler Building, and further downtown, the proud outline of the Freedom Tower. I lean forward in my seat, trying to take it all in, this postcard image above our dashboard. A thrill runs through me as the city unfolds, revealing more of itself the closer we get. This place, as huge and impersonal and overwhelming as it is—it also feels like home, now. It feels like it knows me, like it's always known me, and in that sense I'm coming to truly know myself.

Michael manages to pull into a spot right in front of our stoop and shuts off the engine. We step out into the cold air and he takes my bags from the back seat, setting them down on the sidewalk.

"Alex—" His eyes search mine, then he reaches forward, tucking a strand of hair behind my ear. I close my eyes and rest my cheek against his palm. In the freezing air, the warmth from his hand is enough to send heat coursing through my entire body.

He steps forward, slipping his arms around me and pressing a kiss to my mouth. His forehead rests against mine as he murmurs, "I think I'm really falling for you."

My heart trips, stumbles, then takes off on a running leap in my chest. I stare at him, disbelieving and breathless, trying to contain my huge, euphoric grin. "Yeah, I think... I am too."

My grin is mirrored on his face, and he pulls me tight into his arms. And I know then, I have nothing to worry about.

37

I climb the stairs and give a light knock on Michael's door. When he dropped me home earlier, he invited me to come up and join him and Henry for dinner tonight. I've been so excited all day that I could hardly sit still. I was hoping Cat would be home so I could gush about my amazing week with him, but she's been at work.

And now, as I wait in front of Michael's door, I feel a flutter of nerves. Maybe it's because Henry will be there. I like Henry, and I think he likes me. But now that Michael and I are a couple, I realize it's *essential* he likes me if things are going to work.

The door swings open and Michael stands there, breathless.

"Uh, hi." My gaze locks on his strange expression, trying to read it. His eyes are wide, his face ashen.

"Something is wrong with Henry."

My stomach drops. "What?"

"His face is swollen and he can't breathe."

I push past Michael into the apartment, searching for

Henry. He's at the kitchen table, doubled over, struggling for breath.

Michael appears beside me. He wrings his hands, jittery with panic.

I glance around. "What happened?"

"Nothing! He was just having some dinner and—"

"Is he allergic to anything?"

"No, I—well, I've been waiting on some test results..." Michael turns and paces across the living room. "I've already called 911 but they won't be here for ages."

"What did he eat?" I gesture to the table. "What is this?"

"Chinese. Some chicken and some shrimp..."

I crouch beside Henry. Suddenly the symptoms seem very familiar. I leap to my feet, pointing to the floor. "Michael, lay him down."

He stops pacing and looks at me. "Where are you going?"

"Lay him down! I'll be right back." I dash out the door and fly down the stairs. Bursting into our apartment, I snatch my bag off the counter. Then I take the stairs two at a time back up to Michael's.

He's kneeling beside Henry, holding his hand. "It's going to be okay, bud," he repeats, his voice shaking. "It's going to be okay."

I kneel on the floor. Michael watches as I pull my EpiPen out of my bag.

"What's that?"

"It's an EpiPen, for allergic reactions. I think he's experiencing anaphylaxis." I raise the pen and glance at Michael.

"Wait!"

"It's okay." I put a hand on his arm. "I know about this—I'm allergic to bee stings. You have to trust me."

He hesitates, then nods.

I put the pen against Henry's thigh and press the button. "It's okay, Henry, it's okay," I say, holding the pen against his leg. Michael and I stare wordlessly at each other, not daring to breathe.

I release the pen and we sit still, watching Henry, waiting for something to happen. It feels like an eternity, but gradually his breathing becomes less labored and the redness in his face fades.

My lungs deflate with relief and I sag, waiting for my stampeding heart to slow.

Michael's hand is clasped tightly around Henry's, his mouth a tight line. "You okay, bud?" he asks, his eyes searching Henry's face.

Henry blinks, a little dazed.

There's a buzz at the door and Michael jumps up, letting the paramedics in. I step back and hover in the kitchen while they check over Henry. Then Michael scoops him up in his arms like he's a tiny child, and carries him downstairs to the ambulance.

"Alex," he calls over his shoulder as he heads out the door.

I grab my bag and trail out after him. Agnes is on the landing in a dressing gown, her brow knitted in concern. I try to explain what happened but the words aren't coming out right. My whole body is vibrating with adrenalin.

"Alex!" Michael calls again and I glance at the stairs.

"I'll lock up Michael's," Agnes says. "You go with them."

I clamber down the stairs and out onto the street. Henry is already in the ambulance and Michael goes to climb in with him, but a paramedic stops him.

"You can't ride with us."

"What?!" Michael looks shocked. "He's just a kid. I need to be with him."

"Sorry, sir. We can't have people riding back here. We'll meet you at the Mount Sinai Beth Israel emergency room." He pulls the doors shut before Michael can say anything, and the ambulance peels away from the curb.

Michael turns to me, white-faced and shaking, and for a second I think he's going to cry. Shit.

"Michael, it's okay." I grab his hand and drag him along the street. "I'll find you a cab." Our quiet street opens out onto the much busier Hudson Street, and I scan the road desperately for a cab. I've never actually *hailed* a cab before —it intimidates the shit out of me—but I'll be damned if that's going to stop me now. One sails past with its light on and I throw up my hand, yelling, "*Taxi!*"

It screeches to a stop a few feet ahead of us and I yank Michael towards it, opening the door and pushing him in. I go to close the door but Michael grabs my hand.

"Please come."

I slide into the backseat without hesitating. "Of course."

The taxi pulls away and I turn to Michael. He's gripping the seat and staring at me, breathing hard, his pale face twisted with worry. I reach out and pull him into my arms, holding him close as we bump along towards the hospital.

"It's okay," I murmur, pressing a kiss to his head. "He'll be okay."

I SIT in the corner of Henry's room, watching Michael by the bed. He's clasping Henry's hand, his head bowed. By the time we got to the hospital and located Henry he was pretty much back to normal, but they want to keep him here to do some allergy tests and observe him overnight. We've been here for two hours already and Michael hasn't left Henry's side.

Eventually, Henry falls asleep. Michael strokes his head for a few minutes, watching him sleep, then comes over and slumps into a seat beside me.

"How are you going?" I ask tentatively.

He rakes a hand through his hair, his face solemn. "That was the most terrifying thing that has ever happened to me."

"Yeah, it can be pretty scary." I try to remember my first bee sting, when my parents didn't know what was going on, but I was too young and the memory is all fuzzy and distorted.

Michael twists in his seat towards me. "Alex, thank you. If you hadn't been there, I don't know what..."

I don't say anything. I can't bear to think of what could have happened.

He looks down at his hands. I see him swallow as tears well in his eyes, and I reach for his hand.

"Hey," I say, threading my fingers through his. "It's okay. He's okay now."

He nods, sniffing and squaring his shoulders, squeezing my hand. I feel him relax a little, and we sit there together, not saying anything. Not needing to say anything. After a while I can feel his gaze on me, and my eyes wander to his.

"Thanks for being here," he says. He lifts my hand to his mouth, pressing a soft kiss to the back of it, and my heart swells with emotion.

"Of course," I murmur. I wouldn't be anywhere else but here with him and Henry right now.

Henry makes a sound from the bed and Michael leaps to his feet, running to his side. I smile to myself as Henry simply rolls over and goes back to sleep, and Michael droops with relief. I can't believe this guy thinks he's a bad dad. Not in a million years.

I rest back against my seat, closing my eyes. I'm just about to doze off, but the door to the room swings open with a loud bang and I jump. Blinking, I watch as a tall, slim woman with long mahogany hair strides across the room and over to the bed.

"Henry, my *darling*," she cries theatrically. She turns to Michael beside the bed. "What did you *do* to my baby?"

He starts explaining, but I can't follow his words. Because at Michael's side, stands Mel. Mel, worried about Michael's son, Henry.

Her son, Henry.

Their son.

There's an icy trickle of dread down my spine as I gape at the two of them together, shell-shocked. This cannot be happening.

"How could you do this?" Mel spits at Michael. Her usually friendly voice is laced with venom and I glance at the door beside me, feeling a sudden, desperate urge to not be here. Mel has her back to me, and I send up a silent prayer that I can escape unseen as I carefully lift myself out of the chair.

Michael shakes his head in disbelief. "I've been asking for those allergy test results for weeks."

"Oh, so this is *my* fault?"

"No, but—"

"I can't *believe* you let this happen," Mel hisses, lowering herself into the chair at Henry's bedside.

I'm inching back towards the door now, groping along the wall for the handle. I have to get out of here. This is too surreal.

"I *knew* you couldn't be trusted." Mel glares at Michael

with such hatred I half expect him to burst into flames. "You're so—"

I grasp the handle and the door opens with a loud click. Shit.

Mel's gaze swivels to me, and as she narrows her eyes, I feel my blood run cold. "Why are *you* here, exactly?"

I give her a weak smile before glancing at Michael uncertainly. He takes a step closer, slipping his arm around me and tucking me into his side.

"Alex is my girlfriend. She saved Henry's life. She had her EpiPen, and that's what saved him." He turns to me, remembering his manners. "Sorry, Alex. This is my ex-wife, Melanie."

"Yes," Mel says coldly. "We know each other."

Michael looks between us in confusion.

"Through Cat," I mumble.

"Oh. Yes, of course."

"And she's been writing for our website," Mel adds.

"Oh." Michael glances at me, loosening his arm as realization breaks across his face. "Right."

"Yes," Mel continues as if I'm not even here, "Alex writes about how *fabulous* it is to be single." She gives me a pointed look, and beside me I hear Michael sigh.

"Uh, I'll let you guys talk." I yank the door open and slip out into the hallway, and almost immediately they start arguing. I know I shouldn't, but I hover by the door, anxious to hear what they say.

"Jesus, Michael. This is so fucking typical of you."

"What took you so long to get here, anyway?"

"I had a date. I came as quickly as I could."

There's silence for a beat, then Mel speaks again.

"I can't believe you're dating *Alex*, of all people."

"Don't talk about her. That's none of your business."

"You know she's like half your age, don't you? That's pretty fucking sad, Mike."

"She's not half my age, Melanie."

"Well, she's certainly not in her forties. But this is just the sort of pathetic mid-life crisis I'd expect from you."

There's muttering and I hear a chair scrape back and footsteps heading for the door. I leap across the hall and lean against the wall, inspecting my nails as if I'd been there the whole time.

Michael appears, his face in a scowl. I'm immediately reminded of the man I met—the grumpy man in the suit who was always frowning, the man who was in court battling to be able to see his son. Now I know why he becomes that man. The things she just said to him, the way she spoke to him... My heart aches for him.

His expression softens when he sees me, and he takes my hand. "I'm going to get some coffee. Want to come?"

I nod and we wander down the corridor in silence, coming to a vending machine by the elevators.

Michael turns to me, rubbing the back of his neck. "I'm sorry about Melanie. She's so difficult. But I guess you already know that."

I watch the coffee machine, saying nothing. She hasn't been difficult with me. In fact, she's been lovely to me, and I know she's one of Cat's closest friends. But it was like meeting a different person back there.

Michael hands me a coffee and we head back down the corridor, finding some chairs. I try to sip the hot, bitter liquid, but my head is still spinning. *Mel* is Michael's ex. Stunningly beautiful Mel. Despite everything, I find myself wondering how it's possible he could actually like *me* after being with her.

And then another thought occurs to me, one that pushes

everything else out of my mind: Mel said her ex cheated on her—that she found him in bed with another woman.

I inhale sharply as realization hits me square in the chest. Michael cheated on Mel and that's why their marriage ended.

Fuck.

38

I steal a glance at Michael. He's leaning forward, elbows resting on his knees. His face is tired and drawn, his hair is disheveled. He's cradling his coffee in his hands, gazing down at it. In this moment he looks defeated, even a little broken, and there's a tug in my heart. This kind, sweet man, cheated on his wife and destroyed his family? Is that even possible?

No. I refuse to believe he would do that. I may have only known him a few months, but I feel like I *know* him—the real him. And the Michael I know would never do that.

I stare down into my coffee cup, my mind in free fall. Why would Mel have lied, though? She didn't even know that I knew him when she told me that. And he was weird at Christmas, when I asked him about his marriage. And—oh God—I just remembered Cat, on New Year's Eve, when Michael arrived and she got so hostile...

Unease ripples through me. Because even though we've just spent an amazing week together, that's only the tip of the iceberg. Before all that, I spent a *lot* of time fantasizing about Michael. I've written an entire romance novel about it, for Christ's sake. Is it possible I've missed something everyone else seemed to know? Was I so desperate for my own Prince Charming, I didn't want to see what was right there?

I look at Michael and feel a stab behind my breastbone. Because... my heart. My heart is protesting. My heart is telling me that's all wrong—*he wouldn't do that, he's not that guy.* Not my Michael.

He turns to see me scrutinizing him. When he reaches for my hand, I give an involuntary flinch and he frowns.

"You okay?"

"I..." I gnaw on my bottom lip, wanting to ask him but not even sure where to begin.

"Alex, what's wrong?"

"Nothing," I mumble, glancing away. I can't ask him about this now. He's worried about Henry and this is not the time. This isn't about me.

"Hey." He leans closer to tuck my hair behind my ear. "Something's wrong and I want you to tell me. Please."

When I lift my gaze to his concerned face, my heart protests again, louder. Maybe I should just ask him. He's got enough to worry about right now without me sulking. That's not fair, either.

And if I don't say something, this is going to eat me up.

I set our coffees aside and stand, glancing down the corridor. Finding an empty room, I pull Michael in and close the door. My hands are trembling as I think about what I'm going to ask him. Because this isn't really about Mel or whatever happened in their past—it's about the fact that maybe I don't know him as well as I thought I did. That maybe I've imagined him to be someone he's not.

"Michael..." I shift my weight. "I didn't know that Mel

was your ex-wife. I don't know how I didn't figure it out, but I didn't."

Even though the room is dark, lit only by the light from the tiny corridor window, I can see the apprehension etched on his face as I speak.

"And she told me, a while back..." I swallow. Fuck, how do I say this? "She told me something and I want to know if it's true."

"Okay." He scratches his head. "What was it?"

"She told me..." I draw an uneven breath. "She told me that you cheated on her and broke up your family."

He's quiet. I wait for him to look ashamed, but he doesn't. "Melanie told you I cheated on her?"

I nod.

A muscle ticks in his neck as he clenches his jaw. "What did she say, exactly?"

"She said she caught you in bed with someone else and that you said she wasn't enough for you."

His eyes widen incredulously. "Fucking hell." He slumps down into a chair, pressing his fingertips to his temples. "I cannot believe this."

I lower myself into the chair beside him.

"Did she tell you that so you'd stay away from me?"

"I don't think so. She told me before she even knew that I knew you."

He wipes a hand down his face. "Well, that explains why Cat hates me," he mutters. "Shit, this is so typical of Melanie. I should have known she'd pull a stunt like this."

His words ignite a spark of hope in me. "So it's not true?"

"No," he says, his hands curling into fists in his lap. "*She* cheated. I found texts on her phone. She was having an affair with some guy from her office."

Relief shudders through me. I exhale slowly, trying to make sense of this. "But... why would she lie?"

He gives a harsh laugh. "Because she wants the attention and the sympathy. Because she's too proud to admit she fucked up our whole marriage. Because she's angry with me."

If I think of the way she just spoke to him, "angry" is an understatement. I've never seen someone so enraged, as if Michael had been deliberately trying to poison his own son.

"Why is she angry with *you*?"

"Because I refused to stay with her."

"You couldn't trust her?"

"Yeah, that, and it brought out a nasty side to her. I saw who she really was. I didn't want to break up our family, believe me, but I also didn't want to stay with her just for Henry's sake when I didn't love her, or even respect her, anymore. That's why she's been trying to take Henry away from me. She's angry and bitter."

I run my eyes over Michael's anguished face. This is what she does to him: she breaks him down. There's an ache in my chest and I reach for his hand, squeezing it. "Why didn't you tell me what happened with her?"

He gives a despondent shrug. "I don't know. I guess I didn't feel right bad-mouthing her."

"What?" I marvel at his kindness. "It seems to me like she deserves it. Besides, it's not bad-mouthing if it's *true.*"

He nods sadly, staring at the floor. The hurt in his eyes makes my throat close with sorrow. How could someone be so cruel to this man? And how could I have been so stupid to even consider it could be true?

"Michael." I'm trying to keep the emotion out of my voice, but he hears it and looks at me in surprise.

"Hey," he murmurs, slipping out of his chair and onto

his knees on the floor in front of me. It reminds me of the first time we made love and I reach for him, pulling him close, blinking against tears.

"I'm never going to let you feel like that again," I murmur into his neck, and his arms tighten around me. "You deserve so much better." I smooth my hands over his back, kissing his cheek, holding him tight. I don't know what else to say, how else to show him that it's okay that he's a bit broken—that I'm a bit broken too, and if he lets me, I'll put his pieces back together and keep him safe from that ever happening again.

Well, there is one thing I want to say—something that's been coming to me for a while now—but I don't dare let myself say it.

"Alex, baby." He draws back and his eyes are shining as he brushes his thumb over my cheek. "I know that as long as I'm with you, I won't feel that way again." He presses his mouth to mine in a soft, sweet kiss, then gathers me into his arms.

We hold each other in the dark room for some time, listening to the bustle of the corridor outside. Eventually, Michael lets out a weary sigh and stands, pulling me up.

"It's going to be a long night. You don't have to stay if you don't want to."

I survey his tired face. I don't want to be anywhere else, but I also don't want to overstep. "Do you want me to stay?"

He gives me a tiny nod and I slip my hand into his.

"Then I'm not going anywhere."

We wander back out into the corridor, blinking in the bright light. Hand-in-hand, we turn and head back towards Henry's room. I'm not looking forward to seeing Mel again, but I'm sure Michael wants to confront her about her lies.

Just as we are about to reach Henry's room, the door

swings open and a guy steps out. He's tall and lean, with dark mussed hair and a silver chain glinting from under his leather jacket. He strides past us and my eyes follow him curiously.

He looks so familiar. Where do I know...

Mark. That's Mark. That's Cat's ex-husband.

A chill rushes over my skin as I put the pieces together.

Surely not. She wouldn't.

But when my gaze swings back to Henry's door, Mel is standing there with her arms folded and her eyes narrowed to slits.

I glance at Michael, numb with shock, but he didn't even notice Mark pass us. He's staring at the floor, rubbing his chin, no doubt planning what he's going to say to Mel.

Because she is fucking unbelievable. Not only did she lie about Michael cheating, she's also lying to Cat.

What. A. Bitch.

Mel steps out of the room, pulling Henry's door closed behind her. Her narrowed gaze is trained on me, but I don't care. I haven't done anything wrong, and any second now Michael is going to lay into her.

Her eyes flit to Michael and her beautiful face twists into a scowl. "Mike," she snarls. The way she says his name makes my skin crawl. "The doctor came in and wanted to speak to us. But you were off, fuck knows where."

I watch Michael expectantly, waiting for the anger I saw in him a few moments ago, but he just sighs. "Why didn't you come and find me?"

"Because that's not my job. A decent father would have been here."

My lips part in shock. I can't believe she would say that to him. Anger prickles hot under my skin as she continues her vicious tirade.

"Poor Henry is in there, suffering, but do you care?" She rolls her eyes. "No. You're thinking only about yourself. Typical, selfish Mike, who—"

"What the fuck is wrong with you?" The words slice through the air, stopping Mel mid-rant, and it takes me a second to realize they've come from me. "Don't speak to him like that. Don't you *dare* speak to him like that."

She arches an eyebrow. "Excuse me?"

"You don't get to talk to him like that anymore. He's the best man I've ever met, and *you* are just a liar." I turn to Michael, ready for him to step in, but he's giving me a wary look.

Fine. Alright. I'll get the ball rolling.

"He knows you've been lying, telling people that he was the one who cheated, when—"

"I don't think that's any of your business," Mel snaps, her eyes blazing. "What happens between my husband and I—"

"Your *ex*-husband," I correct. "And it *is* my business if it's a lie that's still causing damage."

Mel opens and closes her mouth, momentarily wrong-footed, then her gaze cuts to Michael. "What did you tell her?"

"I told her the *truth*," he mutters. "She seemed to be under the impression that *I* was responsible for our marriage falling apart."

I squeeze Michael's hand and when he squeezes back, I feel a swell of triumph. Right. Time for him to put her in her place, once and for all.

"Well, you could have tried harder, Mike," Mel spits. "This is your problem—you don't try hard enough."

"Look, I know I'm not perfect," he says. "But—"

There's a noise from Henry's room and Michael drops my hand, pushing past Mel and in through the door. I go to follow after him, but Mel's manicured claws curl around my arm and I freeze.

"We're not done," she hisses as the door to Henry's room swings closed.

I feel a dart of panic at being alone in the corridor with her. It was one thing when I had Michael beside me, but now I begin to shrink.

"It's a shame you're involved with Mike now, right when Justin was about to offer you that column."

What?

I step back to examine her face, trying to read her expression. She has to be lying. Justin would have called or emailed me if I'd gotten the column. No, she's just using something she knows I want to manipulate me. God, Michael was right. She's the worst.

"I don't believe you," I say, squaring my shoulders. "Justin would have contacted me if I'd gotten it."

"Oh, he will. But you, *unfortunately*, will be unable to accept."

I force out a breath, suddenly exhausted. "Fine. Whatever. Then I'll talk to him about writing something else." I glance over her shoulder to Henry's room, hoping he's okay.

"I don't think so. We don't just offer out jobs at random, Alex."

Her words drag my attention back to her and I wonder, for a fleeting second, what if she's *not* lying? What if I *have* been offered the position, after all this work, only to have it taken away from me?

"You know," she continues, watching me carefully, "it's not at all surprising that Mike would try to do this to your career."

My heart jolts. I know she's trying to bait me and I should resist, but for some stupid reason I can't. "What?"

"He tried to sabotage my career, many times. He was always threatened by my success. It's sad that he's still up to his usual tricks."

I swallow. "He's not trying to destroy my career."

"Oh really? He must have known you were trying to get this column. And he'll also be aware that you won't be able to write it if you're not single."

My brain reminds me of the conversation Michael and I had in the car, when he suggested I don't accept the position if I'm offered it, and there's a twist in my gut. But—no. That wasn't him sabotaging me. He's not like that.

I lift my chin, trying not to let her get under my skin. What was it Michael said? She's a master at manipulation. "Mel—"

"If you continue to see Mike, I'll have no choice but to tell Justin. He'll be extremely interested to know what's going on."

"I could say the same to you," I mutter.

Her perfect brows slant together. "I'm sorry?"

"I'm sure Cat would be interested to know what's going on with Mark."

Her eyes narrow. For a second I think she's going to slap me, but she simply says, "Is that a *threat*?"

I open my mouth to speak but she cuts me off.

"I'd be *very* careful if I were you, Alex." She glares at me for another second before stalking off down the corridor.

I stare after her, trying to calm my erratic breathing and racing pulse. I'm not great with confrontation at the best of times, but when it's your new lover's beautiful ex-wife who is dead-set on destroying your career, it's even worse.

No, I tell myself firmly. I'm not going to let her win. She's a liar, and I'm not going to believe a word out of her mouth.

I shake it off and slip into Henry's room, relieved to see

Henry is peacefully asleep, Michael seated beside the bed. I ponder the back of him, slumped forward with his head in his hands, and feel a wash of confusion. Why didn't he stand up to Mel? I expected more from him back there. I know she's terrifying, but fuck—if anyone should be angry about her behavior, it's him. So why didn't he put her in her place?

He looks up, giving me a tired smile as I wander over, then he reaches an arm around my waist and rests his head against my side. I stroke a hand over his hair, leaning to press a kiss to the top of his head.

It doesn't matter about Mel and all her shit. *This* is what matters. This right here.

39

They release Henry in the morning, and Michael and I bring him home in a cab. He's completely fine—his usual, chatty self—and I'm so relieved. When we get in the building, Michael sends him upstairs and pauses with me in the lobby.

"Thanks for staying with us. I'm sorry everything was so weird at the hospital."

I shake my head, pushing Mel's threats from my mind. "Don't be silly. It was a crazy, stressful night. I'm just glad Henry is okay."

"Me too." He leans in to kiss me but stops himself with a yawn.

"Bored of me already?" I joke, and he chuckles.

"Not even close. But right now I need to sleep. Want to come up tonight, once Henry's asleep?"

I nod eagerly.

"Good. I'll text you later." He lowers his mouth to mine in a long, delicious kiss.

There's a noise at the front door, and we draw apart to

see Agnes entering the lobby. Heat paints my cheeks and when I glance at Michael, he's pink too.

"Good morning, Agnes," we mumble in unison, like a pair of children caught doing something naughty.

"Seems like a very good morning indeed," she says wryly as she ambles past.

Michael and I exchange a grin. He takes her arm to help her up the steps, and blows me a kiss over her head.

With a happy sigh, I let myself into the empty apartment. Cat is at work, but when she gets home later I want to talk to her about Mel. I need to tell her about Mark—about *all* the lies Mel has been spinning.

Fuck, I'm exhausted. I pad over to my nook, collapse face-first onto my bed and pass out.

IT'S late afternoon when I'm woken by my phone vibrating on the nightstand. My first thought is that it could be Michael, so I lunge on it without even checking who's calling.

Big mistake.

"Alexis?" Mum's voice comes on the line and I wilt against my pillow.

"Hi, Mum," I mumble.

"Hello, darling! How are you?"

My mind wanders to the kiss from Michael on my doorstep this morning and I smile. "I'm good."

"That's good. And how's the writing going?"

I hesitate, surprised. My parents have never asked about my writing before. I never even told them about the articles I've been writing for Bliss Edition, despite what a big deal it is for me. Perhaps I was worried Mum would fly into a blind panic again and start ranting about how I'm running out of time and need to find a man before my ovaries shrivel to raisins.

My fingers go to the book charm around my neck. Mum does seem to be trying, asking after my writing. Maybe she wants to be more supportive.

"Well, I've been writing a few articles for a high-profile woman's website, and there was talk of it possibly becoming a regular feature."

"That's nice."

"Yeah. But... I don't know. I haven't heard anything, and I thought I would by now." I sigh, thinking of Mel's words. "Maybe it's not meant to be."

"Well, you can't say I didn't warn you."

I feel a zing of irritation. Here we go. "What?"

"You know, moving all the way to New York, thinking you'll build a whole new career as a writer..."

I raise my eyes to the ceiling. "It's not a whole new career, Mum. I did work at the paper for several years, remember?"

"But that was just a little paper, darling. It's a bit unrealistic to think it would lead to some big, fancy New York job."

I give an exasperated sigh. I don't have the energy to explain that it's not a big fancy job—and it's not like she'd listen. She doesn't believe I can do it and that's all there is to it.

Anyway, maybe she's right. After all the articles I've written for Justin, I've heard nothing about the position. I've got nothing to show for my time over here.

Oh, hang on. That's not true at all. I've met a lovely man —a man who makes me feel like anything is possible. Mum was so against the idea of me staying single, so *surely* she'll be excited to hear I've met someone.

"There is something else, though, Mum. I've met a guy."

"Really?"

"Yeah. He's my neighbor. He's a writer as well. He's a great guy and—" I snap my mouth shut. That was close. I almost, without even realizing it, said, "I think he could be the one."

As in *The One*.

Bloody hell. That thought hit me out of nowhere, but now that it's here, I can't help but think, well... shit. I think he is.

There's a flurry of nerves in my stomach and I have to force myself to take a deep breath. When I arrived in the city I promised myself I wouldn't do this again—I wouldn't let myself get swept up in some fairy-tale romance—because I *always* end up hurt and disappointed. It was fine when we were just fooling around at Michael's cabin, but now we are back in the city and I've met his ex-wife and been to hospital with his son and there's no denying we are in a full-on relationship. He told me he was *falling* for me. And I'm... well, I don't even want to think about what I'm feeling. It's terrifying.

But when I picture Michael's face, when I think of the things he says to me and the way he holds me, I don't feel terrified in the slightest. Because this is something else. This is it.

"He's what, Alexis?" Mum barks impatiently, and I jump.

"Sorry. He's just... he's really great," I murmur, smiling to myself. I wait for her reply but the line is thick with silence, and I feel myself bristle. "What?"

"I'm sure you think he's nice, darling. But that's what you thought about Travis, isn't it?"

I frown. "Well, yes. But—"

"You do have a tendency to do this sort of thing. You've

only been over there for a few months and you already think you've found Prince Charming! I thought you went over there to *write*, Alexis. That's what you've been carrying on about this whole time."

"Well..." I swallow down the sense of unease rising inside me. "I can do both."

"But you've already given up on your writing," she says, and anger flares in my chest.

"I haven't given up on it," I snap. For fuck's sake. Here I was thinking she'd be pleased I'd met someone after her negative reaction to me being single, but now she's just finding reasons to be negative about this! Why does nothing I do *ever* make her happy?

My phone pings and I pull it back to see an email from Justin flash up on the screen. My heart jerks. "Mum, I've got to go." I end the call and, with shaking hands, open Justin's email. And there, on the screen, is the news I've been waiting for.

I've got the job.

40

I knock quietly on Michael's door, not wanting to wake Henry. My whole body is fizzling with nervous energy. I've spent all evening thinking about the job offer from Justin. Apparently it *wasn't* so unrealistic to believe I could get a job as a writer over here. I've worked my butt off and earned this, and that feels good.

Well, it's bittersweet. Mel obviously hasn't said anything to Justin about Michael, but it's only a matter of time. There's no doubt in my mind she'll make good on her threat if she wants to.

I'm trying to tell myself it's okay. I've made my choice and that's being with Michael. I feel bad for letting Justin down, and I guess I could ask to write about something else, but Mel did say that was unlikely. Besides, I've spent the past month proving I can write about being single. To ask for something else now wouldn't be fair. I'll just have to let it go. Maybe I'll do what Michael suggested; focus on my romance novel and see if I can do something with that.

I can't deny how torn I feel, though. I wanted this job and now that I've finally got it, I have to give it up. And while

I know that's the right choice, I still feel uneasy about it. Mum's words echo through my head—*I thought you went over there to write*—and I keep trying to push them away. I know that if I can just see Michael, just talk to him about all this, I'll feel better.

The door swings open. He's standing there in a navy blue T-shirt that shows his muscular arms, his hair is slightly mussed, and he's visibly struggling to contain his grin. "Hey, beautiful."

Oh God. I feel better already.

"Hi." I bite my lip at the sight of him, feeling strangely shy. "How's Henry?"

"He's great." Michael's eyes track over me, then without warning he pins me up against the door frame and claims my mouth with a blistering kiss. Heat pools in my belly, spreading out along my limbs. I get a mental image of Agnes catching us and have to stop myself from giggling.

"How is it possible that I missed you so much after only one day?" he murmurs into my hair, his hands snaking their way around my waist and holding me close against him. I can feel how hard he is already, and as he kisses me again, I'm overcome by the urgent need to get his clothes off.

"Sorry." He draws away from me with a sheepish laugh. "I probably shouldn't maul you the second you get in the door. Let's have a drink."

"What?" I blow out a breath in disbelief. "Fuck that. Bedroom." The words slip out before I can stop them and Michael's eyebrows shoot up.

Jesus, what is *wrong* with me?

"Sorry," I mumble, feeling warmth spread over my cheeks. "Just ignore me."

He shakes his head, his eyes sparking as he slides a hand

down to lightly smack me on the butt. "No. Bedroom it is. Now."

Oh, there's that bossy voice. *Fuck.*

I giggle, stumbling into the apartment and finding my way to his room. Then he's peeling my dress off, kissing his way down my chest and slipping a hand into my underwear as I stand, grasping his shoulders because I'm weak at the knees. I reach for his belt buckle impatiently, but he pushes my hands away, nudging me back onto the bed.

"You promised," he murmurs, tugging at my underwear and sliding it down my legs.

"What?"

He kneels on the floor at the foot of the bed, taking my legs and hooking them over his strong shoulders. "I've been waiting *forever* to do this."

I give him a wry smile. "You mean you've been waiting a few days."

"No." His eyes smolder as he gazes at me. "Try three months."

His words send heat searing through me and I drop my head back onto the bed with a moan. He slides his hands under my butt, angling my hips up. I feel the scratch of his beard on my inner thigh as he lowers his mouth onto me, then his tongue sweeps over the throbbing, wet heat between my legs.

"Oh, oh God," I groan, and he immediately stops.

I glance down to see amusement dancing in his eyes. "We have to be quiet, with Henry here."

"Shit." I cringe. "Sorry. You can stop if you want—"

"Fuck no," he growls, then he buries his face between my legs again.

My hands drop to his head, pushing into his hair, holding him right where I want him. And he's happy to comply. He slides his tongue over me greedily, working his fingers into me as he does, and it only takes a few minutes until I'm a panting, heaving mess, arching against his mouth and trying not to scream the roof off.

His grin stretches from ear to ear as he pushes to his feet and drops his pants. He takes his hard length in his hand and strokes, chuckling as I try to gather myself together on the bed. I watch him roll on a condom, feeling the familiar ache to have him inside me again.

He climbs on top of me, pinning my hands above my head and capturing my mouth. His tongue strokes roughly over mine as he nudges my legs apart. When he pushes inside me I gasp in delight, my hands flying down to him, my nails digging into his back as I suppress a moan.

It's not long before I'm writhing beneath him, pulling him deeper into me, and the moan I managed to contain earlier escapes from my lips. He has no choice but to put a hand over my mouth as he watches me with hooded eyes, and it's the hottest thing. A few moments later it's his turn to keep quiet, and I take in the pleasure on his beautiful face as his body tenses and releases, shuddering against me.

Afterward, we lie in bed gazing at each other in the soft lamplight. I run a hand over his cheek, my body still aching to feel him as if I'll never get enough.

"So how was your day, anyway?" Michael asks, and I laugh.

"Shouldn't you ask me that *before* you take my clothes off?"

He flashes me a grin. "I couldn't help myself."

"Me either," I say, leaning in and stealing a kiss. "Um, my day was okay. I slept most of it. Then Mum called." I swallow nervously. "And then, er, I got an email telling me I got the column."

His eyebrows lift, then his lips tip into a smile. "Wow, Alex, that's... Congratulations." His smile slides away as he drags his teeth across his bottom lip, an uneasy silence settling over us. "So what are you going to do?"

"Well..." I hesitate, wondering if I should mention Mel's threats from the hospital. Eventually, I sigh. "Mel told me last night that if I don't stop seeing you, she's going to tell them I'm not single."

His brow furrows but he says nothing, and there's a twinge of annoyance in my gut.

"That's it? I thought you might be a bit more shocked that she threatened me."

He gives a hollow laugh. "Not at all. That's Melanie."

Huh. That's not *quite* what I was expecting. "You don't feel the need to, I don't know, defend me or tell her to back off?"

"I—" He grimaces. "I try not to piss her off. It's not worth going back to court and putting Henry through all that again."

I open my mouth to protest, remembering how reluctant he was to speak up to her last night. But I force myself to stay quiet. I don't want to argue with him about that now.

"Well, anyway," I mumble. "I might not have a choice about the column, thanks to her."

Michael strokes his beard. "Maybe it's for the best? You don't want to write about that stuff anyway, right?"

I pull the sheets up to my armpits and smooth them down over me, trying to ignore the irritation crawling under my skin. "Well... I don't want to lose the chance to be a featured writer on Bliss Edition."

"But you can't write a column about being single if you're not, right? And I don't want you to be." His mouth slants into a smile and he reaches for my hand, lacing his fingers through mine.

"I don't want to be, either," I say, giving his hand a squeeze.

"Exactly. I think you should forget about the column and focus on your romance novel. I read it and I think it's great."

"You read all of it?"

"I did, and I think you have something good there. I love Matthew and Annie and their story."

"Oh." I smile, buoyed by his encouragement. "So you really think I should turn down the column?"

He gives a slow nod and confusion swirls through me. How can he be so supportive of my novel but not the rest of it?

"Michael... you said you'd support whatever I decide to do. Do you remember that?"

"Yeah, I do. But I think you're wanting to write this column for the wrong reasons. I mean, you're not interested in writing it, are you?"

"Well—"

"It's more about proving yourself to your parents."

I pull my hand away. "What?"

"Am I wrong?"

I chew my lip, staying silent. I don't want to think about it like that, but maybe he's got a point.

"Alex, it's okay. But"—he shrugs—"it's a little immature to let that influence your decisions. You just have to get over it."

His words hit me like a slap and I shrink away, feeling a cold, prickly sensation wash over me. I think back to an hour ago when I was anxious to come up here and talk this through with him, certain he'd understand why I'm feeling so torn. Instead, he's just making me feel like shit and expecting me to give everything up without a second thought.

And now I wonder if turning this job down could be a big mistake. This is the best opportunity for my career that I've ever had—which is why I came all the way over here in the first place. Maybe Mum was right: I *am* giving up on my writing. Do I really want to throw it away because I'm hoping for my happily ever after? I might have had an amazing week away with Michael, but if he can't understand why this is important to me then maybe he doesn't know me so well after all.

He studies my face. "What's wrong?"

I stare at him, incredulous. Right. Well. If he doesn't get why I'm upset right now then he *really* doesn't know me.

"I don't know what you thought was going to happen," he says, looking perplexed. "If we want to be together then you can't write the column. You get that, right?"

"Of course I get that!" I blow out a frustrated breath. "It's not even about the job, Michael. It's about the fact that you can't understand why this is difficult for me. I thought out of everyone, *you* understood what my writing means to me, and how complicated things are with my parents. I thought you'd support and encourage me."

"I *do* understand—"

"You don't, because you're telling me to get over all this stuff with my parents and abandon my career, just like that. In fact, you were telling me on the drive home to give up on this. So clearly, you *don't* understand me—"

"Alex, you're being ridiculous. I do—"

"Stop!" I raise my hand, anger boiling hot in my blood. How *dare* he call me ridiculous for defending myself. Fuck —he sounds exactly like my mother.

I climb out of bed, pulling my clothes on with trembling

hands. I've had enough of the people I care about not supporting me. I might not be able to control who my parents are, but I sure as hell can control who I give my heart to. And it's not going to be someone who can't understand what matters to me.

"You know what?" I say, zipping up my dress. "You might be this hot-shot writer with loads of books published, but I'm not sure you should be telling me what to write. What about your historical novel? How can you sit there and tell me what I should or shouldn't write when you won't even take your own advice?" I glare at him, waiting for his retort. But he just stares at me.

I turn to go, thinking I'm done, when more words rush up my throat. "And as for Mel? I can't believe you're okay with her speaking to me like that. I understand you have to look out for Henry, but that's no excuse for letting her push me—or more importantly, *you*—around."

"Fuck, Alex," he growls, sitting up in bed. "I can't believe you're giving me a hard time about Melanie right now. You have no idea what I've been through with her."

"But have you thought about the example you're setting for Henry? He sees you being manipulated by her. He sees her walking all over you."

Michael's jaw tightens. "Oh, so now *you* think I'm a bad father too? I'm sorry I'm not some kind of perfect Prince Charming, Alex, but I do have flaws."

I suck in a shocked breath. "What? Is that what you think I'm looking for? Prince Charming?"

"I don't know." He shrugs. "You've told me you think I'm perfect. And let's face it, *Matthew* is pretty perfect. It's hard to live up to that."

I gape at him in disbelief. Matthew is a fictional character; I don't expect Michael to be faultless. God. It's one thing to hear my mother say that I'm searching for some unrealistic ideal of romance—I expect it from her. But to hear this from *him*?

"Melanie is always giving me shit about how I'm a crap father," Michael mutters. "Always pointing out my flaws. And now you're—"

"You're comparing me to *her*? Are you fucking kidding me?"

A muscle ticks in his neck and his eyes are cold as they move over my face, but he doesn't deny it.

"Wow." I swallow hard, realizing just how wrong I was about him. Because if he truly thinks I'm no better than his cruel ex-wife, then he really, *really* doesn't know me at all.

Fuck, I'm an idiot. Of course there's no such thing as a happy ending. Why on earth did I think this time would be different?

"Okay. Then I'll make this easy for you, Michael." I draw in a shaky breath, forcing myself to meet his gaze. "I choose my writing."

The anger on his face gives way to alarm. "Alex, wait."

"You know," I say bitterly, "I'm surprised you even wanted to be with someone as immature and ridiculous as me in the first place."

He scrambles out of bed and reaches for his pants. "I didn't mean—"

"It doesn't matter. I can't do this, I'm sorry." And as I gaze at his handsome face, his pleading eyes and knitted brow, I know I *am* sorry—sorry that I can't be with this beautiful man. But I'm not going to stay with someone who doesn't understand me or care about the things that matter to me.

With tears escaping down my cheeks, I dash out of his apartment and down the stairs, hoping there might be some way to rescue my career.

41

When I push the front door open, Cat is sitting in the living room and my heart sinks. I haven't seen her in days and I'd been so eager to talk to her about Mel. But now that's the *last* thing I feel like doing.

I try to slip in quietly and go straight to my bedroom nook, but before I can even get in the door she turns to me, her eyes narrowed to slits.

"What the hell is wrong with you?"

I feel a bolt of shock. "What?"

"How could you do that to Mel?"

With a weary sigh, I lower myself onto the chair next to her and wipe my cheeks. "I... have a lot to tell you."

"Yes, you do. Honestly, Alex. Mel went to all that trouble to help you with your writing and then you get together with *Michael*? After everything he did to her?"

I press my fingertips to my eyelids. "First of all, I didn't know she was his ex-wife."

"What? I told you at New Year's."

"No. I think you were *going* to tell me, then Kyle arrived. Anyway, he didn't do anything to her. She was the one who cheated on him."

Cat blinks. "What?"

"*She* was the one who cheated," I repeat. "Not him. He told me everything."

"Are you kidding me? You believe him over her?"

"I do, actually, but it doesn't matter. I made a mistake with him and it's over."

She snorts. "Well that doesn't mean you haven't hurt Mel. I can't believe you would do this to her."

I examine Cat's face and frustration bubbles up inside me. She's so loyal to Mel, but Mel doesn't deserve her loyalty at all. "She's full of shit, Cat."

"What the hell are you talking about?"

I grit my teeth, suddenly at the end of my rope. This hideous woman has no regard for anyone else's feelings and somehow *I'm* the one being crucified. I can't believe Michael thinks I'm like her.

"You know her new secret man? It's *Mark*. She's dating your ex-husband."

Cat's jaw drops. "Wow. I cannot believe you would say that."

"I'm sorry, but it's true."

"No. She would never do that to me." Cat stares at me for a moment, screwing up her face. "I can't believe you're doing this, after all we've done for you."

I jerk back, stunned. She thinks I'm making this up to hurt her? I open my mouth to say something, then close it again as the words die on my tongue. What's the point? She'll never believe me over Mel. Mel is too good a liar.

Cat stands, raking her eyes over me with disgust. "I

thought we were friends, Alex. But obviously I was wrong." And with that she stalks up the hallway to her room, slamming the door.

I stare after her, my heart pounding, my breathing shallow. I know she's just angry, but her words sting all the same. Before I know it, the tears are coming hard and fast, and I bury my head in my hands. It feels like everything is falling apart and I don't know where to turn. I just want to crawl into bed and sleep for a million years; forget I ever came to this bloody city.

I trudge over to my nook and sink down onto my bed, but now this little space that has brought me so much comfort is just making me sad. I don't belong here, in this apartment with someone who doesn't trust me, in this building with the man who hurt me.

I don't belong here at all.

With trembling hands, I reach under the bed and grab my suitcases, quickly gathering my things. I take my clothes down off the rack and empty the drawers, stuffing the contents haphazardly into my bags. As I pack, I remember the day Cat told me I could live here and feel a fresh spasm of hurt. I can't believe she thinks I would lie to her, that I would make up something so hurtful. But she's known Mel for years and I've only been here for a few months. Of course she believes Mel over me.

My cheeks are wet as I finish shoving all of my possessions into my suitcases, wishing so badly that things had turned out differently.

Then I take one last look at the apartment I've called home since I arrived, and with a heavy heart, head out the door for the one place I have left to go in the city.

By the time I'm ringing the buzzer to Geoff's apartment, it's nearly midnight. From the street I can see the lights are on, and he lets me in quickly, waiting at the door when I get to his floor. His face falls when he sees my puffy eyes and he ushers me inside without a word, taking my suitcases and guiding me over to his sofa.

"I'm so sorry to show up unannounced. I didn't know where else to go."

He pats my arm. "Don't you worry about that. Of course you're welcome here."

I sit stiffly, playing with the hem of my dress, holding my breath. I know if I say anything more, I'll burst into tears.

"Is this about Michael?" Geoff asks tentatively.

I nod.

"Oh, hon. What happened?"

Ugh, it's no use. Fresh tears spill onto my cheeks as I tell him about the week away with Michael that wasn't supposed to happen, about everything between him and I in the cabin. I tell him about Mel and the hospital, getting the job and the argument with Michael. And then I tell him about Cat.

"Wait. So Michael's ex-wife is Cat's friend, Mel? What are the odds of that?"

I shrug. "I think Cat knows Mel because she used to live upstairs."

"Oh. Right." He's quiet for a moment, then speaks again. "I have to ask... are you sure you want to end things with him? You two are so good together and I know how much you like him."

"I don't have a choice, Geoff. I thought things with him were real, that he understood me and supported me, but... I was wrong. Like I always am. And as for Cat—" I break off and look down at my hands as my throat tightens. Here I was thinking Cat and I were friends, but she won't believe a word I say. How can you have a friendship with someone who doesn't trust you?

Geoff puts an arm around my shoulder and gives me a squeeze. "She'll come around."

"I'm not so sure."

"If Mel *is* with Mark—if the things you said are true—then she has no reason not to. She might just have to learn it the hard way."

I sag back on the sofa, overwhelmed with exhaustion. Not just from the emotional roller coaster of everything with Michael, or the drama with Mel and my writing, or the argument with Cat; from everything here in New York. It feels too hard, all of a sudden.

"Maybe I should go home," I mumble.

Geoff gives me an encouraging smile. "Yes. I'm sure Cat will—"

"To New Zealand."

His face falls. "Oh, no. Oh, please don't. I know this feels shitty right now, but things will get better."

I swallow as tears fill my eyes again.

"I promise things will get better. Don't leave." He hugs me again, tighter. "Besides, what would the bookstore do without you?"

I give him a watery smile. As much as I love working there, that's the least of my problems now.

"Get some sleep," he says, standing and gathering a pillow and blankets for me. "You'll feel better in the morning."

He takes my hands and hauls me up off the sofa, then sets about pulling out the sofa bed and making it up while I stand there numbly. With another hug, Geoff pads to bed, flicking the lights off as he leaves. An eerie glow falls over the room, cast by the street light outside the window. I shiver as I peel my clothes off and pull on my pajamas. I haven't had a chance to do my laundry since getting back from the cabin, and my clothes smell like Michael after spending so much time wrapped up in his arms. As I climb onto Geoff's sofa bed, my heart hurts so much I can't sleep. Instead, I just curl up in the darkness and sob into the pillow.

WHEN MY EYES open the next morning, there's a blissful moment where I don't yet remember what has happened. But as I gaze around Geoff's apartment, it all comes screaming back to me.

The week at the cabin with Michael, his kisses on my lips, his hands on my skin. Him telling me he's falling for me, then telling me to give up my writing, making me feel stupid about my parents, comparing me to his nasty ex-wife.

It was awful, but despite everything, misery settles over me when I think about the fact that I told him it was over. And lying here now, alone, I physically *ache* with missing him.

Did I make a huge mistake?

No. Because all I have to do is remind myself of his words, and bile rises in my throat. How could he know me at all? And how could he care about me, if he can't care about what matters to me?

God, I was deluded, believing I could have a happily ever after with him. Of course it was just a fantasy. Everything with Michael felt too good to be true. I just didn't want to see it until it was too late.

I prop myself up on my elbows. The sofa bed squeaks beneath me and I let out a weighted sigh. Because I didn't just lose Michael yesterday. I lost Cat and my apartment. And maybe, I also lost my fledgling career.

Pulling myself up, I grab some fresh clothes and head to the bathroom. I'm weak with gratitude when I see Geoff has left a towel out for me. I don't know what I'd do without him.

I step under the stream of water and rinse myself, determined to find a way out of this mess. Things might not have worked out with Michael, but that doesn't mean my life is over. In fact, now that Michael's gone, I *could* write the column for Justin—if Mel hasn't already ruined that opportunity for me. It might not have come about exactly as I wanted, but the important thing here is that I need to do what's right for me. And that's putting my writing first.

My mind drifts to the fight with Cat as I scrub. I so desperately want to talk to her again and explain myself more clearly. I said everything in the heat of the argument; no wonder she didn't believe me. And if she went to Mel afterward, Mel would have simply denied it. But I know if I can explain myself calmly and rationally, Cat will have to listen to me.

And then another thought occurs to me. If Cat *did* talk to Mel after I left, then Mel will know I told Cat about Mark. And that will make Mel even more determined to hurt me. If she thinks I not only hooked up with her ex-husband but also tried to turn her best friend against her, she would have no reason *not* to convince Justin to rescind his offer. She would set out to destroy me.

My gut roils as I step out of the shower, processing this. There's a very good chance, then, that Mel has in fact told Justin everything. And knowing her storytelling abilities, I imagine it's a rather embellished version of what happened. She's probably in tears in Justin's office right now, telling him what a monster I am and how stupid they've been to trust me.

And, if that's the case, I've lost the opportunity to write the column. And that means that, now, I've lost everything that matters to me here in New York.

I try to ignore the anxiety tightening across my chest as I pull my dress and tights on. When I catch sight of myself in the mirror, I pause. The girl gazing back at me is the girl that's always been there: the one from the small town who wasted years in a dead-end job, dreaming of happily ever after, with nothing to show for any of it. She's still there, only now she's in New York.

I throw a bitter laugh at my reflection. Why did I think that coming here would be any different? How on earth did I think that being in a different city would magically make me a different person? What kind of wishful thinking is that?

Biting back tears, I shuffle into the living room and stuff my pajamas back into my suitcase. I pick up my phone to check the time and there it is: a missed call.

From Justin.

My stomach plunges. There's no voicemail, but it doesn't matter. Because there's only one reason he would be calling me this early. Mel's been in touch with him.

I stare at the screen, tears stinging my throat. Well, that's it. I've lost everything I've worked for with my writing. I've lost Cat. And I've lost Michael.

There's only one thing left to do. It's the only sensible thing anyone in my position would do.

I gather my suitcases, scribble Geoff a note to thank him for everything, and head out onto the street, hailing a cab to the airport.

It's time to go home.

42

"There's really nothing?" I tap my credit card on the counter, eying the United Airlines attendant.

She shakes her hair-sprayed head and not a single hair moves. "Sorry, the flight is completely full. I can get you on another flight to Los Angeles, then you'll have a twelve hour layover before the connecting flight to New Zealand."

I frown. A twelve hour layover doesn't sound ideal, but I do want to get out of here—the sooner the better. God, how I wish I could just click my heels together and be home already.

The attendant glances between me and the line of people forming behind me. "What would you like to do?"

I fiddle with my credit card. For some reason I feel myself hesitating, and she purses her lips impatiently.

"Why don't you take a minute to think about it? It doesn't leave for four hours and there's plenty of seats left."

I give her a brittle smile, then drag my suitcases over to a bench and sink down, closing my eyes. Touching the book charm around my neck, I feel another wave of misery. Going back home is hardly what I want to do. I feel like a complete and utter failure, but what choice do I have? There's nothing left for me here.

I should call Mum and tell her I'm coming home, but I can't face her pity, her saying—probably word for word—"I told you so." And worst of all, I'm worried that maybe she was right all along.

Because what the hell have I done? I've wasted thousands of dollars trekking across the planet for nothing. Still, I guess I can always earn more money. Worst of all is the damage I can't undo; the hurt I've caused Cat and the writing career I came so close to having, then threw away. All because some hot guy wanted to get in my pants.

That's the thing that hurts the most. I trusted Michael. I let him see who I really am, let him see the things that have hurt me. And then he just went and hurt me too.

Despite all this, for some reason I'm not marching over and buying a ticket home. I can't put my finger on what it is, but something is keeping me rooted to this plastic chair. It's like I need someone to tell me it's the right thing to do, to push me. But who? I don't want to hear my mother's voice right now. I'm too ashamed to call Emily and tell her I'm about to crawl back home.

Before I know what I'm doing, I thumb through my contacts and lift my phone to my ear.

"Hello?"

"Hey, Harri."

"Hey!" My sister's voice is bright and happy, and I burst into tears. "Shit. What's wrong?"

A woman two seats down from me gives me a peculiar look and I try to pull myself together. "Sorry. I'm just... I'm at the airport. I think I'm going to come back to New Zealand."

She's quiet for a beat. "Okay. Why?"

I tell her everything, trying to keep my emotions in check. When I'm done, I lean back against the plastic seat, feeling hollow and spent. I know she's going to convince me to stay here, keep trying, etcetera, and I don't have the energy to fight her.

"Well, okay then," Harriet says at last. "Come home."

"Oh," I say, taken aback. "You think I should?"

"What's stopping you?"

"I don't know," I mumble. "Mum and Dad will make me feel awful."

"Oh, yeah. They will. But you need to do what's right for you. If that's the only thing stopping you, then you should come home."

I fiddle with the book charm, looking around the airport concourse at the people with excited faces, about to embark on adventures. That was me a few months ago. And now I'm back here, feeling as if I've just given up.

Harriet sighs. "Look, I know you've always struggled with what Mum and Dad think, but you need to find a way to get past that. I had to learn to. Remember when they wanted me to go to university? We had a big fight about it."

"You did?" I ask vacantly. "Why was that, again?"

"They assumed that since you'd gone, I'd go. They couldn't understand why I didn't want to."

"But they were annoyed when I left for uni!"

"I know, I remember," Harriet says with a laugh. "That's my point. It doesn't matter what you do, they'll always find something to complain about."

I think back to the last conversation I had with Mum, when she was negative about me meeting someone—hot on the heels of lamenting me staying single. And what about my writing? When I was making strides with that she had complaints, then when she thought I'd given up on it, she wasn't bloody happy either.

Shit, Harriet is right. It doesn't matter what I do, they'll always find something to pick at. I could write a bestseller or marry a prince and there would be something wrong. There always is.

Ugh, I *do* need to get past this. I need to learn how to do what's right for me and stop letting Mum's voice nag in my ear. My parents have been like a ghost, following me around my whole life, casting a shadow over everything. I even let them follow me all the way to New York, for Christ's sake. But I don't want them here anymore. I've had enough.

"Thanks, Harri," I say, wiping my nose. For a younger sister, she's surprisingly wise.

"So you're coming home?"

Home. The word appears in my mind, glowing and warm, like a marquee sign lit with yellow bulbs. But when I think of my old flat, that tiny town, my parents... I don't feel that warm glow. The last time I felt like that was when Michael and I returned to the city, after our week at the cabin. And while part of that happiness might have had to do with him, I know that a huge part of it had to do with the city. Things might be shitty right now—my career and my roommate and my love life might have all given up on me—but the city hasn't, I know that. New York hasn't given up on me. And somehow, I just *know* it never will.

"No," I say, pushing to my feet and gathering my bags. "I'm not. Because that's not my home anymore. New York is."

I end the call and stash my phone, turning for the exit. I'm not running away this time, because I'm in the right place. I'm where I'm meant to be, and I just have to find a way to make it work.

First thing's first—I need to clear the air with Cat.

Actually, *first*, I need coffee. It's been a nightmare of a morning and I haven't had my usual dose of caffeine. No wonder I'm feeling so shit.

I spot a coffee shop across the airport and pivot, dragging my suitcases along.

"Alex!"

The word rises out of the din around me and I glance across the crowded airport concourse. But it's just travelers, pushing past each other, and I shake my head with a chuckle.

"Alex!"

Okay, hang on. That was definitely my name.

I pause and swivel, looking around again, but I can't see anyone I know. God, I'm so caffeine-deprived I'm hearing things.

Straightening my shoulders, I turn and continue towards the coffee shop.

"Alex! Wait." My suitcase is yanked from my hand and I spin around to see a familiar face.

My heart stops.

"Don't go. Please." Cat looks at me beseechingly.

Geoff appears beside her, his hands on his hips as he doubles over, trying to catch his breath. "You're... so... fast..."

A disbelieving laugh shakes out of me at the sight of my two friends. Cat flaps a hand at Geoff to grab my suitcases and, taking my arm, leads me back over to the bench. Geoff bumbles along with my baggage, dumping it at my feet and collapsing beside us.

"I'm so sorry for what I said." Cat clasps my hands, her expression sincere. "You were right. About everything."

I glance at Geoff and he shrugs. "I'm sorry. When I saw your note, I had to call her."

I fix my attention back on Cat. "You spoke to Mel?"

"Yes. I called her last night and she denied everything, so I figured you were lying. Then when Geoff called in a panic this morning, I called Mark, and he told me the truth. When I called Mel back and told her, she finally confessed."

"I'm sorry for how I told you. I never meant to blurt it out that way and hurt you. I was upset."

Cat shakes her head. "You did the right thing, telling me. I'm so sorry for not believing you. I'd just had an awful evening with Kyle and I shouldn't have taken it out on you."

"It's okay." I pull her into a hug, relief flooding my body. "What happened with Kyle?"

"Ugh, I'll tell you another time. But that's over. Now what's this about you leaving New York?" She looks at me sternly and I let out a long, weary breath.

"I'm not. I thought I should, but—"

"There's no need to leave just because you broke up with a guy," Geoff says.

"Well, I also destroyed my career."

Geoff cocks his head. "What?"

"I got offered that column but Mel told Justin not to give it to me."

Cat winces. "Yes, I think she was going to make sure you didn't get it."

Geoff stares at me wide-eyed. "What a crazy bitch."

I snort in agreement. "It's okay, I'm not going to let her stop me. I'll talk to Justin. I worked hard to prove I'm a good writer, so I'm not just going to walk away."

Geoff grins. "Good."

"Besides, I don't want to leave New York. This is my home, and I don't want to be anywhere else."

Cat exhales in relief. "I'm so glad." Her and Geoff exchange a look and he leans closer.

"And what about Michael?"

I shake my head, swallowing against the sudden sting in my throat. "No, that's... no."

"But why?" Geoff presses. "When I saw you together at New Year's... it just looked like you were meant to be, you know? And the way you're both writers, and you met in this huge city, then you got stranded at a snowy cabin... It's like a fairy tale."

I blink the tears away from my eyes, giving Geoff a humorless laugh. "That's what I thought too. But that's the problem, Geoff. Fairy tales only exist in movies and books. Real life isn't perfect like that."

His brow knits, and he opens his mouth to say more, but Cat puts her hand on his arm, turning to me.

"Will you come home now?"

I grimace. "I can't come back to the building. I can't risk running into Michael."

Her face falls, but she nods in understanding.

"Stay with me," Geoff offers.

I stare at him for a moment, at his kind face regarding me hopefully. Cat is waiting with her eyebrows raised. Gazing at my two friends—the friends who rushed out to the airport in Queens to stop me from leaving the country—I burst into tears of relief. I knew staying was the right thing to do.

43

"You have to let me read it!"

I shake my head at Geoff, pulling my boots on. "Are you kidding? No way." I haven't let myself even *think* about my romance novel, let alone look back over it. I know it will just make me think of Michael, and every time that happens, I cry. It's only been a few days, but I'm beginning to worry that I'm getting severely dehydrated.

Geoff folds his arms. "Okay, I'll make you a deal. I'll let you stay rent-free on my sofa in exchange for a copy of your romance novel."

I straighten up, frowning in confusion. "I'm already staying here rent-free."

"Exactly," he says with a smug smile. "Ooh, I'll sweeten the deal. How about I get you a great job at the bookstore I run?"

I roll my eyes, taking my laptop from his outstretched hand. "Fine, Geoff. I get your point." I flip the lid open and wait for it to boot up. "Just... I don't want to *talk* about it, okay? You can read it but we are not going to discuss it."

He puts his hand on his heart. "Promise."

I send it via email then snap my laptop shut, sliding it into my bag. Smoothing my hands over my dress, I glance at Geoff anxiously. "Okay, how do I look?"

He appraises my outfit. "Like a woman who wasn't secretly hiding a boyfriend from her new boss?"

"Perfect," I say, pulling on my coat. "That's just what I was going for."

I slip out the front door into the cold morning air, tugging my scarf up around my neck as I wander through the Village towards the subway. It's so icy that my nose is numb, but I still look around at the row houses and brick buildings with a smile. I love this part of the city, and seeing it again just reminds me that it's where I'm meant to be. I can't believe I ever doubted that.

As I ride the subway up to Midtown, anxiety burrows under my skin. I'm not sure I want to surprise Justin with a visit, but this needs to be done. I want to fight for the job I earned.

If I'm not too late.

When I step into the elevator and press the button for the fifteenth floor, sandwiched between four other people with a visitor pass slung around my neck, my gut is turning itself inside out. I ride the elevator, picking at a nail until it bleeds. The ping of the opening doors sends my heart skittering, and for a second I stand, frozen.

What am I doing? Justin won't want to see me. I'll probably be escorted off the premises by a security guard, my face scarlet with humiliation. And what if Mel's in there? She no doubt knows how spectacularly things ended with Michael, and will be more than happy to rub salt into the wound.

But as the doors begin to slide closed again, determination grips me and I lunge forward, slipping through the gap. I came here for a reason and I'm not turning back now.

Get it together, Alex. Game face on.

At reception I have to give my name, and the woman tells Justin over the phone that it's me. I'm surprised when she ushers me down a corridor towards his office, instead of asking me to leave. That has to be a good sign.

As I knock on Justin's door, my pulse is thumping in my ears.

Right. I can do this.

"Alex, come in."

I enter the room and Justin gestures to the chair opposite his desk. I sit, taking a deep breath. Any minute now he's going to tell me how disappointed he is, and I'm going to need to do some serious groveling. But that's okay, I knew that. That's why I'm here.

"I'm glad you came in," he says, pushing his chair out and coming to lean against the front of his desk. "Mel spoke to me."

I shrink. Here it comes.

"God, she's a nightmare," he mutters, and confusion weaves through me.

"Er, what?"

"She gave me this whole speech about how you're screwing around with her ex." He raises his eyes to the ceiling. I'm about to begin my groveling when he shakes his head, offering me a smile. "Anyway, did you see my email? We've been so thrilled with your articles."

Wait. What?

"My articles?"

"Yes." He passes a hand through his salt and pepper hair. "Our readers have really connected with your voice and your sense of humor. I think it will make a great regular feature."

"Regular feature?"

He gives me a strange look. "Are you okay?"

"Justin—" I hesitate, wanting to make sure I'm understanding him. "Are you still offering me the column?"

"What? Of course."

"I just thought that Mel—"

"No." He shakes his head with a chuckle. "I ignore her most of the time."

"Oh." I frown, puzzled. "I figured she would convince you not to give it to me, just like she convinced you to read my blog in the first place."

Justin cocks his head. "She didn't convince me to read your blog. She didn't even intend to *show* me your blog, Alex. She sent the link to someone at work to mock your writing and accidentally cc'd me into the email."

I stare at Justin in disbelief. "She was mocking my writing?" I ask quietly, surprised to find myself feeling hurt. Out of everything she's done, I never thought to question her encouraging words about my writing. But now I remember how she said my blog was "hilarious" and I suddenly understand what she meant.

He grimaces. "Sorry, I probably shouldn't have said that. But I clicked on the link in the email, thinking I'd have a good laugh, and instead found a talented writer. That's why I asked you to send me some articles."

"But..." I rub my forehead, trying to make sense of this. "Why was she so nice at brunch when we met?"

"Mel is all about saving face. She could hardly admit she'd passed over your writing when I liked it. She wanted to take credit for finding you, because I was impressed."

"Huh." I'm quiet, processing this. Since I saw the real Mel at the hospital and learned the truth about who she is, I've wondered why she was so nice to me when we met, why she went out of her way to help me with my writing. But it was just saving face in front of Cat and Justin. Of course. That's how she handled her divorce too; by painting herself as the victim.

"Anyway," Justin says, bringing my attention back to him. "Do you have a working visa?"

"Um... no."

"Okay." He shrugs. "I can help you sort that out. So are we good?"

I sigh, deciding to do the mature thing. If I'm going to work with him, I don't want him to think I'm a liar. "What Mel told you was right, though. I was seeing her ex."

"Uh, okay." He brushes at some invisible lint on his pants. "It's not really any of my business."

"But the column you're offering me is about being single. So I thought that if I wasn't, then I wouldn't get it."

"Well..." He rubs his jaw, considering this. "Yeah, that could be a problem. So you're not single, now?"

"I—" Tears tingle in my nose and I look down at my hands, sniffing. "I am now, yes." As the words leave my mouth, there's a little ache, deep in my ribcage. Even after everything Michael said to me, I miss him. God, I know it's stupid—I know that I only miss a *fantasy*, some dream I had of us—but I do.

"Okay, then there's no issue. The column is yours if you want it."

My mouth pushes into a smile, but a weight settles into the pit of my stomach. I want to be a writer for Bliss Edition, but the thought of continuing to write about how fabulous it is to be single after being with Michael doesn't exactly thrill me. In fact, it makes me want to cry.

But it's not just because of Michael. I was over writing about this topic before things even happened with him, I just didn't want to admit it to myself. And if I'm going to stay here in the city and live my life on my own terms, then I need to be honest—with myself and with Justin.

I clear my throat, lifting my gaze to meet his. "I don't mean to be ungrateful, Justin, but I don't want to write about being single anymore. I know that's what the whole column is supposed to be about, but I can't do it. I'm sorry to let you down." I pull my purse onto my shoulder and stand, extending a hand to thank him and leave. But he just looks at my hand then back up at my face.

"Right. Well, what do you want to write about?"

I stare at him, his frame casually leaning against his desk, his arms folded across his chest. "I'm sorry?"

He shrugs. "Alex, you've proven you're a great writer and I'd love to have you on board. So if you don't want to write this column, I'll see if I can create something else to utilize your talents. What do *you* want to write about?"

I lower myself into the chair, my mind spinning. Well, I didn't see this coming. And now, shit, I don't know. What *do* I want to write about?

"The city," I hear myself say. "This city is... something else. It's alive, and breathing, like this living thing, this *loving* thing, welcoming you no matter where you're from. I feel like it wants to know you, like it needs you as much as you need it. It's like a lover calling you back to bed when you leave, and—" I break off as Justin's eyebrows shoot up. Shit, what am I even saying right now? What kind of delusional rant is this?

But Justin nods. "Yes, you're right. That's why I love New York. Why everyone loves New York." He scrubs a hand over his stubbly chin. "You might not want to write about being

single, but what about writing as if the city were your date?"
He pushes away from his desk, pacing as he thinks. "A 'New
York is my boyfriend' kind of thing. You said the city is like a
lover, and you're clearly passionate about it. We could create
a weekly column where you go on some kind of date with
the city and write about it, as if it were a man. It could be
part travel memoir, part dating column, all from a
humorous perspective. What do you think?"

Excitement zips through me and I give Justin a genuine
smile. I love this city and I'd be proud to write about it—to
have New York as my "boyfriend."

And perhaps, best of all, I know New York will never
break my heart.

44

I slide the book back onto the shelf, trying not to let my eyes wander to the section beside me—the section where I discovered Michael's book. I've been trying to avoid this whole aisle, but Geoff keeps giving me things to shelve down here. I'm beginning to wonder if he's doing it on purpose.

With a sigh, I shuffle up to the counter. It's been a long first day back at work, but it's good to return to some sort of normal. Well, I guess it looks normal on the outside, but my chest feels like it's been hollowed out and filled with cement.

"We need to talk," Geoff says as I lean against the counter. He's unboxing some new thrillers and I pick one up absently.

"About what?"

"Your novel."

I set the book down, narrowing my eyes. "No."

"Oh, come on! It's—"

"That wasn't the deal, Geoff! You promised we didn't have to discuss it."

"I know. But that was before I knew how brilliant it is."

I snort. This should be good.

"I'm serious!" He abandons the box to focus his attention on me. "It's fantastic. It's hot, and the story is solid, and that Matthew character—"

"Oh God," I mutter, heat rising to my cheeks. This is exactly what I was trying to avoid.

"I think you need to do something with it."

I twist away, pretending to busy myself with the new arrivals. "I'm not—"

"Alex." Geoff puts his hand on my arm, turning me back to him. "I mean it. I read a lot of books, and I'm not just saying this as a friend. I think you have something here."

I observe his earnest expression and feel a flicker of hope ignite inside me. I trust Geoff, and if he's saying this, maybe, well... is it possible that it *is* good?

"And the ending," Geoff adds with a swoon. "It's adorable."

I mentally douse the flicker of hope, shaking my head. "It's not adorable. It's absurd," I say, and my concrete heart hardens a little more.

I've been trying not to think about the ending I wrote at the cabin, high on Michael's pheromones, dazed from hours of sex and cuddling, unable to think rationally. I'm trying to keep Michael out of my mind altogether, and most of the time it's working. Well, during the day it's working. At night, when I'm in bed alone, I somehow forget how mad I'm supposed to be. Instead, I'm consumed by the physical ache of missing him. I miss his kisses, his hands on me. I miss his woodsy smell and his sweet taste, the way his eyes would light up when he looked at me. I miss the low rumble of his laugh. I miss the way he made me feel safe and sexy and— even if it was just for a little while—happy.

Then, when the morning comes and I have a headache from crying over the happy ending I never got, I remind myself again how angry I am that he wanted me to give up my writing after he'd promised to support me. And when I think about how he compared me to Mel, how he told me I was being ridiculous... my fury returns in full force.

But that's good. It's easier to be angry with him than to feel the emptiness of missing him.

Geoff frowns. "It's a romance novel, Alex. That's how it's supposed to end."

I heave out a sigh. He's right, of course, and I'd hate it if these books ended any other way. I don't want to read about two broken people who fall in love and think they're going to be happy, only to end up with mangled hearts. That's what real life is for.

Geoff smiles at a customer as they enter the store, then turns back to me. "Look. You might not be feeling good about love right now, and I get that. But your book is great, and I hope you do something with it." He follows after the customer and I'm left with his words echoing in my head.

The truth is, I kind of would like to do something with my novel. I'm thrilled to have the column from Justin, but I also want something for me—something that can keep that hopeless, romantic side of myself satisfied, so I'm not tempted to go looking for it in real life again. I'd been reluctant to do anything with my novel because I was worried what my parents might think. But I've decided to do what's best for me now. Taking my romance novel seriously would be a good first step.

Geoff leaves me to lock up for the evening, and I'm relieved when it's time to head home. It's been good to be back at work, but my heart is feeling heavy after thinking about Michael. I wonder if he's thinking about me, or if he's just gone back to his old, grumpy self. He said I helped him to be more optimistic, to feel good. But when I think about the hurt we caused each other, I can't see how that can be true.

I'm just locking up the store, ready to schlep myself home, when I see him. He's standing across the street in a pool of light from a street lamp, his beanie on his head, his hands in his coat pockets.

My eyes lock onto his and my heart lurches. It's only been a week, but I'd forgotten how handsome he is. I'd forgotten how tall he is, how broad his shoulders are, how masculine and sexy his beard is, how beautiful his espresso eyes are. It all comes rushing back in that moment as I step out of the bookstore and pull the door shut behind me with trembling hands.

"Hi," he says uncertainly, approaching me.

"Hello." I rip my gaze away from him and stuff my keys into my bag. I'm afraid that if I look at him, I'll either burst into tears or start yelling. I'm not sure which would be worse.

"Do you have a moment to talk?"

I nod, trying to make sense of the cyclone of emotions inside me. I know I should be mad at him. I should be telling him I don't want to see him, that he hurt me and let me down. But the main thing I'm feeling is misery. Somehow, I'm missing him more than ever now that he's right in front of me.

"Alex, I'm sorry." His voice breaks and I look up in surprise. "I promised to respect your writing—to support your decision—and I broke that promise. I dismissed your feelings about your parents and that was wrong. I shouldn't have told you to just forget it. I know it's not that easy."

My throat constricts with emotion. After my conversation with Harriet I've come to see Michael was right about my parents, I just didn't want to admit it to myself. But seeing the anguish on his face now, I feel the anger I've been keeping stored inside dissipate, like the mist from our breath in the freezing air.

"I should never have told you to give up the column. I was way out of line and I'm sorry. I never meant to hurt you or make you feel like I wasn't taking your writing seriously. Because I *do* take it seriously, and I *do* care about what matters to you."

The sincerity in his eyes sends a tiny ripple of that familiar warm sensation through me; the one I felt when things were good with us, when he made me feel understood. But now it's bittersweet, because everything is different.

"And you were right about me needing to stand up to Melanie," Michael continues, his gaze sliding down to his hands. "I let her push me around for so long because I was afraid that Henry would get caught between us, but what you said was right. I don't want him to see me as a coward." His Adam's apple dips as he swallows, and his jaw tightens. It's then that I realize he's holding back tears.

My heart squeezes and I know I have to say something or I'm going to burst. "I wasn't trying to say you're a bad father. I know Mel says that and she makes you feel awful but, truly, I think you're a great dad. I didn't mean to make you feel like you aren't."

His gaze meets mine. "I know. I was just angry. Not even at *you*—at Melanie, for making everything *so* difficult, all the time. And I shouldn't have taken that out on you. But you are *nothing* like her," he says fiercely. His eyes roam my face and his expression softens. "Because, despite what you think, I *do* know you."

I give him a slow, sad nod, feeling the sting of tears behind my eyes. Seeing him now, hearing his words... I really want to believe him. I want to get back to that place where I felt so seen and so safe with him, where I believed everything would work out. But I don't know how.

"Melanie told me she spoke to Justin," Michael says. "I'm sorry if you lost the job because of me. I never intended for that to happen. I shouldn't have pushed you to be with me."

There's a sharp pain in my heart. How could he say that? He never pushed me to be with him. I wanted all of it—all of *him*. I still do. I open my mouth to say as much but the words lodge in my throat. How do I say that after I told him I was choosing my writing instead? What could make up for that? And worse—what if, after everything, he doesn't want me anymore?

I force myself to meet his gaze. "I didn't lose the job."

"You didn't?"

"No." I'm quiet for a moment, then I draw a wobbly breath. "Michael, you were right. The column... I was doing it for the wrong reasons, and you could obviously see that when I couldn't. I told Justin I don't want to write about being single and he's given me something else. And, even though it was hard to hear, you were right about my parents, too. I need to let go of what they think."

"Yeah, but..." He grimaces. "I should never have said it the way I did. I didn't mean to hurt you like that."

I give a little nod, searching his sad eyes. How could I have thought this man didn't know me, didn't support me? I'm desperate to find some words, to find a way to ask him if there's any chance—

"Anyway," he mumbles, staring down at the sidewalk, "I just... I had to come and apologize. I didn't want to end things like that."

End things.

The words ring in my ears, so final, and my heart drops into my stomach.

"My life is too complicated. It—" His voice catches and he stops, swallowing hard. "It wasn't fair to ask you to get involved with all that."

I wrench my gaze away, trying to ignore the pain ripping through me. Fuck, if I thought it hurt being away from him, I was wrong. Having him right here—and knowing he's given up on me, on *us*—hurts so much I can't breathe.

And now we're just standing woodenly across from each other, separated by a thick wall of regret. He's said his piece and I know I should go, but I can't bring myself to walk away from him. So I say the only thing I can think of.

"I'm going to do something with my romance novel."

Michael's brow lifts. "Oh, wow. What are you thinking?"

"I don't know." I stuff my hands in my coat pockets. "I'll try submitting it to some literary agents, see if anyone is interested." I shiver, watching my breath come out in a cloud in front of me in the cold night air. I'd give anything to step forward into Michael's arms right now, to snuggle into the warmth of him, to have his touch soothe and comfort me. But I know I can't.

I clear my throat. "How's Henry?"

"He's good. Keeps asking about you." A ghost of a smile passes over Michael's mouth and my heart cracks right down the middle. I try to look away but I can't; I just keep staring at Michael, silently begging him to say something to fix it all, something to give me the tiniest drop of hope. But he isn't going to, because life isn't a fairy tale and things don't work out when you fuck them up this badly.

I can't believe I was so stupid to ruin this. This whole time I thought he didn't understand me, didn't care about my writing, and now that I know I was wrong I just want to sob. Sharp, bitter misery slices through me, splintering my heart, and I tear my gaze from his as my vision blurs.

"I have to go," I mutter. I can't stand here for another second, pretending to have a normal conversation when my ribcage is crushing my lungs in despair.

He stiffens in front of me. "Alex—"

"Goodbye, Michael," I say, my voice strangled with tears. I don't let myself look at him again as I turn on my heel and trudge away. As soon as I'm around the corner, the dam bursts and the tears spill down my cheeks.

45

They say that things heal with time, but I don't buy it. It's been a week since Michael came to see me at the bookstore and I don't feel better in the slightest.

The only thing that has helped is being contacted by Hatfield Literary Agency this morning. I was surprised when they called, because I haven't done a single thing with my manuscript, but Geoff has lots of contacts through the store. He's been banging on about how great he thinks my novel is, and obviously believes in it a great deal if he's gone out of his way to get it into the hands of an agent. If I'm lucky, they're calling me in here as more than just a favor to Geoff.

And if I'm really lucky, this will distract me from thinking about Michael.

My stomach pinches with nerves as I glance around the lobby of the Midtown building where I'm meeting Natalie from Hatfield Agency. The marble floor gleams in the afternoon sunlight that streams through the huge glass windows, making the expansive space too bright. It's one of those winter days that looks beautiful, but is so cold and crisp you can't be outside for long.

I pull my phone out, checking the time. I'm early, so I fire off a text to Emily.

Alex: Guess where I am right now? Meeting with a literary agent about my romance novel. Eek!

Emily: Oh hon, that's amazing!

Alex: Yeah. I'm a bit nervous. Don't know what to expect.

Emily: Don't be nervous. Just be your lovely self and you'll wow them! Your book is awesome and they'd be idiots not to love it.

Despite myself, I smile, feeling my nerves settle a little. I emailed a copy of my novel to Emily a few days ago and she's been sending me inappropriate emojis to show me how much she's enjoying it. Needless to say, there have been quite a few eggplants in my inbox.

I slip my phone away as a slim woman comes striding across the lobby towards me, her patent black heels clicking on the marble. She's wearing dress pants and a cute polka-dot blouse, her auburn hair pulled up in a bun, and black square-rimmed glasses on her button nose. She reminds me a little of Harriet, and I immediately like her.

"Alex?"

I stand, extending a hand. "Yes. Hello."

"Natalie. Thanks for coming in." She takes my hand with a smile. "I'm excited to discuss your novel with you. Let's go upstairs." She heads for the elevators and I follow her inside. "How long have you been querying it?"

"Er—" I smooth my hands down my dress, trying not to sound as clueless as I feel. "Not long?"

"Well, I think you have something great here."

A thrill runs through me but I give her a casual smile,

wanting to play it cool. The elevator pings as we arrive at our floor and I follow Natalie to a glass-walled office. By the time I'm sitting opposite her desk, I'm effervescent with excitement. I can't believe I'm here, meeting with a literary agent who likes my novel.

"So, I loved it." Natalie picks up a pen and twirls it. "I love the story and the characters, especially this Matthew character. Boy is he dreamy!" She giggles, pretending to fan herself.

I quickly force a laugh, even though my throat tightens at the mention of Matthew—or as I know him, Michael.

"He sounds sexy, but also sweet. It's good to get a balance of the two."

There's a familiar sting behind my eyes and I nod, looking down at my hands. *Yes, it is. And it's not easy to find.*

"I love how we see Matthew and Annie grow and fall in love," Natalie says, grinning. "And the ending is gorgeous."

"I guess," I mutter, swallowing against the sudden scratchiness in my voice. "But it doesn't always work out like that, does it?"

"Well..." She chews the end of her pen in thought. "Not always, no. But happy endings can—and do—happen. There's nothing wrong with expecting it to work out."

There's a pang my heart. "Yes, there is," I mumble, and Natalie raises an eyebrow.

Shit.

"Uh, what I mean is..." I stammer, scrambling for something reasonable to say without bursting into tears. God, why am I on the verge of tears now? "You know, sometimes people grow apart, or they have differing values, or it's just not meant to be."

"Of course. But there are also plenty of instances where people *do* work things out, where love conquers all.

Surely, if you're writing a romance novel, you must believe that?"

I let out a deep, sad sigh. As Natalie gazes at me, I feel my defenses begin to crumble down, until I'm forced to confront that part of me I've been running from. Because the truth is I *want* to believe that—I certainly used to. I've dreamed for years of having my own happily ever after. It's just that lately, I've begun to worry that won't be part of my story.

"Well, I've always believed that," Natalie says wistfully. "When love is true, there's nothing it can't overcome. That's why I love these books. They teach us that it's okay to believe in love, to want the fairy-tale ending. Because if you don't believe in it, you'll never get it."

There's nothing crazy about believing in love.

Michael's words from our visit to Strand bookstore come back to me, and I remember the way I felt, standing in the poetry aisle, thinking about how cynical I'd gotten. I decided that I *wanted* to believe in love.

But I haven't been, have I? I fought Michael every step of the way. And the minute things got real, I put my walls up and retreated, using my writing or my parents or whatever else I could find as an excuse. In fact, ever since my birthday, I've done everything I can to deny what I truly want, to keep love at bay.

And it found me anyway.

Realization rushes over me and I look down at my hands, blinking against tears. I finally found the one happily ever after I wanted more than anything and I destroyed it myself. All because I was scared—scared that maybe I didn't deserve the thing I wanted so badly. Scared that Michael was too good to be true and I'd end up disappointed all over again.

"That's not the only reason I love these books," Natalie continues, bringing my attention back to her. "They also teach us that it's okay for women to want the things they want, you know? When I was younger, I saw romance novels as a guilty pleasure. People used to tell me they gave women unreasonable expectations. But what's so unreasonable about wanting to be loved, wanting to be happy? Nothing." She chuckles. "And there's *nothing* wrong with wanting great sex."

I can't help a rueful little smile to myself. I've felt ashamed for years for wanting the things I've read about in romance novels—a man I love, a career that fulfills me, sex that rocks my world. Everyone had always told me that was too much to ask for.

But Natalie's right. I think of the shit I've settled for in the past—the job that left me feeling empty, the men who did nothing more than the bare minimum. Hell, I used to think it was unreasonable to hope for an orgasm during sex, until I met Michael. When I reflect on those things, I realize I was settling because I thought I didn't deserve the things I really wanted.

And now I can see that I'm not just miserable because I miss Michael and I fucked everything up with him. I'm hurting because I let myself down, by continually denying what I want and who I am. I'm a romantic, and I want love— true, deep, passionate love. I can't keep turning away from my optimistic, sensitive, dreamy side. Those are the parts of myself I've been trying to ignore—the parts, I think, Michael cherished the most. I was just too scared to believe him.

I meet Natalie's gaze, trying to keep my voice steady. "But what if... what if Annie messed everything up?"

Natalie gives me a bemused look. "Well... if that

happened she'd fix it, because she's in love with him."

Fuck.

Her words hit me hard in the chest and I feel as if I've been punched. She's right—I *am* in love with him. I haven't wanted to admit that to myself, but I can't keep running from it. I'm so in love with him it hurts. I miss him so much, it feels like I'm split open and bleeding everywhere. I thought by now the pain might be dying down, but it's not. Not even a little bit.

"Annie wouldn't let Matthew walk away," Natalie says. "If you're in love with someone, you fight for them. These stories teach you to fight for the things you want—to fight for your happily ever after."

I let my watery eyes meet hers, and as she gazes at me gently, it almost feels like she isn't talking about Matthew and Annie at all anymore.

Fight for your happily ever after.

Her words play on a loop in my head, imprinting themselves along the synapses in my brain. And I realize, slowly, that I never once fought for my happily ever after. I did the exact opposite.

God, how did I not see this? I fought for the other things I wanted—my writing, New York—but not for my dream of falling in love. I was too busy denying I even wanted it.

But I can't do that anymore. I don't *want* to do that anymore. I thought Michael had given up on us, but it was *me* who had given up. He came to see me and apologize—and I didn't tell him how I feel. I didn't tell him that I love him, that I don't care if his life is complicated, that I don't want things to be over. I didn't tell him that, more than anything, I just want to be with him.

I didn't fight for him at all.

"Natalie," I say, rushing to my feet. "I have to go."

hirty minutes later, I find myself standing in front of my old apartment building, shaking from more than just the bitter cold. I was worried Natalie would think I was unprofessional, cutting our meeting short, but boy was I wrong. When I told her that I was going to declare my love to someone, she nearly burst with excitement. She assured me that she wanted to work with me, despite the fact that I was fleeing our meeting in a frenzy, then made me promise to tell her all the details as she hurried me out the door.

Now, I look up at Michael's windows, glowing in the fading evening light. Snow is beginning to fall, but it's nothing compared to the fire inside me, burning to tell Michael how I feel. I climb the front steps and with each footfall, determination drives me forward, faster, until I'm taking the stairs two at a time. I'm breathless by the time I'm at his door, but that's not why my heart is beating so wildly.

I raise a trembling hand to knock. Footsteps approach and my lungs constrict, trapping my breath. Butterflies thrash in my stomach, making me feel sick. The doorknob twists and the door swings open and my heart leaps into my throat.

Michael's eyes meet mine. "Alex..." Concern wrinkles his brow. "Are you okay?"

What? Oh God, I must look an absolute mess. I've been crying since Natalie's office and my eyes are probably puffy and red. My mascara will be in train-tracks down my face.

What the hell am I doing? This is *not* how one is supposed to look when knocking on an estranged lover's doorstep in order to win them back.

"Uh, um... I was just in the neighborhood." I try to give him a smile, but it turns into more of a grimace.

He folds his arms across his chest, cocking his head to one side. I search his face for a hint of a smile, for some sign of happiness at my being here, but there isn't one.

"How've you been?" I try again, desperate for the awkwardness to dissipate. It's like a thick wall between us and I can't get to the other side, I can't get to the real Michael.

He shrugs, shifting his weight.

I press my lips together into a line, feeling a swell of misery. He doesn't want to see me. He told me his life was complicated, and here I am, adding more stress. I let my gaze slide away. What am I even doing here?

"Alex—"

My eyes flit back to him, but he's just staring at the floor, rubbing his jaw in thought. And I decide that whatever I do, I'm at least going to share my good news with him.

"I, um, met with a literary agent about my romance novel. They want to represent me."

A smile touches his mouth. "That's... that's fantastic news."

"Yes. So thank you for your encouragement and support with that."

He looks down at his hands, sighing.

I swallow hard against the lump in my throat. I almost can't breathe, this hurts so much. The ache in my heart is expanding, pressing against the edges of me and threatening to burst out. I can feel my chest rising and falling with my jagged breaths, my pulse throbbing in my ears. I need to get these words out—to know I tried.

"I miss you," I blurt.

His gaze lifts to mine and he studies me, silent.

"I can't sleep. I can't stop thinking about you. Everything feels empty. I never meant to mess you around." I blink against rising tears, searching for the words I need. "At Strand you told me to be optimistic, to believe in love, and I wanted to. But now I can see I was still fighting it. I was scared—scared that my parents were right about me dreaming too much, scared that I'd never get to have the thing I wanted more than anything. Scared that maybe... maybe I didn't deserve it."

There's a glimmer of compassion in his eyes and that gives me the courage I need to continue.

"But I realized it's a choice. I can either deny the part of me that wants those things—I can deny who I *am*—or I can embrace it. And I'm choosing to embrace it. Because you, Michael... you made me believe in myself. You made me believe in love. And..." I wipe at my cheek as a tear escapes, determined to speak the truth, to tell him the thing I should have told him at the cabin, long ago. "I love you."

I hold my breath, waiting for his response, but the silence stretches between us. It feels like an eternity so I speak again, desperately wishing he would tell me what I need to hear. "I don't know if you're still interested in me...?" Despite myself, I gaze at him hopefully.

His eyes dart over my face, then he shakes his head. "I'm not."

Despair washes over me, filling my eyes. Of course he's not. I'm on his doorstep babbling incoherently, my eyes puffy and my cheeks smeared with tears.

But I know it's not really that. I let him down. He's been hurt before and he won't be with someone who hurt him again—who just makes his life harder. I couldn't be the woman he needed me to be.

I glance at my hands as a tear slides down my cheek. I'll never forgive myself for ruining this.

"I'm not *interested* in you, Alex," he says, closing the gap between us. "I'm in *love* with you."

My eyes fly up in surprise to find a little smile forming on his lips. Then before I know what is happening, he slips his arms around me and pulls me close.

"You are?" I whisper.

He reaches a finger up to wipe my tears away, but more just spill down in their place. Only this time, they're happy tears.

"Yes. I'm so in love with you, beautiful girl. I think..." He shakes his head, his eyes gleaming. "I think I have been ever since you kissed me in the poetry aisle at Strand."

I gaze up at him, breathless as his words sink in. "Me too," I say with a disbelieving smile.

"These past couple weeks have been torture. I thought that when I came to see you at the bookstore, you might, I don't know, reconsider. But you were so distant. I thought I'd lost you forever."

"But—" I frown, confused. "At the bookstore, you didn't say anything..."

"I know. I just... I didn't want to push you."

I nod, thinking back to what he said. "You said your life is complicated, and I don't want to add to that. But—"

"What?" His brows pull together. "You don't *add* to the complication, Alex. Is that what you thought I meant?"

I laugh unsteadily. "I don't know, I—"

"No. You make all of that shit better. You make *me* better." He gazes at me affectionately, then tucks me in against his chest. I can hear his heart beating a steady, solid rhythm and it soothes me. My eyes flutter closed as happiness sweeps along my limbs, sinking into my bones. And in the warmth of Michael's arms, I feel my broken heart begin to piece itself back together.

"You really do make me better," he murmurs into the top of my head. "You want to know what I've been working on this evening?"

I draw back to find a smile nudging his mouth. "What?"

"My historical novel."

"Really?"

"Yeah. I decided to have a go at writing it. You were right. I should do it for myself."

"And how is it going?"

"Ah, well." He gives a sheepish laugh. "It's pretty tough. I've never written a novel, so it's a steep learning curve. But so far, I'm loving it."

I beam up at him, buzzing with the knowledge that I helped push him towards one of his dreams. Just like he did for me.

"I'm so glad," I say, loving the excitement on his face. I can feel it pulsing through him, see it in the way his eyes are lit up. "You're a brilliant writer, Michael, and I know that your fiction is going to be amazing. I can't wait to read it, and..."

"Alex," Michael murmurs, his lips hovering over mine.

"Yes?" I say on a sigh, gazing up at him. His dark eyes are hypnotizing me, his masculine scent intoxicating me, his hands on my back radiating warmth through my whole body.

"Stop talking, so I can kiss you." Then, finally, he brings his mouth down to mine.

47

Michael takes my hand and pulls me inside, closing the door behind us. "Did you have dinner?"

I shake my head, unable to curb the huge smile tugging at my mouth. Being back in his apartment, somehow.... it feels like I'm *home*.

He takes my coat. "We were just going to eat, if you'd like to join us?"

I follow him into the kitchen and find Henry pulling plates out of the cupboard.

Shit. I didn't know Henry was here. I hope he didn't hear me pour my heart out to Michael on the doorstep. I quickly wipe at my moist cheeks.

Henry turns to me, grinning. "Hi, Alex! I made—" he breaks off in concern when he sees me trying to compose myself. "Are you okay?"

I glance at Michael in question, and he puts an arm around my waist, pressing a kiss to my temple. He gives me a little nod and I turn back to Henry with an incandescent smile.

"Yes. I'm... Your dad has made me very happy."

Henry looks between the two of us and blushes. "Okay," he says awkwardly, turning away and adding another plate to the pile.

Michael chuckles, releasing me and reaching for a bottle of wine. Henry takes the plates through to the table and I wonder if, perhaps, I should come back later. Poor Henry is obviously finding this whole thing a bit much.

"Sorry," I mumble to Michael. "I didn't know you guys were about to have dinner. I should go."

"What?" Michael sets the wine down and turns to me, taking my hand. "No way. I want you to stay. *We* want you to stay."

I waver, but when I spy Henry looking at me hopefully over Michael's shoulder, a smile slides onto my lips. "Okay."

I stand in the kitchen, watching as Henry serves up three plates of lasagna. Michael pours two glasses of wine and sets them down on the table. Then the two of them turn to me, grinning, and gesture for me to sit. And my heart feels like it will burst when I lower myself into my seat beside Michael, opposite Henry. It reminds me of Christmas, when I spent the evening here with them and Agnes, and felt so warm, so happy. Now I realize why. It's like I've found my place, the place where I'm meant to be. I know I'm getting so far ahead of myself, thinking this, but I can't help it. And as Michael takes my hand under the table and squeezes, I have to blink against happy tears.

"Sorry it's kind of burnt," Henry says, frowning down at his plate.

I shake my head and smile at him. "It's perfect," I say, and Michael squeezes my hand again.

As we eat, Henry tells me about things that have been happening at school, with his friends, how much he's enjoying riding his new bike when it's not snowing. After dinner, Michael does the dishes while Henry and I sit at the table and keep talking. He tells me about the book he's been reading—Bill Bryson's *A Short History of Nearly Everything*, the book he was reading when I first met him, in the hall— and he shares what he's learned and how interesting it is. As he speaks, I'm struck by his curiosity and intelligence— traits I'm certain he got from his dad.

Eventually, Michael finishes up in the kitchen and Henry goes to get ready for bed. I sit at the table, finishing my glass of wine, not wanting to leave but knowing I probably should. I did show up here unannounced, after all. And it's a school night for Henry.

But just as I'm about to rise from my chair, Michael comes over behind me and leans down by my ear, speaking in a low voice. "Don't you even think of going anywhere. I'm just going to see Henry off to bed, then I'll be free. Okay?"

I tilt my face towards him. He's only inches away from me, and I can't stop myself from leaning closer. "Okay."

He brushes his lips over mine, letting out a little sigh.

"Ew, gross." We both turn to see Henry in his dinosaur pajamas, emerging from the hallway.

Michael straightens up, one hand on my shoulder, a wide grin stretching his face. "Get used to it, bud."

I stand from the table, blushing. "Sorry, Henry."

He gives a dramatic eye-roll, but I can see he's smiling.

Michael pads up the hallway with a chuckle, and Henry steps closer to me. "It's nice to have you here again, Alex. Dad hasn't smiled like that for weeks." He reaches out and pulls me into a hug, squeezing me tight. "Goodnight."

"Goodnight, Henry," I say, fighting against another round of tears. Happy tears. Really happy tears.

I sit on the sofa trying to process everything that has

happened over the past hour and a half. I told Michael I love him, and he told me he loves me back. I ate dinner with him and Henry, and it was wonderful. And as Michael finally emerges from the hall and his eyes land on me and smolder, I'm pretty sure I know what's coming next.

He reaches for my hand, pulling me up off the sofa. "Henry's so happy you're back. He might have missed you more than me, actually."

I laugh, feeling joy rush my bloodstream. I know that things with Michael can only work if Henry is on board, so having him want me here is everything. But it's not just that. I've missed Henry too. I've missed them both.

I run my eyes over Michael, taking a second to just look at him. His dark hair is messy and unstyled, his face is tired, but there's a light in his eyes, in the way that he's looking at me—just like that time at the ice-rink. I take a mental picture of him standing there in his long-sleeved tee, faded jeans, bare feet. This man—fuck. He's everything I could ever want. I'll never love another man as much as I love him. Never.

He swallows visibly, pulling me close to him. "Bedroom?"

I nod and turn down the hallway without hesitating. He enters the room behind me and closes the door, then turns to me, peeling my layers off, until I'm naked. His eyes roam over my bare skin while I stand there, but I don't feel the need to hide. Because I know he's seen all of it—all of *me*—and he loves me anyway. He always has.

We make love slowly, passionately, as if we're doing it for the first time all over again. And while he kisses me, holding me close and giving me every piece of him, I wonder how on earth I ever managed to convince myself that believing in love was crazy.

AFTER, he kisses me with those feather-soft kisses that make my toes curl, make me giddy.

"Alex..." He sets his head down on the pillow and gazes at me. His eyes have those deep crinkles in the corners, his mouth is set in a permanent smile. "I can't believe you're here. I thought I'd lost you. I'm never letting you go now. You know that, right?"

"I know. And I'm more than okay with that."

He leans forward to kiss me again. "I love you," he murmurs against my lips.

"I love you too. More than anything." I think of the last time I was here, and regret tugs at me. "I'm so sorry about our fight. I promised not to hurt you and I did."

"Hey, it's okay. I don't expect you to be perfect."

"And I don't expect *you* to be, either," I say quickly, remembering what he'd said last time.

His eyes soften. "I know. I was just scared that I couldn't be what you need me to be. But I know you don't need me to be perfect, and you can't be either. I don't expect us to always see eye to eye. Sometimes we'll fight, and that's fine." He takes my hand and laces his fingers through mine. "What matters is that we keep going. It's not a one-time thing, falling in love. We have to keep choosing each other, over and over again."

"I can do that," I say, knowing it's the truth. And just like that, I understand. Happily ever after is not some fairy-tale ending. It's not a hand-in-hand stroll into the sunset as the credits roll. It's a work in progress, a choice you have to keep making. And that's how I know I'm getting my happy ending —because I'll never choose anyone else again.

Michael runs his thumb across my palm. "When I woke

up beside you at the cabin every morning... that was the happiest I've felt in forever. I want to wake up beside you every day. But..." He lets his breath out in a long stream. "I guess when I said my life is complicated, I meant that I come as a package deal. I know you love me, but it's not just me. It will never be just me. You understand that, right?"

I lift his hand to my mouth and kiss the back of it. "Yes. Of course."

"Because going forward, I need to know you're okay with that. Is that something you want?"

I pause, thinking, and decide to tell him the truth. "Honestly? I never imagined that when I fell in love, it would be with someone who has a kid. Or a terrifying ex-wife. But then, I could never have imagined *you*, or how I feel for you. So, you and your package—"

Michael raises his eyebrows and I giggle.

"What I mean is... I know you come as a package deal, and I'm okay with that. More than okay. Henry is such a sweet kid. I love him too," I say, understanding for the first time that I do. "Because he's yours. Because he matters to you. And that means he matters to me, too."

The creases around Michael's eyes deepen. "Good. Because... look, I can't do anything without talking to Henry first. This is his home too, and I need to make sure he's happy with everything. I'm quite certain he will be, but I need to do everything with him in mind. Does that make sense?"

I nod, smiling. I think I know where he's going with this, but I don't want to get ahead of myself.

"Okay. Because I want you here every night, every morning. I want you as part of our family, Alex. Once I've had a chance to talk to Henry, once I know he's okay with everything, I'm going to ask you to move in."

My pulse accelerates as he keeps speaking.

"And after that... I'm going to ask you something else." His eyes burn into mine, serious and intense. "I'm not kidding around with you. This is it, for me."

My heart takes off in a sprint now. I'm breathless as I stare at him. Is he really saying what I think he is?

"Michael..." I shake my head in disbelief. I want to make sure we aren't getting swept up in the moment, that this is real. Because he's offering me everything I could ever want. "How can you be certain, so soon?"

He gives me a tender smile. "Ever since you came into my life last year, I've been happier than I ever imagined I could be. I never thought I'd feel like this again." He scrubs a hand over his beard, thinking. "And when you've had everything you *don't* want, it becomes pretty fucking clear when the thing you *do* want is right in front of you. And then you don't want to let that go."

I press my eyes shut, feeling tears slip out and down my cheeks. Holy shit, I cannot believe what this man is saying to me. I'm vibrating with happiness. It's coursing through me like an electrical current, lighting every cell in my body. I could power the whole city.

I feel Michael wipe my tears, and when I open my eyes, he's regarding me with concern. "I don't mean to freak you out. I know it's quick, and I don't want to rush you. But—"

"No." I place a hand on his chest, trying to figure out how to put what I'm feeling into words. "From the first day that I arrived in this city, I wanted two things: to build a writing career, and"—I give a little shrug—"you." It's true, I realize. As soon as I saw him in line at Starbucks... He was the most handsome man I'd ever laid eyes on. And even though he was grumpy, maybe a tiny part of me could see what was underneath: a good man who just needed to be loved.

"When I finally got my column, when I met with the agent... it felt like nothing without you. Everything feels like nothing, without you. So I can assure you, whenever you decide to ask me, the answer will be yes. Hell yes."

Michael's mouth pulls into a grin and he glances away from me, huffing a little laugh to himself. "Fuck, I'm a lucky guy."

I shake my head, lifting the covers and climbing on top so I'm straddling him. I lean down and thread my hands into his hair, kissing him softly. "I'm the lucky one."

He slides his hands up my back, holding me down against him as his tongue sweeps into my mouth, hungry for me again. When he releases me, his eyes are twinkling. "So Natalie loved your romance novel, huh?"

"Yes. And—wait." I push up so I'm sitting. "I never told you her name."

"Didn't you?"

"No." I narrow my eyes and his mouth pulls into an impish grin. "It was *you*?"

"Yeah. I hope you're not mad. I know you told me not to show it to anyone but I had to, Alex. I've been with Natalie's agency for years and I knew if I gave it to her, she'd love it."

"But why didn't she tell me it was you?"

"I asked her not to. I didn't want you to think I'd only done it to get your attention. And I didn't want you to think she was just doing it as a favor to me. If she told you she loved it, then she means that."

"Well... I guess I owe you a thank you. Here's hoping someone will publish it."

"I'm sure they will." He lets his hands skate down my bare thighs. "But there is one problem."

"What's that?"

"There are a lot of intimate scenes, involving—well, basically involving us."

I blush, glancing away from him. I guess he has a point there, and it never occurred to me he might be uncomfortable about that.

He takes my chin, turning my face back to him. "I love it, Alex, all of it. But I was just thinking... we don't want to mislead people."

"How?"

"We haven't done even *half* the things in there. You have a very vivid imagination." His mouth tilts into a sly smile and the dimple appears in his cheek. My face burns, but I don't look away this time, because there's a playful spark in his eyes that's making my heart beat harder, making heat shoot out along my limbs.

"I just think we have an obligation," he continues, sliding his hands up to the meeting of my thighs.

"An obligation?" I ask, trying to keep my breathing steady as he lowers his thumb to trace a lazy circle between my legs. Pleasure zings through me, and he grins when he sees it on my face.

"Yes. An obligation to act out every single one of your dirty little fantasies. I think it would be irresponsible not to."

I huff out a breath, arching forward against his hand, noticing that he's ready for me again too. And, oh God—the thought of actually *doing* every single thing I've imagined myself doing with Michael? Fuck, I can't even see straight at the thought.

I lower my mouth down to his and nibble on his bottom lip, delirious with desire. "We definitely have an obligation."

He chuckles, extending an arm to feel about for a

condom on the nightstand. I watch as he rolls it on, feeling the need building between my legs.

"There's probably going to be a sequel too."

His eyes meet mine, dark and hazy, and a naughty grin is dancing on his mouth as he pushes into me again. I close my eyes and submit to the shiver of ecstasy it sends through my body.

"There'd better be a whole fucking series," he says roughly against my ear, letting his teeth nip at my earlobe.

I let out a giggle, but it's swallowed by his mouth, and both of us reach the edge a few minutes later.

Afterward, as I lower myself onto the mattress beside him, a laugh bubbles up in my chest. "You know, there are quite a few scenes in my book that we haven't..."

"I know." He winks at me.

"You really want to do them *all*? It's going to make for a busy week."

He laughs, leaning over to kiss my shoulder. "There's no rush, beautiful." He buries his face in my hair, and I smile, knowing exactly what his next words are going to be, and knowing I have everything I could ever want. "We have the rest of our lives."

EPILOGUE

Head to www.jenmorrisauthor.com/litc-epilogue to get access to an exclusive *Love in the City* epilogue!

Did you enjoy *Love in the City*? Reviews help indie authors get our books noticed!

If you liked this book, please leave a review on Amazon. Or you can leave a review on Goodreads. It doesn't have to be much—even a few sentences helps! Thank you.

ACKNOWLEDGMENTS

Well. I can't believe I'm finally writing my own acknowledgments page. It's a bit surreal, actually. Since this is my first novel, I'm going to be totally self-indulgent and bleat on like I'm accepting an Oscar until they play the music to usher me off the stage. Here we go!

First of all (this is so cheesy but I'm doing it) I have to thank the Alex inside of me—the one who dared me to write my own book, to believe it could be done, to share that book with the world. We did it, girl! (Should we move to Manhattan now?)

My partner Carl—the Michael to my Alex. He pushes me in the right direction when I'm lost, supports me unconditionally, and makes sacrifices so I can go after my dreams. He even sent me on a solo research trip to New York! And don't get me started on all the inspiration he provides for the heroes in my stories.

Our little boy, Baxter. He's taught me so much about myself, including how to focus on what matters most. I hope someday I can encourage him towards his dreams, no matter what they are.

My parents, Helen and Chris, who have always done their best to understand my crazy ways. And thank you for taking me to New York when I was seventeen. I've been obsessed ever since!

Jon Kibzey, the teacher who told me years ago that I could write. I've called upon his kind words many times to keep me going, and I'm quite certain that without them, I wouldn't be here. Thank you.

Amanda Wood, the one person who probably knows my inner Alex better than anyone else. She's loved her all along, pushing me when I need it, supporting me when I need it—always, always believing in me. And I wouldn't know half the things I do about American culture if I hadn't spent so many hours watching *Friends* with her.

Sarah Side, my unofficial editor and close friend. She's put in countless hours reading my work, offering feedback, encouraging me, listening to me blather on into the small hours, working through plot/character/general emotional issues, and being an all-round star. Without her, there is no way you'd have this book in your hands. Seriously.

Louise Ryan, who read the first ever draft version of this book and assured me it wasn't crap. Her encouragement and enthusiasm meant I kept going—even if the book looks *very* different now (thank God).

Gina Burns, for showing me around the East Village and Coney Island, taking me to a boozy brunch, and answering a million and one questions about Americans and New York. Oh, and her pug Mia, who inspired Stevie. (And her friend Jeff, with whom I took *wild* artistic license to create Geoff.)

My sister, Emma, who inspired Harriet's pragmatic nature. She might be four years younger than me but she's wise, like Harriet.

Kira Slaughter, for letting me share many, *many* pictures

of book boyfriend inspiration, and talking with me for hours about Michael and Alex as if they were real people. Her love for this book led us to develop the best kind of friendship, sharing our obsession with New York, books, hot guys and *Friends*.

My critique partners, Lauren H. Mae and Jennifer Evelyn Hayes. They spent a *lot* of time helping me develop and polish a story I'm proud to share. I'm so grateful to have their help and support for my work.

Beta readers—such an important part of this process. So many people put time into reading this work and offering feedback—too many to name—but here are the people who went above and beyond with their support and encouragement: Tammy Eyre, Emma Grocott, Chloe Liese, Kelly Fuller, Caroline Palmer, Caroline Chalmers, Laura Harris, Kristen Fairgrieve, Michele Voss, and Kelly Pensinger. To each and every one of you: your words helped me to improve, push forward, believe in myself. Thank you so much.

My cover designer, Elle Maxwell. She took my ideas and made them into a gorgeous cover, capturing every detail perfectly, and never once complained I was being too pedantic.

The bookstagram and indie author community, who has been so encouraging and supportive. I never imagined I'd find such a wonderful community of people online. I love being part of it.

To anyone who has bought/read/reviewed/shared this book—thank you. I can't even begin to explain what it means to me that you've given up your time and money for my work.

Alright, they're playing the music. I'm off to work on the next book!

ABOUT THE AUTHOR

Jen Morris writes sexy romantic comedies with heat, humor and heart. She believes that almost anything can be fixed with a good laugh, a good book, or a plane ticket to New York.

Her books follow women with big dreams as they navigate life and love in the city. Her characters don't just find love—they find themselves, too.

Jen lives with her partner and son, in a tiny house on wheels in New Zealand. She spends her days writing, dreaming about New York, and finding space for her ever-growing book collection.

Love in the City is her debut novel, and the first book in the *Love in the City* series.

ALSO BY JEN MORRIS

Don't miss book two in the series: *You Know it's Love*. Join Cat as she tries to save her vintage clothing business—and fight her feelings for the cocky new bartender at her brother's bar.

You might also enjoy book three in the series: *Outrageously in Love*. See Harriet visit New York and meet a sexy nerd, watch Alex and Michael get married, and catch up with the rest of the gang.

Follow me on Instagram and Facebook: @jenmorrisauthor

See all the book inspiration on Pinterest:

www.pinterest.com/jenmorrisauthor/

Or subscribe to my newsletter for updates, release info, and cover reveals.

www.jenmorrisauthor.com

Printed in Great Britain
by Amazon